JAROSLAV HAŠEK was born in Prague in 1883,
the son of a schoolmaster. Young Hašek attended the
Prague Commercial Academy, where his first literary
production was characteristically an attack on the
school principal; from there he went to work in a
bank, but repeated absences without leave soon ended
his career as a clerk. A book of his verses appeared
in 1903, and was followed in succeeding years by a
flood of comic short stories and sketches. During this
period, Hašek became editor of the magazine *Animal
World,* whose ingenuous readers proved fair game for
his inveterate love of practical jokes and improbable
hoaxes. In 1915 he was drafted into the Austrian
Army, but soon succeeded in being captured by the
Russians. He spent five years in Russia as a prisoner,
then in the Czech Legion under Russian command,
and finally in the Red Army fighting his former
Russian officers. Returning to Prague in 1920, he
began *The Good Soldier: Schweik,* his final attack in a
lifelong war against the social lie. He planned *Schweik*
to cover six volumes, but had completed only four
when he died in 1923 of tuberculosis contracted
during the war. His creation, however, lived on,
winning ever-increasing popular and critical acclaim,
surpassed only by the supreme tribute paid to
Schweik by several European armies, as they rigorously
banned the book from their barracks.

Jaroslav Hašek

THE GOOD SOLDIER: SCHWEIK

Illustrated by *Joseph Lada*
Translated by *Paul Selver*
With a Foreword by *Leslie A. Fiedler*

A SIGNET CLASSIC

NEW AMERICAN LIBRARY

FOREWORD

The Antiwar Novel and the Good Soldier Schweik

I.

Written in Prague in the twenties about the events of 1914 and 1915, *The Good Soldier: Schweik* first reached America with the Depression, and returns now, after another war and another peace, strangely involved in history: not only the history of the times it describes, but the history of the times through which it has come down to us. What shifts of taste and allegiance it has survived! What collapsed hopes and betrayed dreams!

Perhaps the kind of pacifism it embodies is the sole product of World War I to have lasted into our era. Certainly the official aims in whose names that war was fought, and which were theoretically assured by the Treaty of Versailles, have not come to very much. The dissolution of the League of Nations, the successes of Stalin and Hitler, and the outbreak of World War II made clear that the outward forms of democracy, national self-determination, and international cooperation, imposed by fiat or invoked in piety, had little to do with the inward meaning of the world after 1919. Not peace and order but terror and instability were the heritage of the post-war years: an institutionalized terror and a stabilized instability, in whose honor two minutes of silence were observed for the score of November elevenths between the first Great Armistice and the second great eruption of violence.

But pacifism, too, was a victim of World War II, which saw thousands of young men, who earlier had risen in schools and colleges to swear that they would never bear arms, march off to battle—as often as not with copies of antiwar books in their packs. Those books were real enough, like the passion that prompted them and the zeal with which they were read; only the promises were illusory. The unofficial war-resisters, who for twenty years had pored over evocations of battlefield atrocities to immunize themselves against the appeals of patriotism, found their own slogans finally as irrelevant as the catch phrases they pretended to despise. To be sure, the end of still another war has seen the upsurge of still another pacifism; but this seems by now part of a familiar pattern, the zig which implies a zag before and after.

Perhaps then, one must content himself with saying more moderately that the chief lasting accomplishment of World War I was the invention of the antiwar novel: a fictional record of the mood out of which the pacifism of between-the-wars was born and of the hopes and fears which sustained it through all the horrors of peace. It is certainly true that before the 1920's that genre did not exist, though it had been prophesied in the first two-thirds of Stephen Crane's *The Red Badge of Courage;* and that since the 1920's, it has become a standard form: both a standard way of responding to combat experience and a standard way of starting a literary career.

In the United States, the examples of Hemingway and Faulkner have ensured the continuing popularity of the genre; the latter struggling as early as *Soldier's Pay* and as late as *A Fable* to give shape to his sense of World War I, and the former providing a classic prototype once and for all in *A Farewell to Arms.* No wonder similar books from abroad have always moved us, from Henri Barbusse's *Le Feu* to *All Quiet on the Western Front,* and notably, of course, *The Good Soldier: Schweik.* And no wonder, too, that the generation of Americans who had broken their pacifist oaths in World War II sought to make amends by keeping faith with the sort of novel that had made war real to them before life itself had gotten around to doing it.

Certainly the flood of antiwar novels that generation has been producing since the forties owes more to certain books that their authors had grown up reading than to the actual fighting that many of them did. A typical case in point is Norman Mailer's *The Naked and the Dead,* begun at Harvard before Mailer had lived through any battles but fictional ones; and quite properly so, since for those of his age *the meanings of their wars had already been established by men twenty and thirty years their senior*, by Hemingway and Faulkner and Jaroslav Hašek, among others.

As a matter of fact, the meaning of their wars has been for most generations established before the fact—in our culture, largely by works of art. The writers of Europe and America who were young enough to fight in World War I were, in this light, unique, endowed with a peculiar freedom their successors have vainly tried to emulate by imitating the forms in which it was expressed. Only the former, however, actually lived in the interval between two conventional ways of understanding war, serving as the gravediggers to one and the midwives to the other.

For a thousand years or so, roughly from the time of Charlemagne to 1914, the wars of Christendom, whether fought against external enemies or strictly within the family, had been felt and celebrated in terms of a single continuous tradition. And those who lived within that tradition assumed without question that some battles at least were not only justifiable but holy, just as they assumed that to die in such battles was not merely a tolerable fate but the most glorious of events. Doubts they may have had, but these could scarcely be confessed to themselves, much less publicly flaunted.

Full of internal contradictions (what, after all, had any military code to do with the teachings of Christ?) and pieced together out of the rag bag of history (tales of Old Testament berserkers like Samson, scholarly recollections of Roman *vertu* and Greek *arete*, popular vestiges of the Germanic combat-religion), nonetheless the Christian heroic tradition proved viable for ten centuries, as viable in the high verse of Dante and Shakespeare and Chaucer as in folk ballads and the sermons of country priests. Yet all the while it lived, of course, it was dying, too, dying with the civilization that had nurtured it, already mourned for by the time of Sir Walter Scott. So slowly did it die, however, that only under the impact of total war were those who fought shocked into admitting that perhaps they no longer believed in what they fought for.

Last to learn that the old tradition had in fact died were the heads of state, kings and emperors, prime ministers and presidents. In their mouths, the shabby slogans For God and Country, For Christ and King, *Dulce et decorum est pro patria mori*—rang ever less convincingly. But they were not the simple hypocrites their earliest critics took them for; they were merely dupes of history, in whom self-interest conveniently cooperated with confusion. Even more absurd than they, however, seemed the prelates of churches, on whose lips the more bloody battle cries, always a little ironical, appeared suddenly nothing but ironical. Yet it was not the believers who felt the absurdity, only those for whom God was presumably dead.

Small wonder, then, that priest and potentate alike remained unaware that history had rendered them comic, since no one told them except those whose opinions they discounted in advance. Indeed, some to this very day have not realized that the words they speak in all solemnity have been to others for over forty years household jokes. One function of totalitarianism in its manifold forms is precisely to forestall the moment of awakening, imposing by decree the heroic concepts which once flourished by consent. The totalitarian chief counterfeits ever more grotesque versions of the Hero, and in cell and torture chamber attempts to exact from those who dare laugh at him "confessions" that nothing is funny at all. The earliest record of such an attempt, as well as of its gloriously comic failure, is to be found in *The Good Soldier: Schweik.*

Not only in totalitarian societies, however, is the antiheroic spirit assailed by the guardians of the pseudoheroic. In more democratic nations, mass culture is entrusted with the job assigned elsewhere to the secret police; and where those who snicker at pretension are not hauled off to prison, they find it difficult to make themselves heard above the immensely serious clatter of the press and the ponderous voices of official spokesmen, magnified to thunder by P.A. systems. Yet certain writers, like Hašek before them, continue to feel obliged to carry to the world the comic-pathetic news it is reluctant to hear: the Hero is dead. First to know, such writers are the last to forget that ever since World War I they have been called on to celebrate, with due hilarity, the death of the myth of the heroic, even as their predecessors were called on solemnly to celebrate its life.

In the battle front against war, however, there is these days no more possibility of a final victory or defeat than on the battle fronts of war itself. In the former as in the latter, the end is stalemate; for the antiheroic satirists who have carried the day in the libraries and the literary magazines elsewhere seem to have made little impression. The notion of the Christian Hero is no longer viable for the creative imagination, having been destroyed once and for all by the literature of disenchantment that followed World War I; so that no modern Shakespeare could conceive of presenting warriors and kings in the light shed on them by the chronicle plays, nor can we imagine a contemporary Vergil suggesting that death for the fatherland is sweet. Yet we fight wars still, ever vaster and more efficient wars, while senators and commissars alike speak, and are applauded for speaking, in all seriousness the very lines given caricatured senators and commissars in satirical antiwar novels.

Worse still, the antiheroic revolt has itself become in two or three generations a new convention, the source of a new set of fashionably ridiculous clichés. Shameless politicians are as likely to use the slogans of between-the-wars pacifism to launch new wars as they are to refurbish more ancient platitudes. The wild freedom with which the authors of *The Enormous Room* and *Le Feu, The Good Soldier: Schweik* and *A Farewell to Arms,* challenged millennial orthodoxies has been sadly tamed; its fate is symbolized by Picasso's domesticated dove hovering obediently over the rattling spears of the Soviet war camp. Nevertheless, such books still tell us certain truths about the world in which we live, reveal to us certain ways in which men's consciousness of themselves in peace and war was radically altered some four decades ago.

The antiwar novel did not end war, but it memorializes the end of something almost as deeply rooted in the culture of the West: the concept of Honor. It comes into existence at the moment when in the West men, still nominally Christian, come to believe *that the worst thing of all is to die*—more exactly, perhaps, the moment when for the first time in a thousand years it is possible to *admit* that no cause is worth dying for. There are various mitigated forms of this new article of faith: that no cause is worth the death of all humanity, or of a whole nation, or simply of millions of lives; but inevitably it approaches the formulation: no cause is worth the death of a man, no cause is worth the death of *me!*

There are in the traditional literatures of Europe, to be sure, characters who have believed that death was the worst event and honor a figment; but such characters have always belonged to "low comedy," i.e., they have been comic butts set against representatives of quite other ideals, Sancho Panzas who serve Don Quixotes, Falstaffs who tremble before Prince Hals, Leporellos who cower as the Don Giovanni tempt fate. They have been permitted to blaspheme against the courtly codes precisely because those codes have been so secure. And, in any event, their cowardice has always spoken in prose or dialect, worn the garb of a servant or vassal, bowed the knee before an unchallenged master. They represented not a satirical challenge but precisely a "comic relief" from the strain of upholding—against the promptings of our animal nature, the demands of indolence, and greed, and fear—those high values that were once thought to make men fully human. *Fatti non foste a viver come bruti, ma per seguire virtute e conoscenza.*

What happens, however, when the Leporellos, the Falstaffs, and the Sancho Panzas begin to inherit the earth? When the remaining masters are in fact more egregious Falstaffs and Leporellos and Sancho Panzas, and all that Don Quixote and Prince Hal and Don Giovanni once stood for is discredited or dead? What happens in a time of democracy, mass culture, and mechanization, a time when war itself is transformed by the industrial revolution? *The Good Soldier: Schweik* addresses itself to answering, precisely and hilariously, this question. And the answer is: what happens is what has been happening to us all ever since 1914, what happens is *us*.

We inhabit for the first time a world in which men begin wars knowing their avowed ends will not be accomplished, a world in which it is more and more difficult to believe that the conflicts we cannot avert are in any sense justified. And in such a world, the draft dodger, the malingerer, the gold brick, the crap-out, all who make what Hemingway was the first to call "a separate peace," all who somehow *survive* the bombardment of shells and cant, become a new kind of anti-heroic hero. Of such men, Schweik is the real ancestor. "A great epoch calls for great men," Hašek tell us in a prefatory note. "Today, in the streets of Prague, you can come across a man who himself does not realize what his significance is in the history of the great new epoch. . . . If you were to ask him his name, he would answer . . . 'I am Schweik.' . . . He did not set fire to the temple of the goddess at Ephesus, like that fool of a Herostrate, merely in order to get his name into the . . . school reading books. And that, in itself, is enough."

Not all of Hašek's book, unfortunately, is devoted to portraying a Falstaff in a world without Hotspurs or Prince Hals. Much of it is spent in editorializing rather obviously about the horrors of war and the ironies of being a chaplain, the shortcomings of the Emperor Franz Joseph and the limitations of the military mind; and toward the end it becomes rather too literary in a heavy-handed way, especially after the introduction of Volunteer Officer Marek, a figure obviously intended to speak directly for the author. From time to time, we feel it as dated, say, as *What Price Glory* or *All Quiet on the Western Front*, for we have grown by now as weary of the phrasemongering and self-pity of conventional pacifism as of the attitudinizing and pharisaism of conventional patriotism.

It is not Hašek's anticlericalism or anti-Semitism, not his distrust of Magyars or of the long-defunct Austrian Empire, not his Czech nationalism or his defense of the Czech tongue against German linguistic imperialism that moves us today. The dream of expropriation, too ("After this war, they say, there ain't going to be any more emperors and they'll help themselves to the big royal estates"), rings hollow for us now, who know how it turned into the nightmare from which Jan Masaryk leaped to his death two wars later.

It is only when Hašek turns Schweik loose among scoundrels quite like himself, the police spy Bretschneider or the atheist Jewish chaplain, Otto Katz, and permits him to speak his own language—only, that is to say, when the anarchist intellectual permits himself to be possessed by his *lumpen* antihero—that the book becomes at once wonderfully funny and wonderfully true. Schweik is fortunately one of those mythical creations who escape the prejudices of their creators even as they elude our definitions; and he refuses to speak with the voice of the 1920 revolutionary, even as he refuses to speak with the voice of councilors and kings.

He will not be exploited by his author any more than he will be by the con men and bullies who inhabit his fictional universe; moving through a society of victimizers, he refuses to become a victim. Though Hašek would persuade us that he is surrounded by Pilates ("The glorious history of the Roman domination of Jerusalem was being enacted all over again"), Schweik certainly does not consider himself a Christ. He is neither innocent nor a claimant to innocence. Charged with political crimes by an absurd police spy, he pleads guilty; and to a fellow prisoner who cries, "I'm innocent, I'm innocent," he remarks blandly, "So was Jesus Christ but they crucified Him for all that. Nobody anywhere at any time has ever cared a damn whether a man's innocent or not."

To Schweik malice is simply one of the facts of life, the inexhaustible evil of man a datum from which all speculation about survival must begin. He neither looks back to a Golden Age nor forward to redemption, secular or heavenly, but knows that if he is to survive it must be in a world quite like the one he has always known. A communicant of no church and a member of no party, he considers that neither intelligence nor charity are likely to ameliorate man's condition. "Anybody can make a mistake," he says at one point, "and the more he thinks about a thing, the more mistakes he's bound to make." And at another, he remarks with a straight-faced nihilism before which we can seek refuge only in laughter, "If all people wanted to do all the others a good turn, they'd be walloping each other in a brace of shakes."

Return evil for evil is Schweik's anti-Golden Rule, though often he assumes the guise of nonresistance, along with the semblance of idiocy, to do it. He is, however, neither a pharisee nor a hypocrite, only a simple conniver—in civil life, a peddler of dogs with forged pedigrees; in war, a soldier who will not fight. His resistance to war is based on no higher principles than his business; both are rooted in the conviction that a man must somehow *live* and, if possible, thrive on the very disasters which surround him. In the end, he is a kind of success, as success goes in a society intent on committing suicide; he eats well, drinks well, sleeps with the mistress of one of his masters, and pummels another mercilessly. But above all, he does not die. What more can a man ask?

He is even promoted from a lowly batman to company orderly, though, of course, the one place he will not go to is the Front. No matter how hard history nudges him, no matter what his orders read, nothing will force him into battle. He marches resolutely backward or in circles, but never forward into the sound of shooting; and by the novel's end, he has managed blessedly to be taken prisoner by his own side. Refusing to recognize the reality of disaster, he turns each apparent defeat into a victory, proving himself in the end no more a schlemiel than a Victim, or one of those Little Men so beloved in sentimental protest literature. Yet he seems sometimes all three, for it pleases his native slyness to assume such roles, fooling us as readers, even as he fools his superiors in the fiction they share, and as we suspect he fools the author himself. Indeed, he is fond of speaking of himself as "unlucky," but when he explains what this epithet means, it turns out he is unlucky only to others, especially those unwise enough to entrust him with important commissions.

Schweik's affiliation runs back through all the liars of literature to the father of lies himself, back through Falstaff to the sly parasites of Roman comedy and the Vices, those demidevils of medieval literature. He is, in fact, the spirit that denies, as well as the spirit that deceives: but he plays his part without melodrama, among the clowns, his little finger on the seam of his trousers, and his chin tucked in. So plump, affable, snub-nosed, and idiotically eager to please does he seem, that we are more inclined to pat his head than to cry, "Get thee behind me!"

Yet on his lips the noblest slogans become mockeries. Let him merely cry, "God save the Emperor" and all who listen are betrayed to laughter; for he speaks in the name of the dark margin of ambivalence in us all—that 5 or 10 per cent of distrust and ridicule that lurks in our hearts in regard even to the cause to which we are most passionately committed. And in the world in which Hašek imagines him, there is none to gainsay him, since the spokesman for the 90 or 95 per cent of ordinary affirmation are corrupted or drunken or dumb.

We cannot help knowing, moreover, that not only the slogans of a distant war and a fallen empire, but those most dear to us now—the battle cries of democracy or socialism— would become in that same mouth equally hilarious; our pledges of allegiance intolerable jokes even to us who affirm them. Surely Schweik is not yet dead, but survives in concentration camps and army barracks, in prison cells and before investigating committees, assuring his interrogators of his feeble-mindedness and his good will as their pretenses to virtue and prudence crumble before his garrulous irrelevancies. "Beg to report, sir," he says looking us right in the eye, "I'm an idiot, sir." And the idiocy of our definitions of sanity becomes immediately apparent.

It seems appropriate that Jaroslav Hašek and Franz Kafka lived at the same moment in the same city; for, though their politics differed as did the very language in which they chose to write, though one was mildly anti-Semitic and the other a

Jew, their visions of the world's absurdity were much the same. Perhaps there was no better place from which to watch the decay of Europe and the values which had nurtured it than Prague; no better place to see how *comic* that catastrophe was.

Jewish legend tells us that precisely in Prague, in the attic of that city's ancient synagogue, the *Golem* waits to be reborn: the sleeping man-made Avenger who will awake only when some terror beyond all the Jews have known threatens the world. And maybe, after all, Schweik is no devil, but only that *Golem* in the uniform of a doomed empire, more comic in his second coming than anyone could have foreseen. "Terribly funny," we say putting down the book, and not taking the adverb seriously enough.

Kafka, we remember, thought himself a humorist, yet we shudder reading him. Hašek, it would appear, believed he wrote a tale of terror and was greeted by laughter. Let us leave the final word to Schweik, who reports, getting the names a little wrong, of course, but making his point all the same, "I once knew a Czech author personally, a chap named Ladislav Hajek. . . . He was a cheerful gentleman, he was, and a good sort, too. He once went to a pub and read a lot of his stories there. They were very sad stories and they made everybody laugh, and then he started crying and stood us drinks all around and—"

The account remains unfinished, like the book in which it appears, for the tale of the Good Soldier Schweik can never really be done; and, in any event, Hašek, who roused him from his long sleep in Prague, died at forty of the T.B. he had contracted in the prison camps of World War I.

Leslie A. Fiedler

Fano, Italy
26 July 1962

AUTHOR'S PREFACE

A GREAT EPOCH calls for great men. There are modest unrecognized heroes, without Napoleon's glory or his record of achievements. An analysis of their characters would overshadow even the glory of Alexander the Great. Today, in the streets of Prague, you can come across a man who himself does not realize what his significance is in the history of the great new epoch. Modestly he goes his way, troubling nobody, nor is he himself troubled by journalists applying to him for an interview. If you were to ask him his name, he would answer in a simple and modest tone of voice: "I am Schweik."

And this quiet, unassuming, shabbily dressed man is actually the good old soldier Schweik; that heroic, dauntless man who was the talk of all citizens in the Kingdom of Bohemia when they were under Austrian rule and whose glory will not pass away even now that we have a republic.

I am very fond of the good soldier Schweik, and in presenting an account of his adventures during the World War, I am convinced that you will all sympathize with this modest, unrecognized hero. He did not set fire to the temple of the goddess at Ephesus, like that fool of a Herostrate, merely in order to get his name into the newspapers and the school reading books.

And that, in itself, is enough.

CONTENTS

BOOK I

BOOK I

1.

Schweik, the Good Soldier,
Intervenes in the Great War

"So THEY'VE killed Ferdinand," said the charwoman to Mr. Schweik who, having left the army many years before, when a military medical board had declared him to be chronically feeble-minded, earned a livelihood by the sale of dogs—repulsive mongrel monstrosities for whom he forged pedigrees. Apart from this occupation, he was afflicted with rheumatism, and was just rubbing his knees with embrocation.

"Which Ferdinand, Mrs. Müller?" asked Schweik, continuing to massage his knees. "I know two Ferdinands. One of them does jobs for Prusa the chemist, and one day he drank a bottle of hair oil by mistake; and then there's Ferdinand Kokoska who goes around collecting manure. They wouldn't be any great loss, either of 'em."

"No, it's the Archduke Ferdinand, the one from Konopiste, you know, Mr. Schweik, the fat, pious one."

"Good Lord!" exclaimed Schweik. "That's a fine thing. And where did this happen?"

"They shot him at Sarajevo with a revolver, you know. He was riding there with his Archduchess in a motor car."

"Just fancy that now, Mrs. Müller, in a motor car. Ah, a gentleman like him can afford it and he never thinks how a ride in a motor car like that can end up badly. And at Sarajevo in the bargain, that's in Bosnia, Mrs. Müller. I expect the Turks did it. I reckon we never ought to have taken Bosnia and Herzegovina away from them. And there you are, Mrs. Müller. Now the Archduke's in a better land. Did he suffer long?"

"The Archduke was done for on the spot. You know, people didn't ought to mess about with revolvers. They're dangerous things, that they are. Not long ago there was another gentleman down our way larking about with a revolver and he shot a whole family as well as the house porter, who went to see who was shooting on the third floor."

"There's some revolvers, Mrs. Müller, that won't go off, even if you tried till you was dotty. There's lots like that. But they're sure to have bought something better than that for the Archduke, and I wouldn't mind betting, Mrs. Müller, that the man who did it put on his best clothes for the job. You know, it wants a bit of doing to shoot an archduke; it's not like when a poacher shoots a gamekeeper. You have to find out how to get at him; you can't reach an important man like that if you're dressed just anyhow. You have to wear a top hat or else the police'd run you in before you knew where you were."

"I hear there was a whole lot of 'em, Mr. Schweik."

"Why, of course, there was, Mrs. Müller," said Schweik, now concluding the massage of his knees. "If you wanted to kill an archduke or the Emperor, for instance, you'd naturally talk it over with somebody. Two heads are better than one. One gives one bit of advice, another gives another, and so the good work prospers, as the hymn says. The chief thing is to keep on the watch till the gentleman you're after rides past. . . . But there's plenty more of them waiting their turn for it. You mark my words, Mrs. Müller, they'll get the Czar and Czarina yet, and maybe, though let's hope not, the Emperor himself, now that they've started with his uncle. The old chap's got a lot of enemies. More than Ferdinand had.

A little while ago a gentleman in the saloon bar was saying that there'd come a time when all the emperors would get done in one after another, and that not all their bigwigs and suchlike would save them. Then he couldn't pay for his drinks and the landlord had to have him run in. And he gave him a smack in the jaw and two to the policeman. After that they had to strap him down in the police ambulance, just to bring him to his senses. Yes, Mrs. Müller, there's queer goings on nowadays; that there is. That's another loss to Austria. When I was in the army there was a private who shot a captain. He loaded his rifle and went into the orderly room. They told him to clear out, but he kept on saying that he must speak to the captain. Well, the captain came along and gave him a dose of c.b.[1] Then he took his rifle and scored a fair bull's-eye. The bullet went right through the captain and when it came out the other side, it did some damage in the orderly room in the bargain. It smashed a bottle of ink and the ink got spilled all over some regimental records."

"And what happened to the private?" asked Mrs. Müller after a while, when Schweik was getting dressed.

"He hanged himself with a pair of braces," said Schweik, brushing his bowler hat. "And the braces wasn't even his. He borrowed them from a jailer, making out that his trousers were coming down. You can't blame him for not waiting till they shot him. You know, Mrs. Müller, it's enough to turn anyone's head, being in a fix like that. The jailer lost his rank and got six months as well. But he didn't serve his time. He ran away to Switzerland and now he does a bit of preaching for some church or other. There ain't many honest people about nowadays, Mrs. Müller. I expect that the Archduke was taken in by the man who shot him. He saw a chap standing there and thought: Now there's a decent fellow, cheering me and all. And then the chap did him in. Did he give him one or several?"

"The newspaper says, Mr. Schweik, that the Archduke was riddled with bullets. He emptied the whole lot into him."

"That was mighty quick work, Mrs. Müller, mighty quick. I'd buy a Browning for a job like that. It looks like a toy, but in a couple of minutes you could shoot twenty archdukes with it, thin or fat. Although between ourselves, Mrs. Müller, it's easier to hit a fat archduke than a thin one. You may remember the time they shot their king in Portugal. He was a fat

[1] Confined to barracks.

fellow. Of course, you don't expect a king to be thin. Well, now I'm going to call around at The Flagon and if anybody comes for that little terrier I took the advance for, you can tell 'em I've got him at my dog farm in the country. I just cropped his ears and now he mustn't be taken away till his ears heal up or else he'd catch cold in them. Give the key to the house porter."

There was only one customer at The Flagon. This was Bretschneider, a plain-clothes policeman who was on secret service work. Palivec, the landlord, was washing glasses and Bretschneider vainly endeavored to engage him in a serious conversation.

"We're having a fine summer," was Bretschneider's overture to a serious conversation.

"All damn rotten," replied Palivec, putting the glasses away into a cupboard.

"That's a fine thing they've done for us at Sarajevo," Bretschneider observed, with his hopes rather dashed.

"What Sarajevo's that?" inquired Palivec. "D'you mean the wineshop at Nusle? They have a rumpus there every day. Well, you know what sort of place Nusle is."

"No, I mean Sarajevo in Bosnia. They shot the Archduke Ferdinand there. What do you think of that?"

"I never shove my nose into that sort of thing, I'm hanged if I do," primly replied Mr. Palivec, lighting his pipe. "Nowadays, it's as much as your life's worth to get mixed up in them. I've got my business to see to. When a customer comes in and orders beer, why, I just serve him his drink. But Sarajevo or politics or a dead archduke, that's not for the likes of us, unless we want to end up doing time."

Bretschneider said no more, but stared disappointedly around the empty bar.

"You used to have a picture of the Emperor hanging here," he began again presently, "just at the place where you've got a mirror now."

"Yes, that's right," replied Mr. Palivec. "It used to hang there and the flies left their trade-mark on it, so I put it away into the lumber room. You see, somebody might pass a remark about it and then there might be trouble. What use is it to me?"

"Sarajevo must be a rotten sort of place, eh, Mr. Palivec?"

Mr. Palivec was extremely cautious in answering this deceptively straightforward question. "At this time of the year it's damned hot in Bosnia and Herzegovina. When I was in the army there, we always had to put ice on our company officer's head."

"What regiment did you serve in, Mr. Palivec?"

"I can't remember a little detail like that. I never cared a damn about the whole business, and I wasn't inquisitive about it," replied Mr. Palivec. "It doesn't do to be so inquisitive."

Bretschneider stopped talking once and for all, and his woe-begone expression brightened up only on the arrival of Schweik, who came in and ordered black beer with the remark: "At Vienna they're in mourning today."

Bretschneider's eyes began to gleam with hope. He said curtly: "There are ten black flags at Konopiste."

"There ought to be twelve," said Schweik, when he had taken a gulp.

"What makes you think it's twelve?" asked Bretschneider.

"To make it a round number, a dozen. That's easier to reckon out and things always come cheaper by the dozen," replied Schweik.

This was followed by a long silence, which Schweik himself interrupted with a sigh. "Well, he's in a better land now, God rest his soul. He didn't live to be Emperor. When I was in the army, there was a general who fell off his horse and got killed as quiet as could be. They wanted to help him back onto his horse and when they went to lift him up, they saw he was stone dead. And he was just going to be promoted to field marshal. It happened during an army inspection. No good ever comes of those inspections. There was an inspection of some sort or other at Sarajevo, too. I remember once at an inspection like that there was twenty buttons missing from my tunic and I got two weeks' solitary confinement for it, and I spent two days of it tied up hand and foot. But there's got to be discipline in the army, or else nobody'd care a rap what he did. Our company commander, he always used to say to us, 'There's got to be discipline, you thickheaded louts, or else you'd be crawling about like monkeys on trees, but the army'll make men of you, you thickheaded boobies.' And isn't it true? Just imagine a park and a soldier without discipline on every tree. That's what I was always most afraid of."

"That business at Sarajevo," Bretschneider resumed, "was done by the Serbs."

"You're wrong there," replied Schweik, "it was done by the Turks, because of Bosnia and Herzegovina."

And Schweik expounded his views of Austrian international policy in the Balkans. The Turks were the losers in 1912 against Serbia, Bulgaria, and Greece. They had wanted Austria to help them and when this was not done, they had shot Ferdinand.

"Do you like the Turks," said Schweik, turning to Palivec. "Do you like that heathen pack of dogs? You don't, do you?"

"One customer's the same as another customer," said Palivec, "even if he's a Turk. People like us who've got their business to look after can't be bothered with politics. Pay for your drink and sit down and say what you like. That's my principle. It's all the same to me whether our Ferdinand was done in by a Serb or a Turk, a Catholic or a Moslem, an anarchist or a young Czech liberal."

"That's all well and good, Mr. Palivec," remarked Bretschneider, who had regained hope that one or other of these two could be caught out, "but you'll admit that it's a great loss to Austria."

Schweik replied for the landlord, "Yes, there's no denying it. A fearful loss. You can't replace Ferdinand by any sort of tomfool. Still, he ought to have been a bit fatter."

"What do you mean?" asked Bretschneider, growing alert.

"What do I mean?" replied Schweik composedly. "Why, only just this: If he'd been fatter, he'd certainly have had a stroke earlier, when he chased the old women away at Konopiste, when they were gathering firewood and mushrooms on his preserves there, and then he wouldn't have died such a shocking death. When you come to think of it, for him, the Emperor's uncle, to get shot like that, oh, it's shocking, that it is, and the newspapers are full of it. But what I say is, I wouldn't like to be the Archduke's widow. What's she going to do now? Marry some other archduke? What good would come of that? She'd take another trip to Sarajevo with him and be left a widow for the second time. A good many years ago there was a gamekeeper at Zlim. He was called Pindour. A rum name, eh? Well, he was shot by poachers and left a widow with two children. A year later she married another gamekeeper from Mydlovary. And they shot him, too. Then she got married a third time and said: 'All good things go by threes. If this turns out badly, I don't know what I shall do.' Blessed if they didn't shoot him, too, and by that time she'd had six children with all those gamekeepers. So she went to the Lord of the Manor himself at Hluboka and complained of the trouble she'd had with the gamekeepers. Then she was advised to try Jares, a pond keeper. Well, you wouldn't believe it, but he got drowned while he was fishing and she'd had two children with him. Then she married a pig gelder from Vodnany and one night he hit her with an axe and gave himself up to the police. When they hanged him at the assizes in Pisek, he said he had no regrets and on top of that he passed some very nasty remarks about the Emperor."

"Do you happen to know what he said?" inquired Bretschneider in a hopeful voice.

"I can't tell you that, because nobody had the nerve to repeat it. But they say it was something pretty awful, and that one of the justices, who was in court at the time, went mad when he heard it, and they're still keeping him in solitary confinement so as it shouldn't get known. It wasn't just the ordinary sort of nasty remark like people make when they're drunk."

"What sort of nasty remarks about the Emperor do people make when they're drunk?" asked Bretschneider.

"Come, come, gentlemen, talk about something else," said the landlord, "that's the sort of thing I don't like. One word leads to another and then it gets you into trouble."

"What sort of nasty remarks about the Emperor do people make when they're drunk?" repeated Bretschneider.

"All sorts. Just you have too much to drink and get them to play the Austrian hymn and you'll see what you'll start saying. You'll think of such a lot of things about the Emperor that if only half of them were true, it'd be enough to disgrace him for the rest of his life. Not that the old gentleman deserves it. Why, look at it this way. He lost his son Rudolf at a tender age when he was in the prime of life. His wife was stabbed with a file; then Johann Orth got lost and his brother, the Emperor of Mexico, was shot in a fortress up against a wall. Now, in his old age, they've shot his uncle. Things like that get on a man's nerves. And then some drunken chap takes it into his head to call him names. If war was to break out today, I'd go of my own accord and serve the Emperor to my last breath."

Schweik took a deep gulp and continued, "Do you think the Emperor's going to put up with that sort of thing? Little do you know him. You mark my words, there's got to be

27

war with the Turks. Kill my uncle, would you? Then take this smack in the jaw for a start. Oh, there's bound to be war. Serbia and Russia'll help us. There won't half be a bust-up."

At this prophetic moment Schweik was really good to look upon. His artless countenance, smiling like the full moon, beamed with enthusiasm. The whole thing was so utterly clear to him.

"Maybe," he continued his delineation of the future of Austria, "if we have war with the Turks, the Germans'll attack us, because the Germans and the Turks stand by each other. They're a low lot, the scum of the earth. Still, we can join France, because they've had a grudge against Germany ever since '71. And then there'll be lively doings. There's going to be war. I can't tell you more than that."

Bretschneider stood up and said solemnly, "You needn't say any more. Follow me into the passage and there I'll say something to you."

Schweik followed the plain-clothes policeman into the passage where a slight surprise awaited him when his fellow toper showed him his badge and announced that he was now arresting him and would at once convey him to the police headquarters. Schweik endeavored to explain that there must be some mistake; that he was entirely innocent; that he hadn't uttered a single word capable of offending anyone.

But Bretschneider told him that he had actually committed several penal offenses, among them being high treason.

Then they returned to the saloon bar and Schweik said to Mr. Palivec, "I've had five beers and a couple of sausages with a roll. Now let me have a cherry brandy and I must be off, as I'm arrested."

Bretschneider showed Mr. Palivec his badge, looked at Mr. Palivec for a moment, and then asked, "Are you married?"

"Yes."

"And can your wife carry on the business during your absence?"

"Yes."

"That's all right, then, Mr. Palivec," said Bretschneider breezily. "Tell your wife to step this way. Hand the business over to her, and we'll come for you in the evening."

"Don't you worry about that," Schweik comforted him. "I'm being run in only for high treason."

"But what about me?" lamented Mr. Palivec. "I've been so careful what I said."

Bretschneider smiled and said triumphantly, "I've got you for saying that the flies left their trade-mark on the Emperor. You'll have all that stuff knocked out of your head."

And Schweik left The Flagon in the company of the plain-clothes policeman. When they reached the street Schweik, fixing his good-humored smile upon Bretschneider's countenance, inquired, "Shall I get off the pavement?"

"How d'you mean?"

"Why, I thought now I'm arrested I mustn't walk on the pavement."

When they were passing through the entrance to the police headquarters, Schweik said, "Well, that passed off very nicely. Do you often go to The Flagon?"

And while they were leading Schweik into the reception bureau, Mr. Palivec at The Flagon was handing over the business to his weeping wife, whom he was comforting in his own special manner. "Now stop crying and don't make all that row. What can they do to me on account of the Emperor's portrait where the flies left their trade-mark?"

And thus Schweik, the good soldier, intervened in the World War in that pleasant, amiable manner which was so peculiarly his. It will be of interest to historians to know that he saw far into the future. If the situation subsequently developed otherwise than he expounded it at The Flagon, we must take into account the fact that he lacked a preliminary diplomatic training.

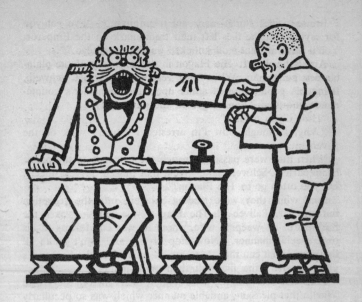

2.

Schweik, the Good Soldier,

at the Police Headquarters

THE SARAJEVO assassination had filled the police headquarters with numerous victims. They were brought in, one after the other, and the old inspector in the reception bureau said in his good-humored voice, "This Ferdinand business is going to cost you dear." When they had shut Schweik up in one of the numerous dens on the first floor, he found six persons already assembled there. Five of them were sitting around the table, and in a corner a middle-aged man was sitting on a mattress as if he were holding aloof from the rest.

Schweik began to ask one after the other why they had been arrested.

From the five sitting at the table he received practically the same reply: "That Sarajevo business." "That Ferdinand business." "It's all through that murder of the Archduke." "That

Ferdinand affair." "Because they did the Archduke in at Sarajevo."

The sixth man who was holding aloof from the other five said that he didn't want to have anything to do with them because he didn't want any suspicion to fall on him. He was there only for attempted robbery with violence.

Schweik joined the company of conspirators at the table, who were telling each other for at least the tenth time how they had got there.

All, except one, had been caught either in a public house, a wineshop, or a café. The exception consisted of an extremely fat gentleman with spectacles and tear-stained eyes who had been arrested in his own home because two days before the Sarajevo outrage he had stood drinks to two Serbian students, and had been observed by Detective Brix drunk in their company at the Montmartre night club where, as he had already confirmed by his signature on the report, he had again stood them drinks.

In reply to all questions during the preliminary investigations at the commissariat of police, he had uttered a stereotyped lament: "I'm a stationer."

Whereupon he had received an equally stereotyped reply: "That's no excuse."

A little fellow, who had come to grief in a wineshop, was a teacher of history and he had been giving the wine merchant the history of various political murders. He had been arrested at the moment when he was concluding a psychological analysis of all assassinations with the words, "The idea underlying assassination is as simple as the egg of Columbus."

Which remark the commissary of police had amplified at the cross-examination thus: "And as sure as eggs are eggs, there's quod in store for you."

The third conspirator was the chairman of the "Dobromil" Benevolent Society. On the day of the assassination the "Dobromil" had arranged a garden party, combined with a concert. A sergeant of gendarmes had called upon the merry-makers to disperse, because Austria was in mourning, whereupon the chairman of the "Dobromil" had remarked good-humoredly, "Just wait a moment till they've played *Hej Slované*." [1]

Now he was sitting there with downcast heart and lamenting, "They elect a new chairman in August and if I'm not

[1] Czech popular song.

31

home by then I may not be re-elected. This is my tenth term as chairman and I'd never get over the disgrace of it."

The late Ferdinand had played a queer trick on the fourth conspirator, a man of sterling character and unblemished scutcheon. For two whole days he had avoided any conversation on the subject of Ferdinand, till in the evening when he was playing cards in a café, he had won a trick by trumping the king of clubs.

"Bang goes the king—just like at Sarajevo."

As for the fifth man, who was there, as he put it, because they did the Archduke in at Sarajevo, his hair and beard were bristling with terror, so that his head recalled that of a fox terrier. He hadn't spoken a word in the restaurant where he was arrested—in fact he hadn't even read the newspaper reports about Ferdinand's assassination, but was sitting at a table all alone, when an unknown man had sat down opposite him and said in hurried tones, "Have you read it?"

"No."

"Do you know about it?"

"No."

"Do you know what it's all about?"

"No, I can't be bothered about it."

"You ought to take an interest in it all the same."

"I don't know what I ought to take an interest in. I'll just smoke a cigar, have a few drinks, have a bit of supper, but I won't read the papers. The papers are full of lies. Why should I upset myself?"

"So you didn't take any interest even in the Sarajevo murder?"

"I don't take any interest in any murders, whether they're in Prague, Vienna, Sarajevo, or London. That's the business of the authorities, the law courts and the police. If anyone gets murdered anywhere, serves him right. Why does he want to be such a damn fool as to let himself get murdered?"

Those were his last words at that conversation. Since then he had kept on repeating in a loud voice at intervals of five minutes, "I'm innocent, I'm innocent."

He had shouted these words in the entrance to the police headquarters, he would repeat them while being conveyed to the Prague sessions, and with these words on his lips he would enter his prison cell.

When Schweik had heard all these dreadful tales of conspiracy he thought fit to make clear to them the complete hopelessness of their situation.

"We're all in the deuce of a mess," he began his words of comfort. "You say that nothing can happen to you, to all of us, but you're wrong. What have we got the police for except to punish us for letting our tongues wag? If the times are so dangerous that archdukes get shot, the likes of us mustn't be surprised if we're taken up before the beak. They're doing all this to make a bit of a splash, so that Ferdinand'll be in the limelight before his funeral. The more of us there are, the better it'll be for us, because we'll feel all the jollier. When I was in the army, sometimes half the company were shoved into clink. And lots of innocent men used to get punished. Not only in the army, in the law courts, too. Once I remember there was a woman who was sentenced for strangling her new-born twins. Although she swore she couldn't have strangled the twins, because she's only had one baby, a female one, that she managed to strangle quite painlessly, she was sentenced for double murder. Once the court takes a thing up, there's trouble. But there's bound to be trouble. It may be that not all people are such crooks as they're taken for. But nowadays how are you going to tell an honest man from a crook, especially now in these grave times when Ferdinand got done in? When I was in the army the captain's pet dog got shot in the wood behind the parade ground. When he heard about it, he called us all out on parade and ordered every tenth man to step one pace forward. Of course, I was a tenth man, and there we stood at attention without moving an eyelash. The captain walked around us and said, 'You blackguards, you ruffians, you scum, you scabby brutes, I'd like to shove the whole gang of you into solitary confinement over that dog. I'd chop you into mincemeat, I'd shoot you and have you turned into stew. But just to show you that I'm not going to treat you leniently, I'm giving you all fourteen days c.b.' You see, that time the trouble was over a dog, but a full-blown archduke's at the bottom of it all. That's why they've got to put the fear of God into people, so as to make the trouble worth while."

"I'm innocent, I'm innocent," repeated the man with the bristly hair.

"So was Jesus Christ," said Schweik, "but they crucified Him for all that. Nobody anywhere at any time has ever cared a damn whether a man's innocent or not. *Maul halten*

33

und weiter dienen,[2] as they used to tell us in the army. That's the best and wisest thing to do."

Whereupon Schweik stretched himself out on the mattress and fell asleep contentedly.

In the meanwhile, two new arrivals were brought in. One of them was a Bosnian. He walked up and down gnashing his teeth. The other new guest was Palivec who, on seeing his acquaintance Schweik, woke him up and exclaimed in a voice full of tragedy, "Now I'm here, too!"

Schweik shook hands with him cordially and said, "I'm glad of that, really I am. I felt sure that gentleman'd keep his word when he told you they'd come and fetch you. It's nice to know you can rely on people."

Mr. Palivec, however, remarked that he didn't care a damn whether he could rely on people or not, and he asked Schweik on the quiet whether the other prisoners were thieves who might do harm to his business reputation.

Schweik explained to him that all except one, who had been arrested for attempted robbery with violence, were there on account of the Archduke.

Mr. Palivec was annoyed and said that he wasn't there on account of any fool of an archduke, but on the Emperor's account. And as this began to interest the others, he told them how the flies had soiled the Emperor.

"They left stains on him, the vermin," he concluded the account of his mishap, "and now I've been put into jail. I'll pay those flies out for this," he added menacingly.

Schweik went back to sleep, but not for long, because they soon came to take him away to be cross-examined.

And so, mounting the staircase to Section 3 for his cross-examination, Schweik bore his cross to the summit of Golgotha, although he himself was unaware of his martyrdom.

On seeing a notice that spitting was prohibited in the corridors, he asked the police sergeant to let him spit into a spittoon, and beaming with good nature, he entered the bureau, saying, "Good evening, gentlemen, I hope you're all well."

Instead of a reply, someone pummeled him in the ribs and stood him in front of a table behind which sat a gentleman with a cold official face and features of such brutish savagery that he looked as if he had just tumbled out of Lombroso's book on criminal types.

[2] "Hold your tongue, and get on with your job."

34

He hurled a bloodthirsty glance at Schweik and said, "Take that idiotic expression off your face."

"I can't help it," replied Schweik solemnly. "I was discharged from the army on account of being weak-minded and a special board reported me officially as weak-minded. I'm officially weak-minded—a chronic case."

The gentleman with the criminal countenance grated his teeth as he said, "The offense you're accused of and that you've committed shows you've got all your wits about you."

And he now proceeded to enumerate to Schweik a long list of crimes, beginning with high treason and ending with insulting language toward His Royal Highness and Members of the Royal Family. The central gem of this collection constituted approval of the murder of the Archduke Ferdinand, and from this again branched off a string of fresh offenses, among which sparkled incitement to rebellion, as the whole business had happened in a public place.

"What have you got to say for yourself?" triumphantly asked the gentleman with the features of brutish savagery.

"There's a lot of it," replied Schweik innocently. "You can have too much of a good thing."

"So you admit it's true?"

"I admit everything. You've got to be strict. If you ain't strict, why, where would you be? It's like when I was in the army—"

"Hold your tongue!" shouted the police commissioner. "And don't say a word unless you're asked a question. Do you understand?"

"Begging your pardon, sir, I do, and I've properly got the hang of every word you utter."

"Who do you keep company with?"

"The charwoman, sir."

"And you don't know anybody in political circles here?"

"Yes, sir, I take the afternoon edition of the *Narodni Politika,* you know, sir, the paper they call the puppy's delight."

"Get out of here!" roared the gentleman with the brutish appearance.

When they were taking him out of the bureau, Schweik said, "Good night, sir."

Having been deposited in his cell again, Schweik informed all the prisoners that the cross-examination was great fun. "They yell at you a bit and then kick you out." He paused a moment. "In olden times," continued Schweik, "it used to be much worse. I once read a book where it said that people charged with anything had to walk on red-hot iron and drink molten lead to see whether they was innocent or not. There was lots who was treated like that and then on top of it all they was quartered or put in the pillory somewhere near the Natural History Museum.

"Nowadays, it's great fun being run in," continued Schweik with relish. "There's no quartering or anything of that kind. We've got a mattress, we've got a table, we've got a seat, we ain't packed together like sardines, we'll get soup, they'll give us bread, they'll bring a pitcher of water, there's a closet right under our noses. It all shows you what progress there's been. Of course, it's rather a long way to the place where you're cross-examined, along three corridors and up one flight of stairs, but the corridors are clean and there's plenty going on in them. Some are being taken one way, others the opposite way, young and old, male and female. It's nice to know you're not alone. They all go wherever they're taken and they're absolutely satisfied, because they're not afraid of being told in the bureau, 'We've talked your case over and tomorrow you'll be quartered or burned alive, according as you prefer.' That must have been a nasty thing to have to look forward to, and I think, gentlemen, that it would have upset a good many of us. Ah, yes, nowadays things have improved for our benefit."

He had just concluded his vindication of the modern imprisonment of citizens when the warder opened the door and shouted, "Schweik, you've got to get dressed and go to be cross-examined."

"I'll get dressed," replied Schweik. "I've no objection to that, but it strikes me there must be some mistake. I've been cross-examined once and they chucked me out. And what I'm afraid is that these other gentlemen who are here along with me are going to have a grudge against me because I've been called for a cross-examination twice running and they've not been there at all yet this evening. It's enough to make them jealous of me."

"Clear out and shut your row," was the reply to Schweik's considerate representations.

Schweik again stood in the presence of the criminal-faced gentleman who, without any preliminaries, asked him in a harsh and relentless tone, "Do you admit everything?"

Schweik fixed his kindly blue eyes upon the pitiless person

36

and said mildly, "If you want me to admit it, sir, then I will. It can't do me any harm. But if you was to say, 'Schweik, don't admit anything,' I'll argue the point to my last breath."

The severe gentleman wrote something on his documents and, handing Schweik a pen, told him to sign.

And Schweik signed Bretschneider's depositions, with the following addition:

> All the above-mentioned accusations against me are based upon truth.
>
> JOSEF SCHWEIK

When he had signed, he turned to the severe gentleman. "Is there anything else for me to sign? Or am I to come back in the morning?"

"You'll be taken to the criminal court in the morning," was the answer.

"What time, sir? You see, I wouldn't like to oversleep myself, whatever happens."

"Get out!" came a roar for the second time that day from the other side of the table before which Schweik had stood.

On the way back to his new abode, which was provided with a grating, Schweik said to the police sergeant escorting him, "Everything here runs as smooth as clockwork."

As soon as the door had closed behind him, his fellow-prisoners overwhelmed him with all sorts of questions, to which Schweik replied brightly, "I've just admitted I probably murdered the Archduke Ferdinand."

And as he lay down on the mattress, he said, "It's a pity we haven't got an alarm clock here."

But in the morning they woke him up without an alarm clock, and precisely at six Schweik was taken away in the Black Maria to the county criminal court.

"The early bird catches the worm," said Schweik to his fellow travelers, as the Black Maria was passing out through the gates of the police headquarters.

3.

Schweik Before the Medical Authorities

THE clean, cozy cubicles of the county criminal court produced a very favorable impression upon Schweik—the white-washed walls, the black-leaded gratings, and the fat warder in charge of prisoners under remand, with the purple facings and purple braid on his official cap. Purple is the regulation color not only here but also at religious ceremonies on Ash Wednesday and Good Friday.

The glorious history of the Roman domination of Jerusalem was being enacted all over again. The prisoners were taken out and brought before the Pilates of 1914 down below on the ground floor. And the examining justices, the Pilates of the new epoch, instead of honorably washing their hands, sent out for stew and Pilsen beer and kept on transmitting new charges to the public prosecutor.

Here, for the greater part, all logic was in abeyance and it was red tape which was victorious, it was red tape which throttled, it was red tape which caused lunacy, it was red tape which made a fuss, it was red tape which chuckled, it was red tape which threatened and never pardoned. They were jugglers with the legal code, high priests of the letter of the law, who gobbled up accused persons, the tigers in the Austrian jungle, who measured the extent of their leap upon the accused according to the statute book.

The exception consisted of a few gentlemen (just as at the police headquarters) who did not take the law too seriously, for everywhere you will find wheat among the tares.

It was to one of these gentlemen that Schweik was conducted for cross-examination. When Schweik was led before him, he asked him with his inborn courtesy to sit down, and then said, "So you're this Mr. Schweik?"

"I think I must be," replied Schweik, "because my dad was called Schweik and my mother was Mrs. Schweik. I couldn't disgrace them by denying my name."

A bland smile flitted across the face of the examining counsel. "This is a fine business you've been up to. You've got plenty on your conscience."

"I've always got plenty on my conscience," said Schweik, smiling even more blandly than the counsel himself. "I bet I've got more on my conscience than what you have, sir."

"I can see that from the statement you signed," said the legal dignitary, in the same kindly tone. "Did they bring any pressure to bear upon you at the police headquarters?"

"Not a bit of it, sir. I myself asked them whether I had to sign it and when they said I had to, why, I just did what they told me. It's not likely I'm going to quarrel with them over my own signature. I shouldn't be doing myself any good that way. Things have got to be done in proper order."

"Do you feel quite well, Mr. Schweik?"

"I wouldn't say quite well, your worship. I've got rheumatism and I'm using embrocation for it."

The old gentleman again gave a kindly smile. "Suppose we were to have you examined by the medical authorities."

"I don't think there's much the matter with me and it wouldn't be fair to waste the gentlemen's time. There was one doctor examined me at the police headquarters."

"All the same, Mr. Schweik, we'll have a try with the medical authorities. We'll appoint a little commission, we'll have you placed under observation, and in the meanwhile you'll have a nice rest. Just one more question: According to the statement, you're supposed to have said that now a war's going to break out soon."

"Yes, your worship, it'll break out at any moment now."

"And do you ever feel run down at all?"

"No, sir, except that once I nearly got run down by a motor car, but that's years and years ago."

That concluded the cross-examination. Schweik shook hands with the legal dignitary and on his return to the cell he said to his neighbors, "Now they're going to have me examined by the medical authorities on account of this murder of Archduke Ferdinand."

"I've already been examined by the medical authorities," said one young man. "That was when I was had up in court over some carpets. They said I was weak-minded. Now I've embezzled a steam-threshing machine and they can't touch me. My lawyer told me yesterday that once I've been reported weak-minded I can make capital out of it for the rest of my life."

"I don't trust the medical authorities," remarked a man of intelligent appearance. "Once when I forged some bills of exchange I went to a lecture by Dr. Heveroch, and when they nabbed me I pretended to have an epileptic fit, just like Dr. Heveroch described it. I bit the leg of one of the medical authorities on the commission and drank the ink out of an inkpot. But just because I bit a man in the calf they reported I was quite well, and so I was done for."

"I am not afraid of their examination," declared Schweik. "When I was in the army, I was examined by a veterinary surgeon and I got on first-rate."

"The medical authorities are a rotten lot," announced a small, misshapen man. "Not long ago they happened to dig up a skeleton on my field and the medical authorities said the skeleton had been murdered by some blunt instrument forty years previously. Now I'm only thirty-eight, but they locked me up, though I've got a birth certificate, a certificate of baptism, and a copy of the entry in the parish register."

"I think," said Schweik, "that we ought to look at everything fair and square. Anybody can make a mistake, and the more he thinks about a thing, the more mistakes he's bound to make. The medical authorities are human beings, and human beings have got their failings. That's like once at Nusle, just by the bridge, a gentleman came up to me one night when I was on my way home and hit me over the head with a horse-whip and when I was lying on the ground he flashed a light on me and said, 'I've made a mistake, that's not him.' And it made him so wild to think he'd made a mistake that he landed me another whack across the back. It's just in the course of nature for a man to keep on making mistakes till he's dead. That's like the gentleman who found a mad dog half-frozen one night and took it home with him and shoved it into his wife's bed. As soon as the dog got warm and came to, it bit the whole family, and the youngest baby that was still in the cradle got torn to pieces and gobbled up by it. Or I can give you another example of a mistake that was made by a cabinetmaker who lived in the same house as me. He opened the church at Podol with his latchkey, thinking he was at home, undressed in the sacristy, thinking it was the kitchen, and lay down on the altar, thinking he was at home in bed, and he covered himself over with some of those counterpanes with scripture texts on them and he put the gospel and other sacred books under his head to keep it propped up. In the morning the verger found him and when he came to his senses, he told him in quite a cheerful sort of way that it was a mistake. 'A fine mistake,' said the verger, 'seeing as now we've got to have the church consecrated all over again because of it.' And here's another example I can give you of a mistake made by a police dog at Kladno. A wolfhound belonging to a Sergeant Roter, whom I daresay you've heard of. This Sergeant Roter used to train these dogs and make experiments on tramps, till at last all the tramps began to give the Kladno district a wide berth. So he gave orders that the gendarmes must run in any suspicious person at all costs. Well, one day they ran in a fairly well-dressed man whom they found sitting on the stump of a tree in the woods. They at once snipped off a piece of his coat tails and let the police dogs have a sniff at it. Then they took the man into a brickworks outside the town and let the trained dogs follow his tracks. The dogs found him and brought him back. Then the man had to climb a ladder into an attic, vault over a wall, jump into a pond, with the dogs after him. In the end it turned out that the man was a Czech radical M.P. who had taken a trip to the woods, through being so sick and tired of Parliament. That's why I say that people have their failings, they make mistakes, whether they're learned men or just damned fools who don't know any better. Why, even cabinet ministers can make mistakes."

41

The commission of medical authorities which had to decide whether Schweik's standard of intelligence did or did not conform to all the crimes with which he was charged, consisted of three extremely serious gentlemen with views which were such that the view of each separate one of them differed considerably from the views of the other two.

They represented three distinct schools of thought with regard to mental disorders.

If in the case of Schweik a complete agreement was reached between these diametrically opposed scientific camps, this can be explained simply and solely by the overwhelming impression produced upon them by Schweik who, on entering the room where his state of mind was to be examined and observing a picture of the Austrian ruler hanging on the wall, shouted, "Gentlemen, long live our Emperor, Franz Josef the First."

The matter was completely clear. Schweik's spontaneous utterance made it unnecessary to ask a whole lot of questions, and there remained only some of the most important ones, the answers to which were to corroboate Schweik's real opinion, thus:

"Is radium heavier than lead?"

"I've never weighed it, sir," answered Schweik with his sweet smile.

"Do you believe in the end of the world?"

"I have to see the end of the world first," replied Schweik in an offhand manner, "but I'm sure it won't come my way tomorrow."

"Could you measure the diameter of the globe?"

"No, that I couldn't, sir," answered Schweik, "but now I'll ask you a riddle, gentlemen. There's a three-storied house with eight windows on each story. On the roof there are two gables and two chimneys. There are two tenants on each story. And now, gentlemen, I want you to tell me in what year the house porter's grandmother died?"

The medical authorities looked at each other meaningly, but nevertheless one of them asked one more question. "Do you know the maximum depth of the Pacific Ocean?"

"I'm afraid I don't, sir," was the answer, "but it's pretty sure to be deeper than what the river is just below Prague."

The chairman of the commission curtly asked, "Is that enough?"

But one member inquired further: "How much is twelve

thousand eight hundred and ninety-seven times thirteen thousand eight hundred and sixty-three?"

"Seven hundred and twenty-nine," answered Schweik without moving an eyelash.

"I think that's quite enough," said the chairman of the commission. "You can take this prisoner back to where he came from."

"Thank you, gentlemen," said Schweik respectfully, "it's quite enough for me, too."

After his departure the three experts agreed that Schweik was an obvious imbecile in accordance with all the natural laws discovered by mental specialists.

The report submitted to the examining judge contained, among other remarks, the following passage:

The undersigned medical authorities base themselves upon the complete mental deficiency and congenital cretinism of Josef Schweik who was brought before the above-mentioned commission and who expressed himself in terms such as "Long Live our Emperor Franz Josef the First," a remark which completely suffices to demonstrate Josef Schweik's state of mind as an obvious imbecile. The undersigned commission therefore makes the following recommendations: 1. The proceedings against Josef Schweik should be suspended. 2. Josef Schweik should be removed to a mental clinic for observation purposes and to ascertain how far his mental state is dangerous to his surroundings.

While this report was being drawn up, Schweik was explaining to his fellow prisoners, "They didn't worry about Ferdinand. All they did was to crack some jokes with me about radium and the Pacific Ocean. In the end we decided that what we'd talked to each other about was quite enough, and then we said goodbye."

"I trust nobody," remarked the little misshapen man on whose field they had dug up a skeleton. "They're all a pack of shysters."

"If you ask me, it's just as well they are," said Schweik, lying down on the straw mattress. "If all people wanted to do all the others a good turn, they'd be walloping each other in a brace of shakes."

43

4.

Schweik Is Ejected from the Lunatic Asylum

WHEN Schweik later on described life in the lunatic asylum, he did so in terms of exceptional eulogy. "I'm blowed if I can make out why lunatics kick up such a fuss about being kept there. They can crawl about stark naked on the floor, or caterwaul like jackals, or rave and bite. If you was to do anything like that in the open street, it'd make people stare, but in the asylum it's just taken as a matter of course. Why, the amount of liberty there is something that even the socialists have never dreamed of. The inmates can pass themselves off as God Almighty or the Virgin Mary or the Pope or the King of England or our Emperor or St. Vaclav, although the one who did him was properly stripped and tied up in solitary confinement. There was a chap there who kept thinking that he was an archbishop, but he did nothing but guzzle. And then there was another who said he was St. Cyril and St. Methodus, just so that he could get double helpings of grub.

One fellow was in the family way and invited everyone to the christening. There were lots of chess players, politicians, fishermen and scouts, stamp collectors and photographers and painters there. They used to keep one man always in a strait waistcoat, to stop him from calculating when the end of the world was coming. Everybody can say what he likes there, the first thing that comes into his head, just like in Parliament. The noisiest of the lot was a chap who said he was the sixteenth volume of the encyclopedia and asked everybody to open him and find an article on sewing machines or else he'd be done for. He wouldn't shut up until they shoved him into a strait waistcoat. I tell you, the life there was a fair treat. You can bawl, or yelp, or sing, or blub, or moo, or boo, or jump, say your prayers or turn somersaults, or walk on all fours, or hop about on one foot, or run around in a circle, or dance, or skip, or squat on your haunches all day long, and climb up the walls. Nobody comes up to you and says, 'You mustn't do this, you mustn't do that, you ought to be ashamed of yourself, call yourself civilized?' I liked being in the asylum, I can tell you, and while I was there I had the time of my life."

And, in good sooth, the mere welcome which awaited Schweik in the asylum, when they took him there from the central criminal court for observation, far exceeded anything he had expected. First of all they stripped him naked, then they gave him a sort of dressing gown and took him to have a bath, catching hold of him familiarly by the arm, during which process one of the keepers entertained him by narrating anecdotes about Jews. In the bathroom they immersed him in a tub of warm water and then pulled him out and placed him under a cold douche. They repeated this three times and then asked him whether he liked it. Schweik said that it was better than the public baths near the Charles Bridge and that he was very fond of bathing. "If you'll only just clip my nails and hair, I'll be as happy as can be," he added, smiling affably.

They complied with this request and when they had thoroughly rubbed him down with a sponge, they wrapped him up in a sheet and carried him off into Ward Number 1 to bed, where they laid him down, covered him over with a quilt, and told him to go to sleep.

Schweik still tells the story with delight. "Just imagine, they carried me, actually carried me along. It was a fair treat for me."

And so he blissfully fell asleep on the bed. Then they woke

him up to give him a basin of milk and a roll. The roll was already cut up into little pieces and while one of the keepers held Schweik's hands, the other dipped the bits of roll into milk and fed him as poultry is fed with clots of dough for fattening. After he had gone to sleep again, they woke him up and took him to the observation ward, where Schweik, standing stark naked before two doctors, was reminded of the glorious time when he joined the army. Almost involuntarily he let fall the word *"Tauglich."*

"What's that you're saying?" remarked one of the doctors. "Take five paces forward and five paces to the rear."

Schweik took ten paces.

"I told you," said the doctor, "to take five."

"A few paces more or less don't matter to me," said Schweik.

Thereupon the doctors ordered him to sit on a chair and one of them tapped him on the knee. He then told the other one that the reflexes were quite normal, whereat the other wagged his head and he in his turn began to tap Schweik on the knee, while the first one lifted Schweik's eyelids and examined his pupils. Then they went off to a table and bandied some Latin phrases.

"Can you sing?" one of them asked Schweik. "Couldn't you sing us a song?"

"Why, with pleasure, gentlemen," replied Schweik. "I'm afraid I haven't got much of a voice or what you'd call an ear for music, but I'll do what I can to please you, if you want a little amusement."

And he struck up:

> *"O the monk in the armchair yonder,*
> *In his hand he bows his head,*
> *And upon his pallid visage,*
> *Two bitter, glowing tears are shed.*

"That's all I know," continued Schweik, "but if you like I'll sing you this:

> *"My heart is brimming o'er with sadness,*
> *My bosom surges with despair,*
> *Mutely I sit and afar I gaze:*
> *My yearning's afar, it is there, it is there.*

[1] "Fit."

"And that's all I know of that one, too," sighed Schweik. "But besides that I know the first verse of 'Where Is My Home?' and 'General Windischgratz and All His Commanders Started the Battle at the Break of Day' and a few of the old popular favorites like 'Lord Preserve Us' and 'Hail We Greet Thee with Thousand Greetings' . . ."

The two doctors looked at each other and one of them asked Schweik, "Has the state of your mind ever been examined?"

"In the army," replied Schweik solemnly and proudly, "the military doctors officially reported me as feeble-minded."

"It strikes me that you're a malingerer," shouted one of the doctors.

"Me, gentlemen?" said Schweik deprecatingly. "No, I'm no malingerer, I'm feeble-minded, fair and square. You ask them in the orderly room of the Ninety-first Regiment or at the reserve headquarters in Karlin."

The elder of the two doctors waved his hand with a gesture of despair, and pointing to Schweik, said to the keepers, "Let this man have his clothes again and put him into Section Three in the first passage. Then one of you can come back and take all his papers into the office. And tell them there to settle it quickly, because we don't want to have him on our hands for long."

The doctors cast another crushing glance at Schweik, who deferentially retreated backward to the door, bowing with unction the while. From the moment when the keepers received orders to return Schweik's clothes to him, they no longer showed the slightest concern for him. They told him to get dressed and one of them took him to Ward Number 3 where, for the few days it took to complete his written ejection in the office, he had an opportunity of carrying on his agreeable observations. The disappointed doctors reported that he was "a malingerer of weak intellect," and as they discharged him before lunch, it caused quite a little scene. Schweik declared that a man cannot be ejected from a lunatic asylum without having been given his lunch first. This disorderly behavior was stopped by a police officer who had been summoned by the asylum porter and who conveyed Schweik to the commissariat of police.

47

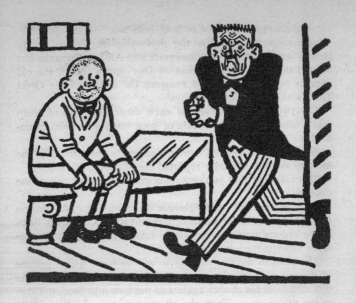

5.

Schweik at the Commissariat of Police

SCHWEIK'S bright sunny days in the asylum were followed by hours laden with persecution. Police Inspector Braun arranged the meeting with Schweik as brutally as if he were a Roman hangman during the delightful reign of Nero. Just as they used to say in harsh tones, "Throw this rascal of a Christian to the lions," Inspector Braun said, "Shove him in the clink."

Not a word more or less. But as he said it, the eyes of Inspector Braun shone with a strange and perverse joy.

Schweik bowed and said with a certain pride, "I'm ready, gentlemen. I suppose that clink means being in a cell and that's not so bad."

"Here, not so much of your lip," replied the police officer, whereupon Schweik remarked:

"I'm an easygoing sort of chap, and grateful for anything you do for me."

In the cell a man was sitting on a bench, deep in meditation. He sat there listlessly, and from his appearance it was obvious that when the key grated in the lock of the cell he did not imagine this to be the token of approaching liberty.

"Good day to you, sir," said Schweik, sitting down by his side on the bench. "I wonder what time it can be."

"Time is not my master," retorted the meditative man.

"It's not so bad here," resumed Schweik. "Why, they took the trouble to plane the wood this bench is made of."

The solemn man did not reply. He stood up and began to walk rapidly to and fro in the tiny space between door and bench, as if he were in a hurry to save something.

Schweik meanwhile inspected with interest the inscriptions daubed upon the walls. There was one inscription in which an anonymous prisoner had vowed a life-and-death struggle with the police. The wording was, "You won't half cop it." Another had written, "Rats to you, fatheads." Another merely recorded a plain fact: "I was locked up here on June 5, 1913, and got fair treatment." Next to this some poetic soul had inscribed the verses:

> I sit in sorrow by the stream.
> The sun is hid behind the hill.
> I watch the uplands as they gleam,
> Where my beloved tarries still.

The man who was now running to and fro between door and bench as if he were anxious to win a marathon race, came to a standstill and sat down breathless in his old place, sank his head in his hands and suddenly shouted, "Let me out!"

Then, talking to himself, "No, they won't let me out, they won't, they won't. I've been here since six o'clock this morning."

He then became unexpectedly communicative. He rose up and inquired of Schweik, "You don't happen to have a strap on you so that I could end it all?"

"Pleased to oblige," answered Schweik, undoing his strap. "I've never seen a man hang himself with a strap in a cell.

"It's a nuisance, though," he continued, looking around about, "that there isn't a hook here. The bolt by the window wouldn't hold you. I tell you what you might do, though. You could kneel down by the bench and hang yourself that way,

49

like the monk who hanged himself on a crucifix because of a young Jewess. I'm very keen on suicides. Go it!"

The gloomy man into whose hands Schweik had thrust the strap looked at it, threw it into a corner, and burst out crying, wiping away his tears with his grimy hands and yelling the while, "I've got children! I'm here for drunkenness and immorality! Heavens above, my poor wife! What will they say at the office? I've got children! I'm here for drunkenness and immorality," and so ad infinitum.

At last, however, he calmed down a little, went to the door, and began to thump and beat at it with his fist. From behind the door could be heard steps and a voice. "What do you want?"

"Let me out," he said in a voice which sounded as if he had nothing left to live for.

"Where to?" was the answer from the other side.

"To my office," replied the unhappy father, husband, clerk, drunkard, and profligate.

Amid the stillness of the corridor could be heard laughter, dreadful laughter, and the steps moved away again.

"It looks to me as if that chap ain't fond of you, laughing at you like that," said Schweik, while the desperate man sat down again beside him. "Those policemen are capable of anything when they're in a wax. Just you sit down quietly if you don't want to hang yourself, and wait how things turn out. If you're in an office, with a wife and children, it's pretty bad for you, I must admit. I suppose you're more or less certain of getting the sack, eh?"

"I don't know," sighed the man, "because I can't remember what I did. I only know I got thrown out from somewhere and I wanted to go back and light my cigar. But it started all right. The manager of our department was giving a birthday spree and he invited us to a pub, then we went to another and after that to a third, a fourth, a fifth, a sixth, a seventh, an eighth, a ninth . . ."

"Wouldn't you like me to count for you?" asked Schweik. "I'm good at figures. I was once in twenty-eight pubs. But I'm bound to say I never had more than three drinks in any of them."

"To cut a long story short," continued the unfortunate clerk whose manager had celebrated his birthday in such magnificent style, "when we'd been in about a dozen different taprooms, we discovered that we'd lost our manager, although we'd tied him with a piece of string and took him with us like a dog. So we went to have a look for him and the end of it was that we lost each other till at last I wound up in a night club, quite a respectable place, where I drank some liqueur or other straight from the bottle. I can't remember what I did after that; all I know is that at the commissariat here, when they brought me in, the two police officers reported that I was drunk and disorderly, that I'd been guilty of immoral conduct, that I'd struck a lady, that I'd jabbed a pocketknife through somebody else's hat that I'd taken from the hatrack. Then I'd chased the ladies' orchestra away, accused the headwaiter in front of everyone of stealing a twenty-crown note, smashed the marble slab of the table where I was sitting, and spat into the black coffee of a stranger at the next table. That's all I did as far as I can remember. And I can assure you that I'm a steady, intelligent man whose only thoughts are for his family. What do you think of that? I'm not one of the rowdy sort."

Schweik did not reply, but inquired with interest, "Did you have much trouble in smashing that marble slab, or did you splash it at one blow?"

"At one blow," replied the man of intelligence.

"Then you're done for," said Schweik mournfully. "They'll prove that you must have trained yourself to do it. And the stranger's coffee you spat in, was it with rum or without rum?" And without waiting for an answer, he proceeded to explain. "If it was with rum, that makes matters worse, because it costs more. In court they reckon up every item, and add them together, so as to make the most of it."

"In court . . ." whispered the conscientious family man dejectedly, and hanging his head he lapsed into that unpleasant state of mind when a man is gnawed by his conscience.

"And do they know at home," asked Schweik, "that you've been locked up, or are they waiting till it gets into the papers?"

"You think it'll be in the papers?" guilelessly inquired the victim of his manager's birthday.

"It's a dead certainty," was the downright answer, for it was not Schweik's way to hide anything from his fellow men. "This prank of yours is going to be a fair treat for newspaper readers. I myself like reading the drunk-and-disorderly bits. Not long ago at The Flagon there was a customer who smashed a glass with his head. He chucked it up into the air and then stood underneath it. They ran him in, and on the very next morning we read about it in the papers. Another time I gave an undertaker's mute a smack in the eye and he gave me one in return. To stop the row they had to run us both in, and the afternoon editions had all about it. Another time at The Dead Man there was a councilor who smashed two glasses. Do you think they hushed it up? Not they—the next day it was reported in all the papers. All you can do is to send from prison a letter to the newspapers saying that the report published about you doesn't refer to you and that you're no relation of the person of that name and have no connection with him. Then you must write home to tell them to cut your letter out of the paper and keep it, so that you can read it when they let you out of quod."

Noticing that the man of intelligence was shivering, Schweik asked, full of concern, "Do you feel cold?"

"It's all up with me," sobbed Schweik's companion. "I've got no chance of promotion now."

"That you haven't," agreed Schweik readily, "and if they don't take you back at the office when you've served your sentence, I bet it won't be easy for you to find another job. Whatever job it is, even if you wanted to work as a knacker's assistant, you'd have to show them some testimonials. Ah, that little spree of yours is going to be an expensive business! And what's your wife and children going to live on while you're doing time?"

The man sobbed, "My poor children, my poor wife!"

Then the wayward penitent stood up and started talking about his children. There were five of them; the eldest was twelve and he was a boy scout. He drank nothing but water and he ought to have been an example to his father, who for the first time in his life had been guilty of such shocking conduct.

"A boy scout!" exclaimed Schweik. "I like hearing about boy scouts. Once when I was in camp for my annual training with the Ninety-first the local farmers started chivvying some boy scouts in the woods where there was regular swarms of them. They collared three. When they were tying up the smallest of the lot, he kicked up such a hullabaloo, bellowing and sniveling so much, that we hardened veterans couldn't stand the sight of it and we made ourselves scarce. While these three scouts was being tied up, they managed to bite eight of the farmers. Afterward in their den in the woods they found piles and piles of gnawed bones of poultry and game, a whole lot of cherry stones, bushels of unripe apple cores and other tidbits like that."

But the boy scout's unhappy father was not to be comforted.

"What have I done?" he wailed. "My reputation's ruined."

"That it is," said Schweik, with his native frankness. "After what's happened you're bound to have a ruined reputation for the rest of your life, because when your friends read about it in the papers, they'll add to it. That's the way it always happens, but don't you take it to heart. There's at least ten times more people with ruined and damaged reputations than those with a clean record. That's a mere fleabite."

Heavy steps could be heard in the passage, the key grated in the lock, the door opened, and the police officer called Schweik.

"Excuse me," said Schweik chivalrously, "I've only been here since twelve o'clock, but this gentleman's been here since six o'clock this morning. And I'm not in any hurry."

There was no reply to this, but the police officer's powerful hand dragged Schweik into the corridor and conveyed him upstairs in silence to the first floor.

In the second room a commissary of police was sitting at a table. He was a stout gentleman of good-natured appearance.

He said to Schweik, "So you're Schweik, are you? And how did you get here?"

"As easy as winking," replied Schweik. "I was brought here by a police officer because I objected to them chucking me out of the lunatic asylum without any lunch. What do they take me for, I'd like to know?"

"I'll tell you what, Schweik," said the commissary affably. "There's no reason why we should be cross with you here. Wouldn't it be better if we sent you to the police headquarters?"

"You're the master of the situation, as they say," said Schweik contentedly. "From here to the police headquarters'd be quite a nice little evening stroll."

"I'm glad to find that we see eye to eye in this," said the commissary cheerfully. "You see how much better it is to talk things over, eh, Schweik?"

"It's always a great pleasure to me to have a little confab with anyone," replied Schweik. "I'll never forget your kindness to me, your worship, I promise you."

With a deferential bow and accompanied by the police

officer he went down to the guardroom, and within a quarter of an hour Schweik could have been seen in the street under the escort of another police officer who was carrying under his arm a fat book inscribed in German *Arrestantenbuch*.

At the corner of Spálená Street Schweik and his escort met with a crowd of people who were jostling around a placard.

"That's the Emperor's proclamation to say that war's been declared," said the policeman to Schweik.

"I saw it coming," said Schweik, "but in the asylum they don't know anything about it yet, although they ought to have had it straight from the horse's mouth, as you might say."

"How d'you mean?" asked the policeman.

"Because they've got a lot of army officers locked up there," explained Schweik, and when they reached a fresh crowd jostling in front of the proclamation, Schweik shouted, "Long live Franz Josef! We'll win this war." Somebody from the enthusiastic crowd banged his hat over his ears and so, amid a regular concourse of people, the good soldier Schweik once more entered the portals of the police headquarters.

"We're absolutely bound to win this war. Take my word for it, gentlemen," and with these few remarks Schweik took his leave of the crowd which had been accompanying him.

And somewhere from the far distances of history there descended upon Europe the realization that the morrow can shatter the plans of today.

6.

Schweik Home Again
After Having Broken the Vicious Circle

THROUGH the premises of the police headquarters was wafted
the spirit of authority which had been ascertaining how far
the people's enthusiasm for the war actually went. With the
exception of a few persons who did not disavow the fact that
they were sons of the nation which was destined to bleed on
behalf of interests entirely alien to it, the police headquarters
harbored a magnificent collection of bureaucratic beasts of
prey, the scope of whose minds did not extend beyond the jail
and the gallows with which they could protect the existence of
the warped laws.

During this process they treated their victims with a spiteful
affability, weighing each word beforehand.

"I'm extremely sorry," said one of these beasts of prey with black and yellow stripes, when Schweik was brought before him, "that you've fallen into our hands again. We thought you'd turn over a new leaf, but we were mistaken."

Schweik mutely assented with a nod of the head and displayed so innocent a demeanor that the black-yellow beast of prey gazed dubiously at him and said with emphasis, "Take that idiotic expression off your face."

But he immediately switched over to a courteous tone and continued, "You may be quite certain that we very much dislike keeping you in custody and I can assure you that in my opinion your guilt is not so very great, because in view of your weak intellect there can be no doubt that you have been led astray. Tell me, Mr. Schweik, who was it induced you to indulge in such silly tricks?"

Schweik coughed and said, "Begging your pardon, sir, but I don't know what silly tricks you mean."

"Well, now, Mr. Schweik," he said in an artificially paternal tone, "isn't it a foolish trick to cause a crowd to collect, as the police officer who brought you here says you did, in front of the royal proclamation of war posted up at the street corner, and to incite the crowd by shouting, 'Long live Franz Josef. We'll win this war'?"

"I couldn't stand by and do nothing," declared Schweik, fixing his guileless eyes upon his inquisitor's face. "It fairly riled me to see them all reading the royal proclamation and not showing any signs that they was pleased about it. Nobody shouted hooray or called for three cheers—nothing at all, your worship. Anyone'd think it didn't concern them a bit. So, being an old soldier of the Ninety-first, I couldn't stand it and that's why I shouted those remarks and I think that if you'd been in my place, you'd have done just the same as me. If there's a war, it's got to be won, and there's got to be three cheers for the Emperor. Nobody's going to talk me out of that."

Quelled and contrite, the black-yellow beast of prey flinched from the gaze of Schweik, the guileless lamb, and plunging his eyes into official documents, he said, "I thoroughly appreciate your enthusiasm, but I only wish it had been exhibited under other circumstances. You yourself know full well that you were brought here by a police officer, because a patriotic demonstration of such a kind might, and indeed, inevitably would be interpreted by the public as being ironical rather than serious."

"When a man is being run in by a police officer," replied Schweik, "it's a critical moment in his life. But if a man even at such a moment don't forget the right thing to do when there's a war on, well, it strikes me that a man like that can't be a bad sort after all."

The black-yellow beast of prey growled and had another look at Schweik.

Schweik met his eye with the innocent, gentle, modest and tender warmth of his gaze.

For a while they looked fixedly at each other.

"Go to blazes, Schweik," said the jack-in-office at last, "and if you get brought here again, I'll make no bones about it, but off you'll go before a court-martial. Is that clear?"

But before he realized what was happening, Schweik had come up to him, had kissed his hand and said, "God bless you for everything you've done. If you'd like a thoroughbred dog at any time, just you come to me. I'm a dog fancier."

And so Schweik found himself again at liberty and on his way home.

He considered whether he ought not first of all to look in at The Flagon, and so it came about that he opened the door through which he had passed a short while ago in the company of Detective Bretschneider.

There was a deathlike stillness in the bar. A few customers were sitting there, among them the verger from St. Apolinnaire's. They looked gloomy. Behind the bar sat the landlady, Mrs. Palivec, and stared dully at the beer handles.

"Well, here I am back again," said Schweik gaily. "Let's have a glass of beer. Where's Mr. Palivec? Is he home again too?"

Instead of replying, Mrs. Palivec burst into tears, and, concentrating her unhappiness in a special emphasis which she gave to each word, she moaned, "They—gave—him—ten—years—a—week—ago."

"Fancy that, now," said Schweik. "Then he's already served seven days of it."

"He was that cautious," wept Mrs. Palivec. "He himself always used to say so."

The customers in the taproom maintained a stubborn silence, as if the spirit of Palivec were hovering about and urging them to even greater caution.

"Caution is the mother of wisdom," said Schweik, sitting

57

down to his glass of beer. "We're living in such queer times that a man can't be too cautious."

"We had two funerals yesterday," said the verger of St. Apolinnaire's, changing the subject.

"Somebody must have died," said another customer, whereupon a third man inquired:

"Did they have a regular hearse?"

"I'd like to know," said Schweik, "what the military funerals are going to be like now that there's a war on."

The customers rose, paid for their drinks, and went out quietly. Schweik was left alone with Mrs. Palivec.

"I never thought," he said, "that they'd sentence an innocent man to ten years. I've already heard of an innocent man getting five years, but ten—that's a bit too much."

"And then my husband admitted everything," wept Mrs. Palivec. "What he said about the flies and the pictures, he repeated it word for word at the police station and in court. I was a witness at the trial, but what could I say when they told me I stood in a relation of kinship to my husband and that I could decline to give evidence? I was so scared of the relation of kinship, thinking it might lead to more trouble, that I declined to give evidence, and, poor fellow, he gave me such a look, I'll never forget the expression on his face, not to my dying day I won't. And then when they passed the sentence and they were taking him off, he shouted in the passage, as if he'd gone off his head, 'Up the rebels!' "

"And does Mr. Bretschneider still come here?" asked Schweik.

"He was here a few times," replied the landlady. "He had one or two drinks and asked me who comes here, and he listened to what the customers were saying about a football match. Whenever they see him, they only talk about football matches. And he fairly had the jumps, as if any minute he'd go raving mad and start rampaging about. But the whole time he only managed to get hold of one gentleman, and he was a paper hanger."

"It's all a matter of practice," remarked Schweik. "Was the paper hanger a soft-headed sort of fellow?"

"Much the same as my husband," she replied, weeping. "Bretschneider asked him if he'd fire against the Serbs. And he said he didn't know how to shoot. He'd been once, he said, to a shooting gallery and had some shots for a crown. Then we all heard Mr. Bretschneider say as he took out his notebook, 'Hello, another nice bit of high treason!' And he took the paper hanger away with him and he never came back."

"There's lots of them'll never come back," said Schweik. "Let me have a glass of rum."

Schweik was just having a second glass of rum when Bretschneider came into the taproom. He glanced rapidly around the empty bar and sat down beside Schweik. Then he ordered some beer and waited for Schweik to say something.

Schweik took a newspaper from the rack, and glancing at the back page of advertisements, he remarked, "Look here, that man Cimpera who lives at Straškov is selling a farm with thirteen roods of land belonging to it situated close to school and railway."

Bretschneider drummed nervously with his fingers, and turning to Schweik, he said, "I'm surprised to find you interested in farming, Mr. Schweik."

"Oh, it's you, is it?" said Schweik, shaking hands with him. "I didn't recognize you at first. I've got a very bad memory for faces. The last time I saw you, as far as I remember, was in the office of the police headquarters. What have you been up to since then? Do you come here often?"

"I came here today on your account," said Bretschneider. "They told me at the police headquarters that you're a dog fancier. I'd like a good ratter or a terrier or something of that sort."

"I can get that for you," replied Schweik. "Do you want a thoroughbred or one from the street?"

"I think," replied Bretschneider, "that I'd rather have a thoroughbred.'

"Wouldn't you like a police dog?" asked Schweik. "One of those that gets on the scent in a jiffy and leads you to the scene of the crime? I know a butcher who's got one. He uses it for drawing his cart, but that dog's missed its vocation, as you might say."

"I'd like a terrier," said Bretschneider with composure, "a terrier that doesn't bite."

"Do you want a terrier without teeth, then?" asked Schweik. "I know of one. It belongs to a man who keeps a public house."

"Perhaps I'd rather have a ratter," announced Bretschneider with embarrassment. His knowledge of dogcraft was in its very infancy, and if he hadn't received these particular instructions from the police headquarters, he'd never have bothered his head about dogs at all.

But his instructions were precise, clear, and stringent. He was to make himself more closely acquainted with Schweik on the strength of his activities as a dog fancier, for which purpose he was authorized to select assistants and expend sums of money for the purchase of dogs.

"Ratters are of all different sizes," said Schweik. "I know of two little 'uns and three big 'uns. You could nurse the whole five of 'em on your lap. I can strongly recommend them."

"That might suit me," announced Bretschneider. "And what would they cost?"

"That depends on the size," replied Schweik. "It's all a question of size. A ratter's not like a calf. It's the other way around with them. The smaller they are, the more they cost."

"What I had in mind was some big ones to use as watchdogs," replied Bretschneider, who was afraid he might encroach too far on his secret police funds.

"Right you are," said Schweik. "I can sell you some big 'uns for fifty crowns each, and some bigger still for twenty-five crowns. Only there's one thing we've forgotten. Do you want puppies or older dogs, and then is it to be dogs or bitches?"

"It's all the same to me," replied Bretschneider, who found himself grappling with unknown problems. "You get them for me and I'll come and fetch them from you at seven o'clock tomorrow evening. Will they be ready by then?"

"Just you come along. I'll have them without fail," answered Schweik drily. "But under the circumstances I shall have to ask you for an advance of thirty crowns."

"That's all right," said Bretschneider, paying the money. "And now let's have a drink on the strength of it. I'll stand treat."

When they had each had four drinks, Bretschneider announced, after telling Schweik not to be afraid of him, that he wasn't on duty that day and so he could talk to him about politics.

Schweik declared that he never talked about politics in a public house, and that politics was a mug's game anyhow.

In opposition to this, Bretschneider was more revolutionary in his views and said that every weak country was predestined to destruction. Then he asked Schweik what *he* thought about this.

Schweik announced that it had nothing to do with the country, but that once he had to look after a weak St. Bernard puppy which he had fed with army biscuits and it had died.

When they had each had five drinks, Bretschneider asserted that he was an anarchist and asked Schweik which organization he ought to join.

Schweik said that once an anarchist had bought a mastiff from him for a hundred crowns and had failed to pay the last instalment.

Over the sixth drink Bretschneider was talking about revolution and against mobilization, whereupon Schweik leaned over toward him and whispered into his ear, "There's a customer just come in, so don't let him hear you or it might be awkward for you. And look, the landlady's crying!"

Mrs. Palivec was, in fact, crying on her chair behind the bar.

"What are you crying for, missus?" asked Bretschneider. "In three months we'll have won the war, there'll be an amnesty, your husband'll come back home, and then we'll have a fine old spree here."

"Don't you think we'll win?" he added, turning to Schweik.

"What's the good of chewing the rag about that the whole time?" said Schweik. "The war's got to be won and there you are. But now I must be off home."

Schweik paid his reckoning and returned to Mrs. Müller, his old charwoman, who was extremely scared when she saw that the man who had let himself in with a key was Schweik.

"I didn't think you'd be back for years and years," she said with her usual frankness. "And so, till further notice, as you might say, I took a new lodger—a porter from a night club, and him not having anywhere to go, I felt sorry for him, like, and then the police came and searched the place three times, but they couldn't find anything, so they said you was done for, through being so artful and all."

Schweik immediately discovered that the unknown lodger had made himself extremely comfortable. He was sleeping in Schweik's bed and he had been magnanimous enough to be satisfied with only half the bed, granting the use of the other half to some member of the opposite sex who was asleep with an arm gratefully encircling his neck, while articles of male and female clothing were scattered in a medley around the bed. From this chaos it was evident that the porter from the night club had been in a merry mood when he had returned with his lady.

"Look here, boss," said Schweik, shaking the intruder, "don't you be late for lunch. I should be very upset if people said I'd chucked you out before you'd had a chance of getting any lunch."

The porter from the night club was very sleepy, and it took a long time before he understood that the owner of the bed had returned home and was laying claim to his property.

In the manner of all porters from night clubs, this gentleman announced his intention of bashing anyone who woke him up, and he endeavored to continue his slumbers.

Schweik meanwhile collected portions of the man's wardrobe, brought them to his bedside, and shaking him vigorously, said, "If you don't get dressed, I'll chuck you out into the street just as you are. It'd be much better to get away from here with your clothes on."

"I wanted to sleep till eight in the evening," announced the porter, somewhat taken aback and putting on his trousers. "I'm paying the landlady two crowns a day for the bed and she lets me bring girls from the club here. Marena, get up."

By the time he had discovered his collar and was arranging his tie, he had sufficiently pulled himself together to assure Schweik that the Mimosa Club was one of the most respectable of its kind, for the only ladies allowed there were those who were properly registered with the police, and he cordially invited Schweik to pay a visit to the establishment.

On the other hand, his female companion was not at all pleased with Schweik and in reference to him made use of some highly select expressions, the most select of which was, "You measly, low-down skunk, you!"

After the departure of the intruders, Schweik went to have it out with Mrs. Müller, but he could discover no sign of her, except a piece of paper, upon which in her scrawly handwriting she had, with unusual ease, recorded her thoughts regarding the unfortunate episode of the loan of Schweik's bed to the porter from the night club.

Pleese sir forgive me for not seeing you agane, becos I shall jump out of the winder.

"Liar," said Schweik, and waited.

Half an hour later the unhappy Mrs. Müller crept into the

kitchen, and from her downcast expression it was evident that she expected Schweik to provide her with words of comfort.

"If you want to jump out of the window," said Schweik, "go into the bedroom. I've opened the window for you. I wouldn't advise you to jump out of the kitchen window, because if you did, you'd fall into the roses in the garden and squash them and then you'd have to pay for them. If you jump out of the bedroom window, you'll land nicely on the pavement, and if you're lucky, you'll break your neck. If your luck's out, you'll just break all your ribs, arms, and legs, and then it'll cost you a pretty penny in the hospital."

Mrs. Müller burst into tears. Quietly she went into the bedroom, closed the window, and came back, saying, "There's a dreadful draft from that window, and it wouldn't do your rheumatism any good, sir."

Then she went to make the bed, putting everything straight with unusual care. When she rejoined Schweik in the kitchen, she remarked with tears in her eyes, "Those two puppies, sir, that we kept in the yard, they've died. And the St. Bernard dog ran away when the police were searching the place."

"Holy Moses!" exclaimed Schweik. "He'll get himself into a nice mess. I'd bet anything he'll have the police after him."

"He did bite one police inspector, when he pulled him out from under the bed while they were looking around the place," continued Mrs. Müller. "It started this way: One of the gentlemen said that there was somebody under the bed and so they called on the St. Bernard in the name of the law to come out and when he wouldn't come, they pulled him out. So he snapped at them and bolted out through the door and he hasn't been back since. They asked me a lot of questions, too, about who comes here and whether we get any money from abroad, and then they started calling me names when I told them that money didn't come from abroad very often, but the last time it was from a gentleman at Brno who sent sixty crowns in advance for an Angora cat that you advertised about in the newspaper and instead of which you sent him a blind fox terrier puppy in a packing case. After that they talked to me as nice as could be and so as I shouldn't be scared at being left all alone here, they said I ought to take the porter from the night club as a lodger. You know, the one you sent about his business."

"I'm having a rough time with all these police officers, Mrs.

Müller. I bet you won't see many people coming here to buy dogs now," sighed Schweik.

I do not know whether the gentleman who inspected the police records after the collapse of Austria could make anything of such items in the secret police funds as: B. 40 cr., F. 50 cr., M. 80 cr., etc., but they would be quite mistaken if they supposed that B., F., and M. are the initials of persons who for 40, 50, or 80 crowns betrayed the Czech nation to the Austrian eagle.

B. stands for St. Bernard, F. for fox terrier and M. for mastiff. All these dogs were taken by Bretschneider from Schweik to the police headquarters. They were hideous freaks which had nothing whatever in common with any of the pure breeds, as which Schweik foisted them off upon Bretschneider.

The St. Bernard was a cross between a mongrel poodle and a sort of dubious cur; the fox terrier had the ears of a dachshund, was the size of a mastiff, and had bandy legs as if it had suffered from rickets. The mastiff had a shaggy head resembling the jowl of a collie and lopped tail; it was no taller than a dachshund, and was shorn behind.

Then Detective Kalous went there to buy a dog and he returned with a cowed monstrosity resembling a spotted hyena, with the mane of a Scottish sheep dog, and to the items of the secret funds was added: R. 90 cr.

This monstrosity was supposed to be a retriever.

But not even Kalous managed to worm anything out of Schweik. He fared the same as Bretschneider. Schweik transferred the most skillful political conversation to the subject of how to cure distemper in puppies, and the only result produced by the most artfully contrived traps was that Schweik foisted off upon Bretschneider another incredibly crossbred canine freak.

7.

Schweik Joins the Army

WHILE the forests by the river Raab in Galicia beheld the
Austrian troops in full flight, and in Serbia the Austrian divisions, one by one, were receiving the drubbing they so richly
deserved, the Austrian Ministry of War suddenly thought of
Schweik as a possible means for helping the monarchy out of
its fix.

When Schweik received notice that within a week he was to
present himself for medical examination, he was in bed with
another attack of rheumatism.

Mrs. Müller was making him coffee in the kitchen.

"Mrs. Müller," came Schweik's tranquil voice from the
bedroom. "Mrs. Müller, come here a moment."

When the charwoman was standing by his bedside, Schweik
said in the same tranquil tones, "Sit down, Mrs. Müller."

There was something mysteriously solemn in his voice.

When Mrs. Müller had sat down, Schweik sat up in bed and announced, "I'm going to join the army."

"My gracious me!" exclaimed Mrs. Müller, "and what are you going to do there?"

"Fight," replied Schweik in a sepulchral voice. "Austria's in a bad way. Up in the north we've got our work cut out to keep them away from Cracow, and down in the south they'll be all over Hungary if we don't get busy soon. Things look very black whichever way you turn, and that's why they're calling me up. Why, only yesterday I read in the paper that clouds are gathering above our beloved country."

"But you can't walk."

"That doesn't matter, Mrs. Müller, I'll join the army in a Bath chair. You know that confectioner around the corner, he's got the kind of thing I want. Years and years ago he used to wheel his lame grandfather—a bad-tempered old buffer he was too—in it, for a breath of fresh air. That's the Bath chair you're going to wheel me to the army in, Mrs. Müller."

Mrs. Müller burst into tears. "Hadn't I better run for the doctor, sir?"

"Not a bit of it. Except for my legs I'm a sound piece of cannon fodder, and at a time when Austria's in a mess, every cripple must be at his post. Just you go on making the coffee."

And while Mrs. Müller, tear-stained and flustered, was straining the coffee, the good soldier Schweik began to warble in bed:

> *"General Windischgraetz and all his commanders*
> *Started the battle at the break of day;*
> *Hop, hop, hop!*
> *They started the battle and began to pray:*
> *Help us, O Lord, with the Virgin Mary;*
> *Hop, hop, hop!"*

Mrs. Müller, scared by this dreadful battle song, forgot about the coffee, and trembling from head to foot, listened in terror to the good soldier Schweik, who went on warbling in bed:

> *"With the Virgin Mary and the four bridges here,*
> *Piedmont, look out, for your end is near;*
> *Hop, hop, hop!*

There at Solferino a battle began,
Lots of blood was shed, knee-deep it ran;
Hop, hop, hop!
Knee-deep ran the blood and corpses by the load,
The boys of the Eighteenth, their derring-do they showed;
Hop, hop, hop!
The boys of the Eighteenth, don't be afraid,
A wagonload of money is coming to your aid;
Hop, hop, hop!"

"Goodness gracious, Mr. Schweik, please don't," could be heard a pitiable voice from the kitchen, but Schweik concluded his war song:

"A wagonload of money and a carful of stew,
What other regiment could do as much as you?
Hop, hop, hop!"

Mrs. Müller rushed out of doors and ran for the doctor. When he returned an hour later, Schweik was dozing. He was aroused from his slumbers by a portly gentleman, who held his hand on Schweik's forehead for a moment and said, "Pray don't be alarmed. I'm Dr. Pavek from Vinohrady—Show me your hand—Put this thermometer under your arm—that's right—Show me your tongue—More of it—Keep it still— What did your father and mother die of?"

And thus it came about that at the time when Vienna desired all the nations of Austria-Hungary to show the most sterling examples of fidelity and devotion, Dr. Pavek was prescribing bromide for Schweik's patriotic enthusiasm and recommending the undaunted and worthy warrior Schweik not to think about the army.

"Continue in a recumbent posture and keep your mind at rest. I will return tomorrow."

When he came the next day, he asked Mrs. Müller in the kitchen how the patient was getting on.

"He's worse, Doctor," she replied, with genuine concern. "In the night, when his rheumatism came on, he was singing the Austrian anthem, if you please."

Dr. Pavek saw himself compelled to counter this new manifestation of his patient's loyalty by increasing the dose of bromide.

On the third day Mrs. Müller reported that Schweik was getting still worse.

"In the afternoon, Doctor, he sent for a map showing what he called the seat of war, and in the night his mind started wandering and he said that Austria would win."

"And is he using the powders in accordance with my prescription?"

"He hasn't sent for them yet, Doctor."

Dr. Pavek departed, after having let loose upon Schweik a tempest of diatribes, with the assurance that never again would he treat a patient who declined to accept his medical assistance with bromide.

Only two days were left before Schweik was to appear before the recruiting medical board.

During this time Schweik made the appropriate preparations. First of all he sent Mrs. Müller for a military cap and secondly he sent her to the confectioner around the corner to borrow from him the Bath chair in which he used to wheel his lame grandfather, that bad-tempered old buffer, for a breath of fresh air. Then he remembered that he needed a pair of crutches. Fortunately the confectioner had also kept a pair of crutches as a family keepsake to remember his grandfather by.

All that he wanted now was the bunch of flowers worn by recruits. This also was obtained for him by Mrs. Müller, who during these few days became remarkably thin and wept wherever she went.

And thus, on that memorable day, the following example of touching loyalty was displayed in the streets of Prague:

An old woman pushing a Bath chair, in which sat a man wearing a military cap with a polished peak and brandishing a pair of crutches. And his coat was adorned with a flamboyant bunch of flowers.

And this man, again and again brandishing his crutches, yelled, as he passed through the streets of Prague, "To Belgrade, to Belgrade!"

He was followed by a crowd of people, the nucleus of which had been an insignificant knot of idlers assembled in front of the house whence Schweik had proceeded to the army.

Schweik duly noted that the police officers stationed at various crossroads saluted him.

In Vaclav Square the crowd around Schweik's Bath chair had increased to several hundred, and at the corner of Kradovska Street it mobbed a German student wearing a cap with the colors of his association, who shouted to Schweik, *"Heil! Nieder mit den Serben!"* [1]

At the corner of Vodickova Street the mounted police interfered and dispersed the crowd.

When Schweik showed the police inspector in black and white that he was to appear that day before the medical board, the inspector was somewhat disappointed, and to restrict the continuance of any disorder he had the Bath chair, with Schweik inside it, escorted by two mounted constables to the headquarters of the medical board.

The *Prague Official News* published the following report on this occurrence:

PATRIOTISM OF A CRIPPLE

Yesterday morning the pedestrians in the main streets of Prague were the witnesses of a scene which bears admirable testimony that in this grave and momentous epoch the sons of our nation also can give the most sterling examples of fidelity and devotion to the throne of our aged ruler. It is not too much to say that we have returned to the times of the ancient Greeks and Romans, when Mucius Scaevola had himself led into battle, regardless of his burned hand. The most sacred emotions and sentiment were touchingly demonstrated yesterday by a cripple on crutches who was being wheeled along in a Bath chair by an old woman. This scion of the Czech nation was, of his own accord and regardless of his infirmity, having himself conveyed to the army in order that he might give up his life and possessions for his Emperor. And the fact that his war cry "To Belgrade!" met with such warm approval in the streets of Prague is only a further proof that the people of Prague are furnishing model examples of love for their country and the Royal Family.

The *Prager Tagblatt* wrote in similar terms and concluded its report by saying that the cripple volunteer had been accompanied by a crowd of Germans who had protected him with their bodies against attempts made to lynch him by Czech agents of the Entente powers.

Bohemia published this report and demanded that the crippled patriot should be rewarded, adding that any gifts from

[1] "Three cheers! Down with the Serbs!"

German citizens for the unknown hero should be sent to the offices of the paper.

While, according to these three papers, the Czech territory was unable to produce a single lofty-minded citizen, the gentlemen on the medical board did not hold this view.

This applies particularly to Dr. Bautze, chairman of the board. He was a man who stood no nonsense and who regarded everything as a fraudulent attempt to escape the army and the front, bullets, and shrapnel.

He is well known for his remark *"Das ganze tschechische Volk ist eine Simulantenbande."* [2]

Within ten weeks of his activities he weeded out 10,999 malingerers from 11,000 civilians and he would have collared the eleven thousandth man, if at the very moment when Dr. Bautze yelled at him *"Kehrt euch!"* [3] the unfortunate fellow had not had a stroke.

"Take this malingerer away," said Dr. Bautze, when he had ascertained that the man was dead.

And now on that memorable day Schweik stood before him stark naked like all the rest, but bashfully hiding his nudity with the crutches on which he was leaning.

"Das ist wirklich ein besonderes Feigenblatt," [4] said Dr. Bautze, "there weren't any fig leaves like that in the Garden of Eden."

"In the lowest category on account of being weak-minded," remarked the sergeant major, examining the official records.

"And what else is wrong with you?" asked Dr. Bautze.

"Beg to report, sir, I've got rheumatism, but I'll serve the Emperor till I'm hacked to pieces," said Schweik modestly. "My knees are swollen."

Bautze glared ferociously at the good soldier Schweik and yelled, *"Sie sind ein Simulant!"* [5] and turning to the sergeant major he said with icy calm, *"Den Kerl sogleich einsperren!"* [6]

Two soldiers with fixed bayonets led Schweik away to the military prison.

Schweik hobbled along on his crutches but with horror he perceived that his rheumatism was disappearing.

When Mrs. Müller, who with the Bath chair was waiting for Schweik on the bridge, saw him escorted by bayonets, she

---

[2] "The whole of the Czech nation is a gang of malingerers."
[3] "About turn."
[4] "That's a very funny kind of fig leaf."
[5] "You are a malingerer."
[6] "Have the fellow locked up immediately."

burst into tears and left the Bath chair in the lurch, never to return to it.

And the good soldier Schweik modestly proceeded in the escort of the state defenders.

The bayonets glittered in the sunshine and when they reached the Radetzky monument Schweik turned to the crowd who was accompanying him.

"To Belgrade! To Belgrade!" he shouted.

And Marshal Radetzky gazed dreamily from his monument at the good soldier Schweik departing with his recruit's nosegay in his coat, as he limped along on his old crutches, while a solemn-looking gentleman informed the people round about that they were taking a deserter to prison.

8.

Schweik as Malingerer

AT THIS momentous epoch the great concern of the military doctors was to drive the devil of sabotage out of the malingerers and persons suspected of being malingerers, such as consumptives, sufferers from rheumatism, rupture, kidney disease, diabetes, inflammation of the lungs, and other disorders.

The torments to which malingerers were subjected had been reduced to a system, and the degrees of torment were as follows:

1. Absolute diet—a cup of tea morning and evening for three days, accompanied by doses of aspirin to produce sweating, irrespective of what the patient complained of.

2. To prevent them from supposing that the army was all beer and skittles, they were given ample doses of quinine in powder.

3. Rinsing of the stomach twice daily with a liter of warm water.

4. The use of the clyster with soapy water and glycerine.

5. Swathing in sheets soaked with cold water.

There were dauntless persons who went through all five degrees of torment and had themselves removed in a simple coffin to the military cemetery. There were, however, others who were fainthearted and who, when they reached the clyster stage, announced that they were quite well and that their only desire was to proceed to the trenches with the next draft.

On reaching the military prison, Schweik was placed in the hut used as an infirmary which contained several of these fainthearted malingerers.

"I can't stand it any longer," said his bed-neighbor, who had been brought in from the surgery where his stomach had been rinsed for the second time.

This man was pretending to be shortsighted.

"I'm going to join my regiment," decided the other malingerer on Schweik's left, who had just had a taste of the clyster, after pretending to be as deaf as a post.

On the bed by the door a consumptive was dying, wrapped up in a sheet soaked in cold water.

"That's the third this week," remarked Schweik's right-hand neighbor. "And what's wrong with you?"

"I've got rheumatism," replied Schweik, whereupon there was hearty laughter from all those round about him. Even the dying consumptive, who was pretending to have tuberculosis, laughed.

"It's no good coming here with rheumatism," said a stout man to Schweik in solemn tones. "Rheumatism here stands about as much chance as corns. I'm anemic, half my stomach's missing, and I've lost five ribs, but nobody believes me. Why, we actually had a deaf and dumb man here, and every half hour they wrapped him up in sheets soaked in cold water, and every day they gave him a taste of the clyster and pumped his stomach out. Just when all the ambulance men thought he'd done the trick and would get away with it, the doctor prescribed some medicine for him. That fairly doubled him up, and then he gave in. 'No,' he says, 'I can't go on with this deaf and dumb business, my speech and hearing have been restored to me.' The sick chaps all told him not to do for himself like that, but he said no, he could hear and talk just like

73

the others. And when the doctor came in the morning, he reported himself accordingly."

"He kept it up long enough," remarked a man, who was pretending to have one leg a quarter of an inch shorter than the other, "not like the man who was shamming a paralytic stroke. Three quinines, one clyster, and a day's fast was enough for him. He owned up, and before they got as far as pumping out his stomach there wasn't a trace of any stroke at all. The man who held out longest here was the one who had been bitten by a mad dog. He bit and howled, not half he didn't; he could manage that a fair treat, but he couldn't foam at the mouth. We helped him all we could. We used to keep on tickling him for a full hour before the doctor came till he got spasms and went blue in front of our very eyes, but there wasn't a trace of any foam. It just wasn't in him. Oh, it was something shocking. Well, when the doctor comes, up he stands by the bed straight as a dart and says, 'Beg to report, sir, that the dog that bit me don't seem to have been mad.' The doctor gives such a funny look at him that he begins to shake all over and goes on talking, 'Beg to report, sir, that I wasn't bitten by any dog at all. I bit my own hand, myself.' After he'd owned up to that, he was had up for biting his hand so as not to get sent to the front."

"All diseases where you want to foam at the mouth," said the stout malingerer, "take a lot of shamming. Take epileptic fits, for instance. There was a chap here who had epileptic fits and he always used to tell us that one fit was nothing to him; he could do ten of 'em a day, if necessary. He used to twist himself in spasms and clench his fists, make his eyes start out of his head till they looked as if they was on the ends of wires, and he could kick and put out his tongue—well, I tell you, it was a first-rate epileptic fit, the real thing. Suddenly he got boils, two on his neck and two on his back, and he had to stop twisting himself and knocking his head on the floor, because he couldn't move his head or sit down or even lie down. Then he got fever and that made him lightheaded, and he gave the game away while the doctor was there. And he gave us a dickens of a time with his boils, because he had to stop among us with them for another three days on diet number two: coffee and roll in the morning, gruel or soup in the evening. And we with our stomachs pumped out and starving on diet number nought had to look on while this chap gobbled up his grub, smacked his lips, fairly puffing and belching through being so chockful of food. He dished three others through that, and they owned up too. They was trying their luck with a weak heart."

"The best thing to do," said one of the malingerers, "is to sham madness. In the next room there are two other men from the school where I teach and one of them keeps shouting day and night, 'Giordano Bruno's stake is still smoldering; renew Galileo's trial!' and the other one yelps, first three times slowly, 'Bow, wow, wow,' and then five times in quick succession, 'Bowwowwowwowow,' and then slowly again, and so on without stopping. They've kept it up for more than three weeks. I meant at first to act the fool and be a religious maniac and preach about the infallibility of the Pope, but finally I managed to get some cancer of the stomach for fifteen crowns from a barber down the road."

"I know a chimney sweep," remarked another patient, "who'll get you such a fever for twenty crowns that you'll jump out of the window."

"That's nothing," said another man. "Down our way there's a midwife who for twenty crowns can dislocate your foot so nicely that you're crippled for the rest of your life."

"I got my foot dislocated for five crowns," announced a voice from the row of beds by the window, "for five crowns and three drinks."

"My illness has run me into more than two hundred crowns already," announced his neighbor, a man as thin as a rake. "I bet there's no poison you can mention that I haven't taken. I'm simply bung full of poisons. I've chewed arsenic, I've smoked opium, I've swallowed strychnine, I've drunk vitriol mixed with phosphorus. I've ruined my liver, my lungs, my kidneys, my heart—in fact, all my inside outfit. Nobody knows what disease it is I've got."

"The best thing to do," explained someone near the door, "is to squirt paraffin oil under the skin on your arms. My cousin had a slice of good luck that way. They cut off his arm below the elbow and now the army'll never worry him any more."

"Well," said Schweik, "you see what you've all got to go through for the Emperor. Even having your stomachs pumped out. When I was in the army years ago, it used to be much worse. If a man went sick, they just trussed him up, shoved him into a cell to make him get fitter. There wasn't any beds and mattresses and spittoons like what there is here. Just a bare bench for them to lie on. Once there was a chap who had typhus, fair and square, and the one next to him had smallpox. Well, they trussed them both up and the M.O. kicked them in the ribs and said they were shamming. When the pair of them kicked the bucket, there was a dust-up in Parliament and it got into the papers. Like a shot they stopped us from reading the papers and all our boxes was inspected to see if we'd got any hidden there. And it was just my luck that in the whole blessed regiment there was nobody but me whose newspaper was spotted. So I was had up in the orderly room and our colonel, silly old buffer, God rest his soul, starts yelling at me to stand to attention and tell him who'd written that stuff to the paper or he'd smash my jaw from ear to ear and keep me in clink till all was blue. Then the M.O. comes up and he shakes his fist right under my nose and shouts, 'You misbegotten whelp; you scabby ape; you wretched blob of scum; you skunk of a Socialist, you!' Well, I looks 'em straight in the face, without moving an eyelid, and there I stood keeping my mouth shut and with one hand at the salute and the other along the seam of my trousers. There they was, running around and yelping at me like a couple of puppies, and I just kept standing there and saying nothing. I keeps my mouth shut, salutes, and holds my left hand along the seam of my trousers. When they'd been carrying on like that for about half an hour, the colonel dashes up to me and yells, 'Are you an idiot or ain't you?' 'Beg to report, sir,' I says, 'that I'm an idiot.' Well, after a lot of rushing about the colonel decides to give me twenty-one days' solitary confinement for being an idiot, two days per week without any grub, a month's c.b., forty-eight hours in irons. 'Lock him up on the spot,' he says. 'Don't give him anything to eat; tie him hand and foot; show him the army doesn't need any idiots. We'll knock the newspaper nonsense out of your head, you ruffian,' he says. Well, while I was serving my time, there was some rum goings on in the barracks. Our colonel stopped the troops from reading at all, and in the canteen they wasn't allowed even to wrap up sausages or cheese in newspapers. That made the soldiers start reading and our regiment had all the rest beat when it came to showing how much they'd learned. We used to read all the papers and in every company there were chaps who made up verses and songs guying the colonel. And whenever anything happened in the regiment there was always some smart chap among the rank and file who wrote a bit about it to the papers and called it 'Soldiers Tortured.' And that wasn't enough for them, mind you. Why, they used to write to our M.P.'s at Vienna asking them to take their part, and so they began to ask questions in Parliament, one after another, all about our colonel being a brute and that sort of stuff. Some minister or other sent a commission to look into it, and in the end a chap named Franta Henclu got two years, because he was the one who had complained to the M.P.'s in Vienna about a smack in the eye that he got from the colonel on the parade ground. Afterward, when the commission had cleared off, the colonel had us all drawn up, the whole blessed regiment, and he says, a soldier's a soldier and he's got to hold his tongue and do his duty, and if there's anything he doesn't like, then it's infringement of subordination. 'You gang of ruffians,' he says, 'you thought the commission was going to help you. Well, it helped you damn well,' he says. 'And now you'll march past me company by company and repeat aloud what I've just said.' So away we went, one company after another, eyes right, with our hands on our rifle straps, and yelled at the colonel, 'You gang of ruffians, you thought the commission was going to help you. Well, it helped you damn well.' The colonel was laughing fit to bust, till the Eleventh Company marches past. Up they came, stamping their feet, but when they got alongside the colonel they never said a word. The colonel turns as red as a beetroot and sends the Eleventh Company back to do it all over again. They march past and keep their mouths shut, but each file as it came up just stares at the colonel as bold as brass. '*Ruht!*'[1] says the colonel and walks across the barrack square, cracking his whip across his top boots. Then he spits and suddenly comes to a standstill and yells '*Abtreten!*'[2] mounts his old nag, and was outside the gate like a shot. We was waiting for the Eleventh Company to cop out, but nothing happened. We waited one day, two days, a whole week, and still nothing happened. There was no sign of the colonel in the barracks, and everybody—men, N.C.O.'s, and officers—was all chortling about it. Then we got a new colonel and we heard that the old one was in a sanatorium or something because he'd written a letter to the Emperor to tell him that the Eleventh Company had mutinied."

The time had now come for the doctor to pay his afternoon

[1] "Halt!"
[2] "Dismiss!"

visit. Dr. Grunstein went from bed to bed, followed by a medical corps orderly with a notebook.

"Macuna."

"Present, sir."

"Clyster and aspirin. Pokorny."

"Present, sir."

"Stomach to be rinsed out and quinine. Kovarik."

"Present, sir."

"Clyster and aspirin. Kotatko."

"Present, sir."

"Stomach to be rinsed out and quinine."

And so the process continued with, one after another, mercilessly, mechanically, incisively.

"Schweik."

"Present, sir."

Dr. Grunstein gazed at the newcomer. "What's the matter with you?"

"Beg to report, sir, I've got rheumatism."

During the period of his activities, Dr. Grunstein had adopted a delicately ironical manner, which proved far more effective than shouting.

"Aha, rheumatism," he said to Schweik. "You've got a frightfully troublesome illness. It's really quite a coincidence to catch rheumatism at the very moment when a war starts and you've got to join the army. I expect you're horribly upset about it."

"Beg to report, sir, I *am* horribly upset about it."

"Just fancy now, he's upset about it. It's frightfully nice of you to think of us with that rheumatism of yours. In peacetime the poor fellow skips about like a goat, but as soon as war breaks out he's got rheumatism and can't use his knees. I suppose your knees hurt you?"

"Beg to report, sir, my knees hurt me something cruel."

"And night after night you can't sleep, eh? Rheumatism is a very dangerous, painful, and troublesome illness. We've had some very satisfactory results with rheumatic patients here. Absolute diet and our other methods of treatment have proved extremely efficacious. Why, you'll be cured quicker here than at Pistany and you'll march up to the front line leaving clouds of dust behind you."

Then, turning to the N.C.O. orderly, he said, "Write this down: 'Schweik, absolute diet, stomach to be rinsed out twice daily, clyster once daily'; and then we'll see in due course what further arrangements are to be made. In the meantime, take him into the surgery, rinse out his stomach, and when he comes to, let him have the clyster, but thoroughly, till he screams blue murder and scares his rheumatism away."

And then, turning to all the beds, he delivered a speech brimful of wise and charming adages: "Don't imagine you're dealing with the sort of nincompoop who lets himself be humbugged by any bit of hanky-panky. Your dodges don't worry me in the least. I know you're all malingerers who want to shirk the army. And I treat you accordingly. I've managed hundreds and hundreds of soldiers like you. These beds have accommodated whole swarms of men who had nothing wrong with them except a lack of the military spirit. While their comrades were fighting at the front, they thought they'd loll about in bed, get hospital diet, and wait till the war stopped. Well, that's where they made a damn big mistake, and you're all making a damn big mistake, too. In twenty years to come you'll still scream in your sleep when you dream you're trying to swing the lead on me."

"Beg to report, sir," announced a quiet voice from the bed near the window, "that I'm quite well again. My asthma sort of disappeared in the night."

"Name?"

"Kovarik, beg to report, sir, I'm for the clyster."

"Good. You'll have the clyster before you go, to help you along on your journey," decided Dr. Grunstein, "so you can't complain we didn't cure you here. And now, all the men whose names I read out are to follow the N.C.O. and get what's coming to them."

And each one received a lavish portion as prescribed. Schweik's bearing was stoical.

"Don't spare me," he urged the myrmidon who was applying the clyster to him. "Remember, you've sworn to serve the Emperor. And if it was your own father or your brother who was lying here, give 'em the clyster without turning a hair. Remember that Austria stands as firm as a rock on these clysters and victory is ours."

On the next day when Dr. Grunstein came around he asked Schweik how he liked the military hospital.

Schweik replied that it was a first-class and well-managed establishment. As a recompense for which he was given the same as on the day before, together with aspirin and three quinine pills, which he had to take in a glass of water there and then.

But Socrates did not drink his cup of hemlock with such composure as Schweik the quinine. Dr. Grunstein now tried all the grades of torment on him.

When Schweik was wrapped up in a wet sheet in the presence of the doctor, and the latter asked him how he liked it, he replied, "Beg to report, sir, that it's like being in a swimming bath or at the seaside."

"Have you still got rheumatism?"

"Beg to report, sir, that it doesn't seem to be getting any better, somehow."

Schweik was subjected to fresh torments.

Now about this time, the Baroness von Botzenheim, the widow of an infantry general, took a lot of trouble to discover the soldier about whom the newspaper *Bohemia* had published an account of how he had, though a cripple, had himself wheeled along in a Bath chair and while in the Bath chair had shouted "To Belgrade!" which demonstration of patriotism had acted as an incentive to the editor of *Bohemia* to invite his readers to collect money for the benefit of the loyal and heroic cripple.

At last, as the result of an inquiry at the police headquarters, she ascertained that it was Schweik, and further inquiries were easy. The Baroness von Botzenheim, accompanied by her lady companion and a footman, proceeded to pay a visit to Schweik with a hamper of food.

The poor baroness did not know what it meant when someone is in the infirmary ward of a military prison. Her visiting card opened all doors and in the office they treated her with extreme courtesy. Within five minutes she was told that "the brave soldier Schweik," for whom she was inquiring, could be found in Hut Number 3, Bed Number 17. Dr. Grunstein, who was flabbergasted at this turn of events, accompanied her in person.

Schweik was just sitting on the bed after the usual daily moil prescribed by Dr. Grunstein, surrounded by a group of starved and emaciated malingerers, who had not yet given in and were stubbornly struggling with Dr. Grunstein upon the basis of absolute diet.

Anyone listening to them would have had the impression that he was in the society of culinary experts, at an advanced school of cookery or at a course of training for gourmets.

"Even plain hashed fat is eatable," one man was just saying—he was there for "chronic catarrh of the stomach"—"if it's warm. When the fat fries, you squeeze it out till it's dry, add salt and pepper, and I tell you, hashed goose fat isn't a patch on it."

"That be blowed for a yarn," said a man with "cancer of the stomach," "there's nothing like hashed goose fat. All your pork dripping and whatnot isn't in the same street with it; of course, it's got to be fried till it's nice and brown, like the Jews do it. You take a fat goose, strip the fat with the skin, and fry it."

"You're all wrong in what you say about pork dripping," said Schweik's neighbor. "Of course, it stands to reason I'm talking about homemade dripping. It's not brown and it's not golden. It's got to be something between the two. And it mustn't be too soft or too hard. It mustn't crackle, that's a sign it's overdone. It ought to melt on your tongue and make you feel as if your chin was being soaked with dripping."

"Did any of you ever eat horse dripping?" inquired a strange voice, to which, however, nobody replied, because the N.C.O. of the medical corps came running in. "Get into bed all of you. There's an archduchess or somebody coming here and don't let anybody show his dirty feet under the blanket."

No archduchess could have entered with such pomp as was displayed by the Baroness von Botzenheim. She was followed by a regular procession, including the quartermaster sergeant of the infirmary. He interpreted this as the hidden hand of a combing-out board which would remove him from his flesh-pots on the home front and fling him under some barbed wire entanglements at the mercy of shrapnel.

He was pale, but Dr. Grunstein was paler still. Before his eyes danced the old baroness's visiting card bearing the words "General's widow," and all that this might involve, such as: connections, influence, complaints, transfer to the front, and other awful things.

"Here's Schweik," he said, preserving an artificial calm and leading the Baroness von Botzenheim to Schweik's bed. "He's bearing up very patiently."

The Baroness von Botzenheim sat down by Schweik's bed on the chair which had been placed there for her and said in broken Czech, "Czech soldier; prave soldier; cripple soldier; prave soldier. Much like Czech Austrian."

So saying, she stroked Schweik's unshaven face and continued, "I read it all in de paper; I pring you something to eat; to smoke; to trink, Czech soldier, prave soldier. *Johann, kommen Sie her.*" [3]

The footman, a person with bristly whiskers, pulled a capacious hamper toward the bed, while the old baroness's lady companion, a tall lady with a lachrymose face, sat down on Schweik's bed and smoothed the straw bolster behind him, under the firm impression that such was the service which should be rendered to sick heroes.

Meanwhile, the baroness was extracting the gifts from the hamper. A dozen roast fowls, wrapped up in pink tissue paper and decorated with a silken black and yellow ribbon, and two bottles of some wartime liqueur bearing a label inscribed *"Gott strafe England."* The other side of the label showed Franz Josef and Wilhelm holding hands as if they were about to play cat's cradle.

She then extracted from the hamper three bottles of wine for convalescents and two boxes of cigarettes. She arranged everything very elegantly on the empty bed next to Schweik, and added a nicely bound book entitled *Episodes from the Life of Our Emperor.* Among the other things on the bed were some packets of chocolate also bearing the inscription *"Gott strafe England,"* and again with the effigies of the Austrian Emperor and the German Kaiser. Then there was a nice toothbrush inscribed *"Viribus unitis,"* so that whenever the owner cleaned his teeth he would be reminded of Austria. An elegant and very suitable gift for the front and the trenches consisted of a manicure set. On the box was a picture which showed some shrapnel bursting and a man in a helmet rushing forward, bayonet in hand. Under this: *"Für Gott, Kaiser und Vaterland!"* There was a box of rusks without any picture, but to make up for that, it was inscribed with the following verse in German, followed by a Czech translation:

> Austria, O thou noble land,
> Let thy banners now be scanned
> Let them flutter far and wide,
> Austria must evermore abide.

The last gift consisted of a white hyacinth in a flowerpot. When all this was unpacked and arranged on the bed, the Baroness von Botzenheim could not restrain her tears, so

[3] "John, come here."

82

touched was she. The mouths of several starving malingerers began to water. The baroness's lady companion propped Schweik up and also shed tears. It was so quiet that you could have heard a pin drop, when suddenly Schweik, clasping his hands together, interrupted the hush.

"'Our Father, which art in heaven, hallowed be thy name . . .' Excuse me, ma'am, that's not what I mean: 'Lord God, our heavenly Father, bless these gifts which we shall enjoy from Thy bounty, Amen'!"

Whereupon, he took a chicken from the bed and started devouring it, under the horrified gaze of Dr. Grunstein.

"Oh, how he's enjoying it, the brave fellow," whispered the old baroness ecstatically to Dr. Grunstein. "I'm sure he's quite well now and fit to go to the front. I'm really delighted to think I brought it to him just at the right moment."

Then she went from bed to bed distributing cigarettes and chocolates. After which errand she returned to Schweik. smoothed his hair, saying *"Behüt euch Gott"* [4] the while, and departed with all her retinue.

Before Dr. Grunstein could return from below, whither he had accompanied the baroness, Schweik had distributed the fowls, which were devoured by the patients so rapidly that, where the fowls had been, Dr. Grunstein discovered only a heap of bones, picked as clean as if the fowls had fallen alive into a lair of vultures and their fleshless bones had then been exposed for several months to the blazing sun.

The wartime liqueur and the three bottles of wine had also vanished. The packet of chocolate and the parcel of rusks had likewise passed away. Somebody had even drunk the small bottle of nail polish belonging to the manicure set and had chewed the tooth paste which went with the toothbrush.

When Dr. Grunstein had returned, he again struck up a martial attitude and delivered a long speech. A load fell from his mind when the visitor had gone. The pile of gnawed bones confirmed his idea that they were all incorrigible.

"If you'd had any glimmerings of sense," he fulminated. "you'd have kept your hands off all that food and you'd have said to yourselves, if we eat all this up, the doctor won't believe we're seriously ill. What you've done has only showed me that you don't appreciate my kindness. I pump your stomachs; I give you clysters; I try to keep you going on absolute diet and then you go and overeat yourselves. Do you

[4] "God preserve you."

83

want to get inflammation of the intestines? But you're making a big mistake. Before your stomachs begin to digest all you've eaten, I'll clear you out so thoroughly that you'll remember it to your dying day. So now you'll follow me, one by one, just to remind you that I'm not so big a fool as you are, but that I've got more sense than the whole lot of you put together. Furthermore, let me inform you that tomorrow I'm sending a commission here to attend to you, because you've been lolling about quite long enough and there's nothing the matter with any of you. Quick march!"

When it was Schweik's turn, Dr. Grunstein looked at him and a vague recollection of the mysterious visit that day urged him to inquire, "Do you know the baroness?"

"She's my stepmother," replied Schweik calmly, "she abandoned me at a tender age and now she's found me again."

And Dr. Grunstein remarked curtly, "Let Schweik have some more clyster afterward."

In the evening the occupants of the mattresses were in a dismal mood. A few hours earlier their stomachs had been filled with various savory viands and now they contained only weak tea and a slice of bread.

Number 21 called out from the window, "I say, you mightn't believe it, but if I have to choose between braised chicken and roast, give me braised every time."

Someone growled, "Shove a blanket over him," but they were all so weak after their fiasco of a banquet that nobody moved a limb.

Dr. Grunstein kept his word. The next morning a number of military doctors from the famous commission made their appearance.

They solemnly passed along the rows of beds and all they said was "Let's see your tongue."

Schweik thrust out his tongue so far that his countenance produced a fatuous grimace and his eyes blinked. "Beg to report, sir, that's all the tongue I've got."

There ensued an interesting colloquy between Schweik and the commission. Schweik asserted that he had made that statement because he was afraid they might think he was hiding his tongue from them.

The members of the commission, on the other hand, formed remarkably divergent judgments about Schweik.

A half of them asserted that Schweik was *"ein blöder*

Kerl," [5] while the other half took the view that he was a humbug who wanted to poke fun at the army.

"I'll eat my hat," the chairman of the commission yelled at Schweik, "if we don't get even with you."

Schweik gazed at the whole commission with the godly composure of an innocent child.

The chief of the medical staff came close up to Schweik. "I'd like to know what you think you're up to, you porpoise, you!"

"Beg to report, sir, I don't think at all."

"Himmeldonnerwetter!" bellowed one of the members of the commission, clanking his sword. "So he doesn't think at all, doesn't he? Why don't you think, you Siamese elephant?"

"Beg to report, sir, I don't think because soldiers ain't allowed to. Years and years ago, when I was in the Ninety-first Regiment, the captain always used to tell us: 'Soldiers mustn't think. Their superior officers do all their thinking for them. As soon as a soldier begins to think, he's no longer a soldier, but a lousy civilian.' Thinking doesn't lead—"

"Hold your tongue," the chairman of the commission interrupted Schweik fiercely. "We've heard all about you. You're no idiot, Schweik. You're artful, you're tricky, you're a humbug, a hooligan, the scum of the earth, do you understand?"

"Beg to report, sir, yes, sir."

"I've already told you to hold your tongue. Did you hear?"

"Beg to report, sir, I heard you say I was to hold my tongue."

"Himmelherrgott, hold your tongue then. When I say the word, you know full well we don't want any of your lip."

"Beg to report, sir, I know you don't want any of my lip."

The military gentlemen looked at each other and called for the sergeant major.

"Take this man," said the chief of the medical staff, pointing to Schweik, "into the office and wait there for our decision and report. The fellow's as sound as a bell. He's malingering and on top of that he keeps on jabbering and laughing up his sleeve at his superior officers. He thinks he's here just for his amusement and that the army's a huge joke, a sort of fun palace. When you get to the detention barracks, they'll show you the army's no frolic."

Schweik departed with the sergeant major and as he passed across the courtyard he hummed to himself:

[5] "An idiot."

85

"I always thought in the army,
I'd have the time of my life:
I'd stay here a week or a fortnight,
And then go back to my wife."

And while the officer on duty in the orderly room was yelling at Schweik to the effect that fellows like him ought to be shot, the commission was laying the malingerers low in the wards upstairs. Of seventy patients, only two were saved. One whose leg had been blown off by a shell and the other who was a genuine case of caries.

They were the only ones to whom the word *"tauglich"* was not applied. All the rest, not excepting three in the last stages of consumption, were declared fit for general service, and the chief of the medical staff, in making this pronouncement, improved the shining hour by holding forth on the subject.

His speech was interwoven with the most varied terms of abuse and its contents were concise in character. They were all foul brutes and only if they fought staunchly for the Emperor would it be possible for them to be admitted into decent society again, and for them after the war to be forgiven for having tried to shirk the army by malingering. He himself, however, did not believe this to be the case, and held the opinion that they would all come to a bad end on the gallows.

There was a very youthful military doctor, a guileless and still unspoiled creature, who asked the chief of the medical staff for permission to say a few words also. His speech differed from that of his superior officer by reason of its optimistic and simple-minded tone. He spoke in German.

He talked at great length of how all of them, on leaving the hospital and joining their regiments at the front, must be gallant and intrepid. He was, he said, convinced that they would be skillful with rifle and bayonet in the field, and honorable in all their dealings, military and private. They would be invincible warriors, mindful of the glory of Radetzky and Prince Eugene of Savoy. With their blood they would enrich the broad fields of the monarchy's glory and victoriously fulfill the task predestined for them by history. With unflinching courage, heedless of their lives, they would rush forward beneath the shot-riddled banners of their regiments to new glory, to new victories.

Afterward, in the corridor, the chief of the medical staff said to this guileless young man, "My dear fellow, I can assure you it's all sheer waste of breath. Not Radetzky, not Prince Eugene of Savoy whom you're so keen on, could have made soldiers out of these skunks. It doesn't matter whether you talk to them like an angel or like a devil. They're a hopeless gang."

9.

Schweik at the Detention Barracks

THE last resort of people who were unwilling to go to the front was the detention barracks. I knew a schoolmaster who was not anxious to use his mathematical knowledge to assist the artillery in its shooting operations, and so he stole a watch from a lieutenant so as to get into the detention barracks. He did so with complete deliberation. The war did not impress or attract him. He considered it stark lunacy to fire at the enemy, and with shrapnel and shells to slaughter unfortunate teachers of mathematics, just like himself, on the other side, and so he calmly stole the watch.

They first investigated his state of mind, and when he said he had wanted to enrich himself, they dispatched him to the detention barracks. There were quite a lot of people who served their time there for theft or fraud. Idealists and non-idealists. People who looked upon the army as a source of revenue, all those various quartermaster sergeants at the base and at the front who committed all kinds of fraud with rations and pay, and also petty thieves who were a thousand times more honest than the persons who sent them there. Then too, the detention barracks contained those soldiers who had committed various other offenses of a purely military character, such as insubordination, attempted mutiny, desertion. A special branch comprised the political prisoners, 80 per cent of whom were quite innocent and 99 per cent of whom were condemned.

There was a magnificent legal staff, a mechanism such as is possessed by every state before its political, economic, and moral collapse.

Every military unit contained Austria's hirelings who lodged information against the comrades who slept on the same mattresses with them and shared their bread with them on the march.

The police also supplied material to the detention barracks. The military censors of correspondence used to dispatch there those who had written letters from the front to the ones whom they had left at home in distress. The gendarmes even handed over old retired farmers who sent letters to the front, and the court-martial rewarded them with twelve years' imprisonment for their words of comfort and the descriptions of the misery at home.

From the Hradcany detention barracks there was also a road which led by way of Brevnov to the exercise ground at Motol. In front went a man escorted by soldiers, with gyves on his hands, and behind him a cart containing a coffin. And on the exercise ground at Motol a curt order, *"An! Feuer!"* [1] And in all the regiments and battalions they read in the regimental orders that another man had been shot for mutiny.

In the detention barracks a trinity comprising Staff Warder Slavik, Captain Linhart, and Sergeant Major Repa, nicknamed "the hangman," were already carrying out their duties, and nobody knows how many they beat to death in solitary confinement.

On receiving Schweik, Staff Warder Slavik cast at him a glance of mute reproach, as much as to say, "So your reputation's damaged, is it? Is that why you've joined us? Well, my

[1] "Take aim! Fire!"

lad, we'll make your stay here a happy one, the same as we do to all who fall into our hands."

And in order to lend emphasis to this figure of speech, he thrust a muscular and beefy fist under Schweik's nose, saying, "Sniff at that, you damned swab."

Schweik sniffed and remarked, "I shouldn't like a bash in the nose with that; it smells of graveyards."

This calm, thoughtful remark rather pleased the staff warder.

"Ha," he said, prodding Schweik in the stomach, "stand up straight. What's that you've got in your pockets? If it's cigarettes, you can leave 'em here. And hand over your money so's they can't steal it. Is that all you've got? Now then, no nonsense. Don't tell any lies or you'll get it in the neck."

"Where are we to put him?" inquired Sergeant Major Repa.

"We'll shove him in Number Sixteen," decided the staff warder, "among the ones in their underclothes. Can't you see that Captain Linhart's marked his papers 'Streng behüten, beobachten'?[2] Oh, yes," he remarked solemnly to Schweik, "riffraff have got to be treated like riffraff. If anybody raises Cain, why, off he goes into solitary confinement and once he's there we smash all his ribs and leave him till he pops off. We're entitled to do that. What did we do with that butcher, Repa?"

"Oh, he gave us a lot of trouble, sir," replied Sergeant Major Repa dreamily. "He was a tough 'un and no mistake. I must have been trampling on him for more than five minutes before his ribs began to crack and blood came out of his mouth. And he lived for another ten days after that. Oh, he was a regular terror."

"So you see, you swab, how we manage things here when anyone starts any nonsense or tries to do a bunk," Staff Warder Slavik concluded his pedagogical discourse. "Why, it's practically suicide and that's punished just the same here. And God help you, you scabby ape you, if you take it into your head to complain of anything at inspection time. When there's an inspection on, and they ask you if there are any complaints, you've got to stand at attention, you stinking brute, salute and answer, 'I beg to report, sir, no complaints, and I'm quite satisfied.' Now, you packet of muck, repeat what I said."

[2] "To be kept under strict watch and observation."

"Beg to report, sir, no complaints and I'm quite satisfied," repeated Schweik with such a charming expression on his face that the staff warder was misled and took it for a sign of frankness and honesty.

"Now take everything off except your underclothes and go to Number Sixteen," he said in quite civil tones, without adding such phrases as damned swab, packet of muck, or stinking brute, as he usually did.

In Number 16 Schweik encountered twenty men in their underclothing. They were the ones whose papers were marked *"Streng behüten, beobachten!"* and who were now being looked after very carefully to prevent them from escaping.

If their underclothing had been clean and if there had been no bars on the windows, you might have supposed at a first glance that you were in the dressing room of some bathing establishment.

Sergeant Major Repa handed Schweik over to the "cell manager," a hairy fellow in an unbuttoned shirt. He inscribed Schweik's name on a piece of paper hanging on the wall, and said to him, "Tomorrow there's a show on. We're going to be taken to chapel to hear a sermon. All of us chaps in underclothes, we have to stand just under the pulpit. It won't half make you laugh."

As in all prisons and penitentiaries, the chapel was in high favor among the inmates of the detention barracks. They were not concerned about the possibility that the enforced attendance at chapel might bring them nearer to God, or that they might become better informed about morality. No such nonsense as that entered their heads. What the divine service and the sermon did offer was a pleasant distraction from the boredom of the detention barracks. They were not concerned about being nearer to God, but about the hope of discovering the stump of a discarded cigar or cigarette on their way along the corridors and across the courtyard. God was thrust completely into the background by a small butt drifting about hopelessly in a spittoon or somewhere on the dusty floor. This tiny reeking object triumphed over God and the salvation of the soul.

And then too, the sermon itself, what a treat, what fun! Otto Katz, the chaplain, was such a jolly fellow. His sermons were so very attractive and droll, so refreshing amid the boredom of the detention barracks. He could prate so entertainingly about the infinite grace of God, and uplift the vile captives, the men without honor. He could hurl such delightful terms of abuse from the pulpit. He could bellow his *"Ite, missa est"* so gorgeously from the altar, officiate with such utter originality, playing ducks and drakes with Holy Mass. When he was well in his cups, he could devise entirely new prayers, a liturgy of his own which had never existed before.

Oh, and it was too funny for words when he sometimes slipped and fell over with the chalice, the holy sacrament or the missal in his hand, whereupon he would loudly accuse the ministrant from the gang of convicts of having deliberately tripped him up, and would there and then hand out a dose of solitary confinement or a spell in irons. And the recipient thoroughly enjoyed it, for it was all part of the frolics in the prison chapel.

Otto, the most perfect of military chaplains, was a Jew. He had a very checkered past. He had studied in a business college, and there he acquired a familiarity with bills of exchange and the law appertaining to them which enabled him within a year to steer the firm of Katz & Company into such a glorious and successful bankruptcy that old Mr. Katz departed to North America, after arranging a settlement with his creditors, unbeknown to them and unbeknown also to his partner, who proceeded to the Argentine.

So when young Otto Katz had distinterestedly bestowed the firm of Katz & Company upon North and South America, he was in the position of a man who has not where to lay his head. He therefore joined the army.

Before this, however, he did an exceedingly noble thing. He had himself baptized. He applied to Christ for help in his career. He applied to him absolutely confident that he was striking a business bargain with the Son of God. He successfully qualified for a commission, and Otto Katz, the new-fledged Christian, remained in the army. At first he thought he was going to make splendid progress, but one day he got drunk and took Holy Orders.

He never prepared his sermons, and everybody looked forward to hearing them. It was a solemn moment when the occupants of Number 16 were led in their underclothes into chapel. Some of them, upon whom fortune had smiled, were chewing the cigarette ends which they had found on the way to chapel, because, being without pockets, they had nowhere to keep them. Around them stood the rest of the prisoners and they gazed with relish at the twenty men in underclothing beneath the pulpit, into which the chaplain now climbed, clanking his spurs.

"Habt Acht!" [3] he shouted. "Let us pray, and now all together after me. And you at the back there, you hog, don't blow your nose in your hand. You're in the Temple of the Lord, and you'll be for it, mark my words. You haven't forgotten the Lord's Prayer yet, have you, you bandits? Well, let's have a shot at it. Ah, I knew it wouldn't come off. Lord's Prayer, indeed; two cuts from the joint with veg., have a regular blowout, with a snooze to follow, pick your noses, and be hanged to the Lord God, that's more in your line, isn't it?"

He stared down from the pulpit at the twenty bright angels in underclothing, who, like all the rest, were thoroughly enjoying themselves. At the back they were playing put-and-take.

"This is a bit of all right," whispered Schweik to his neighbor, who was suspected of having, for three crowns, chopped off all his comrade's fingers with an axe to get him out of the army.

"You wait a bit," was the answer. "He's properly oiled again today. He's going to jaw about the thorny path of sin."

True enough, the chaplain was in an excellent mood that day. Without knowing why he was doing it, he kept leaning over the side of the pulpit and was within an ace of losing his balance.

"I'm in favor of shooting the lot of you. You pack of rotters," he continued. "You won't turn to Christ and you prefer to tread the thorny path of sin."

"I told you it was coming. He's properly oiled," whispered Schweik's neighbor gleefully.

"The thorny path of sin, you thickheaded louts, is the path of struggle against vice. You are prodigal sons, who prefer to loll about in solitary confinement than return to your Father. But fix your gaze further and upward unto the heights of heaven, and you will be victorious and will harbor peace in your souls, you lousy crew. I'd be glad if that man would stop snorting at the back there. He's not a horse and he's not in a stable—he's in the Temple of the Lord. Let me draw your

[3] "Attention!"

attention to that, my beloved hearers. Now then, where was I? *Ja, über den Seelenfrieden, sehr gut.*[4] Bear in mind, you brutes, that you are human beings and that you must see through a glass darkly into distant space and know that all lasts here only for a time, but God abideth forevermore. *Sehr gut, nicht wahr, meine Herren?*[5] I ought to pray for you day and night, asking merciful God, you brainless louts, to pour out His soul into your cold hearts and wash away your sins with His holy mercy, that you may be His forevermore and that He may love you always, you thugs. But that's where you're mistaken. I'm not going to lead you into paradise." The chaplain hiccoughed. "I won't lift a finger for you," he continued obstinately. "I wouldn't dream of such a thing, because you are incorrigible blackguards. The goodness of the Lord will not guide you upon your ways, the spirit of God's love will not pervade you, because the Lord wouldn't dream of worrying His head about such a gang of rotters. Do you hear me, you down there, yes, you in your underclothes?"

The twenty men in underclothes looked up and said, as with one voice, "Beg to report, sir, we hear you."

"It's not enough just to hear," the chaplain continued his sermon. "Dark is the cloud of life in which the smile of God will not remove your woe, you brainless louts, for God's goodness likewise has its limits, and you hog over there, don't you belch, or I'll have you put away till you're black in the face. And you down there, don't run away with the idea that you're in a taproom. God is most merciful, but only to decent people and not to the scum of the earth who don't follow His rules and regulations. That's what I wanted to tell you. You don't know how to say your prayers, and you think you go to chapel to have some fun, as if it was a music hall or a cinema. And I'm going to knock the idea out of your heads that I'm here to amuse you and give you a good time. I'll shove each and every one of you into solitary confinement, that's what I'll do, you blackguards. Here am I wasting my time with you, and I can see it's all no use. Why, if the field marshal himself was here, or the archbishop, you wouldn't care a damn. You wouldn't turn to God. All the same, one of these days you'll remember me and then you'll realize that I was trying to do you good."

---

[4] "Yes, about the peace of the soul, very good."
[5] "Very good, gentlemen, eh?"

Among the twenty in underclothes a sob was heard. It was Schweik who had burst into tears.

The chaplain looked down. There stood Schweik wiping his eyes with his fist. Around him were signs of gleeful appreciation.

The chaplain, pointing to Schweik, went on: "Let each of you take an example from this man. What is he doing? He's crying. Don't cry, I tell you, don't cry. You want to become a better man. That's not such an easy job, my lad. You're crying now, but when you get back to your cell, you'll be just as big a blackguard as you were before. You'll have to ponder a lot more on the infinite grace and mercy of God; you'll have to make a great effort before your sinful soul is likely to find the right path in this world upon which it should proceed. Today with our own eyes we see a man here moved to tears in his desire for a change of heart, and what are the rest of you doing? Nothing at all. There's a man chewing something as if his parents had brought him up to chew the cud and another fellow over there is searching his shirt for fleas, and in the Temple of the Lord, too. Can't you do all your scratching at home? Must you leave it till you're at Divine Service, of all places? And you're very slack about everything, too, Staff Warder Slavik. You're all soldiers and not a pack of damn silly civilians. So you ought to behave in a soldierly manner, even though you are in church. Damn it all, get busy seeking God, and look for fleas at home. That's all I've got to say, you loafers, and I want you to behave properly at Mass, and not like the last time, when some fellows at the back were swapping government linen for grub."

The chaplain descended from the pulpit and entered the sacristy, followed by the staff warder. After a while the staff warder made his appearance, came straight up to Schweik, removed him from the bevy of men in underclothes, and led him away into the sacristy.

The chaplain was sitting very much at his ease on a table, rolling a cigarette.

When Schweik entered, he said, "Yes, you're the man I want. I've been thinking it over and I rather fancy I've seen through you, my lad. Do you get me? That's the first time anyone's ever shed tears here as long as I've been in this church."

He jumped down from the table, and shaking Schweik by

95

the shoulder, he shouted beneath a large, dismal picture of St. Francis of Sales, "Now then, you blackguard, own up that you were only shamming."

And the effigy of St. Francis of Sales gazed interrogatively at Schweik. On the other side, from another picture, another martyr, whose posterior was just being sawn through by Roman soldiers, gazed distractedly at him.

"Beg to report, sir," said Schweik with great solemnity, staking everything on one card, "that I confess to God Almighty and to you, Reverend Father, that I was shamming. I saw that what your sermon needed was the reformed sinner whom you was vainly seeking. So I really wanted to do you a good turn and let you see there's still a few honest people left, besides having a bit of a lark to cheer myself up."

The chaplain looked searchingly at Schweik's artless countenance. A sunbeam frisked across the dismal picture of St. Francis of Sales and imparted a touch of warmth to the distracted martyr on the wall opposite.

"Here, I'm beginning to like you," said the chaplain, returning to his seat on the table. "What regiment do you belong to?" He began to hiccough.

"Beg to report, sir, I belong to the Ninety-first Regiment and yet I don't, if you follow me. To tell the honest truth, sir, I don't properly know how I stand."

"And what are you here for?" inquired the chaplain, continuing to hiccough.

From the chapel could be heard the strains of a harmonium which took the place of an organ. The musician, a teacher imprisoned for desertion, was making the harmonium wail the most mournful hymn tunes. These strains blended with the hiccoughing of the chaplain to form a new Doric mode.

"Beg to report, sir, I really don't know why I'm here and why I don't complain about it. It's just my bad luck. I always look at everything in a good light, and then I always get the worst of it, like that martyr there in the picture."

The chaplain looked at the picture, smiled and said, "Yes, I really like you. I must ask the provost marshal about you, but I can't stop here talking any longer now. I've got to get that Holy Mass off my chest. *Kehrt euch!* [6] Dismiss!"

When Schweik was back again among his fellow worshippers in underclothes beneath the pulpit, they asked him what

[6] "About turn!"

the chaplain had wanted him in the sacristy for, whereupon he replied very crisply and briefly, "He's tight."

The chaplain's new performance, the Holy Mass, was followed by all with great attention and unconcealed approval. There was one man beneath the pulpit who laid a wager that the monstrance would fall out of the chaplain's hand. He wagered all his bread rations against two punches in the eye and he won his bet.

What filled the minds of all in chapel at the sight of the chaplain's ceremonials was not the mysticism of believers or the piety of the faithful. It was the same feeling that we have in a theater when we are about to see a new play, the plot of which we do not know. Complications ensue and we eagerly wait to see how they will be disentangled.

With esthetic gusto the congregation feasted their eyes upon the vestments which the chaplain had donned inside out, and with a fervid appreciation they watched everything that was being done at the altar.

The red-haired ministrant, a deserter from the 28th Regiment and a specialist in petty theft, was making an honest endeavor to extract from his memory the whole routine and technique of the Holy Mass. He acted not only as ministrant, but also as prompter to the chaplain, who with absolute aplomb mixed up whole sentences and blundered into the service for Advent, which, to everybody's delight, he began to sing. As he had no voice and no musical ear, the roof of the chapel began to re-echo with a squealing and grunting like a pigsty.

"He's well oiled today," those in front of the altar were saying with complete satisfaction and relish. "He isn't half canned. He's been out on the booze with the girls and no mistake."

And now for about the third time the chaplain could be heard chanting *"Ite, missa est"* from the altar, like the war cry of Red Indians. It made the windows rattle. He then looked into the chalice once more to see whether any wine was left, whereupon with a gesture of annoyance he turned to his hearers.

"Well, now you can go home, you blackguards, that's the lot. I have noticed that you do not show the sort of piety you should when you're in church before the countenance of the Holy of Holies, you worthless loafers. Face to face with God

Almighty, you make no bones about laughing, coughing, and sniggering, shuffling with your feet, even in my presence, although I here represent the Virgin Mary, Jesus Christ, and God the Father, you thickheaded louts. If that occurs again, I'll make things as hot for you as you deserve, and you'll discover that the hell I preached to you about not so long ago isn't the only one, but that there's a hell upon earth, and even if you save yourselves from the first one, I'll see you aren't saved from the other. *Abtreten!*"

The chaplain departed to the sacristy, changed his clothes, poured some sacramental wine from a demijohn into a tankard, drank it up, and with the help of the redheaded ministrant mounted his horse which was tied up in the courtyard. But then he suddenly remembered Schweik, dismounted, and went to the provost marshal's office.

Bernis, the provost marshal, was a man about town, an accomplished dancer, and a thoroughpaced bounder. His work bored him terribly. He was always losing documents containing particulars of charges, and so he had to invent new ones. He tried deserters for theft and thieves for desertion. He devised the most varied forms of hocus-pocus to convict men of crimes they had never dreamt of. He trumped up cases of lese majesty, and the imaginary incriminating evidence which he thus produced he always assigned to somebody, the charge or evidence against whom had got lost in the inextricable muddle of official papers.

"Hello," said the chaplain, shaking hands. "How goes it?"

"Rotten," replied Bernis. "They've got my papers into a mess and now it's the devil's own job to make head or tail of them. Yesterday I sent upstairs all the evidence against some chap who was charged with mutiny, and now they've sent it back because, according to them, he's not charged with mutiny, but with pinching jam." Bernis spat with disgust.

"What about a game of cards?" asked the chaplain.

"I've blued every bean I had at cards. A day or two ago we were playing poker with that bald-headed colonel and he cleaned me right out. On the other hand, I've picked up a tasty bit of skirt. And what about your Holiness?"

"I need an orderly," said the chaplain. "I used to have an old chap, an accountant, but he was a smug brute. He kept on snuffling and praying to God to spare him, so I sent him off to the front. I've since heard that his particular crowd got cut to pieces. After that they sent me another fellow, but all he did was to go out boozing and charging it up on my account. He was a decent sort but he had sweaty feet, so I shoved him on a draft, too. Now today I've just discovered a chap who started crying just to rag me. That's the kind of fellow I want. His name's Schweik and he's in Number Sixteen. I'd like to know what he's there for and whether I couldn't wangle him out of it."

Bernis started looking for the documents relating to Schweik but, as usual, he could find nothing.

"Captain Linhart's got it, I expect," he said, after a long search. "God knows how all these papers manage to get lost here. I must have sent them to Linhart. I'll telephone to him at once. Hello, Lieutenant Bernis speaking, sir. I say, do you happen to have any documents relating to a man called Schweik? . . . Schweik's papers must be in my hands? That's odd. . . . I took them over from you? Most odd. He's in Number Sixteen. . . . I know, sir, I've got the records of Number Sixteen. But I thought that Schweik's papers might be kicking around somewhere in your office. . . . Pardon? I'm not to talk to you like that? Things don't kick around in your office? Hello, hello . . ."

Bernis sat down at his table and heatedly expressed his disapproval of the careless way in which investigations were carried out. He and Captain Linhart had been on bad terms for some time past, and in this they had been thoroughly consistent. If Bernis received a file belonging to Linhart, he stowed it away, the result being that nobody could ever get to the bottom of anything. Linhart did the same with the files belonging to Bernis. Also, they lost each other's enclosures.[7]

(Schweik's documents were found among the court-martial records only after the end of the war. They had been placed in a file relating to someone named Josef Koudela. On the envelope was a small cross and beneath it the remark "Settled," together with the date.)

"Well, Schweik's file has got lost," said Bernis. "I'll have him sent for, and if he doesn't own up to anything, I'll let him go and arrange for him to be transferred to your care. Then you can settle his hash when he's joined his unit."

After the chaplain had gone, Bernis had Schweik brought

---

[7] Thirty per cent of the prisoners in the detention barracks remained there throughout the war without having their cases even heard. —Author.

in, but left him standing by the door, because he had just received a telephone message from police headquarters that the receipt of requisite material for charge Number 7267, concerning Private Maixner, had been acknowledged in Office Number 1 under Captain Linhart's signature.

Meanwhile, Schweik inspected the provost marshal's office.

The impression which it produced could scarcely be called a favorable one, especially with regard to the photographs on the walls. They were photographs of the various executions carried out by the army in Galicia and Serbia. Artistic photographs of cottages which had been burned down and of trees, the branches of which were burdened with hanging bodies. There was one particularly fine photograph from Serbia showing a whole family which had been hanged. A small boy with his father and mother. Two soldiers with bayonets were guarding the tree on which the execution had been carried out, and an officer was standing victoriously in the foreground smoking a cigarette. On the other side of the picture, in the background, could be seen a field kitchen at work.

"Well, what's the trouble with you, Schweik?" asked Bernis, putting the slip of paper with the telephone message away into a file. "What have you been up to? Would you like to admit your guilt, or wait until the charge is brought against you? We can't go on forever like this. Don't imagine you're going to be tried in a law court by a lot of damn fool civilians. A court-martial is what you'll be up against—a *k. u. k. Militär-gericht.*[8] The only way you can possibly save yourself from a severe but just sentence is to admit your guilt."

Bernis adopted a peculiar method when he had lost the charge papers against the accused. He considered himself so perspicacious that, although he was not in possession of the written evidence against a man and, indeed, even if he did not know what he was charged with, he could tell why he had been brought to the detention barracks merely by observing his demeanor. His perspicacity and knowledge of men were so great that on one occasion a gypsy who had been sent from his regiment to the detention barracks for stealing shirts was charged by him with political offenses, to wit, he had discussed with some soldiers in a taproom somewhere or other the establishment of an independent national state, composed of the territories of the crowns of Bohemia and Slovakia, with a Slav king to rule over them.

[8] "Imperial and Royal Court-martial."

"We have documents," he said to the unfortunate gypsy. "The only thing left for you to do is to admit your guilt, to tell us where you said it and to what regiment the soldiers belonged who heard you and when it was."

The unfortunate gypsy invented date, place, and the regiment of his alleged audience.

"So you won't admit anything?" said Bernis, when Schweik remained as silent as the grave. "You won't say why you're here? You might at least tell me before I tell you. Once more I urge you to admit your guilt. It'll be better for you because it'll make the proceedings easier and you'll get off with a lighter sentence."

"Beg to report, sir," said Schweik's good-humored voice, "I've been brought here as a foundling."

"How do you mean?"

"Beg to report, sir, I can explain it to you as easy as pie. In our street there's a watchmaker and he had a little boy of two. Well, one day this little boy went off for a walk by himself and got lost and a policeman found him sitting on the pavement. He took the little chap to the police station and there they locked him up. You see, though this little fellow was quite innocent, he got locked up all the same. And even if he'd been able to speak and he'd been asked why he was locked up, he wouldn't have known. And I'm in the same boat as he was. I'm a foundling, too."

The provost marshal's keen glance scrutinized Schweik's face and figure, but he was baffled by them. Such unconcern and innocence radiated from the personality standing before him that he began to pace furiously to and fro in his office, and if he had not promised the chaplain to send Schweik to him, Heaven alone knows how Schweik would have fared.

At last he came to a standstill by his table.

"Now just you listen," he said to Schweik, who was staring unconcernedly into vacancy. "If you cross my path again, I'll give you something to remember me by. Take him away."

When Schweik had been taken back to Number 16, Bernis sent for Staff Warder Slavik.

"Schweik is to be sent to Mr. Katz pending any further decision about him," he said curtly. "Just see that the discharge papers are made out and then have Schweik escorted to Mr. Katz by two men."

"Is he to be put in irons for the journey, sir?"

101

The provost marshal banged his fist on the table.

"You're a damned fool. Didn't I tell you plainly to have the discharge papers made out?"

And all the bad temper which Bernis had been accumulating during the day as a result of his dealings with Captain Linhart and Schweik was now vented like a cataract upon the head of the staff warder and concluded with the words, "You're the biggest bloody fool I've ever come across."

This upset the staff warder and on his way back from the provost marshal's office, he relieved his feelings by kicking the prisoner on fatigue duty who was sweeping the passage.

As for Schweik, the staff warder thought he might as well spend at least one night in the detention barracks and have a little more enjoyment, too.

The night spent in the detention barracks will always be one of Schweik's fondest memories.

Next door to Number 16 was a cell for solitary confinement, a murky den from which issued, during that night, the wailing of a soldier who was locked up in it and whose ribs were being broken by Sergeant Major Repa, at the orders of Staff Warder Slavik, for some disciplinary offense.

When the wailing stopped, there could be heard in Number 16 the crunching noise made by the fleas as they were caught between the fingers of the prisoners.

Above the door in an aperture in the wall an oil lamp, provided with wire netting to protect it, gave a faint light and much smoke. The smell of the oil blended with the natural effluvia of unwashed bodies and with the stench from the bucket.

In the corridors could be heard the measured tread of the sentries. From time to time the aperture in the door opened and through the peephole the turnkey looked in.

At eight o'clock in the morning Schweik was ordered to go to the office.

"On the left-hand side of the door leading into the office there's a spittoon and they throw butts into it," one man informed Schweik. "And on the first floor you'll pass another one. They don't sweep the passages till nine, so you're sure to find something."

But Schweik disappointed their hopes. He did not return to Number 16. The nineteen men in their underclothes wondered what could have happened to him and made all sorts of wild guesses.

A freckled soldier belonging to the defense corps, whose imagination was extremely lively, declared that Schweik had tried to shoot an officer and that he was being taken off that day to the exercise ground at Motol for execution.

10.

Schweik Becomes the Chaplain's Orderly

I.

ONCE more began his odyssey under the honorable escort of two soldiers with bayonets, who had to convey him to the chaplain.

By reason of their physical peculiarities, his escort supplemented each another. While one was lanky, the other was stumpy and fat. The lanky one limped with the right foot, the stumpy warrior with the left. They were both home-service men, having been entirely exempted from military service before the war.

They jogged on solemnly alongside the pavement and from time to time took a peep at Schweik, who marched between them and saluted everybody. His civilian clothing, including the military cap in which he had answered his calling-up notice, had got lost in the storeroom at the detention barracks. But before discharging him, they gave him an old military uniform which had belonged to some potbellied fellow who must have been a head taller than Schweik. Three more Schweiks could have got into the trousers he was wearing. They reached beyond his chest and their endless folds attracted the notice of the passers-by. A vest tunic with patches on the elbows, and covered with grease and grime, dangled around Schweik like a coat on a scarecrow. The military cap, which had also been issued in exchange at the detention barracks, came down over his ears.

Schweik replied to the smiles of the passers-by with sweet smiles of his own and glances which beamed with warm good-nature.

And so they proceeded on their way to Karlin, where the chaplain lived.

It was the stumpy, stout one who first addressed Schweik.

"Where are you from?" he inquired.

"Prague."

"You won't give us the slip?"

The lanky man joined in the conversation. It is a most remarkable thing that while short, fat men are mostly apt to be good-humored optimists, the lanky spindle-shanked ones, on the other hand, are of a more skeptical turn of mind.

And so the lanky fellow said to the dumpy little man, "He'd run away if he could."

"Why should he?" retorted the fat little man. "He's practically free, now that they've let him out of the detention barracks. It's all in the doings I've got here."

"And what's in the doings you've got for the chaplain?" inquired the lanky man.

"I don't know."

"There you are, you don't know and yet you're talking about it."

They crossed the Charles Bridge in complete silence. In Charles Street the fat little man again addressed Schweik: "Don't you know why we're taking you to the chaplain?"

"For confession," said Schweik casually. "They're going to hang me tomorrow. It's always done. They call it spiritual comfort."

"And why are you going to . . . ?" the lanky fellow asked cautiously, while the fat man gazed at Schweik pityingly.

"I don't know," replied Schweik with a good-humored smile. "It's all a mystery to me. I suppose it's fate."

"You must have been born under an unlucky star," remarked the little man sympathetically and with the air of an expert.

"If you ask me," said the lanky man skeptically, "they don't hang a man for nothing at all. There must be some reason for it."

"Yes, when there isn't a war on," remarked Schweik, "but when there's a war, they don't care whether a man gets killed at the front or is hanged at home. As far as they're concerned it's six of one and half a dozen of the other."

"I say, you're not one of those political prisoners, are you?" asked the lanky man. From the tone of his voice it was clear that he was beginning to take to Schweik.

"I should jolly well think I am," said Schweik with a smile.

"You're not a National Socialist, are you?" The fat little man was beginning to get cautious now. He thought he'd better have his say. "It's no business of ours, anyway, and there's lots of people about who've got their eyes on us. It's these blessed bayonets that make them stare so. We might manage to unfix them in some place where we can't be seen. You won't give us the slip? It'd be damned awkward for us if you did. Wouldn't it, Tonik?" he concluded, turning to the lanky man, who said in a low voice:

"Yes, we might unfix our bayonets. After all, he's one of our chaps."

He had ceased to be a skeptic and he was brimming over with pity for Schweik. So they looked for a convenient spot where they unfixed their bayonets, whereupon the fat man allowed Schweik to walk by his side.

"You'd like to have a smoke, wouldn't you?" he said. "That is, if . . ." He was about to say, "If they let you have a smoke before you're hanged," but he did not complete the sentence, feeling that under the circumstances it would scarcely be a tactful remark.

They all had a smoke and Schweik's escort began to tell him about their wives and children, and about their five acres and a cow.

"I'm thirsty," said Schweik.

The lanky man and the fat man looked at each other.

"We might drop in somewhere for a quick one," said the little man, who knew by a sort of intuition that the lanky man would agree. "But it must be some place where we shouldn't be noticed."

"Let's go to The Gillyflower," suggested Schweik. "You can shove your harness in the kitchen. Serabona, the landlord, belongs to the Sokols, so you needn't be afraid of him.

"They play the fiddle and harmonica there," continued Schweik. "The company's good too—tarts and people like that who wouldn't go to a really swell place."

The lanky man and the little man looked at each other again and then the lanky man said, "Well, let's go there then. It's a good step yet to Karlin."

On the way Schweik told them some good stories and they were in good spirits when they reached The Gillyflower. There they did as Schweik had suggested. They put their rifles in the kitchen and went into the taproom where fiddle and harmonica were filling the premises with the strains of a song then much in vogue.

A girl was sitting on the lap of a jaded youth with his hair carefully parted, and singing hoarsely:

> *"I had a girl, I had a girl*
> *But now another man's got her."*

A drunken vendor of herrings was sleeping at a table, and every now and then he woke up, banged his fist on the table, mumbled, "It's gotter stop," and fell asleep again. Behind a billiard table and beneath a mirror three girls were pestering a tram conductor: "Come on, kid, let's have a drop of gin." By the door a soldier was sitting with a number of civilians and telling them about the way he was wounded in Serbia. His arm was bandaged up, and his pockets were full of the cigarettes they had given him. He said he couldn't drink any more and one of the company, a bald-headed old man, kept on urging him. "Have another with me, lad, who knows when we'll meet again? Shall I get them to play you something? Is 'The Orphan Child' one of your favorites?"

This was the tune which the bald-headed old man liked best, and presently the fiddle and harmonica were reproducing its lachrymose melody. The old man became tearful and with quavering voice joined in the chorus.

From the other table somebody said, "Stow it, can't you? Go and eat coke. Buzz off, you with your bloody orphan child."

107

And to emphasize these suggestions, the hostile table began
to sing:

> *"Oh, it's hard, it's hard to part,*
> *Sorrow's gnawing at my heart."*

"Franta!" they called to the wounded soldier when, after
another spell of singing, they had succeeded in outdinning
"The Orphan Child." "Give 'em a miss and come over to us.
Bring some cigarettes along. Never mind those bastards."

Schweik and his escort watched all these goings on with interest. Schweik remembered how he used to go there often
before the war. But his escort had no such reminiscences. For
them it was something entirely new and they began to take a
fancy to it. The first to attain complete satisfaction there was
the little fat man, for such as he, besides being optimistic,
have a very great propensity for epicurism. The lanky man
was still struggling with himself. And as he had already lost
his skepticism, so too he was gradually losing his reticence
and what was left of his forethought.

"I'm going to have a dance," he said after his fifth drink,
when he saw the couples dancing a polka.

The little man was now having a thoroughly good time.
Next to him sat a girl who was talking smut. His eyes were
fairly sparkling.

Schweik kept on drinking. The lanky man finished his dance
and returned with his partner to the table. Then they sang and
danced, drinking the whole time and cuddling the girls who
had joined them. In the afternoon a soldier came up to them
and offered to give them blood poisoning for five crowns. He
said he had a syringe on him and would squirt petroleum into
their legs or hands.[1] That would keep them in bed for at least
two months, and possibly if they kept applying spittle to the
wound, as much as six months, with the chance of getting
completely out of the army.

When it was getting toward evening, Schweik proposed that
they should resume their journey to the chaplain. The little
fat man, who was now beginning to babble, urged Schweik to
wait a little longer. The lanky man was also of the opinion

[1] This is quite an efficacious method of getting into hospital. But the
smell of the petroleum which remains in the swelling gives the game
away. Benzine is better because it evaporates more quickly. Later on,
a mixture of ether and benzine was used for this purpose and, later
still, other improvements were devised.—Author.

that the chaplain could wait. But Schweik had now lost interest in The Gillyflower and threatened that if they would not come, he would go off by himself.

So they went, but he had to promise them that they would all make one more halt somewhere else. And they stopped at a small café where the fat man sold his silver watch to enable them to continue their spree. When they left there, Schweik led them by the arm. It was a very troublesome job for him. Their feet kept slipping and they were continually evincing a desire for one more round of drinks. The little fat man nearly lost the envelope addressed to the chaplain and so Schweik was compelled to carry it himself. He also had to keep a sharp lookout for officers and N.C.O.'s. After superhuman efforts and struggles, he managed to steer them safely to the house where the chaplain lived. He fixed their bayonets for them, and by pommeling them in the ribs, made them lead him instead of having to lead them.

On the first floor a visiting card bearing the inscription "Otto Katz, *Feldkurat*" [2] showed them where the chaplain lived. A soldier opened the door. From within could be heard voices and the clinking of glasses and bottles.

"We—beg—to—report—sir," said the lanky man laboriously in German, and saluting the soldier. "We have—brought —an envelope—and a man."

"In you come," said the soldier. "Where did you manage to get so top-heavy? The chaplain's a bit that way, too." The soldier spat and departed with the envelope.

They waited in the passage for a long time, and at last the door opened and in rushed the chaplain. He was in his shirt sleeves and held a cigar between his fingers.

"So you're here, are you?" he said to Schweik, "and these are the chaps who brought you. I say, got a match?"

"Beg to report, sir, I haven't."

"Here, I say, why not? Every soldier ought to have matches to light up with. A soldier who's got no matches is—What is he?'

"Beg to report, sir, he's without matches," replied Schweik.

"Splendid, he's without matches and can't give anyone a light. Well, that's one thing, and now for the next item on the program. Do your feet stink, Schweik?"

"Beg to report, sir, they don't stink."

[2] Army chaplain.

"So much for that. And now the third point. Do you drink brandy?"

"Beg to report, sir, I don't drink brandy, only rum."

"Good. Just have a look at that chap there. I borrowed him for today from Lieutenant Feldhuber. He's his batman. And he doesn't drink. He's a tee-tee-teetotaler and that's why he's been put on a draft. Be-because a man like that's no use to me. He only drinks water and bawls like a bull."

"You're a teetotaler," he said, turning to the soldier. "You ought to be ashamed of yourself, you bloody fool. For two pins I'd punch you in the jaw."

The chaplain now turned his attention to the men who had escorted Schweik and who, in their endeavor to stand up straight, were wobbling about, vainly trying to prop themselves up with their rifles.

"Y—you're dr-drunk," said the chaplain. "You're drunk while on duty and now you'll be for it. I'll see to that. Schweik, take their rifles away; march them off to the kitchen and mount guard over them until the patrol comes for them. I'll tel-tel-telephone at once to the barracks."

And thus Napoleon's saying "In war the situation changes from one moment to another" was again amply confirmed. In the morning they had escorted him with fixed bayonets to prevent him from giving them the slip; then he himself had led them along; and now, here he was, mounting guard over them.

They first became fully aware of this change in the situation when they were sitting in the kitchen and saw Schweik standing at the door with rifle and bayonet.

"I could do with a drink," sighed the little optimistic man, while the lanky fellow again had a fit of skepticism and said that the whole business was a piece of low treachery. He started loudly accusing Schweik of having landed them in their present plight and reproached him for having promised them that he would be hanged the next day. Now they could see that what he had said about the confession and the hanging was all a hoax.

Schweik made no reply but walked to and fro by the door.

"We haven't half got ourselves in a mess," exclaimed the lanky man.

At last, having heard all their accusations, Schweik remarked, "Now you can see that the army's no picnic. I'm just doing my duty. I got into this just the same as what you did, but fortune smiled on me, as the saying is."

"I could do with a drink," repeated the optimist desperately.

The lanky man stood up and staggered to the door.

"Let's go home, mate," he said to Schweik. "Don't act the fool."

"You go away," said Schweik. "I've got to guard you. We ain't on speaking terms now."

The chaplain suddenly appeared in the doorway.

"I can't get through to the barracks. So you'd better go home and re-remember you mustn't boo-booze when you're on duty. Quick march!"

In fairness to the chaplain it should be added that he had not telephoned to the barracks, for the simple reason that he had no telephone and was talking to a lamp stand.

II.

Schweik had been the chaplain's orderly for three whole days, and during this period he had seen him only once. On the third day an orderly arrived from Lieutenant Helmich telling Schweik to come and fetch the chaplain.

On the way, the orderly told Schweik that the chaplain had had a row with the lieutenant, had smashed a piano, was dead drunk, and refused to go home. Lieutenant Helmich, who was also drunk, had thrown the chaplain into the passage, where he was dozing on the ground by the doorway.

When Schweik reached the spot, he shook the chaplain, and when the latter opened his eyes and began to mumble, Schweik saluted and said, "Beg to report, sir, I'm here."

"And what do you want here?"

"Beg to report, sir, I've come to fetch you."

"So you've come to fetch me, have you? And where are we going?"

"Home, sir."

"And what have I got to go home for? Aren't I at home?"

"Beg to report, sir, you're on the floor in somebody else's home."

"And—how—did—I get here?"

"Beg to report, sir, you were paying a call."

"Not—not—not paying a call. You're—you're—wrong there."

Schweik lifted the chaplain and propped him up against the

wall. While Schweik was holding him, the chaplain floundered from side to side and clung to him, saying, "You're letting me fall." And then, once more, with a fatuous smile, he repeated, "You're letting me fall." At last Schweik managed to squeeze the chaplain up against the wall, whereupon he began to doze again in his new posture.

Schweik woke him up.

"What d'you want?" asked the chaplain, making a vain attempt to drag himself along by the wall and to sit up. "Who are you, anyway?"

"Beg to report, sir," replied Schweik, pushing the chaplain back against the wall, "I'm your batman, sir."

"I haven't got a batman," said the chaplain with some effort, making a fresh attempt to tumble on top of Schweik. There was a little tussle which ended in Schweik's complete victory. Schweik took advantage of this to drag the chaplain down the stairs into the entrance hall, where the chaplain tried to stop Schweik from taking him into the street. "I don't know you," he kept telling Schweik during their tussle. "Do you know Otto Katz? That's me.

"I've been to the Archbishop's," he yelled, catching hold of the door in the entrance hall. "The Vatican takes a great interest in me. Is that clear to you?"

Schweik assented and began to talk to the chaplain as man to man. "Let go of that, I tell you," he said, "or I'll give you such a wallop. We're going home; so now stow your gab."

The chaplain let go of the door and clung to Schweik, who pushed him aside and then carried him out into the street, where he drew him along the pavement in a homeward direction.

"Who's that bloke?" asked one of the onlookers in the street.

"That's my brother," replied Schweik. "He came home on leave and when he saw me, he was so happy that he got tight, because he thought I was dead."

The chaplain, who caught the last few words, stood up straight and faced the onlookers. "Any of you who are dead must report themselves to headquarters within three days so that their corpses can be consecrated."

And he lapsed into silence, endeavoring to fall nose-first onto the pavement, while Schweik held him under the arm and drew him along homeward. With his head thrust forward and his feet trailing behind and dangling like those of a cat with a broken back, the chaplain was muttering to himself, *"Dominus vobiscum—et cum spiritu tuo. Dominus vobiscum."*

When they reached a cab rank, Schweik propped the chaplain in a sitting posture up against a wall and went to negotiate with the cabmen about the fare. One of the cabmen declared that he knew the chaplain very well, that he'd driven him home once and would never do it again.

"He spewed all over my cab," he announced in plain terms, "and then he never paid his fare. I was carting him around for more than two hours before he found out where he lived. And a week later, when I'd been after him about three times, he paid me five crowns for the whole lot."

After long discussions, one of the cabmen agreed to take them.

Schweik went back to the chaplain, who had now fallen asleep. Somebody had removed his bowler hat (for he usually put on civilian clothing when he went for a walk) and taken it away.

Schweik woke him up and with the help of the cabman got him inside the cab. There the chaplain collapsed in a complete torpor and took Schweik for Colonel Just of the 75th Infantry Regiment. He kept muttering, "Don't be too hard on me, sir. I know I'm a bit of a cad." At one moment, it seemed as if the jolting of the cab against the curb was bringing him to his senses. He sat up straight and began to sing snatches from some unrecognizable song. But then he lapsed once again into a complete torpor and turning to Schweik with a wink he inquired, "How are you today, dear lady?"

Then, after a brief pause, "Where are you going for your summer holidays?"

Evidently he saw everything double, for he then remarked, "So you've got a grown-up son," and he pointed to Schweik.

"Sit down," shouted Schweik, when the chaplain started trying to climb onto the seat, "or I'll teach you how to behave, see if I don't."

The chaplain thereupon became quiet and his little piglike eyes stared out of the cab in a state of complete bewilderment as to what was happening to him. Then, with a melancholy expression, he propped his head up in his hands and began to sing:

> *"I seem to be the only one*
> *Whom nobody loves at all."*

But he immediately broke off and remarked in German, "Excuse me, sir, you don't know what you're talking about. I can sing whatever I like." Whereupon he attempted to whistle some tune or other, but the noise which issued from his lips was so loud that the cab came to a standstill. Schweik told the cabman to drive on and the chaplain then tried to light his cigarette holder.

"It won't burn," he said despondently, when he had used up all his matches. "You keep on blowing at it."

But again he at once lost the thread of continuity and started laughing.

"This is no end of a lark. We're in a tram, aren't we?"

He began to search his pockets.

"I've lost my ticket," he shouted. "Stop the tram. I must find my ticket."

And with a gesture of resignation, "All right. Let them drive on."

Then he began to babble. "In the vast majority of cases . . . Yes, all right . . . In all cases . . . You're wrong . . . Second floor . . . That's only an excuse . . . That's your concern, not mine, dear lady . . . Bill, please . . . I've had a black coffee."

In a semidream he began to squabble with an imaginary adversary who was disputing his rights to a seat by the window in a restaurant. Then he began to take the cab for a train and leaning out, he yelled in Czech and German, "Nymburk, all change." Schweik thereupon pulled him back and the chaplain forgot about the train and began to imitate various farmyard noises. He kept up the cock crow longest and his clarion call was trumpeted forth in fine style from the cab. For a while he became altogether very active and restless, trying to get out of the cab and hurling terms of abuse at the people past whom they drove. After that he threw his handkerchief out of the cab and shouted to the cabman to stop, because he had lost his luggage. Next he started telling a story: "At Budejovice there was a drummer. He got married. A year later he died." He burst out laughing. "Isn't that screamingly funny?"

All this time Schweik treated the chaplain with relentless severity. Each time that he made various frolicsome attempts to get out of the cab, to smash the seat and so on, Schweik gave him one or two hard punches in the ribs, which treatment he accepted with remarkable lethargy. Only once did he put up any sort of resistance by trying to jump out of the cab.

He said that he wouldn't go a step further, because he knew that they were on their way to Podmokly and not to Bude-jovice, as they ought to be. Within a minute Schweik had settled his attempt at mutiny and forced him to resume his previous posture on the seat, at the same time taking care to stop him from falling asleep. His mildest remark in this connection was, "Keep awake, or you'll be a dead'un."

All at once the chaplain was overcome by a fit of melancholy and he began to cry. Tearfully he asked Schweik whether he had a mother.

"I'm all alone in the world, my friends," he shouted from the cab. "Take pity on me!"

"Stop that row," said Schweik. "Shut up, or everybody'll say you're boozed."

"I've not drunk a thing, old boy," replied the chaplain. "I'm as sober as a judge."

But suddenly he stood up and saluted. "Beg to report, sir, I'm drunk," he said in German. And then he repeated ten times in succession, with a heartfelt accent of despair, "I'm a dirty dog." And turning to Schweik he persistently begged and entreated, "Throw me out of the cab. What are you taking me with you for?"

He sat down again and muttered, "Rings are forming around the moon. I say, Captain, do you believe in the immortality of the soul? Can a horse get into heaven?"

He started laughing heartily, but after a while he began to mope and gazed apathetically at Schweik, remarking, "I say, excuse me, but I've seen you before somewhere. Weren't you in Vienna? I remember you from the seminary."

For a while he amused himself by reciting Latin verses:

"Aurea prima satas aetas, qual vindice nullo."

"This won't do," he then said. "Throw me out. Why won't you throw me out? I shan't hurt myself.

"I want to fall on my nose," he declared in a resolute tone. Then, beseechingly, he continued, "I say, old chap, give me a smack in the eye."

"Do you want one or several?" inquired Schweik.

"Two."

"Well, there you are then."

The chaplain counted out aloud the smacks as he received them, beaming with delight.

"That does you good," he said, "it helps the digestion. Give me another on the mouth.

115

"Thanks awfully," he exclaimed, when Schweik had promptly complied with his request. "Now I'm quite satisfied. I say, tear my waistcoat, will you?"

He manifested the most diverse desires. He wanted Schweik to dislocate his foot, to throttle him for a while, to cut his nails, to pull out his front teeth. He exhibited a yearning for martyrdom, demanding that his head should be cut off, put in a bag, and thrown into the river.

"Stars around my head would suit me nicely," he said with enthusiasm. "I should need ten of them."

Then he began to talk about horse racing and rapidly passed on to the topic of the ballet, but that did not detain him for long, either.

"Can you dance the czardas?" he asked Schweik. "Can you do the bunny hug? It's like this. . . ."

He wanted to jump on top of Schweik, who accordingly began to use his fists on him and then laid him down on the seat.

"I want something," shouted the chaplain, "but I don't know what. Do you know what I want?" And he drooped his head in complete resignation.

"What's it matter to me what I want?" he said solemnly. "And it doesn't matter to you, either. I don't know you. How dare you stare at me like that? Can you fence?"

For a moment he became more aggressive and tried to push Schweik off the seat. Afterward, when Schweik had quieted him down by a frank display of his physical superiority, the chaplain asked, "Is today Monday or Friday?"

He was also anxious to know whether it was December or June and he exhibited a great aptitude for asking the most diverse questions, such as: "Are you married? Do you like Gorgonzola cheese? Have you got any bugs at home? Are you quite well? Has your dog had the mange?"

He became communicative. He said that he had not yet paid for his riding boots, whip, and saddle, that some years ago he had suffered from a certain disease which had been cured with permanganate.

"There was no time to think of anything else," he said with a belch. "You may think it's a nuisance, but, hm, hm, what am I to do? Hm, hm. Tell me that. So you must excuse me.

"Thermos flasks," he continued, forgetting what he had just been talking about, "are receptacles which will keep beverages

116

and food stuffs at their original temperature. Which game do you think is fairer, bridge or poker?

"Oh yes, I've seen you somewhere before," he shouted, trying to embrace Schweik. "We used to go to school together.

"You're a good chap," he said tenderly, stroking his foot. "You've quite grown up since I saw you last. The pleasure of seeing you makes up for all my troubles."

He waxed poetic and began to talk about the return to the sunshine of happy faces and warm hearts.

Then he knelt down and began to pray, laughing the whole time.

When finally they reached their destination, it was very difficult to get him out of the cab.

"We aren't there yet," he shouted. "Help, help! I'm being kidnapped. I want to drive on."

He had to be wrenched out of the cab like a boiled snail from its shell. At one moment it seemed as if he were going to be pulled apart, because his legs got mixed up with the seat. At last, however, he was dragged through the entrance hall and up the stairs into his rooms, where he was thrown like a sack onto the sofa. He declared that he would not pay for the cab because he had not ordered it, and it took more than a quarter of an hour to explain to him that it was a cab. Even then he continued to argue the point.

"You're trying to do me down," he declared, winking at Schweik and the cabman. "We walked all the way here."

But suddenly, in an outburst of generosity, he threw his purse to the cabman. "Here, take the lot, *ich kann bezahlen.*[3] A kreutzer more or less doesn't matter to me."

To be strictly accurate, he ought to have said that thirty-six kreutzers more or less didn't matter to him, for that was all the purse contained. Fortunately, the cabman submitted it to a close inspection, referring the while to smacks in the eye.

"All right, then, you give me one," replied the chaplain. "Do you think I couldn't stand it? I could stand five from you."

The cabman discovered a five-crown piece in the chaplain's waistcoat pocket. He departed, cursing his fate and the chaplain, who had wasted his time and reduced his takings.

The chaplain got to sleep very slowly, because he kept making fresh schemes. He was anxious to do all kinds of

[3] "I can pay."

117

things, to play the piano, to have a dancing lesson, to fry some fish, and so on. But at last he fell asleep.

III.

When Schweik entered the chaplain's room in the morning, he found him reclining on the sofa in a very dejected mood.

"I can't remember," he said, "how I got out of bed and landed on the sofa."

"You never went to bed, sir. As soon as we got here, we put you on the sofa. That was as much as we could manage."

"And what sort of things did I do? Did I do anything at all? Was I drunk?"

"Not half you wasn't," replied Schweik. "Canned to the wide, sir. In fact, you had a little dose of the D.T.'s. It strikes me, sir, that a change of clothes and a wash wouldn't do you any harm."

"I feel as if someone had given me a good hiding," complained the chaplain, "and then I've got an awful thirst on me. Did I kick up a row yesterday?"

"Oh, nothing to speak of, sir. And as for your thirst, why, that's the result of the thirst you had yesterday. It's not so easy to get rid of. I used to know a cabinetmaker who got drunk for the first time in 1910 on New Year's Eve and the morning of January first he had such a thirst on him and felt so seedy that he bought a herring and then started drinking again. He did that every day for four years and nothing can be done for him because he always buys his herrings on a Saturday to last him the whole week. It's one of those vicious circles that our old sergeant major in the Ninety-first Regiment used to talk about."

The chaplain was thoroughly out of sorts and had a bad fit of the blues. Anyone listening to him at that moment would have supposed that he regularly attended those teetotal lectures, the gist of which was, "Let us proclaim a life-and-death struggle against alcohol which slaughters the best men," and that he was a reader of that edifying work *A Hundred Sparks From the Ethical Anvil*. It is true that he slightly modified the views expressed there. "If," he said, "a chap drank high-class beverages, such as arak, maraschino, or cognac, it'd be all right. But what I drank yesterday was gin. It's a marvel to me how I can swallow so much of the stuff. The taste of it's

118

disgusting. It's got no color and it burns your throat. And if it was at least the real thing, distilled from the juniper like I've drunk in Moravia—but the gin I had yesterday was made of some sort of wood alcohol mixed with oily bilge. Just listen to the way I croak.

"Brandy's poison," he decided. "It must be the real original stuff and not produced at a low temperature in a factory by a pack of Jews. It's the same with rum. Good rum's a rarity. Now, if I only had some genuine cherry brandy here," he sighed, "it'd put my stomach right in no time. The sort of stuff that Captain Schnabel's got."

He began to search in his pockets and inspected his purse. "Holy Moses! I've got thirty-six kreutzers. What about selling the sofa?" he reflected. "What do you think? Will anyone buy a sofa? I'll tell the landlord that I've lent it or that someone's pinched it from me. No, I'll leave the sofa. I'll send you to Captain Schnabel to see if you can get him to lend me a hundred crowns. He won some money at cards the day before yesterday. If he won't fork out, try Lieutenant Mahler in the barracks at Vrsovice. If that's no go, try Captain Fischer at Hradcany. Tell him I've got to pay for the horse's fodder and that I've blued the money on booze. And if he don't come up to scratch, why we'll have to pawn the piano, and be blowed to them. I'll write a note that'll do just as well for one as the other. Don't let them put you off. Say that I'm absolutely stony broke. You can pitch any yarn you please, but don't come back empty-handed or I'll send you to the front. And ask Captain Schnabel where he gets that cherry brandy, and then buy two bottles of it."

Schweik carried out his task in brilliant style. His simplicity and his honest countenance aroused complete confidence in what he said. He deemed it inexpedient to tell Captain Schnabel, Captain Fischer, and Lieutenant Mahler that the chaplain owed money for the horse's fodder, but he thought it best to support his application by stating that the chaplain was at his wit's end about a paternity order. And he got the money from all of them.

When he produced the 300 crowns on his victorious return from the expedition, the chaplain, who in the meanwhile had washed and changed, was very surprised.

"I got the whole lot at one go," said Schweik, "so as we shouldn't have to worry our heads about money again tomorrow or the next day. It was a fairly easy job, although I had to beg and pray of Captain Schnabel before I could get anything out of him. Oh, he's a brute. But when I told him about our paternity case—"

"Paternity case?" repeated the chaplain, horrified.

"Yes, paternity case, sir. You know, paying girls so much a week. You told me to pitch any yarn I pleased, and that's all I could think of. Down our way there was a cobbler who had to pay money like that to five different girls. It fairly drove him crazy and he had to go and borrow from people, but everyone took his word for it that he was in the deuce of a fix. They asked me what sort of a girl it was and I told them she was a very smart little bit, not fifteen yet. Then they wanted to have her address."

"You've made a nice mess of it, I must say," sighed the chaplain and began to pace the room.

"This is a pretty kettle of fish," he said, clutching at his head. "Oh, what a headache I've got."

"I gave them the address of a deaf old lady down our street," explained Schweik. "I wanted to do the thing properly, because orders are orders. I wasn't going to let them put me off and I had to think of something. And now there's some men waiting in the passage for that piano. I brought them along with me, so as they can take it to the pawnshop for us. It'll be a good thing when that piano's gone. We'll have more room and we'll have more money, too. That'll keep our minds easy for a few days. And if the landlord asks what we've done with the piano, I'll tell him some of the wires are broke and we've sent it to the factory to be repaired. I've already told that to the house porter's wife so as she won't think it funny when they take the piano away in a van. And I've found a customer for the sofa. He's a secondhand furniture dealer— a friend of mine, and he's coming here in the afternoon. You can get a good price for leather sofas nowadays."

"Is there anything else you've done?" inquired the chaplain, still holding his head and showing signs of despair.

"Beg to report, sir, I've brought five bottles of that cherry brandy like Captain Schnabel has, instead of the two you said. You see, now we'll have some in stock and we shan't be hard up for a drink. Shall I see about that piano before the pawnshop closes?"

The chaplain replied with a gesture signifying his hopeless plight. And in a trice the piano was being stowed away in the van.

When Schweik got back from the pawnshop he found the chaplain sitting with an open bottle of cherry brandy in front of him, and fuming because he had been given an underdone cutlet for lunch. He was again tipsy. He declared to Schweik that on the next day he would turn over a new leaf. Drinking alcoholic beverages was, he said, rank materialism and man was made to live the life of the spirit. He talked in a philosophical strain for about half an hour. When he had opened the third bottle, the secondhand furniture dealer arrived and the chaplain sold him the sofa for a mere song. He asked him to stop and have a chat and he was very disappointed when the dealer excused himself, as he had to go and buy a night commode.

"I'm sorry I haven't got one," said the chaplain regretfully, "but a man can't think of everything."

After the secondhand furniture dealer had gone, the chaplain started an affable little talk with Schweik, in the course of which he drank another bottle. A part of the conversation dealt with the chaplain's personal attitude toward women and cards. They sat there for a long time. And when evening came, it overtook Schweik and the chaplain in friendly discourse.

In the night, however, there was a change in the situation. The chaplain reverted to the state in which he had been on the previous day. He mixed Schweik up with somebody else and said to him, "Here, don't go away. Do you remember that redheaded cadet in the transport section?"

This idyllic interlude continued until Schweik said to the chaplain, "I've had enough of this. Now you're going to toddle along to bed and have a good snooze, see?"

"I'll toddle along, my dear boy, of course I will," babbled the chaplain. "Do you remember we were in the Fifth together and I used to do your Greek exercises for you? You've got a villa at Zbraslav. And you can go for the steamer trips on the Vltava. Do you know what the Vltava is?"

Schweik made him take his boots off and undress. The chaplain obeyed, but addressed a protest to unknown persons: "You see, gentlemen," he said to the cupboard, "how my relatives treat me.

"I refuse to asknowledge my relatives," he suddenly decided, getting into bed. "Even if heaven and earth conspire against me, I refuse to acknowledge them."

And the room resounded with the chaplain's snoring.

It was about this time that Schweik paid a visit to Mrs. Müller, his old charwoman. The door was opened to him by Mrs. Müller's cousin, who amid tears informed him that Mrs. Müller had been arrested on the same day on which she had taken Schweik in a Bath chair to the army medical board. They had tried the old lady before a court-martial, and as they had no evidence against her, they had taken her to the internment camp at Steinhof. There was a postcard from her. Schweik took this household relic and read:

DEAR ANINKA,

We are Very comfortable hear and are all well. The Woman on the bed next to mine has Spotted . . . and their are also some with small . . . Otherwise, all is well.

We have plenty to eat and collect Potato . . . for Soup, I have heard that Mr. Schweik is . . . so find out some-how wear he is berried so that after the War we can put some Flowers on his grave. I forgot to tell you that in the Attic in a dark corner there is a box with a little Dog, a terrier puppy, in it. But he has had nothing to eat for several Weeks ever since they came to fetch me to . . . So I think it must be to late and the littel Dog is also . . .

Across the letter had been stamped a pink inscription: *"Zensuriert k. k. Konzentrationslager, Steinhof."* [4]

"And the little dog *was* dead," sobbed Mrs. Müller's cousin. "And you'd never recognize the place where you used to live. I've got some dressmakers lodging there. And they've turned the place into a regular drawing room. Fashion pictures on all the walls and flowers in the windows."

Mrs. Müller's cousin was thoroughly upset.

Amid continued sobbing and lamentation she finally expressed the fear that Schweik had run away from the army and wanted to bring about her downfall also and plunge her into misery. She wound up by talking to him as if he were an infamous adventurer.

"That's one of the best jokes I've heard," said Schweik. "I'm fairly tickled to death by it. Well, I don't mind telling you, Mrs. Kejr, you guessed it right, first go. I have done a bunk. But first of all I had to do in fifteen sergeants and sergeant majors. Only don't tell anyone. . . ."

[4] "Censored, Imperial & Royal Internment Camp, Steinhof."

And as Schweik departed from the home which had given him so chilly a welcome, he said, "Mrs. Kejr, there's some collars and shirt fronts of mine at the laundry. You might go and fetch them for me, so that when I come back from the army, I'll have some civilian togs to put on. And see that the moths don't get at my things in the wardrobe. Well, give me best respects to the young ladies who are sleeping in my bed."

Then Schweik went to see what was going on at The Flagon. When Mrs. Palivec saw him, she said that she wouldn't serve him with any drink, because he'd probably taken French leave.

"My husband," she said, beginning to harp upon a now ancient topic, "he was as careful as could be and there he is, poor fellow, in prison, though as innocent as a babe unborn. And yet there's people going about scot-free who've run away from the army. They were looking for you here again last week.

"We was more careful than you," she concluded her discourse, "and now look at the bad luck we've had. It ain't everyone who's as lucky as what you are."

An elderly man, a locksmith from Smichow, had overheard these remarks and he now came up to Schweik, saying, "Do you mind waiting for me outside? I'd like to have a word with you."

In the street it turned out that from what Mrs. Palivec had said he took Schweik for a deserter. He told him he had a son who had also run away from the army and was hiding with his grandmother. Although Schweik assured him that he was not a deserter, he pressed a ten-crown piece into his hand.

"Just to keep you going for a bit," he explained, taking him into a wineshop around the corner. "I know how things are with you. Don't you worry. I won't give you away."

It was late at night when Schweik got back, but the chaplain was not yet at home. He did not turn up till the morning, when he woke Schweik up and said, "Tomorrow we're going to celebrate Mass for the troops. Make some black coffee and put some rum into it. Or better still, brew some grog."

11.

Schweik Accompanies the Chaplain
to the Celebration of Mass

I.

PREPARATIONS for the slaughter of human beings have always been made in the name of God or of some alleged higher being which mankind has, in its imaginativeness, devised and created.

Before the ancient Phoenicians cut a captive's throat, they performed religious ceremonies with just the same magnificence as did the new generations a few thousand years later before they marched into battle and destroyed their enemies with fire and sword.

The cannibals of New Guinea and Polynesia, before sol-

124

emnly devouring their captives, or superfluous persons such as missionaries, travelers, and agents of various business firms, or those merely prompted by idle curiosity, offer up sacrifices to their gods and perform the most diverse religious ceremonies. As the refinement of canonicals has not yet reached them, they decorate their thighs with festoons of gaudy plumage.

Before the Holy Inquisition burned its victims, the most magnificent religious ceremonies were held—High Mass with choral accompaniments.

When criminals are hanged, priests always officiate, annoying the malefactors by their presence.

In Prussia a pastor conducts the poor wretch to the block; in Austria a Catholic priest escorts him to the gallows; in France to the guillotine; in America a clergyman accompanies him to the electric chair; in Spain to the ingenious appliance by which he is strangled, etc.

Everywhere they have to carry a crucifix about on these occasions, as if to say, "You're only having your head chopped off, you're only being hanged, you're only being strangled, you're only having fifteen thousand volts shoved into you, but don't forget what He had to go through."

The shambles of the World War would have been incomplete without the blessings of the clergy. The chaplains of all armies prayed and celebrated Mass for the victory of the side whose bread they ate. A priest was in attendance when mutineers were executed. A priest put in his appearance at the execution of Czech legionaries.

Throughout Europe, men went to the shambles like cattle, whither they were driven by butchers, who included not only emperors, kings, and other potentates, but also priests of all denominations. Mass at the front was always held twice, when a contingent was moving up to the front line and then again before going over the top, before the bloodshed and slaughter. I remember that on one such occasion, while Mass was being celebrated, an enemy airplane dropped a bomb right on top of the altar and nothing was left of the chaplain but a few bloodstained rags.

Afterward he was mentioned in dispatches as a martyr, while our airplanes were preparing similar glory for the chaplain on the other side.

Schweik brewed a splendid dose of grog, far better than all the grog imbibed by old sailors. Such grog as his might have been drunk by eighteenth-century pirates to their complete satisfaction.

The chaplain was delighted.

"Where did you learn to brew such fine stuff as that?" he asked.

"When I was on tramp years ago," replied Schweik, "in Bremen, from a sailor, a regular tough 'un he was. He said grog ought to be strong enough to keep a man afloat from one side of the English Channel to the other. If a man fell into the sea with weak grog inside him, he said, he'd sink like a stone."

"With grog like that inside us, Schweik, we'll have a first-rate Mass," remarked the chaplain. "I think I ought to say a few parting words first, though. A military Mass is no joke. It's not like Mass in the detention barracks or preaching to that scurvy crowd of scalawags. Oh, no, you've got to have all your wits about you. We've got a field altar. It's a folding contraption that'll fit into your pocket. Do you know where I used to keep that folding altar? In the sofa that we sold."

"Whew, that's awkward and no mistake, sir," said Schweik. "Of course, I know that secondhand furniture dealer, but the day before yesterday I met his wife. He's in prison on account of a wardrobe that was stolen and now our sofa's in the hands of a teacher at Vrsovice. That field altar's going to be a nuisance. The best thing we can do is to drink up the grog and go to look for it, because, as far as I can see, we can't have Mass without an altar."

"The field altar's really the only thing that's missing," said the chaplain dismally. "Everything's ready in the exercise ground. The carpenters have knocked up a platform. We'll get the monstrance on loan from Brevnov. I ought to have a chalice of my own, but where the deuce . . ."

He lapsed into thought. "Supposing I've lost it. Well, we could get the challenge cup from Lieutenant Wittinger of the 75th Regiment. He won it a long time ago in a running competition as a representative of the Favorite Sports Club. He used to be a good runner. He did the twenty-five miles cross-country marathon from Vienna to Mödling in one hour forty-eight minutes. He's always bragging about it to us. I settled that with him yesterday. I'm a silly chump to put everything off till the last moment. Why didn't I look into that sofa? Oh, what a fathead I am!"

Under the influence of the grog, prepared according to the recipe of the sailor, that "regular tough 'un," he began to call himself names bluntly, and he uttered the most diverse dicta to indicate where he really ought to be.

"Well, we'd better go and have a look for that field altar," suggested Schweik. "It's broad daylight. I must just get my uniform and drink another glass of grog."

At last they went. The wife of the secondhand furniture dealer, who was half asleep, gave them the address of the teacher at Vrsovice, the new owner of the sofa. The chaplain became extremely affable. He pinched the lady's cheek and chucked her under the chin.

They made their way to Vrsovice on foot, as the chaplain announced that he needed a walk in the fresh air to distract his mind. When they reached the abode of the teacher, a pious old person, an unpleasant surprise was awaiting them. On discovering the field altar in the sofa, the old fellow had jumped to the conclusion that this must be some divine dispensation and he had presented it to the local church for the sacristy there, stipulating that on the other side of the folding altar they should put the following inscription:

PRESENTED FOR THE PRAISE AND HONOR OF GOD
BY MR. KOLARIK, TEACHER
IN THE YEAR OF OUR LORD 1914.

He showed much embarrassment, because when they arrived he was in his underclothes. From their conversation with him it was plain that he regarded the discovery as a miracle and a divine portent. He said that when he bought the sofa, there was a voice within him saying, "Look inside the flap of that sofa"; and he had, he said, also dreamed about an angel who had ordered him in so many words, "Open the flap of the sofa." He had done so.

And when he saw the miniature folding altar in three sections, with a recess for the tabernacle, he had knelt in front of the sofa and had continued long in fervid prayer, praising God. He had, he continued, looked upon this as a sign from heaven, showing him that he was to use his find to decorate the church at Vrsovice.

"That's no use to us," said the chaplain. "Here was a thing that didn't belong to you, and you ought to have handed it over to the police and not to some confounded sacristy."

"This here miracle," added Schweik, "may lead to a fine old mess. You bought a sofa and not an altar, which is government property. This sign from God may turn out to be an expensive business for you. You oughtn't to have taken any notice of the angels. I heard of a man who dug up a chalice in a field, and this chalice had been stolen from a church and buried till the trouble had blown over. Well, he thought it was a sign from God, and instead of melting it down, he went to the parson with this chalice and said he wanted to present it to the church. The parson thought it was his conscience moving him and he sent for the mayor, the mayor put the police on the job, and the upshot was that this chap, who was as innocent as a babe unborn, got shoved into quod for robbing a church, because he would keep on talking about a miracle. He tried to defend himself and started pitching some yarn about an angel, and the Virgin Mary was mixed up in it, too. So he got ten years. The best thing you can do is to come with us to the local parson and get him to give us back that government property. A field altar isn't a stray cat or a stocking that you can give away to anyone you please."

The old gentleman trembled from head to foot, and he began to dress himself, his teeth chattering the while.

"I assure you," he said, "I had not the slightest bad or wrong intention or purpose. I assumed that as the result of what I deemed a divine dispensation it would be vouchsafed me to further the adornment of our humble church."

"Yes, at the government's expense. That's all very fine," said Schweik with relentless severity. "That sort of divine dispensation be blowed. There was a fellow I knew who once had the same idea about a divine inspiration when his hand managed to grab hold of a noose with somebody else's cow attached to it."

The poor old fellow was quite bewildered by these remarks and made no further attempts to defend himself. His sole concern now was to get dressed as quickly as possible and to settle the whole business.

The local parson was still asleep, and being awakened by

128

the noise, he began to use strong language, as in his drowsiness he thought he had to go and administer the last rites to someone.

"I've had enough of this extreme unction business," he muttered, dressing with repugnance. "Some of these people take it into their heads to die when a man's sound asleep. And then he has to haggle with 'em about the fee."

So they met in the passage—one, the representative of the Lord among the Catholic civilians of Vrsovice and the other, the representative of God upon earth, attached to the military organization.

On the whole, however, it was a dispute between a civilian and a military man.

While the parson maintained that the altar did not belong to the sofa, the chaplain declared that, if such were the case, still less could it be transferred from the sofa to the sacristy of a church which was attended solely by civilians. Schweik supplied an accompaniment in the form of remarks, saying, for example, that it was an easy job to furnish a humble church at the expense of the army funds. He uttered the word "humble" in quotation marks.

Finally they adjourned to the sacristy and the parson handed over the altar in return for the following acknowledgment:

Received, a field altar which by chance got into the church at Vrsovice.

(signed) OTTO KATZ, *Army Chaplain.*

The field altar, the cause of all the fuss, had been manufactured by a Jewish firm, Messrs. Moritz Mahler of Vienna, which turned out all kinds of accessories for Holy Mass and religious appliances, such as rosaries and images of saints. The altar consisted of three parts, liberally provided with sham gilding, like the glory of the Holy Church as a whole. It was not possible without a good deal of imagination to discover what the pictures painted on these three parts actually represented. There was only one figure which stood out prominently. It consisted of a naked man with a halo and a body turning green. On either side of him were two winged creatures, intended to represent angels. They looked like legendary monsters, a cross between a wildcat with wings and the apocalyptic beast.

129

Opposite this group was an effigy depicting the Holy Trinity. On the whole, the painter had let the dove off lightly. He had drawn a bird which might have been a dove or might equally well have been a female Wyandotte. God the Father, on the other hand, looked like a bandit from the Wild West, as seen in a thrilling crook film. The Son, to counterbalance this, was a jolly young man with a well-developed corporation, draped in something which resembled bathing drawers. Altogether, he produced the impression of being a devotee of sport. In his hand was a cross, which he held with as much elegance as if it had been a tennis racket.

Seen from afar, however, all these details were merged together and had the appearance of a train entering a railway station. What the third image represented was beyond all conjecture. Beneath it was the inscription *"Heilige Maria, Mutter Gottes, erbarme dich unser."* [1]

Schweik deposited the field altar safely in the cab and then joined the cabman on the box, while the chaplain made himself comfortable inside the cab with his feet on the Holy Trinity.

Schweik chatted with the cabman about the war.

The cabman was a rebel. He made various remarks about the Austrian victory, such as, "They gave you a hot time in Serbia," and the like.

When they reached the octroi, the official inquired what they were carrying. Schweik replied, "The Holy Trinity and the Virgin Mary with an army chaplain."

Meanwhile, on the exercise ground the drafts were waiting impatiently. And they waited for a long time. For Schweik and the chaplain first had to fetch the challenge cup from Lieutenant Wittinger and then they went to the monastery at Brevnov for the monstrance, the pyx, and other accessories of the Mass, including the bottle of consecrated wine. That only shows you that it is not at all easy to celebrate Mass.

"We're sort of getting this job done by fits and starts, like," said Schweik to the cabman.

He was right. For when they reached the exercise ground and were alongside the platform with the wooden framework at the side and a table on which the field altar was to be placed, it turned out that the chaplain had forgotten about the ministrant. This duty had hitherto been performed by an

[1] "Holy Mary, Mother of God, have pity upon us."

infantryman who had managed to get himself transferred to the signal service and had gone to the front.

"Never mind, sir," said Schweik. "That's a job that I can manage, too."

"Do you know how to do it?"

"I've never done it before," replied Schweik, "but there's no harm in trying. There's a war on, and people are doing things they never dreamed about before. All that silly stuff about *et cum spiritu tuo* after your *Dominus vobiscum*—I'll see to that, all right. And afterward it's a pretty soft job to walk around you, like a cat on hot bricks. And then to wash your hands and pour out the wine from the goblets. . . ."

"All right," said the chaplain, "but don't pour out any water for me. I think I'd better put some wine into the second goblet this very minute. Anyhow, I'll tell you all the time whether you've got to step to the right or the left. If I whistle very softly, once, that means to the right; twice, to the left. And you needn't worry much about the missal, either. But the whole thing's no end of a lark. You don't feel nervous, do you?"

"I'm not scared of anything, sir. I could do this ministrant job on my head, as you might say."

The chaplain was right when he said that it was "no end of a lark."

The whole matter passed off without the least hitch.

The chaplain's speech was very concise.

"Soldiers! We have met here in order that, before proceeding to the field of battle, you may turn your hearts toward God, that He may give us victory and keep us safe and sound. I am not going to detain you for long, and I wish you all the best."

"Stand at ease!" shouted the old colonel on the left flank.

A field Mass is called thus because it is amenable to the same laws as military tactics in the field. During the long maneuvers of the armies in the Thirty Years' War field Masses were apt to be extremely lengthy.

As the result of modern tactics, when the movements of armies are rapid and smart, field Masses also have to be rapid and smart.

This particular one lasted exactly ten minutes and those who were close to the center of operations wondered very much why the chaplain whistled while he was officiating.

Schweik showed a smart mastery of the signals. He walked to the right-hand side of the altar, the next moment he was on the left, and all he kept saying was, *"Et cum spiritu tuo."*

It looked like a Red Indian war dance around a sacrificial stone. But it produced a satisfactory effect by relieving the boredom of the dusty, dismal exercise ground with its avenues of plum trees at the back, and the latrines, the odor of which replaced the mystical perfume of incense in Gothic churches.

They all enjoyed themselves immensely.

The officers standing around the colonel were telling each other stories, and this was as it should be. Here and there among the rank and file could be heard the words, "Give us a puff."

And blue clouds of tobacco smoke arose like the smoke of a burnt offering from the assembled companies. All the N.C.O.'s started smoking when they saw that the colonel himself had lit up.

At last came the order, "Let us pray." There was a whirl of dust and a gray rectangle of uniforms bowed the knee before Lieutenant Wittinger's challenge cup, which he won as a representative of the Favorite Sports Club in the Vienna-Mödling cross-country marathon.

The cup was filled to the brim and the general opinion with regard to the result of the chaplain's manipulations was summed up in the remark which passed along the ranks: "He's swigged the lot."

This performance was repeated. Then once more, "Let us pray," whereupon the band trotted out. "Lord preserve us," they formed fours and were marched off.

"Collect all the doings," said the chaplain to Schweik, pointing to the field altar, "so as we can take 'em back to their proper place."

So back they went with their cabman, and honestly restored everything except the bottle of sacramental wine.

And when they were back home again, after having told the unfortunate cabman to apply to the military command about his fare for the long drive, Schweik said to the chaplain, "Beg to report, sir, but must the ministrant be of the same denomination as the one who's doing the communion service with him?"

"Certainly," replied the chaplain, "or else the Mass wouldn't be valid."

"Well, then, there's been a big mistake, sir," announced Schweik. "I'm of no denomination. It's just my luck."

The chaplain looked at Schweik, was silent for a while, and then he patted him on the shoulder and said, "You can drink up what's left of the sacramental wine in the bottle, and imagine you've joined the Church again."

12.

Religious Debate

IT USED to happen that for days at a time Schweik saw nothing of the custodian of warriors' souls. The chaplain divided his time between his duties and his frolics, and on the very rare occasions when he came home, he was bedraggled and unwashed, like a tomcat meowing on his trips across the house tops.

When he did get back, if he was capable of speech, he would talk to Schweik before dropping off to sleep, his favorite topics being high aims, enthusiasm, the pleasures of the mind. Sometimes he tried to recite poetry and to quote passages from Heine.

Schweik cooperated with the chaplain in one more field Mass, this time for the Engineers. By mistake another chaplain, a former catechist and an extremely pious man, had been invited to attend. He eyed his colleague with amazement when the latter offered him a gulp of cognac from the field flask, which Schweik always took with him to religious functions of this kind.

"It's a good brand," said Otto Katz. "Have a drink and then go home. I'll see to this business myself, because I need a breath of fresh air. I've got a bit of a headache today."

The pious chaplain departed, shaking his head dubiously, and Katz, as usual, fulfilled his task with consummate skill.

This time it was a mixture of wine and soda water which was transformed into the blood of the Lord, and the sermon was longer, every third word being "and so forth" or "assuredly."

"Today, soldiers, you are going to the front, and so forth. Now you are turning your thoughts to God and so forth, assuredly. You do not know what will befall you, and so forth and assuredly."

And from the altar "and so forth" and "assuredly" continued to be heard in tones of thunder, alternating with God and all the saints.

In his excitement and the verve of his oratory, the chaplain referred to Prince Eugene of Savoy as a saint who would protect them when they were building bridges across rivers.

Nevertheless, the field Mass concluded without any untoward incident. It was agreeable and entertaining. The Engineers enjoyed themselves very much.

On the way back an attempt was made to stop them from taking the folding altar with them into a tram car.

"I'll give you a wallop over the head with this holy contraption," remarked Schweik to the conductor.

When at last they reached home, they discovered that somewhere on their way they had lost the tabernacle.

"That doesn't matter," said Schweik. "The Early Christians polished off their Mass without a tabernacle. If we was to advertise our loss, the honest person who found it would expect us to stump up. If it was money we'd lost, I don't suppose there'd be any honest person to find it, though there are people like that still knocking about. In the regiment I used to be in there was a soldier, a damn fool like that, who found six hundred crowns in the street one day, and the newspapers called him an honest fellow, which properly blackened his character. Everybody kept out of his way and his girl gave him the chuck. When he went home on leave, his pals kicked him out of the bar parlor where they were having a jollification. He began to look very seedy, and in the end he threw himself under a railway train. Then there was a tailor down our street, and one day he found a gold ring. He was warned not to take it to the police, but he didn't take any notice. At the police station they were very nice to him, and said that somebody had already reported the loss of a gold ring with a brilliant, but when they had a look at the stone, they said, 'Why, my good fellow, that's glass; that's not a brilliant. How much did you get for the brilliant? We've met honest fellows like you before.' Afterward it turned out that there was another man who'd lost a gold ring with a sham brilliant, a family heirloom, but the tailor spent three days in quod for getting excited and abusing the police. He got a reward of ten per cent, according to the regulations, and that came to one crown twenty hellers, because the sham jewelry was only worth twelve crowns, and he chucked this reward into some chap's face and this chap had him up for slander and the tailor had to pay an extra fine of ten crowns.

"It strikes me that nobody's going to bring back our tabernacle, even though it's got the regimental badge on the back of it, because nobody wants to be mixed up with military doings. They'd rather throw it into the river, so as not to have any bother."

In the evening they had a visitor. This was the pious army chaplain who also wished to officiate at the Mass for the pioneer detachment the next morning. Once he had been a catechist. He had a slight limp, the result of an encounter with the father of a pupil whose ears he had boxed for evincing doubts about the Holy Trinity. Now he had come to lead his colleague onto the right path and to take him seriously to task.

He began the proceedings by the remark, "I'm surprised you have no crucifix hanging here. Where do you pray from your breviary? Why, not the single image of a saint adorns the walls of your room. What's that you've got above the bed?"

Katz smiled.

"That's Susanna in the Bath, and the naked female underneath is an old friend of mine. On the right is a bit of Japanese art representing a geisha in bed with an old samurai. An uncommon little thing, isn't it? My breviary's in the kitchen. Schweik, bring it here and open it at page three."

136

Schweik departed, and from the kitchen could be heard the popping of a cork, three times in succession.

The pious chaplain was aghast when three bottles made their appearance on the table.

"That's light sacramental wine, my dear fellow," said Katz. "First-rate quality. The flavor is something like Moselle."

"I have no intention of drinking," announced the pious chaplain obdurately. "I have come to take you seriously to task."

"You'll find that a dry job, my dear fellow," said Katz. "Have a drink and I'll listen. I'm a very tolerant person and quite capable of seeing the other man's point of view."

The pious chaplain took a sip and his eyes started out of his head.

"A deuced good drop of wine, eh, my dear fellow?" said Katz.

The pious chaplain said coldly, "I observe that you are in the habit of using profane language."

"That's just a habit," replied Katz. "Sometimes I actually catch myself being blasphemous. Schweik, fill up his Reverence's glass. I wouldn't mind betting that when you've been in the army as long as I have, you'll do the same. Drink up, my dear fellow."

The former catechist sipped mechanically. It was evident that he wanted to say something but could not. He was collecting his thoughts.

"My dear fellow," continued Katz, "cheer up; don't look so down in the mouth, as if you were going to be hanged in five minutes. Drink up. That's it. Do you feel better now? Tell me, do you hold progressive views about hell? Are you keeping abreast of the spirit of the age? You know the idea. Instead of the usual cauldrons of sulfur for miserable sinners, there are Papin's digesters and high-tension boilers, the sinners are fried in margarine, the spits are driven by electricity, steam rollers squash the sinners flat for millions of years at a time, the gnashing of teeth effect is produced by dentists with special apparatus, the wailing is reproduced by gramophone, and the records are sent up to paradise to amuse the righteous. In paradise there are appliances for spraying eau de Cologne and the philharmonic orchestra plays Brahms for such a length of time that you'd rather be in hell or purgatory. Drink up, my dear fellow. Schweik, give him some cognac. He doesn't seem to be well."

When the pious chaplain had recovered himself somewhat, he whispered, "Religion is a matter for solemn deliberation. If a man does not believe in the Holy Trinity—"

"Schweik," said Katz, interrupting him, "give his Reverence another glass of cognac to bring him around."

The pious chaplain saw spots before his eyes and he restored himself with another glass of cognac, which went to his head. Blinking his eyes, he asked Katz, "Don't you believe in the Immaculate Conception of the Virgin Mary? Don't you even believe in God? And if you don't believe, why are you an army chaplain?"

"My dear fellow," replied Katz, slapping him familiarly on the back, "the government has decided that soldiers need God's blessing before proceeding to die in battle, and as an army chaplain's job is a decently paid occupation which doesn't involve overwork, I find it a jolly sight better than running about on parade grounds or going to maneuvers. I used to get orders from my superiors, but now I do what I like. I represent someone who doesn't exist and I'm a little tin god all on my own. If I don't choose to forgive a man his sins, why, I just don't, even if he begs me on his bended knees. I'm bound to say that there's precious few of 'em who'd go to those lengths."

"I'm fond of God," announced the pious chaplain, beginning to hiccough. "I'm very fond of Him. Give me a little wine.

"I respect God," he then continued. "I respect and esteem Him highly. There's nobody I respect as much as Him."

He brought his fist down on the table and made the bottles rattle.

"God," he said, "is a sublime, a superterrestrial being. He is honorable in all His ways. He is a radiant phenomenon—nobody will ever persuade me of the contrary. I respect St. Joseph, too; in fact, I respect all the saints, except St. Serapion. He's got such an ugly name."

"He ought to apply to have it altered," suggested Schweik.

"I'm fond of St. Ludmilla and St. Bernard," continued the ex-catechist. "He's saved lots of travelers on the St. Gothard. He carries a bottle of cognac around his neck and searches for people who've got lost in the snow."

The entertainment now took a new turn. The pious chaplain began to talk at random.

"I esteem the innocents. Their feast day is on December

138

twenty-eighth. I detest Herod. If a hen sleeps, you can't get newly laid eggs."

He burst out laughing and began to sing, " 'God the holy, God the mighty.' " But he immediately broke off and, turning to Katz, asked him sternly, as he stood up, "You don't believe that we celebrate the ascension of the Virgin Mary on August fifteenth?"

The entertainment was now in full swing. Further bottles made their appearance and from time to time the voice of Katz was heard: "Say you don't believe in God, or I won't fill up your glass any more."

It looked as if the persecution of the Early Christians had been resumed. The ex-catechist was warbling a song about the martyrs in the Roman arena, and then yelled, "I believe in the Lord God, I will not deny Him. Let me have my wine. I can send for some myself."

At last they put him to bed. Before he fell asleep, he raised his right hand, as if he were taking an oath, and declared, "I believe in God the Father, the Son, and the Holy Ghost. Bring me a breviary."

Schweik shoved into his hand some book or other, the result being that the pious chaplain went to sleep with Boccaccio's *Decameron* in his arms.

13.

Schweik Administers Extreme Unction

OTTO KATZ sat meditating upon a circular which he had just brought from the barracks. It was a set of instructions from the War Office:

For the duration of the war the Minister of War cancels the regulations hitherto in force concerning the administration of extreme unction to the troops and issues the following instructions to army chaplains:

1. Extreme unction is abolished at the front.
2. Troops who are seriously ill or wounded are not permitted to proceed to the base for the purpose of extreme unction. Army chaplains are obliged to hand such persons over immediately to the appropriate military authorities for further action.
3. In military hospitals at the base extreme unction can be administered collectively on the basis of an M.O.'s certificate, as long as such extreme unction is not in

the nature of an encumbrance to the military body concerned.

4. In special cases the O.C. military hospitals at the base can allow individuals to receive extreme unction.

5. Army chaplains are obliged, if called upon by the O.C. military hospitals at the base, to administer extreme unction to individuals designated by the commanding officer.

The chaplain then once more read the communication informing him that on the next day he was to proceed to the military hospital in Charles Square for the purpose of administering extreme unction to the seriously wounded.

"Look here, Schweik," shouted the chaplain, "isn't this a dirty trick? As if I was the only army chaplain in the whole of Prague. Why don't they send that pious chap who slept here a few days ago? We've got to go and administer extreme unction, and I've quite forgotten how to do it."

"Then we'll buy a catechism, sir. It's sure to be there," said Schweik. "That's a sort of guide for sky pilots. At the Emaus monastery there used to be a jobbing gardener, and when he wanted to become a lay preacher and they gave him a cowl to save his clothes from getting torn, he had to buy a catechism to learn how to make the sign of the cross, who's the only one to be saved from original sin, what a pure conscience is, and other little trifles like that. Then he went and sold half the cucumbers in the monastery garden without telling them about it, and he left the monastery in disgrace. When I met him, he said, 'I could have sold the cucumbers even if I'd never set eyes on the catechism.' "

When Schweik arrived with the copy of the catechism which he had bought, the chaplain perused it and said, "I say, extreme unction can be administered only by a priest and with oil which has been consecrated by a bishop. So, you see, Schweik, you can't administer extreme unction. Just read the bit to me about how the extreme unction is done."

Schweik read:

"It is administered thus: The priest anoints the sick person on the various organs of his senses, at the same time uttering this prayer: 'By this holy unction and by His goodly mercy may God forgive you for all your transgressions by sight, hearing, smell, taste, speech, and touch.' "

141

"I'd like to know, Schweik," remarked the chaplain, "what transgression can be committed by touch. Can you explain that to me?"

"Lots of things, sir. For instance, you may touch somebody else's pocket. Or, again, at dances—you know the sort of thing I mean."

After further philosophical speculations on this subject, the chaplain said, "Well, anyway, we need oil, consecrated by a bishop. Here's ten crowns. Go and buy a bottle. They don't seem to have any of the stuff in the military stores."

So Schweik set off on his quest for the oil consecrated by a bishop. He called at several grocers' shops but as soon as he said, "I want a bottle of oil consecrated by a bishop," they burst out laughing or else hid themselves in alarm behind the counter. Schweik kept a straight face the whole time. Next he decided to try his luck in the chemists' shops. In the first one they had him put outside by a dispenser. In the second they wanted to telephone for an ambulance. In the third the manager told him that Polák and Co., in Long Street, oil and color merchants, would be sure to have in stock the oil he was after.

And, true enough, Polák and Co., in Long Street, proved to be a smart firm. They never let a customer leave the shop without satisfying his requirements. If anyone wanted copaiba balsam they served him with turpentine, and that did just as well.

When Schweik arrived and asked for ten crowns' worth of oil consecrated by a bishop, the manager said to the assistant, "Give him half a pint of hempseed oil, number three."

And as the assistant was wrapping the bottle up in a piece of paper, he said to Schweik in a strictly mercantile voice, "It's first-rate quality. Should you require any brushes, varnish, or lacquers, let us have your orders. You can rely on being served to your best satisfaction."

Meanwhile the chaplain was recapitulating in the catechism what he had forgotten at the seminary. He took a great fancy to the highly sagacious phrases which made him laugh heartily. Thus: "The term 'extreme unction' is derived from the circumstance that this unction is usually the last or extreme of all unctions which the Church administers to man." Or: "Extreme unction may be received by every Christian Catholic who is seriously ill and has reached years of discretion." Or:

142

"The patient should receive extreme unction, if possible, while he is still in full possession of his senses."

Then an orderly arrived with a packet containing a communication to notify the chaplain that on the next day the administration of extreme unction at the hospital would be attended by the "Society of Genteel Ladies for the Religious Training of Soldiers." This society consisted of hysterical old women and it supplied the soldiers in hospital with images of saints and tales about the Catholic warrior who dies for his emperor. On the cover of the book containing these tales was a colored picture representing a battlefield. Corpses of men and horses, overturned munition wagons, and cannon with the limber in the air were scattered about on all sides. On the horizon a village was burning and shrapnel was bursting, while in the foreground lay a dying soldier with his leg torn off, and above him an angel descended with a wreath bearing this inscription on a piece of ribbon: "This day thou shalt be with Me in paradise." And the dying soldier smiled blissfully, as if they were bringing him ice cream.

When Otto Katz had read the contents of the communication, he spat and muttered to himself, "I'm going to have a hell of a time again tomorrow."

He knew that gang, as he called them, from St. Ignatius' Church, where some years before he had delivered sermons to the troops. At that time he used to take a lot of trouble over his sermons, and the society had a pew behind the colonel. It consisted of two lanky females dressed in black, with a rosary, who had once come up to him after the sermon and had talked for two hours on end about the religious training of soldiers, until it had got on his nerves, and he said to them, "Excuse me, ladies; the colonel's waiting for me to play a rubber of two-handed bridge with him."

"Well, there's the oil," said Schweik solemnly, on his return from Polák and Co. "Hempseed oil, number three, first-class quality. There's enough to anoint a whole blessed battalion. A reliable firm, that. They sell varnish, lacquers, and brushes, too. Now all we want is a bell."

"What's the bell for, Schweik?"

"We've got to keep ringing it on our way to the hospital, so as the people can take off their hats to us, seeing as how we're carrying this hempseed oil number three along with us, sir. That's always done, and plenty of people have been shoved into quod for being disrespectful about it and not taking off their hats. Why, down at Zizkov there was a parson who once gave a blind man a good hiding for not taking off his hat on one of these jobs, and he got shoved into quod on top of that because at the police court it was proved that he was only blind and not deaf or dumb, so that he could hear the bell ringing all right. So, if you don't mind, sir, I'll go and fetch a bell this very minute."

The chaplain agreed, and half an hour later Schweik returned with a bell.

"I got it from the front door of a pub, The Cross Tavern. For about five minutes it was touch and go, and I had to wait a long time first, because people kept passing by."

"I'm just going out for a drink, Schweik. If anyone comes, tell them to wait."

After about an hour a gray-headed elderly man arrived. His bearing was erect and his expression severe. His whole appearance was sheer doggedness and malice. He looked as if he had been sent by fate to destroy our wretched planet and to wipe out every trace of it in the universe.

His speech was uncouth, curt, and churlish.

"Not at home? Gone out for a drink? I've got to wait? All right, I'll wait till tomorrow morning. He can afford drinks, but pay his debts, oh dear no! A fine parson, and no mistake!"

He spat in the kitchen.

"I say, don't spit there!" protested Schweik, gazing with interest at the stranger.

"I'll spit again, I'm dashed if I won't," said the dogged and churlish gentleman, spitting again on the floor. "An army chaplain, too. Disgraceful!"

"If you've been properly brought up," demurred Schweik, "you'd better drop the habit of spitting in other people's houses. Or perhaps you think that because there's a war on, you can do what you like. You've got to behave properly and not like a hooligan. You've got to be polite, you've got to keep a civil tongue in your head and not start any of your bully-ragging tricks here, you blithering idiot. You ought to be in the army."

The severe gentleman rose from his chair, began to shake with excitement, and shouted, "How dare you! Do you mean to say that I'm not a gentleman? What am I, then? Tell me that."

"You're a lousy swine," replied Schweik, looking him full

144

in the face. "You spit on the floor as if you was in a tram or a train or some other public place. I've always wondered why they have notices hanging up everywhere to say that spitting on the floor is prohibited, and now I see that it's for the benefit of chaps like you. I expect you're pretty well known everywhere."

The severe gentleman began to turn red in the face and tried to retaliate with a flood of invective against Schweik and the chaplain.

"Have you quite finished your speechifying?" asked Schweik calmly (when he ended up with, "You're a fine pair of blackguards. Like master, like man"), or would you like to add a few words before I kick you downstairs?"

As the severe gentleman had now so exhausted his powers that no suitable term of abuse occurred to him, he held his peace, and Schweik therefore assumed that it would be useless to wait for any supplementary remarks. Accordingly, he opened the door, placed the severe gentleman in the doorway with his face to the passage, and achieved a goal kick of which the champion player of a champion international football team need not have been ashamed.

And the movement of the severe gentleman downstairs was accompanied by Schweik's voice: "The next time you pay a visit to well-bred people, just see that you behave yourself properly."

The severe gentleman walked up and down outside for a long time, awaiting the return of the chaplain.

Schweik opened the window and watched him.

At last the chaplain arrived, took the visitor into his room, and sat down opposite him.

Schweik silently brought a spittoon in and placed it in front of the visitor.

"What's that you're doing, Schweik?"

"Beg to report, sir, that there's already been a little unpleasantness with this gentleman about spitting on the floor."

"You can go, Schweik. We have some business to attend to."

Schweik saluted. "Beg to report, sir, I'm going."

He went into the kitchen and a very interesting conversation then ensued.

"You've come about that note of hand, I suppose?" the chaplain asked his visitor.

"Yes, and I hope——"

The chaplain sighed. "Man often is reduced to such a plight that the only thing left to him is hope. How lovely is that tiny word 'hope,' one of the three things which uplift man from the chaos of life. Faith, hope, charity."

"I hope, sir, that the money due—"

"Assuredly," the chaplain interrupted him, "and let me repeat once more that the word 'hope' strengthens man in his struggle with life. Nor need you either lose hope. How fine it is to have a definite ideal, to be a pure, innocent creature who lends money on a note of hand and hopes that he will get it back in due course! To hope, unremittingly to hope, that I will pay you twelve hundred crowns, when I have scarcely a hundred in my pocket."

"Then you—" stammered the visitor.

"Yes, then I—" replied the chaplain.

The visitor's face once more assumed a dogged and malicious aspect.

"Sir, this is fraud," he said, rising from the chair.

"Calm yourself, my good sir."

"This is fraud," shouted the visitor stubbornly. "You have misused my confidence."

"Sir," said the chaplain, "a change of air would certainly do you good. It's too stuffy here.

"Schweik," he shouted into the kitchen, "this gentleman would like to go out into the fresh air."

"Beg to report, sir," said the voice from the kitchen, "that I've thrown this gentleman out once already."

"Then do it again!" came the order which was uttered quickly, sharply, and curtly.

"It's a good thing, sir," said Schweik, on his return from the passage, "that we settled up with him before he had a chance of kicking up a row here."

"Yes, Schweik, you see what happens to a man who does not honor a priest," said the chaplain, smiling. "St. Chrysostom said: 'He who honors a priest honors Christ; he who humiliates a priest humiliates Christ the Lord, whose deputy the priest is.' We must get everything ready for tomorrow. Fry some eggs with ham, brew some claret punch, and then we'll devote ourselves to meditation, for, as it says in the evening prayer, 'By God's mercy all snares of the enemy have been turned aside from this dwelling.' "

There are some people who will not take no for an answer.

The man who had twice been ejected from the chaplain's flat was one of them. Just as supper was ready there was a ring at the bell.

Schweik went to the door, came back a moment later, and announced, "He's here again, sir. I've shut him up in the bathroom for the time being, so as we can have our supper in peace."

"That was wrong of you, Schweik," said the chaplain. "A guest's a guest, you know. In ancient times they used to have freaks to amuse them at banquets. Bring him in and let him amuse us."

Schweik came back presently with the pertinacious gentleman, who was staring gloomily in front of him.

"Take a seat," said the chaplain affably. "We're just finishing supper. We've had lobster, salmon, and now we're having a peck at some fried eggs and ham. We can afford to do ourselves well when people lend us money."

"I hope you are not making fun of me," said the gloomy man. "This is the third time today I've been here. I hope that now everything is going to be put right."

"Beg to report, sir," remarked Schweik, "that there's no choking this chap off. He's like a fellow named Bousek from Liben. Eighteen times he got chucked out of Exner's, and every time he went back because he said he'd forgotten his pipe. He crawled back through the window, through the door, out of the kitchen, over the wall into the saloon bar, across the cellar into the taproom, and I expect he'd have got through the chimney if the fireman hadn't cleared him off the roof. A chap who can stick to it like that might have been an M.P. or even a cabinet minister. They did what they could for him."

The persistent man, as if he were taking no notice of Schweik's remarks, repeated obstinately, "I want to have things clear and I must ask you to hear what I have to say."

"Your wish shall be granted," said the chaplain. "Speak your mind, my dear sir. Speak as long as you like, and meanwhile we will continue our feast. I hope that won't prevent you from telling your story. Schweik, serve the next course."

"As you are aware," said the persistent man, "there is a war on. I lent you this money before the war, and if there were no war, I should not insist on payment. But I have had some distressing experiences."

He took a notebook from his pocket and continued: "I've

147

got it all here in black and white. Lieutenant Janata owed me seven hundred crowns, and then went and fell in action on the Drina. Lieutenant Prasek was taken prisoner on the Russian front, and he owes me two thousand crowns. Captain Wichterle, who owed me a similar amount, got killed at Rawa Ruska by his own troops. Lieutenant Machek was taken prisoner in Serbia, and he owes me fifteen hundred crowns. And there are more people like that. One gets killed in the Carpathians without paying me his I.O.U., another gets taken prisoner, another gets drowned in Serbia, another dies in a hospital in Hungary. Now you realize my fears that this war will ruin me unless I put my foot down firmly. You may object that you are in no immediate danger. Just look here."

He thrust his notebook beneath the chaplain's nose: "Here you are: Chaplain Matyás died in the isolation hospital at Brno a week ago. It's enough to drive a man off his head. He owed me eighteen hundred crowns, and then he goes into a cholera ward to administer extreme unction to a man whom I don't know from Adam."

"He was only doing his duty, my dear sir," said the chaplain. "I am going on the same errand tomorrow."

"Into a cholera ward, too," remarked Schweik. "You can come along with us, to see what it means to sacrifice your life."

"Sir," said the persistent man, "you can take my word for it that I'm in a tight corner. Is this war being waged only to dispatch all my creditors into the next world?"

"When you get called up and go to the front," observed Schweik once more, "the chaplain and me'll celebrate a Mass asking the Lord to let the first shell blow you to pieces."

"This is no laughing matter, sir," said the dauntless one to the chaplain. "Kindly ask your servant not to interfere in our business and let us get the matter settled."

"Look here, sir," said Schweik, "just you say the word and I won't interfere in your business. Otherwise I shall go on sticking up for your interests, as it's right and proper for a soldier to do. This gentleman's absolutely right. He wants to get away from here alone. I'm not fond of scenes, either. I'm all for good manners, I am."

"Schweik, I'm beginning to get sick of this," said the chaplain, as if unaware of the visitor's presence. "I thought this fellow was going to amuse us by telling us funny stories, but he wants me to order you not to interfere, although you've twice come into contact with him. On the very evening before an important religious ceremony, when I ought to be directing my whole mind to God, he comes and worries me with some absurd tale about a paltry twelve hundred crowns, prevents me from searching my conscience, turns my thoughts away from God, and wants me to tell him once more that I won't give him anything. I refuse to say another word to him. I don't want this sacred evening to be spoiled. Schweik, tell him yourself: 'The chaplain won't give you a brass farthing.' "

Schweik fulfilled the order, yelling the words into the victim's ear.

The persistent visitor, however, remained seated.

"Schweik," said the chaplain, "ask him how much longer he thinks he's going to dawdle about here?"

"I won't budge an inch until I get my money," declared the dauntless one obdurately.

The chaplain stood up, went to the window, and said, "Then in this case I leave him to you, Schweik. Do with him whatever you think fit."

"Come along, sir," said Schweik, grabbing the visitor by the shoulder. "Three's a lucky number."

And he repeated his previous performance with dispatch and elegance while the chaplain drummed the funeral march on the windowpane.

The evening, which was devoted to meditation, comprised several stages. The chaplain was so devout and fervid in his approach to God that at midnight the sound of song could still be heard from his quarters:

> *"When we were marching away*
> *All the girls wept with dismay."*

And the good soldier Schweik was singing in chorus with him.

There were two persons who were looking forward eagerly to the afternoon's extreme unction ceremony in the military hospital: an old major and a bank manager, a reserve officer. They had both been shot through the stomach in the Carpathians and were now lying side by side. The reserve officer considered it his duty to receive the offices for the dying because his superior officer was anxious to obtain extreme unction. He thought it would be an act of insubordination not to

149

obtain extreme unction also. The devout major was prompted by cunning, as he supposed that a prayer of faith will heal the sick. But in the night before the extreme unction was to be administered, they both died, and when the chaplain arrived with Schweik in the morning, they were lying beneath a shroud, with their faces blackened like all those who die of strangulation.

"We did things in style, too, sir, and now they've spoiled everything," grumbled Schweik, when they were told in the office that the two officers no longer needed any attention.

And they really had done things in style. They had driven in a cab, Schweik had rung the bell, and the chaplain had held a bottle of oil wrapped up in a cloth, with which he had solemnly blessed all the passers-by who had raised their hats.

It is true that there were not many of them, although Schweik had done his best to make a huge din with the bell.

A few urchins ran after the cab, and one of them perched himself on the back of it, whereupon his comrades yelled in chorus, "Whip behind! Whip behind!"

Schweik brandished the bell, the cabman cracked his whip behind, in Vodicková Street a house porter's wife, a member of the Marian congregation, galloped up and overtook the cab, received a blessing while on the run, made the sign of the cross, spat, and returned panting to her former place.

The sound of the bell caused the greatest concern to the cabman's nag, which it evidently reminded of bygone years, because the animal kept looking around and from time to time made efforts to dance on the cobbles.

This is what Schweik was referring to when he said that they had done things in style. The chaplain went into the office to settle the financial side of the extreme unction and supplied the pay-corps sergeant with an account showing that the military exchequer owed him 150 crowns for consecrated oil and traveling expenses.

Then ensued a dispute between the officer in charge of the hospital and the chaplain, in the course of which the chaplain banged his fist on the table several times and remarked, "Don't run away with the idea that extreme unction can be had for nothing. When an officer of the dragoons is detailed for stable duty on a stud farm, he's paid allowances. I'm sorry those two didn't live long enough for extreme unction. It would have meant fifty crowns more."

Schweik meanwhile waited downstairs in the guardroom

with the bottle of holy oil, in which the soldiers evinced a keen interest. One of them expressed the view that this oil would be very good for cleaning rifles and bayonets.

One young soldier from the Moravian highlands, who still believed in the Lord, said that wasn't the way to talk about such things, and sacred mysteries shouldn't be dragged into the discussion. We must, he said, live in hope, like Christians.

An old reservist looked at the raw recruit and retorted, "Damn fine hopes! All you can hope is to have your head blown off by a shell. We've been diddled. One day there was a clerical bloke came here and talked about the peace of God that was spreading over the earth, and how God objects to war but wants everyone to live in peace like brothers. Oh, yes, not half! And the minute the war broke out, they started praying in all the churches for victory. The way they talk, anyone'd think the Lord was a kind of super brass hat who's managing the whole blessed show. I've seen plenty of funerals in this hospital and the arms and legs they've cut off taken away by the cartload."

"And they bury the soldiers naked," said another soldier, "and then another chap puts on the old uniform, and then another, and so it goes on."

"Until we win," observed Schweik.

"You're a fine one to talk about winning," retorted a corporal from a corner. "Your job is to get to the front, into the trenches, and then at 'em for all you're worth, past the barbed wire, the mines, and the machine guns. It's easy to talk when you've got a cushy job at the base."

"I think it's a bit of all right to have a bayonet shoved through you," said Schweik, "and it's not so bad to be shot through the belly. But what's better still is when a shell blows you up and you see how your legs and your guts have got separated from you. And it strikes you as so queer that you die before anyone can explain it to you."

The young recruit sighed from the depths of his heart. He was filled with distress at having got mixed up in a ghasty muddle which meant that he was to be slaughtered like an ox in the shambles. What was it all for?

Another soldier, a schoolmaster in civil life, seemed to have read his thoughts, for he remarked, "There are scientists who say that war is due to sunspots. Whenever a sunspot makes its appearance, some disaster or other is bound to happen. The capture of Carthage—"

"Oh, you shut up and keep all that scientific muck to yourself," interposed the corporal. "The best thing you can do is to sweep the room out. You're on fatigue duty today. We don't care damn-all about sunspots. I wouldn't take a dozen of 'em, not if they was offered to me as a gift."

"These here sunspots are jolly important," intervened Schweik. "Once there was a sunspot and on that very same day I got an awful walloping in a pub down at Nusle. Ever since then, if I have to go anywhere, I always have a look in the papers to see whether another spot's been spotted, so to speak. And if it has, why, I don't go nowhere, no, not me, thanks all the same. When that volcano blew up the whole of the island of Martinique, there was a professor chap wrote in the *Narodni Politika* that he'd been warning readers for quite a long time about a big sunspot. Only the *Narodni Politika* didn't get to the island in time, and so the people on the island got done in."

Meanwhile, upstairs in the office the chaplain had met one of the ladies belonging to the "Society for the Religious Training of Soldiers," a repulsive old harridan, who from early morning used to parade the hospital, distributing images of saints which the sick and wounded soldiers threw into the spittoons. On her rounds she irritated everyone by her nonsensical chatter, the purport of which was that they should repent of their sins and become better men in order to receive eternal salvation after death.

When conversing with the chaplain, she was livid as she told him how the war, instead of making the soldiers nobler, was turning them into brutes. The convalescents downstairs put out their tongues and called her a frump and a canting old geezer.

"Das ist wirklich schrecklich, Herr Feldkurat, das Volk ist verdorben," [1] she said. And she went on to expound her idea of the religious training which soldiers should receive. A soldier could not fight gallantly for his emperor unless he believed in God and was religiously minded. Then he did not fear death because he knew that paradise was in store for him. She continued to drivel in this way and she evidently meant to stick to the chaplain, who, however, took his leave in a most ungallant spirit.

"We're going home, Schweik," he shouted into the guardroom.

[1] "Oh, it's shocking, Chaplain, how depraved they are."

On the homeward journey they didn't do things in style.

"Another time somebody else can go and do their extreme unction for them, and welcome," said the chaplain. "Upon my word, it's a fine thing for a man to have to haggle with them before he can get his money for every blessed soul he wants to save. A pack of damned chartered accountants, that's what they are."

And, noticing that Schweik was carrying the bottle of consecrated oil, he growled, "The best thing you can do with that oil is to clean my boots with it. And your own as well."

"I'll try it on the lock, too," added Schweik. "It creaks something terrible when you come home at night."

And so ended the administration of extreme unction which didn't come off.

14.

Schweik Becomes Batman to Lieutenant Lukash

I.

SCHWEIK'S good fortune did not last long. Unrelenting fate severed the friendly relations between him and the chaplain. While up to this incident, the chaplain had been a likable personality, what he now perpetrated was enough to strip him of all likable quality.

The chaplain sold Schweik to Lieutenant Lukash, or, to put it more accurately, he lost him at cards. Just as they used to dispose of the serfs in Russia. It happened quite unexpectedly. Lieutenant Lukash gave a party and they were playing poker.

The chaplain kept on losing, and at last he said, "How much will you advance me on my batman? He's a champion idiot and a regular card, quite unique in his way. I bet you've never come across a batman like him."

"I'll advance you a hundred crowns," said Lieutenant

Lukash, "and if I don't get them back by the day after tomorrow, you'll let me have this rare specimen. My present batman's an awful fellow. He goes about pulling a long face, he's always writing home, and on top of all that he steals every blessed thing he can lay hands on. I've tried giving him a good hiding, but it isn't the slightest use. I clump his head every time I see him, but he's as bad as ever. I knocked out a few of his front teeth, but there's no curing the fellow."

"Right you are, then," said the chaplain recklessly. "A hundred crowns or Schweik the day after tomorrow."

He lost the hundred crowns and went sadly home. He was quite certain, beyond all manner of doubt, that he would never manage to scrape together the hundred crowns within the specified time, and to all intents and purposes he had basely and despicably sold Schweik.

"I might just as well have said two hundred," he grumbled to himself, but as he changed trams he was overcome by a sentimental feeling of self-reproach.

"It was a rotten thing for me to do," he pondered, as he rang his bell. "For the life of me I don't know how I'm to look him in the face, damn him."

"My dear Schweik," he said when he was indoors, "a very unusual thing happened. I was most infernally unlucky at cards. I blued every cent I had."

There was a short silence, and he continued, "And I wound up by losing you. I got an advance of a hundred crowns with you as security, and if I don't give it back by the day after tomorrow, you won't belong to me but to Lieutenant Lukash. I'm really very sorry about it."

"I've got a hundred crowns left," said Schweik. "I can lend it to you."

"Give it here," said the chaplain, brightening up. "I'll take it to Lukash on the spot. I should really be sorry to part with you."

Lukash was very surprised to see the chaplain again.

"I've come to pay you that debt," said the chaplain, gazing around him triumphantly. "Let's have a flutter."

"Double or quits," declared the chaplain, when his turn came.

And at the second round he once more went the whole hog.

"Twenty wins," announced the holder of the bank.

"My total's nineteen," said the chaplain, very crestfallen, as he put into the bank the last forty crowns left over from the hundred-crown note which Schweik had lent him to redeem himself from fresh serfdom.

On his way home the chaplain came to the conclusion that this settled matters once and for all, that nothing could now save Schweik, that it was predestined for him to become the orderly of Lieutenant Lukash.

And when Schweik let him in, he said to him, "It's all no use, Schweik. Nobody can go against his fate. I've lost you and your hundred crowns as well. I've done everything I could, but fate was too much for me. It's thrown you into the clutches of Lieutenant Lukash, and the time has come for us to part."

"And was there a lot in the bank?" asked Schweik with composure. Whereupon he plunged into a long rigmarole about a tinker named Vejvoda and his gambling misadventure with a chimney sweep, which had led to a raid by the police.

"The bank amounted to millions and millions in I.O.U.'s," said Schweik, "and there was fifteen hundred in ready cash. When the police inspector saw what a lot there was, he didn't half stare. 'Why,' he says, 'I never saw the like of this before. It's worse than Monte Carlo.'"

Schweik then went to brew some grog and the end of it was that the chaplain, when Schweik succeeded, late at night and with some difficulty, in getting him into bed, burst into tears and sobbed, "I have sold you, comrade, shamefully sold you. Overwhelm me with curses, strike me. I will endure it. I throw myself at your mercy. I cannot look you in the face. Maul me, bite me, destroy me. I deserve no better fate. Do you know what I am?"

And the chaplain buried his tear-stained face in the pillow, as in a soft and gentle voice he murmured, "I'm a thorough-paced blackguard," and fell sound asleep.

The next day the chaplain avoided Schweik's glance, went away early, and did not return until nightfall, with a fat infantryman.

"Show him, Schweik," he said, again avoiding Schweik's glance, "where the things are kept, so as he can find his way about, and teach him how to brew grog. Report yourself to Lieutenant Lukash early tomorrow morning."

Schweik and the new man spent a pleasant night together brewing grog. In the morning the fat infantryman was standing on one leg and was mumbling to himself a queer medley of various popular songs. "Oh, there's a tiny stream that flows, my sweetheart serves the crimson beer, O mountain, mountain, thou art lofty. The maidens fared along the highroad. On the White Hill the peasants till."

"There's no need for me to worry about you," said Schweik. "A chap like you is bound to get on with the chaplain like a house afire."

And so it came about that in the morning Lieutenant Lukash beheld for the first time the frank and honest countenance of Schweik, who quoth, "Beg to report, sir, I'm Schweik who the chaplain lost at cards."

II.

Officers' orderlies are of very ancient origin. It would appear that Alexander the Great had his batman. I am surprised that nobody has yet written a history of batmen. It would probably contain an account of how Fernando, Duke of Almavir, during the siege of Toledo, ate his batman without salt. The duke himself has described the episode in his *Memoirs* and he adds that the flesh of his batman was tender, though rather stringy, and the taste of it was something between that of chicken and donkey.

Among the present generation of batmen there are few so self-sacrificing that they would let their masters eat them without salt. And there are cases where officers, engaged in a regular life-and-death struggle with the modern type of orderly, have to use all possible means to maintain their authority. Thus, in 1912, a captain was tried at Graz for kicking his batman to death. He was acquitted, however, because it was only the second time he had done such a thing. On the other hand, a batman sometimes manages to get into an officer's good graces, and then he becomes the terror of the battalion. All the N.C.O.'s try to bribe him. He has the last say about leave, and by putting in a good word for anyone who has been crimed he can get him off. During the war, it was such batmen as these who gained medals for bravery. I knew several in the 91st Regiment. There was one who got the large silver medal because he was an adept at roasting geese which he stole. And his master worded the proposal in support of the decoration as follows:

"He manifested exceptional bravery in the field, showing a complete disregard for his own life and not budging an inch

157

from his officer while under the heavy fire of the advancing enemy."

Today these batman are scattered far and wide throughout our republic, and tell the tale of their heroic exploits. It was they who stormed Sokal, Dubno, Nish, the Piave. All of them are Napoleons: "So I up and tells our colonel as how he ought to telephone to brigade headquarters that it was high time to get a move on."

III.

Lieut. Jindrich Lukash was a typical regular army officer of the ramshackle Austrian monarchy. The cadet school had turned him into a species of amphibious creature. In company he spoke German, he wrote German, but he read Czech books, and when he was giving a course of instruction to a group of volunteer officers, all of them Czechs, he would say to them in a confidential tone, "I'm a Czech just the same as you are. There's no harm in it, but nobody need know about it."

He looked upon the Czech nationality as a sort of secret organization which was best given a wide berth. In other respects he was not a bad fellow. He was not afraid of his superior officers, and at maneuvers he looked after his squad, as was right and proper. He always found comfortable quarters for them in a barn, and although his pay was modest enough he often treated his men to a barrel of beer. He was popular with the rank and file because he was extremely fair to everyone. When in his presence the N.C.O.'s shivered in their shoes and within a month he could turn the most cantankerous sergeant major into a lamb.

Although he could shout if he wanted to, he never bullied. He always was most careful in his choice of words and phrases. "You see," he would say, "I don't like having to punish you, but I can't help myself, because the efficiency of the army depends on discipline. If your uniform isn't just as it should be, if the buttons are not properly sewn on or are missing, that shows you are forgetting the duty you owe to the army. It may be that you cannot understand why you should get c.b. because a button was missing from your tunic on parade yesterday. You may think it's a trifling little detail which in civil life you'd never worry about. Yet you see, in the army, neglect of your appearance brings punishment in its train. And why? The point is not that you have a button missing but that you must accustom yourself to discipline. Today you omit to sew on a button and you begin to get slack. Tomorrow you'll decide that you can't be bothered to take your rifle to pieces and clean it, the day after that you'll leave your bayonet in a pub or even go to sleep while on sentry-go, simply because you began to get slack over this wretched button. That's how it is, and that's why I'm punishing you, so as to save you from a worse punishment for some breach of discipline you might commit through slowly but surely forgetting your duties. So I'm going to give you five days' c.b. and I should like you, over your bread and water, to reflect that punishment is not revenge, but a means of training, the purpose of which is to correct and improve the soldier who is thus punished."

He ought to have been a captain long ago, but his cautious attitude toward racial matters was of no advantage to him, because he was very outspoken toward his superior officers. In regimental affairs he never toadied. This was his heritage from the peasant stock in southern Bohemia, where his birthplace was—a village among the dark forests and the fishponds.

While he acted fairly toward the rank and file, he detested his orderlies, because it had always been his luck to get hold of the most objectionable batmen. And he refused to regard them as soldiers. He used to smack their faces or cuff their heads, and altogether tried, by word and deed, to make them mend their ways. He had pursued this plan unsuccessfully for several years. They came and went continuously and at last he used to sigh to himself when a new one arrived, "Here's another low brute been palmed off on me."

He was remarkably fond of animals. He had a Harz canary, an Angora cat, and a stable dog. All his previous orderlies had treated these pets about as badly as Lieutenant Lukash treated the orderlies when they had done something sneakish.

When Schweik came to report himself to Lieutenant Lukash, the latter took him into his room and said, "Mr. Katz recommended me to you, and I want you to live up to his recommendation. I've had a dozen or more orderlies, and there wasn't one of them settled down properly with me. I give you fair warning that I'm strict and I drop very sharply on all meanness and lying. I want you always to speak the truth and to carry out all my orders without any back answers. If I say, 'Jump into the fire,' why, into the fire you've got to jump, even if you don't want to. What are you looking at?"

Schweik was gazing with interest at that side of the wall where the cage with the canary was hanging, and now, fixing his good-humored eyes on the lieutenant, he said in that kindly voice of his, "Beg to report, sir, that's a Harz canary."

And having thus interrupted the lieutenant's oration, Schweik looked him straight in the face without moving an eyelid and standing stiffly at attention.

The lieutenant was about to make some scathing remark, but perceiving the guileless expression on Schweik's countenance, he merely said, "The chaplain recommended you as a champion idiot, and I'm inclined to think he wasn't far wrong."

"Beg to report, sir, the chaplain as a matter of fact wasn't far wrong. When I was doing my regular service, I was discharged as feeble-minded, a chronic case, too. There were two of us discharged from the regiment for the same reason— me and a Captain von Kaunitz. He was a rum old buffer, he was, sir, if you'll pardon me saying so. When he came with us on the parade ground, he always drew us up as if there was going to be a march-past and then he'd say, 'Now then, er, remember, er, that today's, er, Wednesday, because, er, to-morrow'll be Thursday, er.' "

Lieutenant Lukash shrugged his shoulders like a man who is at a loss to find words to express his thoughts adequately. He paced the room from the door to the window, walking right around Schweik and back again, during which process Schweik, according to where the lieutenant happened to be, faced eyes right or eyes left with such an emphatic expression of innocence on his face that Lieutenant Lukash looked at the carpet as he remarked, "Yes, I must have everything clean and tidy. And I can't stand lies. Honesty's the thing for me. I hate a lie and I punish it without mercy. Is that clear?"

"Beg to report, sir, it's quite clear. The worst thing a man can do is to tell lies. As soon as he begins to get in a muddle and contradict himself, he's done for. I think it's always best to be straightforward and own up, and if I've done anything wrong, I just come and say, 'Beg to report, sir, I've done so-and-so.' Oh yes, honesty's a very fine thing, because it pays in the long run. An honest man's respected everywhere; he's satisfied with himself, and he feels like a newborn babe when he goes to bed and can say, 'Well, I've been honest again today.'"

During this speech Lieutenant Lukash sat on a chair, looking at Schweik's boots and thinking to himself, "Ye gods, I suppose I often talk twaddle like that, only perhaps I put it a bit differently."

However, not wishing to impair his authority, he said, when Schweik had concluded, "Now that you're with me, you've got to keep your boots clean, your uniform spick-and-span, with all the buttons properly sewn on, and, in fact, your get-up must be smart and soldierly. I don't want you to look like a civilian clodhopper. It's a funny thing, but there's none of you can carry himself like a soldier. Of all the orderlies I ever had there was only one who had a soldierly bearing, and he stole my dress uniform and sold it to an old-clothes dealer."

He paused for a while, and then continued, explaining to Schweik all his duties and laying special stress on how essential it was for him to be trustworthy and never to gossip about what went on in the lieutenant's quarters.

"There are ladies who come to see me," he added, "and sometimes one or the other of them stays all night, when I'm not on duty in the morning. In a case like that, you'll bring coffee for two into the bedroom, when I ring. Do you follow me?"

"Beg to report, sir, I follow you. If I came into the bedroom unexpected-like, it might be awkward for the lady. I remember once I took a young woman home with me, and just as we were getting on fine together, my charwoman brought in the coffee. She didn't half have a fright and poured all the coffee down my back. Oh, I know what's what when a lady's in bed."

"That's right, Schweik. We must always be extremely tactful where ladies are concerned," said the lieutenant, who was now getting more cheerful because the subject was one which occupied all his leisure between barracks, parade ground, and gambling.

His quarters revealed marked feminine influence. Numerous ladies had left knickknacks and other adornments as mementos of their visits. One lady had embroidered a charming antimacassar for him, besides stitching monograms on all his underwear. She would probably have completed a set of wall decorations if her husband had not put a stop to the proceedings. Another had littered his bedroom with all sorts

161

of bric-a-brac and had hung a picture of a guardian angel over his bed. A third had left her traces in the kitchen in the form of various utensils which, together with her passionate attachment, she had brought with her. There were an appliance for chopping vegetables, an apparatus for slicing bread, a mincemeat machine, casseroles, baking pans, tureens, ladles, and heaven knows what else.

Lieutenant Lukash also carried on an extensive correspondence. He had an album containing photographs of his lady friends, together with a collection of keepsakes, such as numerous garters, four pairs of embroidered knickers, three camisoles of very delicate material, a number of cambric handkerchiefs, one corset, and several stockings.

"I'm on duty today," he said. "I shan't be home till late. Tidy up the place and see that everything's put straight. The last orderly was no good at all, and he's leaving today with a draft for the front."

When Lieutenant Lukash had gone, Schweik put everything straight, so that when he returned at night, Schweik was able to announce, "Beg to report, sir, everything's been put straight, except for one little hitch. The cat got into mischief and gobbled up your canary."

"How did that happen?" bellowed the lieutenant.

"Beg to report, sir, it was like this. I knew that cats don't like canaries and do them harm if they get half a chance. So I thought I'd make them better acquainted and if the creature showed signs of getting up to any tricks, I'd give her a walloping that'd make her remember to her dying day how to behave when canaries are about, because I'm as fond of dumb animals as can be. Where I live there's a hatter who's trained a cat so well that whereas she used to gobble up three canaries without turning a hair, she won't touch 'em now, and even lets 'em sit on her tail. Well, I wanted to try my hand at that, so I took the canary out of the cage and let the cat sniff at it. But before I knew what was happening, the damned brute had bitten off the canary's head. Really, I never thought she'd be as low-down as that. Now if it'd been a sparrow, sir, I wouldn't have said it, but such a nice Harz canary. And you'd never believe how greedy she was, too. Gobbled it up, feathers and all, and purred away the whole time, as jolly as could be. I've heard that cats haven't got a musical ear and they can't stand a canary singing, because the brutes can't appreciate it. I gave that cat a bit of my mind, that I did, but as God's my witness, I never laid a finger on her. I thought I'd better wait till you decided what's to be done to the mangy brute."

While narrating this, Schweik looked the lieutenant in the face so frankly that the latter, who at first had approached him with intent to do him grievous bodily harm, moved away again, sat on a chair and asked, "Look here, Schweik, are you really such a prize lunatic?"

"Beg to report, sir," replied Schweik solemnly, "I am. I've always been unlucky ever since I was a little kid. Whenever I wanted to do something properly and make a good job of it, it always turned out wrong and got me in a mess. I really did want those two animals to get better acquainted and understand each other, and it's not my fault if the cat gobbled up the canary and spoiled everything. I know a house where some years ago a cat actually gobbled up a parrot, because it laughed at her and mimicked the way she meowed. But cats are tough brutes, and no mistake. If you want me to do that cat in, sir, I'd have to squash her in the door. That's the only thing that'd do the trick."

And Schweik, with the most innocent face and the kindliest of smiles, explained to the lieutenant how cats can be done in. If the Society for the Prevention of Cruelty to Animals had heard him, it would assuredly have foamed at the mouth.

He revealed such expert knowledge that Lieutenant Lukash, forgetting his anger, asked, "Do you know how to treat animals? Are you really fond of them?"

"Well, sir," said Schweik, "I like dogs best, because it's a paying game if you know how to sell them. It's not in my line, because I'm too honest, but people used to come bothering me all the same, because they said I sold them a pup, as you might say, sir, instead of a sound, thoroughbred dog. As if all dogs can be sound and thoroughbred. And then they always wanted a pedigree, so I had to have pedigrees printed and turn a mongrel that was born in a brickworks into a purebred pedigree dog. Oh, you'd be surprised, sir, at the way all the big dog fanciers swindle their customers over pedigrees. Of course, there ain't many dogs that could truthfully call themselves out-and-out thoroughbreds. Sometimes the mother or the grandmother got mixed up with some mongrel or other, or maybe several, and then the animal takes after each of them. Ears from one, tail from another, whiskers from another, jowls from a fourth, bandy legs from a fifth, size from a sixth; and if a dog had a dozen connections of that sort, you can just about imagine, sir, what he looks like. I once bought a dog like that, Balaban his name was, and he had so many parents he was that ugly that all the other dogs kept out of his way and I only bought him because I was sorry for the animal being deserted, like. And he used to squat at home all day long in a corner, and he was always so down in the mouth that I had to sell him as a fox terrier. What gave me the most trouble was dyeing him to make him piebald. The man who bought him took him away to Moravia, and I haven't laid eyes on him since."

The lieutenant began to take a great interest in this doggy lore, and so Schweik was able to continue without hindrance. "Dogs can't dye their own hair, like ladies do, so that's always a job for the one who wants to sell him. When a dog's so old that he's all gray, and you want to sell him as a one-year pup, you buy some silver nitrate, pound it up, and then paint the dog black so that he looks like new. And to give him more strength you feed him with arsenic like they do horses, and you clean his teeth with emery paper like they use to clean rusty knives with. And before you show him to a customer, you make him swallow brandy, so that he gets a bit tipsy and then he's merry and bright and barks as jolly as can be, and chums up with everyone, like people do when they're boozed. But this is the most important part of the business, sir. You must talk to the customers, keep on talking to 'em, till they're sort of flabbergasted. If a man wants to buy a house dog and all you've got is a greyhound, you've got to have the gift of the gab, as they say, to talk the man over, so that he takes the greyhound instead of a house dog. Or supposing someone wants a savage bulldog to keep burglars away, you've got to bamboozle him so that instead of a bulldog he takes one of these here midget lap dogs away in his pocket. When I used to deal in animals, there was a lady came one day and said that her parrot had flown away into the front garden and that some boys who were playing at Indians in front of her house had caught this parrot and torn all the feathers out of its tail and decorated themselves with them like policemen. Well, this parrot felt so ashamed at losing his tail that he fell ill and a vet had finished him off with some powders. So she wanted to buy a new parrot, a well-behaved one, not one of those vulgar birds that can do nothing but swear. Well, what was I to do, not having any parrot and not knowing where to lay hands on one? But I had a bad-tempered bulldog, quite blind he was, too. And I give you my word, sir, I had to talk to that lady from four in the afternoon till seven in the evening, before she bought the blind bulldog instead of the parrot. That was a more ticklish job than any of their diplomatic stuff, and when she was going away, I said to her, 'Those little boys had better not try to pull *his* tail off.' And that's the last words I spoke to that lady, because she had to move away from Prague on account of that bulldog, because he bit everyone in the house. You wouldn't believe, sir, how hard it is to get hold of a really first-rate animal."

"I'm very fond of dogs," said the lieutenant. "Some of my pals who're at the front have got dogs with them, and they write and tell me that the company of a faithful and devoted animal makes life in the trenches quite pleasant. Well, you seem to have a thorough knowledge of dogs, and I hope that if I have one you'll look after him properly. What breed do you consider the best? I mean, for a dog as a companion. I once had a fox terrier, but I don't know—"

"Oh, I think a fox terrier is a very nice dog, sir. Of course, it's not everyone who takes to them, because they've got bristles and tough whiskers that make them look like discharged convicts. They're so ugly that it makes them look quite handsome, and they're clever animals, too. St. Bernards ain't in it with them. Oh, yes, they're clever and no mistake. I once knew one—"

Lieutenant Lukash looked at his watch and interrupted Schweik's flow of talk. "Well, it's getting late and I must be off to bed. Tomorrow I'm on duty again, so you've got the whole day to find your fox terrier."

He went off to bed, and Schweik lay down on the sofa in the kitchen, where he read the newspapers which the lieutenant had brought with him from the barracks.

"Just fancy," said Schweik to himself, scanning with interest the summary of the day's news, "the Sultan's awarded a war medal to the Kaiser, and I haven't even got the M.M. yet."

Suddenly he thought of something, and rushed into the lieutenant's bedroom. Lieutenant Lukash was now fast asleep, but Schweik woke him up.

"Beg to report, sir, you didn't give me any instructions about the cat."

And the lieutenant, half-asleep and half-awake, turned over on the other side and mumbled drowsily, "Three days' c.b."

Then he fell asleep again.

Schweik tiptoed out of the room, dragged the unfortunate cat from under the sofa and said to her, "You've got three days' c.b. *Abtreten.*"

And the Angora cat crawled back under the sofa.

IV.

Schweik was just getting ready to go and look for the fox terrier when a young lady rang the bell and said she wanted to speak to Lieutenant Lukash. Beside her lay two heavy trunks, and Schweik just caught sight of a cap belonging to a porter who was going downstairs.

"He's not at home," said Schweik stolidly, but the young lady was already in the passage and said to Schweik in a peremptory tone:

"Take these trunks into the bedroom."

"It can't be done without the lieutenant's permission," said Schweik. "The lieutenant said I was never to do anything without it."

"Why, you must be mad," exclaimed the young lady. "I've come to pay the lieutenant a visit."

"I don't know nothing about that," replied Schweik. "The lieutenant's on duty, he won't be home till tonight, and my orders are to find him a fox terrier. I don't know nothing about any trunks or any lady. Now I'm going to lock up the place, so perhaps you wouldn't mind getting outside. I ain't had any instructions and I can't leave any stranger here whom I don't know anything about. Down our street there was a confectioner who once let a man in and he forced the wardrobe open and cleared off.

"Of course I don't mean any disrespect to you, miss," continued Schweik, when he saw that the young lady showed signs of getting upset and was crying, "but you absolutely can't stay here; you must see that for yourself, because I'm in charge of the whole place, and I'm responsible for the least thing that happens. So I'll ask you once more not to make any unnecessary fuss. Until I get my orders from the lieutenant, I couldn't let you stay here, not if you was my own brother. I'm sorry I've got to talk to you like this, but in the army we have to have proper discipline."

Meanwhile the young lady had recovered herself somewhat.

She took a visiting card out of her bag, wrote a few lines on it in pencil, put it into a dainty little envelope, and said in tones of distress, "Take this to the lieutenant and I'll wait here for an answer. Here's five crowns to pay your fare."

"It ain't a bit of use," replied Schweik, annoyed by the obstinacy of the unexpected guest. "Keep your five crowns; here they are, on the chair, and if you like you can come with me to the barracks; you wait for me while I take your note and I'll bring back the answer. But you can't wait here, that's a dead cert."

With these words he dragged the trunks into the passage, and rattling the key like the warder of a castle, he said with solemn emphasis, as he stood in the doorway, "Time to lock up."

The young lady dejectedly drifted into the passage; Schweik locked the door and strode ahead. The fair visitor trotted after him like a little pet dog, and did not catch him up till he stopped at a tobacconist's to buy cigarettes.

Now she walked along by his side and made efforts to start a conversation.

"You're sure you'll hand it to him?"

"If I say I will, I will."

"And will you be able to find him?"

"I don't know."

They again walked on side by side in silence, until after some time the young lady resumed. "So you think you'll be able to find him?"

"No, I don't."

"And where do you think he's likely to be?"

"I don't know."

This put a stop to the conversation for quite a long while, until the young lady again continued it by inquiring, "You haven't lost the note?"

"Not yet I haven't."

"You're sure you'll hand it to him?"

"Yes."

"And you'll be able to find him?"

"I've told you I don't know," replied Schweik. "What beats me is how people can be so nosy and keep asking the same question. It's like as if I was to stop every other person in the street and ask him what the date is."

This concluded the attempt to engage in conversation with Schweik, and the rest of the way to the barracks was traversed

167

in complete silence. When they reached the barracks, Schweik told the young lady to wait, and then began to discuss the war with the soldiers at the gateway. The young lady walked nervously to and fro on the pavement with a very distressed look on her face. She saw Schweik continuing his disquisition with an expression about as fatuous as that on the photograph published just about that time in the *Chronicle of the Great War* and entitled "Austrian Heir Apparent Talking to Two Airmen Who Shot Down a Russian Airplane."

Schweik sat down on the bench in the doorway and explained that on the Carpathian front the attacks had failed, but on the other hand, the commander of Przemyśl, General Kusmanek, had proceeded to Kiev, and that the Austrian troops had left eleven pivotal centers behind them in Serbia, so that the Serbians would not be able to keep running after them much longer. He then plunged ino a criticism of the various fighting operations, and made the sensational discovery that a detachment which is entirely surrounded has to surrender.

Having had his say, he thought he had better go out and tell the young lady, who by now was at her wits' end, that he wouldn't be long and that she was not to go away. Thereupon he went upstairs into the office, where he discovered Lieutenant Lukash. He was just expounding a scheme of trenches for the benefit of an officer whom he was taking to task for being unable to draw and not having the least idea of geometry.

"You see, this is the way to draw the diagram. If we have to drop a perpendicular onto a given straight line, we have to do it so that it forms a right angle with it. Do you follow? If that's done, you'll get your trenches in a proper position, and they won't reach as far as the enemy. You'll keep at a distance of six hundred yards from him. But the way you've drawn it, you'd shove our position into the enemy's lines, and you'd have your trenches right on top of the enemy, whereas you need an obtuse angle. Simple enough, isn't it?"

And the reserve officer, who in civil life was a bank cashier, gazed distractedly at the diagrams of which he understood nothing, and heaved a sigh of relief when Schweik approached the lieutenant.

"Beg to report, sir, there's a lady sent you this note and she's waiting for an answer."

He winked in a knowing and confidential manner.

Lieutenant Lukash was not altogether pleased when he read the following:

LIEBER HEINRICH!
Mein Mann verfolgt mich. Ich muss unbedingt bei dir ein paar Tage gastieren. Dein Bursch ist ein grosses Mistvieh. Ich bin unglücklich.

DEINE KATY[1]

Lieutenant Lukash sighed, led Schweik into an empty inner office, closed the door, and began to pace to and fro between the tables. At last he came to a standstill in front of Schweik and said, "This lady says you're a horrid beast. What have you been doing?"

"Beg to report, sir, I didn't do anything to her. I was as polite to her as could be, but she wanted to settle down in your quarters there and then. And as you never gave me any instructions about it, I wouldn't let her. And on top of all that she brought two trunks with her, as if she was going to make herself at home."

The lieutenant gave another loud sigh, which Schweik repeated after him.

"What's that?" shouted the lieutenant in a tone of menace.

"Beg to report, sir, it's a ticklish business. Two years ago down our street there was a young lady moved into a paper hanger's lodgings and he couldn't put her out, and in the end he had to poison himself, and her as well, with coal gas. It was no joke. Women are a nuisance. They don't catch me napping."

"It is a ticklish business," repeated the lieutenant, and never had Schweik spoken a truer word. Dear Jindrich was in the deuce of a fix. Here was a young lady whose husband was after her, and who had come to pay him a visit for several days, at the very moment when he was expecting Mrs. Micek from Trěbon on one of her quarterly shopping trips to Prague. Then, the next day but one another young lady was coming to see him. After having thought the matter over for a week, she had definitely promised to be his, because the following month she was going to marry an engineer.

The lieutenant now dejectedly sat down on the table, and

[1] "DEAR HENRY!
"My husband's after me. You simply must put me up for a few days. Your orderly is a horrid beast. I am so miserable.
"YOUR KATY"

lapsed into silent thought, but all that he could think of for the time being was to sit down and write on an official form:

DEAR KATY,

On duty till 9 P.M. Shall be home at 10. Please make yourself at home. As regards Schweik, my orderly, I have now instructed him to carry out all your wishes.

YOURS, JINDRICH

"Now," said the lieutenant, "you'll hand this note to the young lady. And let me impress upon you that you are to be respectful and tactful in your behavior toward her, and you must carry out all her wishes, which you are to treat as commands. You must treat her courteously and look after her requirements to the best of your ability. Here's a hundred crowns, for which you must account to me after having ordered lunch, supper, and so on for her, should she send you to fetch anything. Also, you'll buy three bottles of wine and a box of Memphis cigarettes. Well, that's all for the present. Now you can go, and once more let me urge upon you the necessity to do everything you can see she wants, even if she doesn't actually ask for it."

The young lady had already given up all hope of seeing Schweik again, and so she was very surprised when she observed him emerging from the barracks and proceeding in her direction with a letter.

Having saluted, he handed her the letter and said, "The lieutenant's instructions to me, miss, are that I am to be respectful and tactful in my behavior toward you, and I'm to look after your requirements to the best of my ability, and to do everything I can see you want, even if you don't actually ask for it. I've got to feed you and to buy whatever you'd like. The lieutenant gave me a hundred crowns to pay for it all, but out of that I've got to buy three bottles of wine and a box of Memphis cigarettes."

When she had read the letter, she recovered her strength of will, which she manifested by ordering Schweik to fetch a cab, and when that was done, she told him to sit on the box with the driver.

They drove home. When they got there, she admirably acted her part as lady of the house. Schweik had to carry the trunks into the bedroom, besides beating the carpets in the yard, and a tiny cobweb behind the mirror made her extremely angry. There was every indication that she intended to dig

170

herself in thoroughly, with a view to a lengthy stay in this strategical position.

Schweik sweated. When he had beaten the carpets, she remembered that the curtains would have to be taken down and dusted. Then he received orders to clean the windows in the bedroom and kitchen. Thereupon she began to rearrange the furniture, which made her very nervous, and when Schweik had dragged it from one corner to another, she was dissatisfied and started devising new groupings and arrangements. She turned everything upside down and slowly, as the cozy snuggery took shape, her supply of energy began to ebb and the harrying gradually came to an end. When everything else was finished, she took clean bed linen from the cupboard, and as she arranged the fresh pillow cases and mattresses, it was clear that she did so with genuine devotion.

Then she sent Schweik for lunch and wine. And before he returned, she put on a filmy gown which made her extremely attractive and alluring. At lunch she drank a bottle of wine and smoked several Memphis cigarettes. And while Schweik was in the kitchen feasting on army bread which he soaked in a glass of brandy, she retired to rest.

"Schweik," she shouted from the bedroom. "Schweik!"

Schweik opened the door and beheld the young lady in an enticing attitude among the cushions.

"Come here."

He stepped up to the bed, and with a peculiar smile she scrutinized his sturdy build. Then, pulling aside the thin covering which had hitherto concealed her person, she said sternly, "Take off your boots and trousers. Let me——"

And so it came about that when the lieutenant returned from the barracks, the good soldier Schweik was able to inform him, "Beg to report, sir, I carried out all the lady's wishes and treated her courteously, just as you instructed me."

"Thank you, Schweik," said the lieutenant. "And did she want many things done?"

"About six," replied Schweik. "And now she's sound asleep. I expect the journey tired her out. I did everything I saw she wanted, even though she didn't actually ask for it."

v.

While whole armies, clinging to the forests on the Dunajec and Raab, were standing in a downpour of shells, and heavy artillery was cutting up and scattering company after company in the Carpathians, and the horizon in all battle areas was aglow with the blazing of villages and towns, Lieutenant Lukash, together with Schweik, was having unpleasantly idyllic experiences with the lady who had run away from her husband and who had now made herself thoroughly at home.

When she had gone out for a walk, Lieutenant Lukash held a council of war with Schweik to discuss how he should get rid of her.

"The best thing, sir," said Schweik, "would be if her husband who she ran away from and who's looking for her, according to what you said was in that note I brought you, was to know where she is, so that he could come and fetch her. Send him a telegram telling him she's staying with you and that he can come and take her away. There was a similar sort of mix-up last year in a villa at Vsenory. But then it was the woman who sent the telegram to her husband, and he came to fetch her and gave the pair of them a good hiding. They was both civilians, but you being an officer, I don't suppose that's likely to happen here. Anyhow, you're not to blame, because you never invited anyone, and when she ran away she did it on her own account. You'll see, a telegram's a very useful wheeze. And if the worst comes to the worst, and there is a bit of a rumpus—"

"Oh, he's a very shrewd fellow," said Lieutenant Lukash. "I know him personally. He's a wholesale hop merchant. Yes, I must have a talk to him. I'll send a telegram."

The telegram which he sent was very brief and businesslike: "Your wife's present address is—" and the address of Lieutenant Lukash completed the message.

And so Madame Katy had a very unpleasant surprise when the hop merchant rushed in. He looked very gentlemanly and solicitous when Madame Katy, as cool as a cucumber, introduced the two of them.

"My husband—Lieutenant Lukash."

That was all she could think of.

"Please take a seat, Mr. Wendler," said Lieutenant Lukash affably, taking a cigarette case out of his pocket. "May I offer you a cigarette?"

The hop merchant, the very shrewd fellow, helped himself courteously to a cigarette and, puffing smoke from his mouth, said solemnly, "You'll be off to the front soon, I suppose?"

"I've applied for a transfer to the 91st Regiment and I expect my application'll be granted as soon as I've finished my job of training volunteer officers. We need a huge number of officers, and it's disheartening to see how many young men who are entitled to be volunteer officers don't come forward to claim their rights. They'd rather stay in the ranks than try and become cadets."

"The hop business has been badly hit by the war, but I suppose it won't last long," remarked the hop merchant, gazing by turns at his wife and the lieutenant.

"We're in a very strong position," said Lieutenant Lukash. "Nobody can doubt for a moment today that the war will end with the victory of the Central Powers. France, England, and Russia haven't enough strength to do anything against the hard fight that Austria, Turkey, and Germany are putting up. Of course, we've had trifling reverses on a few fronts. But as soon as we break through the Russian front between the ridge of the Carpathians and the Dunajec there can be no doubt that the war will come to an end. In the same way the French are faced with the imminent loss of the whole of eastern France and the entry of the German army into Paris. That's absolutely certain. In addition to that, our maneuvers in Serbia are making very successful progress, and the withdrawal of our troops, as a matter of fact, is only a rearrangement of fighting forces, and the conclusions many people are apt to draw from it are not at all such as self-composure in war demands. Before very long we shall see that our carefully planned maneuvers in the southern battle area will bear fruit. Just look here—"

And Lieutenant Lukash took the hop merchant gently by the shoulder and leading him to a map of the battle area hanging on the wall, showed him, with a running commentary, the various pivotal centers.

"The Eastern Bezkyds form an excellent pivotal center for us. In the Carpathian sectors, as you see, we have a strong support. A strong blow on this line and we shan't stop till we get to Moscow. The war will be over before we think."

"And what about Turkey?" asked the hop merchant, wondering how he was to come to grips with the subject which had brought him there.

"The Turks are doing well," replied the lieutenant, leading him back to the table. "Hali Bey, the speaker of the Turkish Parliament, and Ali Bey have come to Vienna. Field Marshal Liman von Sanders has been appointed commander-in-chief of the Turkish army at the Dardanelles. Golz Pasha has proceeded from Constantinople to Berlin and our Emperor has conferred special distinctions upon Enver Pasha, Vice Admiral Usedom, and General Djevad Pasha. Quite a lot of distinctions for so short a period of time."

They all sat looking at each other in silence, until the lieutenant thought he had better relieve the awkward situation by asking, "When did you arrive, Mr. Wendler?"

"This morning."

"I'm very glad you discovered where I am and found me at home, because every afternoon I go to barracks and at night I'm on duty. As my quarters are practically empty all day, I was able to offer your wife my hospitality. While she's staying in Prague she can go in and out, just as she pleases, and nobody will be in her way. Our acquaintance is of such long standing that—"

The hop merchant coughed, "Katy is a bit of a handful and I must thank you most heartily for everything you've done for her. She took it into her head at scarcely a moment's notice to go to Prague, because she said she must have her nerves seen to. I was away at the time and when I got back the house was empty. Katy had gone."

Endeavoring to look as matter-of-fact as he could, he wagged a threatening finger at her and with a forced smile he asked, "I suppose you thought that because I was traveling about, you could travel about, too. Of course, it didn't occur to you that—"

Lieutenant Lukash, seeing that the conversation was taking an awkward turn, again led the hop merchant to the map of the battle area and pointing to the places which were underlined, he said, "I forgot to draw your attention to one very interesting circumstance. I mean this large curve facing southwest, where this mountain range forms a large bridgehead. That is the point to which the Allied offensive is being directed. By cutting off this railway track which connects the bridgehead with the enemy's main line of defense, the communication between the right flank and the northern army on the Vistula must be interrupted. Do I make myself clear?"

The hop merchant replied that all was quite clear to him, and as, in his anxiety to be tactful, he was afraid of making any remark which might be regarded as offensive, he went back to his place and said, "Our hop trade has lost some foreign markets through the war. France, England, Russia, and the Balkans have been lost, as far as the hop trade is concerned. We're still sending hops to Italy, but I'm afraid that it won't be long before Italy butts in, too. But when we've won, we'll make them pay our prices for goods."

"Italy will preserve a strict neutrality," said the lieutenant, to reassure him. "That is—"

"Then why don't the Italians admit that they are bound by the Triple Alliance Treaty between Austria-Hungary and Germany?" burst forth the hop merchant, who suddenly lost his temper as he realized the full extent of his troubles: hops, wife, war. "I was expecting Italy to join in against France and Serbia. If they'd done that, the war would have been over by now. Now my hops are rotting in the warehouse, home orders are few and far between, the export trade has practically stopped, and Italy's remaining neutral. Why didn't Italy renew the Triple Alliance with us in 1912? Where's the Italian Minister of Foreign Affairs, the Marquis de San Giuliano? What's he doing? Is he asleep, or what? Do you know what my annual turnover was before the war and what it is now?

"Don't you imagine I'm not keeping abreast of what's happening," he continued, gazing furiously at the lieutenant, who was placidly puffing smoke rings, each of which collided with the preceding one and dispersed it. "Why did the Germans withdraw to the frontier when they were so close to Paris? Why is such heavy artillery fighting going on between the Maas and the Mosel? Do you know that at Combres and Woewre near Marche they've burned down three breweries which we used to supply with over five hundred sacks of hops annually? And in the Vosges they've burned down the brewery at Hartsmannsweiler, and the huge brewery at Niederaspach near Mülhausen has been completely destroyed? That means a loss of twelve hundred sacks of hops for my firm annually. The Germans fought the Belgians six times for the brewery at Klosterhoek. There you have another three hundred and fifty sacks of hops lost annually."

He now became speechless with indignation. Presently he stood up, walked across to his wife, and said, "Katy, you'll come home with me immediately. Get dressed."

"I'm so upset by all these goings on," he then remarked apologetically. "I used to be as easygoing as could be."

And when she had gone to get dressed, he whispered to the

lieutenant, "This isn't the first time she's done this sort of thing. Last year she ran away with an usher in a school. I had to go right down to Zagreb before I found them. And when I got there, I got an order from the Municipal Brewery at Zagreb for six hundred sacks of hops. Ah, yes, the south was a regular gold mine. Our hops went as far as Constantinople. Now we're half ruined. If the government restricts the production of beer in the bargain, that'll be the last straw."

And lighting the cigarette which the lieutenant had offered him, he said in a stricken voice, "The only big order came from Warsaw—two thousand three hundred and seventy sacks of hops. The biggest brewery there is the Augustinian. Their representative used to come and see me every year. Oh, it's something awful. It's a good thing I haven't got any children."

This logical inference from the annual visit to the representative of the Augustinian brewery in Warsaw caused the lieutenant to smile to himself. The hop merchant noticed this and accordingly continued his statement, "The Hungarian breweries at Sopron and Great Kanizsa used to take on an average one thousand sacks of hops annually from my firm for their export beers that went as far as Alexandria. Now on account of the blockade they refuse to place a single order. I offer them hops 30 per cent cheaper, but they won't order a single sack. Stagnation, anxiety, ruin, and then on top of it all I get these household worries."

The hop merchant lapsed into silence, but this silence was interrupted by Madame Katy, now ready to go.

"What are we to do about my trunks?"

"They can be sent for, Katy," said the hop merchant contentedly, now cheering up at the thought that the episode had passed off without any annoying scenes. "If you want to do any shopping, it's high time we went. The train leaves at two-twenty."

They both amicably took their leave of the lieutenant, and the hop merchant was so glad his ordeal was now over, that when they were saying goodbye in the passage, he remarked to the lieutenant, "If you are wounded, though please God you won't be, you must come and stay with us when you are convalescent. We'll do all we can for you."

When he returned to the bedroom, where Madame Katy had dressed for the journey, the lieutenant found four hundred crowns and the following letter in the wash-hand stand:

LIEUTENANT LUKASH,

You were not man enough to stand up for me against my fool of a husband and you let him drag me away as if I were a mere object he had left behind by mistake. And you had the cheek to say that you had offered me hospitality. I hope I have not run you into more than the enclosed four hundred crowns, which kindly share with your orderly.

For a moment Lieutenant Lukash stood with the letter in his hand, and then he gradually tore it into pieces. With a smile he looked at the money on the wash-hand stand, and noticing that in her indignation she had left her comb on the table, he put it away among his collection of keepsakes.

Schweik came back in the afternoon. He had gone to find a fox terrier for the lieutenant.

"Schweik," said the lieutenant, "you're in luck's way. The lady who was staying with me has gone. Her husband took her away with him. And to show how pleased she is with all you did for her, she left four hundred crowns on the wash-hand stand for you. You must write and thank her, or rather her husband, because it's his money she took with her when she left home. I'll dictate you a letter."

And he dictated:

"DEAR SIR,

"Kindly express to your wife my hearty thanks for the four hundred crowns with which she presented me for all I did for her during her stay in Prague. It was a great pleasure for me to do it and I therefore cannot accept this money and I am sending it—

"Now then, go on writing, Schweik. What are you fidgeting like that for? Where did I leave off?"

"'And I am sending it—'" said Schweik in the quavering voice of tragedy.

"That's right.

"—I am sending it back and beg to remain, with best respects to your wife and yourself, Yours truly,

"JOSEF SCHWEIK,
"ORDERLY TO LIEUTENANT LUKASH"

"Got it all down?"

"Beg to report, sir, there's the date to go in yet."

"'December twentieth, 1914.' That's it, and now address the envelope and put these four hundred crowns inside and take it to the post office. Here's the address."

And Lieutenant Lukash began to whistle blithely to himself a tune from *The Lady Who Was Divorced*.

"There's just one thing more, Schweik," said the lieutenant when Schweik was leaving for the post office. "What about that dog you went to look for?"

"I've got my eye on one, sir, and a very fine animal it is, too. But it's going to be a hard job to get hold of him. All the same, I hope I'll manage to bring him along tomorrow. He don't half bite."

VI.

Lieutenant Lukash did not hear the last few words, and yet they were very important. "The brute bites for all he's worth," was what Schweik was going to add, but then he thought, "What's it matter to him? He wants a dog, and he'll get one."

Now it is all very well to say, "Get me a dog," but the owners of dogs are very careful of their pets, even though they may not be thoroughbreds. The dog is a faithful animal, but only in schoolbooks or natural history primers. Let even the most faithful dog sniff at a fried sausage and he's done for. He'll forget his master, by whose side he was just trotting along. He'll turn around and follow you, his mouth watering, his tail wagging, his nostrils quivering with gusto in anticipation of the sausage.

In that quarter of Prague near the steps leading to the castle there is a small beer shop. One day two men were sitting there in the dim light at the back. One was a soldier and the other a civilian. They were sitting close together and whispering mysteriously. They looked like conspirators at the time of the Venetian Republic.

"Every day at eight o'clock," whispered the civilian, "the skivvy takes him along Havlicek Square on the way to the park. But he's a fair terror. Talk about bite! There's no doing anything with him."

And bending down still closer to the soldier, he whispered into his ear, "He don't even eat sausage."

"Not when it's fried?" asked the soldier.

"No, not even when it's fried."

They both spat.

"What does the brute eat, then?"

"Blowed if I know. Some of these dogs are as pampered and petted as a blessed archbishop."

The soldier and the civilian clinked glasses and the civilian went on whispering. "There was a black Pomeranian once that I was after, and he wouldn't touch sausage either. I followed him about for three days till I got sick of it, and so I went as bold as brass and asked the lady who was taking him around what they fed him on to make him look so nice. That tickled her no end and she says his favorite grub was cutlets. So I bought him a cutlet. I thinks to myself, that'll do the trick. And believe me or believe me not, that bloody tyke wouldn't even look at it, because it was a veal cutlet and he'd been brought up on pork. So I had to buy him a pork cutlet. I let him have a sniff at it and then I starts running, and the dog follows me. The lady yells, 'Puntik, Puntik,' but he'd done a bunk. He follows the cutlet around the corner and when he gets there I put him on the lead, and then next day he was where I wanted him to be. He had some white tufts under his chin, a sort of patch, but they blacked it over and nobody recognized him. All the other dogs I've ever come across, and there's been a tidy few of them, fell for a fried sausage. So the best thing you can do is to ask her what the dog's favorite grub is. You're a well-set-up chap, and with your uniform and all, she'll tell you quick enough. I asked her, but she looked daggers at me and said. 'What's that got to do with you?' She's not much to look at, in fact, if you ask me she's a bit of a frump, but she'll talk to a soldier all right."

"Is it a real fox terrier? The lieutenant won't take any other sort."

"Oh, it's a fox terrier all right. A very fine dog, too. Pepper-and-salt, an out-and-out thoroughbred, as sure as your name's Schweik and mine's Blahnik. All I want to know is what grub he eats and I'll bring him to you."

The two friends again clinked glasses. It was from Blahnik that Schweik had obtained his supply of dogs when he used to deal in them before joining the army. And now that Schweik was a soldier, Blahnik considered it his duty to assist him in a disinterested spirit. He knew every dog in the whole of Prague and environs, and on principle he stole only thoroughbred dogs.

At eight o'clock the next morning the good soldier Schweik might have been seen strolling along by the Havlicek Square and the park. He was waiting for the servant girl with the Pomeranian. At last his patience was rewarded. Around her frisked a dog with whiskers, a bristly, wiry-haired animal with knowing eyes.

The servant girl was rather elderly, with her hair tastefully twisted into a bun. She whistled to the dog and flourished a leash and an elegant hunting crop.

Schweik said to her, "Excuse me, miss. Which is the way to Zizkov?"

She stopped and looked at him to see whether he was in earnest, and Schweik's good-natured face convinced her that this worthy soldier did really want to go to Zizkov. Her expression showed signs of relenting, and with great readiness she explained to him how he could get to Zizkov.

"I've only just been transferred to Prague," said Schweik. "I'm from the country. You're not from Prague either, are you?"

"I'm from Vodnany."

"Then we're almost neighbors," replied Schweik. "I'm from Protivin."

Schweik's familiarity with the topography of southern Bohemia, which he had once acquired during the maneuvers in that region, caused the servant girl's heart to warm to her fellow townsman.

"Then I expect you know Pejchar, the butcher on the market square at Protivin?"

"I should think I do. Why, he's my brother. He's a regular favorite in the whole neighborhood," said Schweik. "He's a good sort, an obliging fellow, he is. Sells good meat and gives good weight."

"Then don't you belong to the Jaresh family?" asked the servant girl, beginning to take to the unknown warrior.

"Yes, of course."

"Which Jaresh is your father, the one at Kertsch or the one at Razice?"

"The one at Razice."

"Does he still go around selling beer?"

"Yes."

"Why, he must be well over sixty."

"He was sixty-eight last spring," replied Schweik with composure. "Now he's got a dog to pull his cart for him. Just like

180

the one that's chasing those sparrows. A nice dog, a beautiful little animal."

"That's ours," explained his new lady friend. "I'm in service at the colonel's. You don't know our colonel, do you?"

"Yes, I do. He's a fine chap, clever, too. We used to have a colonel like him at Budejovice."

"Master's very strict, and a little while ago, when people were saying we'd been beaten in Serbia, he came home in a regular paddy and threw all the plates about in the kitchen and wanted to give me notice."

"So that's your dog, is it?" Schweik interrupted her. "It's a pity that my lieutenant can't stand dogs, because I'm very fond of them."

He lapsed into silence, but suddenly blurted out, "Of course, it's not every dog that'll eat anything you give it."

"Our Lux is awfully dainty. There was a time he wouldn't eat any meat at all, but he will now."

"And what's he like best?"

"Liver, boiled liver."

"Calves' liver or pig's liver?"

"He doesn't mind which," said Schweik's fellow country-woman, with a smile, for she regarded his last question as an unsuccessful attempt at a joke.

They strolled along together for a while, and then they were joined by the Pomeranian. He seemed to take a great fancy to Schweik and tried to tear his trousers as best he could through his muzzle. He kept jumping up at him, but suddenly, as if he guessed Schweik's intentions toward him, he stopped jumping and ambled along with an air of sadness and anxiety, looking askance at Schweik, as much as to say, "So that's what's in store for me, is it?"

The servant girl meanwhile was telling Schweik that she came this way with the dog every evening at six o'clock as well, that she did not trust any man from Prague, that she had once put a matrimonial advertisement in the paper and a locksmith had replied with a view to marriage, but had wheedled eight hundred crowns out of her for some invention or other and had then disappeared. In the country the people were more honest, of that she was certain. If she were to marry, it would have to be a man from the country, but not until the war was over. She thought that war marriages were a mistake, because it generally meant that the woman was left a widow.

Schweik assured her it was highly probable that he would

181

turn up at six o'clock, and he then took his leave, to inform Blahnik that the dog would eat liver of any species.

"I'll let him have ox. liver, then," decided Blahnik. "That's what I collared a St. Bernard dog with, and he was a shy animal, he was. I'll bring that dog along tomorrow all right."

Blahnik kept his word. In the afternoon, when Schweik had finished tidying up, he heard a barking noise at the door, and when he opened it, Blahnik came in, dragging with him a refractory Pomeranian which was more bristly than his natural bristliness. He was rolling his eyes wildly and his scowl was such that it suggested a starving tiger in a cage being inspected by a well-fed visitor to the Zoological Gardens. He gnashed his teeth and growled, as if expressing his desire to rend and devour.

They tied the dog to the kitchen table, and Blahnik described the procedure by which he had acquired the animal.

"I purposely hung about near him with some boiled liver wrapped up in a piece of paper. He began sniffing and jumping up at me. When I got as far as the park I turns off into Bredovska Street and then I gives him the first bit. He gobbles it up, but keeps on the move all the time so as not to lose sight of me. I turns off into Jindrichska Street and there I gives him another helping. Then, when he'd got that inside him, I puts him on the lead and took him across Vaclav Square to Vinohrady and then on to Vrsovice. And he didn't half lead me a dance. When I was crossing the tram lines he flops down and wouldn't budge an inch. Perhaps he wanted to get run over. I've brought a blank pedigree form that I got at a stationer's shop. You'll have to fill that up, Schweik."

"It's got to be in your handwriting. Say he comes from the Von Bülow kennels at Leipzig. Father, Arnheim von Kahlsberg, mother, Emma von Trautensdorf, and connected with Siegfried von Busenthal on his father's side. Father gained first prize at the Berlin Exhibition of Pomeranians in 1912. Mother awarded a gold medal by the Nürnberg Thoroughbred Dogs' Society. How old do you think he is?"

"Judging by his teeth, I should say two years."

"Put him down as eighteen months."

"He's been badly cropped, Schweik. Look at his ears."

"That can be put right. We can clip them when he's got used to us. He'd show fight if we was to try it now."

The purloined dog growled savagely, panted, wriggled about, and then, tired out, he lay down with tongue hanging out, and waited what would befall him. Gradually he became quieter, only from time to time he whined piteously.

Schweik offered him the rest of the liver which Blahnik had handed over. But he refused to touch it, eyeing it disdainfully and looking at both of them, as much as to say, "I've been had once. Now eat it yourselves."

He lay down with an air of resignation and pretended to be dozing. Then suddenly something flashed across his mind; he got up and began to stand on his hind legs and to beg with his front paws. He had given in.

This touching scene produced no effect on Schweik.

"Lie down," he shouted at the wretched animal, which lay down again, whining piteously.

"What name shall we shove into his pedigree?" asked Blahnik. "He used to be called Fox, or something of that sort."

"Well, let's call him Max. Look how he pricks up his ears. Stand up, Max."

The unfortunate Pomeranian, which had been deprived both of home and name, stood up and awaited further orders.

"I think we might as well untie him," suggested Schweik. "Let's see what he'll do."

When he was untied, the first thing he did was to make for the door, where he gave three short barks at the handle, evidently relying on the magnanimity of these evil people. But when he saw that they did not fall in with his desire to get out, he made a small puddle in the doorway, thinking, most probably, that they would throw him out, as had always happened on similar occasions when he was a puppy and the colonel, with military severity, had taught him elementary manners.

But instead of that, Schweik remarked, "He's an artful one, he is, as artful as they make 'em," gave him a whack with a strap, and wetted his whiskers so thoroughly in the puddle that it was all he could do to lick himself clean.

He whined at this humiliation and began to run about in the kitchen, sniffing desperately at his own tracks. Then, unexpectedly changing his mind, he sat down by the table and devoured the rest of the liver which was on the floor. Whereupon he lay down by the fireplace and ended his spell of adventure by falling asleep.

"What's the damage?" Schweik asked Blahnik, when he got up to go.

"Don't you worry about that, Schweik," said Blahnik tenderly. "I'd do anything for an old pal, especially when he's in the army. Well, so long, lad, and never take him across Havlicek Square, or you'd be asking for trouble. If you want any more dogs, you know where I hang out."

Schweik let Max have a good long nap. He went to the butcher's and bought half a pound of liver, boiled it, and waited till Max woke up, when he gave him a piece of the warm liver to sniff at. Max began to lick himself after his nap, stretched his limbs, sniffed at the liver, and gulped it down. Then he went to the door and repeated his performance with the handle.

"Max!" shouted Schweik. "Come here."

The dog obeyed gingerly enough, but Schweik took him on his lap and stroked him. Now for the first time since his arrival Max began to wag the remainder of his lopped tail amicably, and playfully grabbed at Schweik's hand, holding it in his paw and gazing at Schweik sagaciously, as much as to say, "Well, it can't be helped; I know I got the worst of it."

Schweik went on stroking him and in a gentle voice began to tell him a little story:

"Now there was once a little dog whose name was Fox, and he lived with a colonel. The servant girl took him for a walk and up came a gentleman who stole Fox. Fox got into the army, where his new master was a lieutenant, and now they called him Max. Max, shake hands. Now you see, you silly tyke, we'll get on well together if you're good and obedient. If you ain't, why, you'll catch it hot."

Max jumped down from Schweik's lap and began to frisk about merrily with him. By the evening, when the lieutenant returned from the barracks, Schweik and Max were the best of friends.

As he looked at Max, Schweik reflected philosophically, "When you come to think of it, every soldier's really been stolen away from his home."

Lieutenant Lukash was very pleasantly surprised when he saw Max, who on his part also showed great joy at again seeing a man with a sword.

When asked where he came from and how much he cost, Schweik replied with the utmost composure that the dog was a present from a friend of his who had just joined up.

"That's fine, Schweik," said the lieutenant, playing with

Max. "On the first of the month I'll let you have fifty crowns for the dog."

"I couldn't take the money, sir."

"Schweik," said the lieutenant sternly, "when you entered my service, I explained to you that you must obey me implicitly. When I tell you that you'll get fifty crowns, you've got to take the money and go on the spree with it. What will you do with the fifty crowns, Schweik?"

"Beg to report, sir, I'll go on the spree with it, as per instructions."

"And if I should happen to forget it, Schweik, you are to remind me to give you the fifty crowns. Do you understand? Are you sure the dog hasn't got fleas? You'd better give him a bath and comb him out. I'm on duty tomorrow, but the day after tomorrow I'll take him for a walk."

While Schweik was giving Max a bath, the colonel, his former owner, was kicking up a terrible row and threatening that when he found the man who had stolen his dog, he would have him tried by court-martial, he would have him shot, he would have him hanged, he would have him imprisoned for twenty years, and he would have him chopped to pieces.

"There'll be hell to pay when I find the blackguard who did it," bellowed the colonel till the windows rattled. "I know how to get even with low scoundrels like him."

Above the heads of Schweik and Lieutenant Lukash was hovering a catastrophe.

15.

The Catastrophe

COLONEL KRAUS, who also had a handle to his name, to wit,
Von Zillergut, from a village near Salzburg which his ancestors
had stripped bare in the eighteenth century, was an estimable
booby. Whenever he gave an account of anything, he confined himself to concrete details, and stopped every now and
then to ask whether his hearers all understood the most elementary terms, as: "So, as I was just saying, gentlemen, there
was a window. You know what a window is, don't you?" Or:
"A road with ditches along both sides of it is called a highway. Yes, gentlemen. Do you know what a ditch is? A ditch
is a sort of cavity dug by a gang of laborers. It's a deep gutter.
Yes, that's what it is. And they dig it out with shovels. Do you
know what a shovel is?"

He had a mania for explaining things and he indulged in
it with the enthusiasm of an inventor telling people about
the apparatus he has made.

186

"A book, gentlemen, consists of several quarto sheets of paper, cut into various sizes, covered with print and arranged in proper order, bound and pasted together. Yes. Do you know what paste is, gentlemen? Paste is used for sticking one thing to another."

He was so immoderately idiotic that officers gave him a wide berth, in order not to be informed that the pavement separates the street from the roadway and that it consists of a raised stretch of stonewalk alongside the house fronts. And a house front is that part of a house which we see from the street or the pavement. We cannot see the back part of a house from the pavement, as we can immediately ascertain for ourselves if we step into the roadway.

This interesting fact he was prepared to demonstrate on the spot. And he would stop officers to embark on interminable conversations about omelettes, sunlight, thermometers, puddings, windows, and postage stamps.

The remarkable thing was that such an imbecile as this should have gained comparatively rapid promotion. During maneuvers he performed regular miracles with his regiment. He never got anywhere in time, he led the regiment in column formation against machine-gun fire, and on one occasion several years previously, during the imperial maneuvers in southern Bohemia, he and his regiment had got completely lost. They turned up in Moravia, where they wandered about for several days, after the maneuvers were all over.

Once at a banquet in the officers' club, when a conversation was started on the subject of Schiller, Colonel Kraus von Zillergut, without the slightest warning, held forth as follows:

"Well, gentlemen, yesterday I saw a steam plow, driven by an engine. Just imagine, gentlemen, an engine, or rather, not one engine but two engines. I saw smoke, I went nearer, and there was an engine, and on the other side another one. Now, gentlemen, don't you think that was ridiculous? Two engines, as if one wasn't enough."

He lapsed into silence, but after a moment announced, "If the benzine gets used up, the motor car comes to a standstill. It must be so. I saw the thing happen yesterday. And then people talk a lot of twaddle about persistence of forces. Isn't it ridiculous?"

He was extremely devout. He often went to confession, and since the outbreak of the war he had prayed regularly for the success of Austria and Germany. He always flew into a temper when he read in the paper that more prisoners had been captured. He would bellow, "What's the good of taking prisoners? Shoot the lot. No mercy. Pile up the corpses. Trample on 'em. Burn every damned civilian in Serbia alive. Every man jack of 'em. And finish the babies off with bayonets."

Having finished his classwork at the training school for volunteer officers, Lieutenant Lukash went for a walk with Max.

"I hope you don't mind me telling you, sir," said Schweik solicitously, "but you got to be careful with that dog, or he'll run away. I expect he's fretting a bit after his old home, and if you was to untie him, he might take his hook. And if I was you I wouldn't take him across Havlicek Square, because there's a butcher's dog always hanging about around there and he's a terror, he is. The minute he sees a strange dog on his beat, he gets that angry, thinking the other dog's going to sneak some of his grub. And he don't half bite."

Max frisked about merrily and got under the lieutenant's feet, entangling his leash in the officer's sword and altogether displaying extreme delight at being taken for a walk.

They went out into the street and Lieutenant Lukash made for the Prikopy. He had an appointment with a lady at the corner of Panská Street. He was engrossed in official thoughts. What was he to lecture about to the volunteer officers the next day? How is the elevation of a given hill determined? Why is the elevation always measured above the sea level? How can the simple elevation of a hill from its base be determined from the elevation above the sea level? Confound it, why on earth did the War Office include such rot in its syllabus? That's all very well for the artillery. Besides, there are the general staff maps. If the enemy is on Hill 312, there's no point in wondering why the elevation of the hill is measured above the sea level or in calculating how high it is. You just look at the map, and there you are.

He was disturbed from these reflections by a stern "Halt!" just as he was approaching Panská Street. At the same instant the dog tried to scuttle away from him, lead and all, and gleefully barking, it hurled itself upon the man who had shouted "Halt!"

The lieutenant found himself face to face with Colonel Kraus von Zillergut. He saluted and apologized to the colonel for not having noticed him earlier.

"An officer of lower rank, sir," thundered Colonel Kraus, "must always salute officers of higher rank. That is a regulation which, I believe, is still in force. And there is another thing. Since when have officers been in the habit of promenading in the streets with stolen dogs? Yes, with stolen dogs, I said. A dog which belongs to someone else is a stolen dog."

"This dog, sir—" began Lieutenant Lukash.

"Belongs to me, sir," said the colonel, interrupting him curtly. "That's my dog Fox."

And Fox alias Max remembered his old master, and completely repudiated his new one. He left Lieutenant Lukash in the lurch and began to jump up at the colonel with every appearance of delight.

"To walk about with stolen dogs, sir, is incompatible with an officer's honor. You didn't know? An officer cannot purchase a dog unless he has convinced himself that he can do so without fear of any untoward consequences." Colonel Kraus continued to bellow as he stroked Max, who now basely began to snarl at the lieutenant and to show his teeth, as if saying to the colonel, "Give it him hot!"

"Would you consider it right, sir," continued the colonel, "to ride on a stolen horse? Didn't you read my advertisement in *Bohemia* and the *Prager Tageblatt* about the loss of my Pomeranian? You didn't read the advertisement that your superior officer put into the papers?"

The colonel banged the fist of one hand into the palm of the other.

"Upon my word, what are these young officers coming to? Where's their sense of discipline? A colonel puts advertisements in the paper and they don't read them."

"By Jove, wouldn't I like to land him a couple across the jaw, the silly old buffer!" thought Lieutenant Lukash to himself as he looked at the colonel's whiskers, which reminded him of an orangutan.

"Just step this way a moment," said the colonel. So they walked along together, engaged in a highly pleasant conversation.

"When you get to the front, you won't be able to get up to tricks of that sort. I've no doubt it's very nice to lounge about at the base and go for walks with stolen dogs. Oh yes! With a dog belonging to your superior officer. At a time when we are losing hundreds of officers every day on the battlefields. And catch them reading advertisements. Not they! Why, damn it all, I might go on advertising for a hundred years that I've lost a dog. Two hundred years, three hundred years!"

The old colonel blew his nose noisily, which in his case was always a sign of great indignation, and said, "You can continue your walk."

Whereupon he turned on his heel and departed, savagely slashing his riding whip across the ends of his greatcoat.

Lieutenant Lukash crossed the road, and there again he heard that yell of "Halt!" The colonel had just stopped an unfortunate infantry reservist who was thinking of his mother and had not noticed him.

With his own hands the colonel conducted him into barracks for punishment, calling him a blithering jackass.

"What am I to do with that fellow Schweik?" thought the lieutenant. "I'll bash his jaw in, but that's not enough. Why, if I was to slice him into strips, it would be too good for a skunk like him."

And disregarding his appointment with the lady, he wrathfully made his way home.

"I'll murder that blighter, that I will," he said to himself, as he got into a tram.

Meanwhile the good soldier Schweik was engrossed in a conversation with an orderly from the barracks who had brought a number of documents for the lieutenant to sign and was now waiting.

Schweik treated him to coffee and the pair of them were telling each other that Austria would get the worst of it. Almost every word they uttered would have brought them to the gallows for high treason if they had been overheard.

"The Emperor must be off his chump by now," announced Schweik. "He never was what you'd call brainy, but the war will about put the lid on it."

"He's off his chump all right," assented the soldier from the barracks, "absolutely barmy. Why, I don't suppose he even knows there's a war on. I shouldn't be surprised if they jibbed at telling him about it. And if his signature's on the manifesto to the country, why it's been faked. They had it printed without telling him. By this time I expect his mind's an absolute blank."

"He's done for," added Schweik with the air of a man who knows. "They have to feed him like a baby. A few days ago there was a chap in a pub telling us he's got two wet nurses."

"I wish it was all over," sighed the soldier from the barracks. "If they'd only give us a good hiding, perhaps we'd have a little peace."

And they continued their conversation in this strain, till Schweik dismissed Austria once and for all: "This silly, rotten country ought to be done away with," to which he added, "I won't half be glad when I get to the front."

Then they recalled the wars of long ago, and Schweik pointed out that when stinkpots were thrown into a besieged castle, it was no picnic to fight with all those smells about. He would probably have made more such profound remarks, if at that point the conversation had not been interrupted by the return of Lieutenant Lukash.

He glared ferociously at Schweik, signed the documents and, having dismissed the messenger, beckoned Schweik to follow him into the next room. The lieutenant's eyes flashed fire. Sitting down on a chair, he gazed at Schweik and meditated on the beginning of the slaughter.

"First of all I'll land him a couple across the mouth," he reflected; "then I'll bang his nose in and pull his ears. After that, we'll see."

And he found himself confronted by the kindly and guileless eyes of Schweik, who interrupted the calm before the storm, as follows: "Beg to report, sir, you've lost your cat. She ate up the boot polish and now she's gone and kicked the bucket. I threw her into the cellar—the next one, that is. You'll have a job to find another Angora cat like that. She was a nice little animal, that she was."

"What am I to do with him?" was the question which darted across the lieutenant's mind. "Good God, what an utter imbecile he looks!"

And Schweik's good-natured, guileless eyes beamed with a blend of tenderness and complacency at the thought that all was well, and nothing had happened, and even if anything had happened, all was well just the same.

Lieutenant Lukash jumped up, but he did not hit Schweik as he had originally intended. He brandished his fist under his nose and bellowed, "You stole that dog, Schweik."

"Beg to report, sir, that you went for a walk with Max this afternoon, so I couldn't have stole him. I thought it was funny when you came back without him, and it struck me at the time that something was up. That's what's called a situation. I knew a bagmaker named Kunesh and he could never go for a walk with a dog without losing him. Generally he left him in some pub or other, or someone stole him or borrowed him and never brought him back, or—"

"Schweik, you misbegotten numskull, for God's sake hold your tongue. Either you're a thoroughpaced rascal or else you're a champion, double-dyed, blithering idiot. But I warn you, don't try any of your tricks on me. Where did you get that dog from? How did you get hold of him? Do you know that he belongs to our colonel? Tell me the truth. Did you steal him or didn't you?"

"Beg to report, sir, I didn't steal him."

"Did you know he was stolen?"

"Beg to report, sir, yes, I knew that, sir."

"Then, Schweik, you prize ass, you thickheaded booby, you lousy skunk, I'll shoot you, by heaven I will. Are you really such a blithering idiot?"

"Beg to report, sir, I am, sir."

"Why did you bring me a stolen dog? What did you palm the brute off on me for?"

"I wanted to please you, sir."

And Schweik's eyes gazed kindly and tenderly at the lieutenant, who dropped into a chair and lamented, "My God, what have I done to have this bloody fool inflicted on me?"

He sat there in silent resignation and felt too limp even to give Schweik a smack in the face. At last he rolled a cigarette and without knowing why, he sent Schweik for the *Bohemia* and the *Prager Tageblatt* so that he could read the colonel's advertisement about the stolen dog.

Schweik returned with the newspapers opened at the advertisement page. His face was beaming and he announced with the utmost joy:

"Here it is, sir. The colonel gives a grand description of that stolen Pomeranian. It's a fair treat to read it, that it is. And on top of that he offers a reward of a hundred crowns to anyone who brings the dog back to him. Generally they only offer fifty crowns reward. I knew a man who earned his living that way. He'd steal a dog, then look in the lost, stolen, or strayed advertisements and go to the owner's address. Once he stole a fine black Pomeranian and as the owner didn't advertise, he thought he'd put an advertisement in the papers himself. So he had a whole five crowns' worth, and at last some fellow came along and said it was his dog that he'd lost, but he thought it wouldn't be any use looking for the animal because he didn't trust people's honesty. But now he could see that there were a few honest people left and he was very glad of it. And he said that it was against his principles to reward honesty, but as a slight token of his appreciation he'd give him a copy of his book on cultivating flowers in home and garden. My friend took this black Pomeranian by the hind legs and hit this chap on the head with him. Ever since that time he's given up advertising in the papers. He'd rather sell the dogs to the knacker if nobody wants to advertise for 'em."

"You go and lie down, Schweik," ordered the lieutenant. "You'd go on driveling away till the morning, if I'd let you."

He also went to bed, and in the night he dreamed that Schweik had stolen also the horse belonging to the heir apparent, had brought it to him, and that during an inspection the heir apparent had recognized the horse when he, the unfortunate Lieutenant Lukash, was riding on it in front of his company.

In the morning the lieutenant felt as if he had been on the spree all night, in the course of which he had been knocked about. He was weighed down by a nightmare feeling which he could not shake off. Then, exhausted by his horrible dream, he fell into a doze from which he was aroused by a knocking at the door. Schweik's good-humored face peeped in, and he asked when he was to wake the lieutenant up.

The lieutenant moaned, "Get out, you blithering jackass. This is too terrible for words."

And when he was up and Schweik brought him his breakfast, the lieutenant was taken aback by another of Schweik's questions. "Beg to report, sir, would you like me to get you a dog, sir?"

"I'll tell you what, Schweik. I've a damned good mind to send you before a court-martial," said the lieutenant with a sigh, "but they'd only let you off, because I'll bet they've never come across such a ghastly idiot as you. Look at yourself in the glass. Doesn't it make you feel sick to see what a blithering jackass you look? You're the most appalling freak of nature I've ever seen. Now, be frank about it, Schweik. Don't you hate the sight of your own face?"

"Beg to report, sir, I do. In this glass I look sort of lopsided, like. This glass wasn't properly cut. That's like the curved glass they used to have at the Fun Palace, and when you looked at yourself in it, it made you want to spew. Mouth like that, head like a bilge pail, belly like a bombardier when he's boozed. Oh, a regular fright, I tell you, sir."

The lieutenant turned away, sighed, and came to the conclusion that this would be a fitting moment to attend to his coffee rather than to Schweik, who, however, was already puttering about in the kitchen. Lieutenant Lukash could hear him singing:

> *"We soldiers, we're a jolly crew,*
> *The girls all love us, that they do,*
> *We draw our pay, by night and day*
> *And everywhere we get our way."*

"You seem to get your way all right, you blighter," muttered the lieutenant and spat with disgust.

Schweik's head suddenly appeared in the doorway.

"Beg to report, sir, they've come for you from the barracks. You've got to go at once to the colonel. An orderly's just brought the message."

And he added confidentially, "It may be something to do with that dog."

"I know all about it," said the lieutenant, when the orderly was about to deliver his message.

He said it dejectedly and departed, with a withering glance at Schweik.

This was not an orderly-room affair, but something far worse. The colonel was sitting very glumly in his armchair when the lieutenant entered his office.

"Two years ago," said the colonel, "you applied to be transferred to the Ninety-first Regiment at Budejovice. Do you know where Budejovice is? On the Vltava, yes, the Vltava, and the Ohre or some such river flows into it just there. The town is large and, if I may say so, cheerful, and if I am not mistaken there is an embankment alongside the river. Do you know what an embankment is? It's a sort of rampart, built up above the water. Yes. However, that's neither here nor there. We once had maneuvers in the neighborhood."

The colonel was silent for a while and then, staring into his inkpot, passed on to another subject.

"You've upset that dog of mine. He won't eat anything. Look, there's a fly in the inkpot. Funny that a fly should fall into the inkpot in the winter. It's the result of slack discipline."

"Out with it, for God's sake, you bloody old idiot," thought the lieutenant.

The colonel stood up and paced to and fro in his office.

"I have given much thought to the question of how I ought to deal with you so that this may not occur again, and I remembered that you applied to be transferred to the Ninety-first Regiment. The supreme command informed me quite recently that there is a considerable shortage of officers in the Ninety-first Regiment, because they have all fallen victims to the Serbians. I give you my word of honor that within three days you will be in the Ninety-first Regiment at Budejovice, where drafts are being formed. You need not thank me. The army needs officers who . . ."

And being now at a loss as to what he should say next, he looked at his watch and remarked, "It's half past ten. It's high time for me to be off to the orderly room."

This concluded their pleasant chat, and the lieutenant heaved a sigh of profound relief as he left the office and proceeded to the officers' training school, where he announced that within a day or two he would be going to the front and was therefore arranging a farewell party.

On his return home he said to Schweik portentously, "Schweik, do you know what a draft is?"

"Beg to report, sir, when you're on draft it means you're going to be sent to the front."

"Exactly, Schweik," said the lieutenant solemnly, "and so allow me to inform you that you are going on draft with me. But don't you imagine you'll be able to get up to any of your silly tricks there. Well, are you glad?"

"Beg to report, sir, I'm as glad as I can be," replied the good soldier Schweik. "It'll be a grand thing if you and me was to fall together fighting for the Emperor and his family."

BOOK II

1.

Schweik's Misadventures on the Train

THERE were three passengers in a second-class compartment of the Prague-Budejovice express. Lieutenant Lukash, opposite whom an elderly and entirely bald gentleman was sitting, and Schweik, who was standing modestly in the corridor and was just preparing to listen to a fresh storm of abuse from Lieutenant Lukash, who, regardless of the presence of the bald-headed civilian, kept yelling at Schweik throughout the journey, that he was a Godforsaken idiot and similar things.

The cause of the trouble was a trifling matter, a slight discrepancy in the number of pieces of luggage that Schweik was looking after.

"One of our trunks has been stolen, you say," snarled the lieutenant at Schweik. "That's a fine thing to tell anyone, you jackass."

"Beg to report, sir," announced Schweik softly, "it has been stolen, all the same. There's a lot of crooks knocking about at railway stations, and I expect one of them most likely took a fancy to your trunk and then he most likely took advantage of my back being turned when I left the luggage to come and tell you that the luggage was all right. He must have pinched that trunk just at a moment when the coast was clear. They're always on the lookout for a chance like that. Two years ago, at the northwestern station, they stole a young lady's perambulator with a baby girl wrapped up inside, and they went and handed the baby over at the police station in our street, where they said they'd found it left in a doorway. And then the papers called that poor young lady an inhuman monster."

And Schweik declared with emphasis, "People always have pinched things at railway stations and they always will. You just can't get away from it."

"It strikes me, Schweik," observed the lieutenant, "that you'll come to a very bad end. I still can't make out whether you only act the fool or whether you were born a fool. What was in that trunk?"

"Nothing at all, sir," replied Schweik, with his eyes glued to the bald head of the civilian, who was sitting opposite to the lieutenant and who appeared to be taking no interest whatever in the matter, but was reading the *Neue Freie Press*. "All that was in that trunk was a looking glass from the bedroom and an iron clothes hanger from the passage, so that we didn't really lose anything, because the looking glass and the hanger belonged to the landlord."

Seeing the lieutenant make a very wry face, Schweik continued in an affable tone, "Beg to report, sir, that I never knew beforehand that they'd pinch that trunk, and as regards the looking glass and the hanger, I sent word to the landlord that we'd let him have them back when we come home from the war. There's plenty of looking glasses and hangers in the enemy countries, so we needn't be out of pocket with the landlord. As soon as we take a town—"

"Shut up, Schweik," the lieutenant shouted. "I'll deal with you when we get to Budejovice. Do you know I'm going to have you locked up?"

"Beg to report, sir, I don't," said Schweik blandly. "You never mentioned anything to me about it before, sir."

The lieutenant gritted his teeth, sighed, took a copy of the *Bohemia* from his pocket, and began to read news about great victories, the exploits of the German submarine "E" in the Mediterranean, and when he had come to a report about a new German invention for blowing cities up by means of special triple detonating bombs dropped from airplanes, he was interrupted by the voice of Schweik, who was addressing the bald-headed gentleman.

"Excuse me, guv'nor, but ain't you Mr. Purkrábek, agent of the Slavia Bank?"

When the bald-headed gentleman made no reply, Schweik said to the lieutenant, "Beg to report, sir, I once read in the paper that the average man has sixty thousand to seventy thousand hairs on his head and that many examples show black hair is thinner as a rule."

And he continued remorselessly, "Then there was a doctor who said that loss of hair was due to mental disturbance during confinements."

But now a dreadful thing happened. The bald-headed gentleman jumped toward Schweik and shouted, *"Marsch heraus, du Schweinskerl,"* [1] and having hustled him into the corridor, returned to the carriage, where he gave the lieutenant a little surprise by introducing himself.

Evidently there had been a mistake. The bald-headed man was not Mr. Purkrábek, agent of the Slavia Bank, but merely Major General von Schwarzburg. The major general was just proceeding in mufti on a series of garrison inspections and was now about to pay a surprise visit to Budejovice.

He was the most fearsome inspector general who had ever walked the earth, and if he found anything amiss, the following dialogue would ensue between him and the garrison commandant:

"Have you got a revolver?"

"Yes, sir."

"All right, then. If I were in your place, I'd know what to do with it. This isn't a garrison, it's a pigsty."

And, as a matter of fact, there were always a certain number who shot themselves after one of his inspections, whereupon Major General von Schwarzburg would always observe with satisfaction, "That's the style! That's what I call a soldier."

It looked as if he disliked anyone to remain alive after his inspection. He had a mania for transferring officers to the most unpleasant places. On the slightest pretext, an officer was already saying goodbye to his garrison and was on his way to the frontiers of Montenegro or to some drink-sodden, forlorn outpost in the filthy wilds of Galicia.

[1] "Get out of it, you dirty swine."

200

He now said to Lieutenant Lukash, "Where did you attend the cadet school?"

"At Prague."

"So you attended a cadet school and are not aware that an officer is responsible for his subordinate? That's a nice state of affairs. And then you carry on a conversation with your orderly as if he were a close friend of yours. You allow him to talk without being asked. That's an even nicer state of affairs. In the third place, you allow him to insult your superior officers. And that caps all. What is your name?"

"Lukash."

"And what regiment are you in?"

"I was—"

"I'm not asking where you were but where you are."

"In the Ninety-first Regiment, sir. They transferred me—"

"Oh, they transferred you, did they? Quite right, too. It won't do you any harm to get to the front as soon as possible with the Ninety-first Regiment."

"That's already settled, sir."

The major general now held a lecture about how, of recent years, he had observed that officers talk to their subordinates in a familiar manner and this he held to be a dangerous tendency, inasmuch as it promoted the spread of democratic principles. The private soldier must keep himself to himself, he must tremble before his superior officer, he must fear him. Officers must keep the rank and file at a distance of ten paces from them and not allow them to think independently or, indeed, to think at all. There was a time when officers put the fear of God into the rank and file, but nowadays—

The major general made a hopeless gesture with his hand.

"Nowadays the majority of officers absolutely coddle the rank and file. That's all I wanted to say."

The major general picked up his newspaper again and engrossed himself in it. Lieutenant Lukash, as white as a sheet, went out into the corridor to settle accounts with Schweik.

He found him by the window, looking as blissful and contented as a baby a month old who has drunk its fill and is now dropping off to sleep.

The lieutenant stopped, beckoned to Schweik, and pointed to an empty compartment. He entered at Schweik's heels and closed the door.

"Schweik," he said solemnly, "the time has now come for

you to get the biggest hiding on record. What on earth did you interfere with that bald-headed gentleman for? Do you know that's Major General von Schwarzburg?"

"Beg to report, sir," announced Schweik, with the air of a martyr, "never in my life have I had the least intention of insulting anyone and it's news to me about him being a major general. As true as I stand here, he's the living image of Mr. Purkrábek, agent of the Slavia Bank. He used to come to our pub and once, when he fell asleep at a table, some joker wrote on his bald head with a copying-ink pencil: 'Please note our scheme for safeguarding your children's future as per Schedule III-c enclosed.' Well, they all cleared off, and I was left alone with him, and it was just my luck that when he woke up and saw himself in the glass, he didn't half get ratty and he wanted to give me a good hiding, too."

The word "too" glided with such a touchingly gentle accent of reproach from Schweik's lips that the lieutenant let his arm drop.

But Schweik continued, "There was no need for that gentleman to get into such a wax over a little mistake like that. It's an absolute fact he's supposed to have sixty thousand to seventy thousand hairs, like the average man has, just as the article said. It never struck me there was such a thing as a bald-headed major general. Well, that's what they call a tragic mistake, the same as anybody might make when he passes a remark and somebody else takes it in a wrong way without giving him a chance to explain. I used to know a tailor who—"

Lieutenant Lukash gave one more look at Schweik and then left the compartment. He returned to his former seat, and after a few minutes Schweik's guileless countenance appeared in the doorway. "Beg to report, sir, we'll be at Tábor in five minutes. The train stops there for five minutes. Wouldn't you care to order a little snack of something? Years and years ago they used to have very good—"

The lieutenant jumped up furiously and in the corridor he said to Schweik, "Let me tell you once more that the less I see of you, the better I shall like it. If I had my way I'd never set eyes on you again, and you can take it from me that I won't if I can damn well help it. Don't let me see anything of you. Keep out of my sight, you blithering jackass, you."

"Very good, sir."

Schweik saluted, turned smartly to the right-about in the military manner, and then went to the end of the corridor, where he sat down in a corner on the guard's seat and entered into a conversation with a railwayman.

"There's a question I'd like to ask you, boss."

The railwayman, who evidently was in no mood for conversation, nodded listlessly.

"I used to know a chap named Hofmann," began Schweik, "and he always made out that these alarm signals never act, what I mean to say, that nothing would happen if you pulled this handle. To tell you the honest truth, I never gave the matter another thought, but as soon as I spotted this alarm outfit here, I thought I'd like to know what's what, like, in case I should ever need it."

Schweik stood up and accompanied the railwayman to the alarm brake marked "In case of danger."

The railwayman considered it his duty to explain to Schweik exactly what the alarm mechanism consisted of.

"He was right when he said you've got to pull this here handle, but he was kidding you when he made out it don't act. The train always stops, because this is connected with all the carriages and the engine. The alarm brake has to act."

While he was saying this, they both had their hands on the handle of the lever and then——how it happened must remain a mystery—they pulled it and the train stopped.

They were quite unable to agree as to who had actually done it and made the alarm signal work.

Schweik declared that he couldn't have done it, not being a guttersnipe.

"It's a fair marvel to me," he said good-humoredly to the guard, "why the train stopped so sudden. It was going, then all at once it stopped. I'm more upset about it than what you are."

A solemn gentleman took the guard's part and said he'd heard the soldier start a conversation about alarm signals.

On the other hand, Schweik kept harping upon his good name and insisted that it was no advantage to him for the train to be late, because he was on his way to the front.

"The station master'll tell you all about it," declared the guard. "This'll cost you twenty crowns."

Meanwhile the passengers could be seen climbing down from the carriages, the head guard blew a whistle, and a lady in a panic started running with a portmanteau across the railway track into the fields.

"It's well worth twenty crowns, that it is," said Schweik

203

stolidly, maintaining complete composure. "It's cheap at the price."

Just then the head guard joined the audience.

"Well, it's about time we made a move," said Schweik. "It's a nuisance when a train's late. If it was in peacetime it wouldn't matter so much, but now that there's a war on, all the trains are carrying troops, major generals, lieutenants, orderlies. It's a risky business being late like that. Napoleon was five minutes late at Waterloo and, emperor or no emperor, he got himself into a mess just the same."

At this moment Lieutenant Lukash pushed his way through the group. He was ghastly pale and all he could utter was the word "Schweik!"

Schweik saluted and explained: "Beg to report, sir, they're making out I stopped the train. The railway company have got very funny plugs on their emergency brakes. It's better to keep away from them or else something'll go wrong and they'll ask you to fork out twenty crowns, the same as they're asking me."

The head guard had already blown his whistle and the train was starting again. The passengers returned to their seats and Lieutenant Lukash, without another word, also went back to his compartment. The other guard remained with Schweik and the railwayman. He took out a notebook and began to draw up a report on the whole affair.

The railwayman gazed spitefully at Schweik, who coolly asked, "How long have you been working on the railway?"

As the railwayman did not reply, Schweik proceeded to explain that he had known a certain Frantisek Mlicek of Uhrineves near Prague who had also pulled an emergency brake and it had so scared him that he had lost his speech for a fortnight and only recovered it when he was paying a visit to a gardener named Vanek at Hostivar, and had a fight with someone there. "That happened," added Schweik, "in May, 1912."

The railwayman thereupon went and locked himself in the lavatory.

The guard now called upon Schweik to pay a fine of twenty crowns, as otherwise he would have to take him before the station master at Tábor.

"That's all right," said Schweik. "I like talking to educated people. It'll be a fair treat for me to see that stationmaster at Tábor."

204

When the train arrived at Tábor, Schweik with all due ceremony went to Lieutenant Lukash and said, "Beg to report, sir, I'm being taken before the station master."

Lieutenant Lukash did not reply. He had become completely indifferent to everything. It struck him that the best thing he could do was not to care a rap about anybody, whether it was Schweik or the bald-headed major general, and to sit quietly where he was, to leave the train at Budejovice, to report himself at the barracks, and to proceed to the front with a draft. At the front, if the worse came to the worst, he would be killed and thus get away from this appalling world in which such monstrosities as Schweik were knocking about.

When the train started again, Lieutenant Lukash looked out of the window and saw Schweik standing on the platform and engrossed in a solemn colloquy with the station master. Schweik was surrounded by a crowd of people in which several railway uniforms were visible.

Lieutenant Lukash heaved a sigh. It was not a sigh of pity. His heart felt lighter at the thought that Schweik had been left behind on the platform. Even the bald-headed major general did not seem to be quite such a horrid bugbear.

The train had long since puffed its way into Budejovice, but there was no diminution in the crowd of people around Schweik.

Schweik was asserting his innocence and had so convinced the assembly that one lady remarked, "They're bullying another soldier again."

The assembly accepted this view and a gentleman announced to the station master that he was prepared to pay Schweik's fine for him. He was convinced that the soldier had not done what he was accused of.

Then a police sergeant made his appearance and, having grabbed hold of a man in the crowd, led him away, saying, "What d'you mean by causing all this disturbance? If that's the way you want soldiers treated, how d'you expect Austria to win the war?"

Meanwhile, the worthy person who believed in Schweik's innocence had paid the fine for him and had taken Schweik into the third-class refreshment room, where he had treated him to beer. And having ascertained that all his papers, including his railway warrant, were in the possession of Lieutenant Lukash, he generously presented him with the sum of five crowns for a ticket and sundry expenses.

When he was leaving, he said confidentially to Schweik, "Look here, if you happen to get taken prisoner in Russia, remember me to Zeman, the brewer at Zdolbunov. I've written it down on a bit of paper for you. And keep your wits about you so as you won't have to stay long at the front."

"Don't you worry about that," said Schweik. "It's a good wheeze to see foreign parts for nothing."

Schweik stayed where he was, and while he was quietly drinking his way through the five crowns, the people on the platform who had not witnessed Schweik's interview with the station master and had only seen a crowd in the distance, were telling each other that a spy had been caught taking photographs of the railway station, but a lady contradicted this rumor by declaring that it wasn't a spy at all, but she had heard that a dragoon had struck an officer near the ladies' lavatory because the officer was following his (the dragoon's) sweetheart. These fantastic conjectures were brought to an end by the police, who cleared the platform. And Schweik went on quietly drinking; he wondered with a tender concern what Lieutenant Lukash had done when he reached Budejovice and found no signs of his orderly anywhere.

Before the departure of the slow train, the third-class refreshment room became packed with travelers, consisting mostly of soldiers belonging to the most varied units and nationalities. The tide of war had swept them into the hospital and now they were again leaving for the front to be wounded, mutilated, and tortured once more, so as to qualify for a wooden cross on their graves. One of these hapless wretches, who had just been discharged from the hospital after an operation, in a uniform stained with patches of blood and mud, came and sat down next to Schweik. He was undersized, skinny, woebegone. He put a small bundle on the table, took out a tattered purse, and counted his money.

Then he looked at Schweik and asked, *"Magyarul?"* [1]

"I'm a Czech," said Schweik. "Have a drink, mate."

"Nem tudon, baratom." [2]

"Never mind that, mate," urged Schweik, putting his full glass in front of the woebegone soldier. "Just you have a good drink of that."

He understood, drank, and said *"Kessenem szivesen"* by way of thanks. Then he went on examining the contents of his

[1] "[Do you speak] Hungarian?"
[2] "I don't understand, friend."

purse and ended with a sigh. Schweik realized that the Magyar would have liked to get himself some beer, but had not enough money, and so he ordered some for him, whereupon the Magyar again thanked him and began to explain something to Schweik with the help of gestures. He pointed to his wounded arm and said in an international language, "Piff, paff, puff."

Schweik nodded sympathetically and the undersized convalescent informed Schweik, by lowering his left hand to within half a yard from the floor, and then raising three fingers, that he had three little children.

"Nincs ham, nincs ham," he continued, by which he meant that they had nothing to eat at home, and he wiped tears from his eyes with the dirty sleeve of his military greatcoat, where the hole made by the bullet which had entered his body in the interests of the King of Hungary could still be seen.

It was not surprising that as a result of this entertainment Schweik gradually lost possession of his five crowns and that he slowly but surely cut himself off from Budejovice, since every glass of beer to which he treated himself and the Magyar convalescent lessened his chances of buying a railway ticket.

Another Budejovice train passed through the station and Schweik was still sitting at the table and listening to the Magyar, who repeated his "Piff, paff, puff! *Három gyermek* [3] *nincs ham, éljen."* He uttered the last word, when they clinked glasses.

"Drink away, old chap," replied Schweik. "Shift the booze. You Magyar blokes wouldn't treat us like that."

"Ihre Dokumente, vasi tokúment," a sergeant major of the military police now remarked to Schweik in German and broken Czech. He was accompanied by four soldiers with fixed bayonets. "You sit, *nicht fahren,* sit, drink, keep on drink," he continued in his elegant jargon.

"Haven't got none, *milacku,"* [4] replied Schweik. "Lieutenant Lukash of the Ninety-first Regiment took them with him and left me here in the station."

"Was ist das Wort: milacek?" [5] asked the sergeant major, turning to one of his soldiers, an old defense corps man, who replied:

"Milacek, das ist wie: Herr Feldwebel." [6]

[3] "Three children."
[4] "Darling."
[5] "What does '*milacek*' mean?"
[6] *"Milacek,* that's the same as sergeant major."

The sergeant major continued his conversation with Schweik. "Papers, every soldier without papers, lock up *auf Bahnhofsmilitarkommando, den lausigen Bursch, wie ein toller Hund.*" [7]

They took Schweik accordingly to the military transport headquarters. The guardroom was decorated with lithographs which at that time were being distributed by the War Office among all military departments. The good soldier Schweik was welcomed by a picture which, according to the inscription, represented Sergeant F. Hammel and Corporals Paulhart and Bachmayer of the Imperial and Royal 21st Artillery Regiment, encouraging their men to hold out.

The sergeant major now appeared on the scene and pointing to Schweik, told the corporal of the defense corps to take the lousy so-and-so to the lieutenant, as soon as he arrived.

"The lieutenant's larking about again with the telegraph operator at the station," explained the corporal after the sergeant had left. "He's been after her for the last fortnight and he's always in a hell of a temper when he gets back from the telegraph office. Says he: *Das ist aber eine Hure; sie will nicht mit mir schlafen.*" [8]

On this occasion too he was in a hell of a temper, and when, after an interval, he arrived, he could be heard banging books on the table.

"It's no use, chum, you've got to get it over. So in you go," said the corporal to Schweik in a sympathetic tone.

And he led Schweik into an office where behind a table littered with papers sat a small lieutenant who looked exceedingly fierce. When he saw Schweik with the corporal, he remarked "Aha!" in a significant manner.

Whereupon the corporal explained, "Beg to report, sir, this man was found in the station without any papers."

The lieutenant nodded as if to indicate that years and years ago he had guessed that precisely on that day and at that hour Schweik would be found in the station without papers, for anyone looking at Schweik at that moment could not help feeling convinced that it was quite impossible for a man of such appearance and bearing to have any papers on him. At that moment Schweik looked as if he had fallen from heaven or from some other planet and was now gazing with artless

[7] "In the military headquarters in the station, the lousy fellow, like a mad dog."
[8] "She is a whore; she doesn't want to sleep with me."

wonder at a new world in which he was being asked for papers, some species of nonsense hitherto unknown to him.

The lieutenant nodded as if to indicate that he should say something and he should be questioned about it.

At last he asked, "What were you doing in the station?"

"Beg to report, sir, I was waiting for the train to Budejovice, because I want to get to my regiment where I'm orderly to Lieutenant Lukash, but I got left behind on account of being taken to the station master to pay a fine through being suspected of stopping the express we were traveling in, by pulling the alarm signal."

"Here, I can't make head or tail of this," shouted the lieutenant. "Can't you say what you've got to say in a straightforward manner, without driveling away like a lunatic?"

"Beg to report, sir, that from the very first minute I sat down with Lieutenant Lukash in that train that was to take us to our Ninety-first Imperial Royal Infantry Regiment without any hanging about we had nothing but bad luck. First of all we lost a trunk, then by way of a change, there was a major general, a bald-headed cove—"

"Oh, good Lord!" sighed the lieutenant.

"Beg to report, sir, but I got to go into all this so as I can sort of get it off my chest and give you a proper idea of the whole business like a friend of mine used to say, a cobbler he was and his name was Petrlik, but he's dead now, well, before he began to give his boy a good walloping, he always told him to take his trousers down."

And while the lieutenant fumed, Schweik continued, "Well, somehow or other this bald-headed major got his knife into me at the very start, and Lieutenant Lukash, that's the officer I'm orderly to, he sent me out into the corridor. Then in the corridor I got accused of doing what I've told you. And while they were looking into it, I got left behind on the platform. The train was gone, the lieutenant with his trunks and his papers and with my papers was gone too, and there I was left in the lurch like an orphan, with no papers and no nothing."

Schweik gazed at the lieutenant with such a touching air of gentleness that the latter was quite convinced of the absolute truth of what he was hearing from the lips of this fellow who, to all appearances, was a congenital idiot. He now enumerated to Schweik all the trains which had left for Budejovice since the departure of the express, and he asked him why he had missed them as well.

"Beg to report, sir," replied Schweik, with a good-humored smile, "that while I was waiting for the next train, I got into more trouble through having a few drinks."

"I've never seen such a fool," pondered the lieutenant. "He owns up to everything. I've had plenty of them here and they all swear blind they've never done anything. But this chap comes up as cool as a cucumber and says: I lost all the trains through having a few drinks."

He summed up these considerations in a single sentence, with which he now addressed Schweik, "You're a degenerate. Do you know what it means when anyone's called a degenerate?"

"Beg to report, sir, down our way there was another degenerate. His father was a Polish count and his mother was a midwife. He was a crossing sweeper and in all the pubs he used to go to he made everyone call him 'Count.' "

The lieutenant decided that the time had now come to settle the matter once and for all. He therefore said in emphatic tones, "Now then, you blithering idiot, you fatheaded lout, go to the booking office, buy a ticket, and clear off to Budejovice. If I see any more of you, I'll treat you as a deserter. *Abtreten!*"

As Schweik did not move, but kept his hand at the salute at the peak of his cap, the lieutenant bellowed, "Quick march outside, *abtreten*, didn't you hear what I said? Corporal Palánek, take this driveling idiot to the booking office and buy him a ticket to Budejovice."

After a short interval Corporal Palánek again appeared at the lieutenant's office. Behind Palánek, through the open door, peeped Schweik's good-humored countenance.

"What is it now?"

"Beg to report, sir," whispered Corporal Palánek mysteriously, "he's got no money for a ticket and I've got none, either. They won't let him ride free because he's got no papers to show he's going to the regiment."

The lieutenant promptly delivered a judgment of Solomon to settle the quandary.

"Then let him walk there," he decided, "and when he gets there they can shove him in the clink for being late. We can't be bothered with him here."

"It's no use, chum," said Corporal Palánek to Schweik when they were outside the office again, "you'll have to walk to

Budejovice, old sport. We've got some bread rations in the guardroom. I'll give you some to take with you."

And half an hour later, when they had treated Schweik to black coffee and besides the bread rations had given him a packet of army tobacco to take with him to the regiment, he left Tábor at dead of night, singing a song, an old army song:

> *"When we're marching on our way,*
> *Marvelous it is to say—"*

And heaven knows how it happened that the good soldier Schweik, instead of turning southward toward Budejovice, went due west. He trudged through snow, wrapped up in his army greatcoat, like the last of Napoleon's guards returning from the march on Moscow, the only difference being that he sang blithely:

> *"Oh, I went out for a stroll, for a stroll*
> *Into the grassy meadows—"*

And in the stillness of the night it re-echoed among the snow-covered woods till the dogs began to bark in the village.

When he got tired of singing, Schweik sat down on a pile of gravel, lit his pipe, and after having a rest, trudged on, toward new adventures.

2.

Schweik's Anabasis

XENOPHON, the warrior of antiquity, tramped all over Asia Minor, and heaven knows where else, without any maps. The ancient Goths likewise achieved their expeditions without any topographical knowledge. An anabasis involves marching straight ahead, penetrating unknown regions, being surrounded by enemies who are on the lookout for a chance of wringing your neck. Anyone who has his head screwed on properly, like Xenophon or all the tribes of marauders who poured into Europe from the Lord knows where as far as the Caspian Sea or the Sea of Azov, can do miracles on the march.

When Caesar's legions were somewhere up in the remote north, which incidentally they had managed to reach without maps, they decided they would get back to Rome by a different road, so as to see a little more of the world. And they got there, too. Hence, probably, the saying that all roads lead to Rome.

In the same way all roads lead to Budejovice, a circumstance of which the good soldier Schweik was fully persuaded when instead of the region of Budejovice he beheld a village in the vicinity of Milévsko. But Schweik kept trudging on in a westerly direction and on the road between Kvetov and Vraz he met an old woman who was returning from church and who hailed him with the Christian salutation. "Good day, soldier, which way are you going?"

"I'm off to Budejovice to my regiment," replied Schweik. "I'm off to the war, Ma."

"But you're on the wrong road, soldier," said the old woman with alarm. "You'll never get there that way. If you keep straight on, you'll come to Klatovy."

"Well, I expect I can get to Budejovice from Klatovy," said Schweik with an air of resignation. "It's a tidy step, of course, especially when I'm in such a hurry to join my regiment, because it'd be rough luck on a man like me who wants to do his duty if I was to get into trouble for not turning up in good time."

The old woman looked at Schweik pityingly and said, "You wait in that thicket and I'll bring you some potato soup to warm you. You can see our cottage from here, just behind the thicket a little bit to the left. You can't go yonder past our village, the police are as thick as flies down that way. You go afterward as far as Malcin, but when you leave there, keep away from Cizová. The place swarms with police and they're on the watch for deserters. You go straight through the woods to Sedlec near Horaždovice. The policeman there's a decent fellow, he lets 'em pass through the village. Have you got any papers on you?"

"No, Ma."

"Well, don't go there, then. You better go to Radomyśl, but see you get there in the evening, because all the policemen are at the village inn by then. You'll come to a cottage lower down the road, painted blue, and you can ask there for Melicharek. That's my brother. Tell him I sent you and he'll show you how to get to Budejovice from there."

Schweik waited more than half an hour in the thicket for the old woman, and when he had warmed himself with the potato soup which the poor old woman brought him in a basin tied up in cloth to keep it from getting cold, she took from a bundle a hunk of bread and a piece of bacon which she slipped into Schweik's pocket, made the sign of the cross over him, and said that she had two grandsons at the front. She then repeated very carefully the names of the villages he was to pass through and those he was to avoid. Finally she took a crown-piece from her skirt pocket and gave it to him to buy himself some brandy with, because it was a long way to Radomyśl.

Schweik followed the route recommended by the old woman. When he got to Malcin he was joined by an itinerant concertina player whom he met at the village inn, where he was refreshing himself with brandy because it was a long way to Radomyśl. The concertina player thought Schweik was a deserter and offered to go with him to Horažďovice, where he had a married daughter, whose husband was also a deserter. The concertina player had evidently had a drop too much.

"She's got her husband hidden away in a stable for the last two months, and she'll hide you there, too, till the war's over," he urged Schweik, "and with two of you there, it'll make things more cheerful for both."

When Schweik politely declined this offer, the concertina player flew in a temper and threatened to denounce Schweik to the police at Cizová. He then made off across the fields.

When Schweik reached Radomyśl toward evening, he made his way to Melicharek and gave him the old woman's message. But Melicharek was not at all pleased. He kept asking Schweik for his papers.

"It's all very well," he grumbled, "for a chap like you to run away from the army. You shirk your duty and then you go traipsing about the country, picking up whatever you can lay your hands on. If there was nothing against you, you'd show your papers without beating about the bush and saying you haven't got—"

"That's all right, Dad. Goodbye."

"Goodbye to you and let's hope the next man you meet'll be a bit greener than me."

When Schweik went out into the darkness, the old man still went on muttering to himself.

"He says he's going to Budejovice to join his regiment. From Tábor. And the vagabond goes first to Horažďovice and then to Pisek. Why, drat me if he ain't going round the blessed world!"

Schweik walked on nearly all night, till somewhere near Putim he came across a haystack in a field. He was pulling the straw away when he heard a voice at his elbow, "What regiment are you from? Where are you going?"

"The Ninety-first. I'm off to Budejovice."

"What for?"

"My officer's there."

Close at hand could be heard laughter, proceeding not from one but three. When the mirth subsided, Schweik asked from what regiment they were. He discovered that two were from the 35th and one was from the artillery, also at Budejovice. The men of the 35th had escaped a month previously from a draft, and the artillery man had been on his travels ever since his mobilization. Putim was his home and the haystack belonged to him. At night he always slept there. The day before he had found the other two in the woods, and had taken them with him to his haystack.

They all hoped that the war would be over in a month or two. They imagined that the Russians had practically reached Budapest and Moravia. That was the general belief at Putim. In the morning before daybreak, the dragoon's mother would bring them breakfast. The men of the 35th would then proceed to Strakonice, because one of them had an aunt there and she knew someone in the hills who owned a sawmill where they could easily hide.

"And *you* can come with us if you like," they suggested to Schweik. "Tell your officer to go to hell."

"That's not so easy," replied Schweik, and burrowed out a place for himself well inside the haystack.

When he woke up in the morning, they had all gone, and someone, apparently the dragoon, had left a hunk of bread for him to take away.

Schweik trudged on through the woods, and near Steken he encountered an old tramp, who invited him to have a swig of brandy as if he had known him for years.

"Don't go about in those togs," he warned Schweik. "That there uniform'll land you, as like as not, in a devil of a mess. It fairly stinks of police around here, and you can't do any cadging while you've got that on. The police don't worry us like what they used to. It's only you chaps they're after now.

"It's only you chaps they're after now," he repeated, with such insistence that Schweik thought he had better say nothing about the 91st Regiment. Let him go on thinking that Schweik was what he took him for. Why destroy the good old fellow's illusions?

"And where are you off to?" asked the tramp presently,

when they had both lit their pipes and were walking slowly through the village.

"To Budejovice."

"Holy Moses!" said the tramp in alarm. "If you go there, they'll collar you before you know where you are. Why, you won't have the ghost of a chance. What you want is a suit of civvy clothes, with plenty of stains on 'em. Nice and dirty. Then you can pass yourself off as a cripple. But don't you be afraid. Now we'll hoof it to Strakonice, Volyne, Dub, and I bet you what you like we'll manage to lay our hands on a suit of civvies. Down Strakonice way there's plenty of mugs and pious people who don't lock their doors at night, and in the daytime they don't even shut 'em. In the winter they go to have a bit of a chat with one of their neighbors, and there's a suit of civvies for you on the spot. What do you want? You've got some boots. All you want is a few more togs. Is your army coat an old one?"

"Yes."

"Then you can stick to it. You can wear that all right among the yokels. You only want a pair of breeches and a coat. When we've got hold of that civvy suit we'll sell the breeches and coat you're wearing now. Herman the Jew, at Vodnany, he buys up government stuff and sells it again in the villages.

"Today we'll make a start from Strakonice," he continued, elaborating his plan. "Four hours hoofing it from here'll bring us to a place where an old shepherd, a pal of mine, hangs out. We can stay there overnight and in the morning we'll get to Strakonice and find those togs for you somewhere in the neighborhood."

The shepherd turned out to be an affable old fellow who could remember the tales his grandfather used to tell about the French wars.

"Yes, me lads," he explained, when they were sitting around a stove, on which potatoes were cooking in their jackets, "in those days my granddad, he done a bunk the same as this soldier here. But they copped him at Vodnany and walloped his backside for him till the skin peeled off in strips. And he got off lightly, he did. Why, there was a chap down Protivin way, he was the granddad of old Jaresh, the pondkeeper, he got a dose of powder and shot at Pisek for slinging his hook. And before they put the bullets through him on the ramparts at Pisek, he had to run the gauntlet and got six hundred whacks with sticks. When they'd finished with him, he was glad of the bullets to put him out of his misery. And when did you do a bunk?" he asked Schweik.

"When they were marching us off to barracks, just after I'd been called up," replied Schweik, who realized that he must not shake the old shepherd's faith in him.

"Did you climb over the wall?" inquired the shepherd eagerly, no doubt recalling that his grandfather had told him how he too had climbed over the wall of the barracks.

"Couldn't manage it any other way."

"And did the sentries fire on you?"

"Not half they didn't."

"And where are you off to now?"

"He's fair daft, that's what he is," the tramp replied on Schweik's behalf. "He wants to go to Budejovice of all places. That's the way a young chap without experience does for himself. I shall have to teach him a thing or two. First of all we're going to scrounge some civvy clothes, and then it'll be all right. We'll keep ourselves going till the spring, and then we'll do a bit of farm work somewhere. People are going to have a rough time of it this year, and a chap told me that they're going to nab all the tramps and make them work in the fields. So it strikes me we may as well go of our own free will. There won't be many men left. They'll be done in wholesale."

"You think it'll all be over this year?" asked the shepherd. "Ah, you're right there, lad. The old wars, they was long wars, if you like. Napoleon's wars, and afterward the Swedish wars, as I've heard say, and the Seven Years' War."

The water containing the potatoes now began to boil and after a short silence the old shepherd said in prophetic tones, "But he won't win this war, our Emperor won't, me lads. He hasn't got the people on his side. You ought to hear 'em when they get together at Skocice. That'd show you. After this war, they say, there ain't going to be any more emperors and they'll help themselves to the big royal estates. The police have collared a few of 'em for that sort of talk. Ah, the police are having it all their own way now."

The shepherd then strained the potatoes and poured sour sheep's milk into the dish. After a hasty meal, they soon went to sleep in the warm shanty.

In the night Schweik dressed quietly and crept out. The moon was rising in the east and in its encouraging light

Schweik stepped out eastward, saying to himself, "I'm bound to get to Budejovice sooner or later."

When he emerged from the woods he saw a town on the right, and he therefore turned aside in a more northerly direction. After that he went due south, where another town became visible (this was Vodnany). He adroitly kept clear of it by cutting across the fields, and the morning sun welcomed him on the snowy slopes above Protivin.

"Straight ahead, straight ahead," said the good soldier Schweik to himself. "Duty calls. I must get to Budejovice."

But by an unfortunate chance, after leaving Protivin, instead of bearing to the south for Budejovice, Schweik turned his steps northward in the direction of Pisek. Toward noon he saw a village close by and as he walked down a small hill, he thought to himself, "This'll never do. I'd better ask the way to Budejovice."

And on entering the village he was extremely surprised to see a board on the first cottage bearing the inscription "Putim."

"Crikey," sighed Schweik. "Why, I'm back again in Putim. That's where I slept in the haystack."

He was, however, not at all surprised when from a white cottage behind a pond a policeman stepped forth, like a spider lurking in its web. He went straight up to Schweik and said, "Where are you off to?"

"To Budejovice, to join my regiment."

The policeman gave a sarcastic smile. "But you're coming away from Budejovice. You've left Budejovice behind you," and he drew Schweik into the police station.

"Well, we're pleased to see you," began the police sergeant of Putim, who had the reputation of being very tactful, but at the same time very shrewd. He never bullied persons who were arrested or detained, but subjected them to the kind of cross-examination which made even the innocent admit their guilt.

"Sit down and make yourself at home," he continued. "I expect you're tired after your long tramp. Now tell us where you're going to."

Schweik repeated that he was going to Budejovice to join his regiment.

"Then you've missed your way," said the police sergeant with a smile, "because you're coming from Budejovice, as I'll show you presently. There's a map of Bohemia hanging above your head. Now just you have a look at it. Here, to the south of us, is Protivin. To the south of Protivin is Hluboká, and to the south of that there's Budejovice. So you see you're not going to Budejovice but coming away from it."

The police sergeant gazed indulgently at Schweik, who replied in a calm and dignified tone, "But I am going to Budejovice for all that."

It was more significant than Galileo's famous remark, "But it does move nevertheless," because he must have said it in a fit of exasperation.

"Now, look here," said the police sergeant to Schweik, still in a very friendly tone, "I'll prove to you that you're wrong, and in the end you'll realize that every denial only makes it more difficult to own up."

"You're right there," said Schweik. "Every denial only makes it more difficult to own up."

"There you are; now you can see it for yourself. I want you to tell me quite frankly where you came from when you started off for this Budejovice of yours. I say 'of yours' deliberately, for it seems evident that there must be another Budejovice situated somewhere to the north of Putim and not yet marked in any map."

"I started from Tábor."

"And what were you doing at Tábor?"

"I was waiting for the train to Budejovice."

"Why didn't you take the train to Budejovice?"

"Because I hadn't got a ticket."

"And why didn't they give you a free railway warrant? You're entitled to one, being a soldier."

"Because I hadn't got any papers on me."

"Aha, there you are," said the police sergeant triumphantly to one of the constables. "He's not such a fool as he pretends to be. He's beginning to get himself in a nice muddle."

The police sergeant began again, as if he had not heard Schweik's last reply about his papers. "So you left Tábor. Where did you make for then?"

"Budejovice."

The expression on the police sergeant's face became somewhat stern and his gaze fell on the map. "Can you show us on the map which way you went to get to Budejovice?"

"I can't remember all the places. But I remember that I've been in Putim once before."

The whole staff of the police station eyed each other significantly, and the police sergeant continued, "So you were at the railway station in Tábor. Have you anything in your pockets? Let's see what you have."

When they had searched Schweik thoroughly and found nothing except a pipe and some matches, the police sergeant asked him, "Tell me why it is you've got nothing whatever in your pockets."

"Because I don't need anything."

"Heavens alive!" sighed the police sergeant. "You're a devil of a nuisance. You said you'd been in Putim once. What did you do here the first time?"

"I went around Putim on my way to Budejovice."

"You see what a muddle-headed fellow you are. You yourself say that you were going to Budejovice, and now we just have made it perfectly clear to you that you're coming away from Budejovice."

"I suppose I must have walked around in a circle, like."

The police sergeant again exchanged a meaning glance with the whole of his staff.

"In a circle, eh? It strikes me you've been loitering about the neighborhood. Did you stay long in the railway station at Tábor?"

"Till the last train left for Budejovice."

"And what did you do there?"

"Had a bit of a chat with some soldiers."

Another significant exchange of glances between the police sergeant and his staff.

"And what did you talk to them about? What sort of questions did you ask them?"

"I asked them what regiment they were from and where they were going to."

"I see. And didn't you ask them how many men there are in the regiment and how it is divided up?"

"No, I didn't ask them that, because I know it all inside out. Learned it years ago."

"So you know a lot about our army arrangements?"

"I should think I do."

And then, glancing around at his subordinates, the police sergeant triumphantly played his trump card. "Can you speak Russian?"

"No."

The police sergeant nodded to his right-hand man and when they were both in the adjoining room, he rubbed his hands as he gloated over the thoroughness and certainty of his triumph, and declared: "Did you hear that? He doesn't speak Russian. The chap's as artful as a cartload of monkeys. He's admitted everything except the most important point. Tomorrow we'll hand him over to the district superintendent at Pisek. The secret of dealing with wrongdoers is to keep your wits about you and to treat 'em kindly. Did you see how I put him through it? A fair deluge of questions. You wouldn't think he was that sort, would you? He looks like a village idiot, but those are just the people you've got to be most cautious with. Well, just put him under lock and key and I'll go and draw up a report about it."

And later in the afternoon the police sergeant with an enraptured smile was drawing up a report every sentence of which contained the word *"Spionageverdächtig."* [1]

As he wrote on, the situation became clearer and clearer, and when he had concluded in his queer bureaucratic German, "I therefore herewith beg to report that the enemy officer this day will be handed over to the district police superintendent at Pisek." He smiled at what he had accomplished and called out to his right-hand man, "Have you given the enemy officer anything to eat?"

"In accordance with your instructions, sir, we only supply food to persons who are brought up and cross-examined before twelve o'clock."

"This is a very exceptional case," said the police sergeant impressively. "This is a higher officer, one of the staff. The Russians don't use lance corporals for spying jobs. You can send out to The Tomcat to get him some lunch. Then let them make some tea with rum in it, and send the whole lot here. Don't say who it's for. In fact, don't tell anyone who we've got here. That's a military secret. And what's he doing now?"

"He asked for a bit of baccy. He's sitting in the guardroom and looks as pleased as if he was at home. 'It's nice and warm here,' he says, 'and your stove don't smoke. I feel quite snug here. If your stove was to smoke, you should have the chimney swept. But only in the afternoon, never when the sun's right on top of the chimney,' he says."

"Ah, that only shows his artfulness," said the police sergeant in a voice brimful of satisfaction. "He pretends not to mind. All the same, he knows he's going to be shot. You can't help respecting a man like that, even though he is an

[1] Suspected of espionage.

enemy. There he is, practically face to face with death, as you might say. I'm not so sure whether we'd have the nerve to do it. We might shilly-shally and then back out of it. But there he sits and says, 'It's nice and warm here and your stove don't smoke.' That's what I call pluck. Yes, sir. A man's got to have nerves of steel, he's got to be full of guts, before he can do a thing like that. Guts and pluck. We could do with a little of it in Austria. Not that we haven't got any heroes. I was reading in the paper about— But here we are, wasting our time talking. Just go down and order that meal and on your way send him in to me."

When Schweik was brought in, the police sergeant with an affable nod invited him to sit down, and then asked him whether he had any parents. Schweik said that he hadn't.

It at once occurred to the police sergeant that it was better that there was nobody to weep over the fate of this hapless man. With this thought in his mind he gazed at Schweik's good-humored countenance and suddenly, in a burst of cordiality, he patted him on the shoulder, bent down toward him and asked in a paternal tone, "Well, and how do you like being in Bohemia?"

"First-rate," replied Schweik. "I've never met such nice people anywhere."

The police sergeant nodded assent.

"Yes, the people here are very kind and pleasant. A little thieving or a bit of a row now and then, but that doesn't amount to much. I've been here for the last fifteen years, and when I come to reckon things out, there's only three quarters of a murder every year."

"Do you mean a murder that they didn't make a proper job of?" asked Schweik.

"No, I don't mean that. In the last fifteen years we've only had eleven murders. Five of them were with robbery and the rest were just ordinary ones that hardly count."

The police sergeant paused for a moment, and then proceeded to apply his method of cross-examination.

"And what were you going to do at Budejovice?"

"Join the Ninety-first Regiment."

The police sergeant told Schweik to return to the guardroom, and quick, before he forgot it, he added to the report he was drawing up for the superintendent of police at Pisek: "He knows the Czech language perfectly and wanted to enter the Ninety-first Infantry Regiment at Budejovice."

The police sergeant gleefully rubbed his hands, delighted at the abundance of the material he had collected and at the detailed results achieved by his method of inquiry. He smiled with satisfaction and from a pigeonhole in his desk he took out a schedule of secret instructions issued by the chief of police in Prague. It was marked with the usual "Strictly Confidential" and read as follows:

All police authorities are urgently reminded that they must keep an extremely careful watch on all persons passing through the area of their jurisdiction. The operations of our troops in eastern Galicia have caused a number of Russian units, who have crossed the Carpathians, to occupy positions within the territories of our Empire, thus shifting the battle front further to the west of the Monarchy. This new situation has made it possible for Russian spies, owing to the instability of the battle front, to penetrate further into the territories of our Monarchy, especially in Moravia and Silesia, from which, according to confidential reports, large numbers of Russian spies have proceeded to Bohemia. It has been ascertained that among them there are many Czechs from Russia, trained in Russian military academies and with a perfect knowledge of the Czech language, who seem to be particularly dangerous persons, since they can, and undoubtedly do, spread treasonable propaganda among the Czech population. The police authorities are therefore instructed to detain all suspicious persons and in particular to keep a strict watch on localities in the neighborhood of military garrisons, centers, and stations through which troop trains pass. Persons thus detained are to be immediately subjected to a cross-examination and handed over to the appropriate higher authorities.

The police sergeant again smiled contentedly, and put the secret schedule back again into the pigeonhole labeled "Secret Instructions." There were many of them and and they had been drawn up by the Ministry of the Interior in cooperation with the Ministry of Defense. The police headquarters at Prague were kept busy all day long duplicating and distributing them. They included:

Instructions for keeping in touch with the disposition of the local population.
Hints how, by means of conversation, to trace the effects

of the news from the front upon the disposition of the local population.

Questionnaire on the attitude of the local population toward the war loans and subscriptions.

Questionnaire on the feeling among those called up and about to be called up.

Questionnaire on the feeling among members of the local council.

Instructions for an immediate inquiry to ascertain what political parties the local population belongs to and in what numerical proportions the individual parties are represented in this respect.

Instructions for keeping in touch with the activities of the leaders of the local political parties.

Questionnaire on the manner in which newspapers, periodicals, and pamphlets reach the respective police areas.

Orders relating to an inquiry to discover the associates of persons suspected of disloyalty and to ascertain how their disloyalty is exhibited.

Orders relating to methods for securing informers from among the local population.

Orders for paid informers from among the local population duly registered for service.

Every day brought fresh orders, regulations, questionnaires, and instructions. Swamped by this glut of contrivances which emanated from the Austrian Ministry of the Interior, the police sergeant was harassed with large quantities of arrears, and he dealt with the questionnaires in a stereotyped manner by replying that everything was all right and the loyalty among the local population was up to the I-a standard. The Austrian Ministry of the Interior had devised the following standards to indicate degrees of loyalty and devotion to the Monarchy: I-a, I-b, I-c; II-a, II-b, II-c; III-a, III-b, III-c; IV-a, IV-b, IV-c. The latter standard on the "a" grade denoted treason and gallows, "b" implied internment, while "c" meant observation and imprisonment.

The police sergeant often shook his head despairingly when he saw the accumulation of documents and circulars which relentlessly assailed him with every post. As soon as he saw the familiar envelopes stamped "Official, paid," his heart sank, and in the night, when he was brooding over the whole business, would come to the conclusion that he was not going to survive the war. He was at his wits' end through being bombarded day after day by inquiries from police headquarters, demanding the reason why he had not replied to questionnaire number $\dfrac{72345}{721 \text{ alf}}$d, or what he had done with regard to instructions number $\dfrac{88892}{822 \text{ gfeh}}$z, or what particular results had accrued from orders number $\dfrac{123456}{19222 \text{ bfr}}$V, and so on.

Yes, the police sergeant had passed many sleepless nights. He was continually awaiting inspections, investigations. He used to dream about ropes and about being led to the gallows. And in his dream, just before he was going to be hanged, the Minister of National Defense in person asked him, "Sergeant, what have you done with the reply to circular number $\dfrac{1789678}{23792}$X. Y. Z.?"

But now the outlook was far rosier. The police sergeant did not doubt that the district superintendent of police would tap him on the shoulder and say, "Congratulations, Sergeant." In his mind's eye he saw other delightful prospects, such as distinctions, rapid promotion, and a wide recognition of his efficiency in tracking down wrongdoers, which would pave the way to a brilliant career.

He called his right-hand man and asked him, "Did that lunch arrive?"

"They brought him some smoked pork with cabbage and dumplings. There wasn't any soup left. He's had some tea and wants some more."

"Then get it for him," was the sergeant's liberal decision, "and when he's had it, bring him to me."

"Well, did you enjoy it?" asked the sergeant, when half an hour later Schweik, who had eaten to his heart's content, was brought to him.

"Oh, it wasn't so bad, only there ought to have been a little more cabbage. Still, it can't be helped—I know you wasn't expecting me. The smoked pork was well done. I wouldn't mind betting it was home-cured stuff. And the tea with rum did me a world of good."

The sergeant looked at Schweik and began, "They drink a lot of tea in Russia, don't they? And have they got rum, too?"

"You can get rum all over the world."

"Now don't wriggle out of it," thought the sergeant to himself. "You ought to have been more careful about what you said before." And bending over toward Schweik, he asked in a confidential manner, "I suppose there are pretty girls in Russia, eh?"

"There are pretty girls all over the world."

"Ah, my fine fellow," thought the sergeant, "now you'd like to get out of it, wouldn't you?" And he rapped out like a machine gun, "What did you want to do in the Ninety-first Regiment?"

"I wanted to go to the front."

The sergeant gazed with satisfaction at Schweik and remarked, "That's right. That's the best way of getting to Russia," and he thought to himself, beaming with delight, "That was a smart bit of brain work, that was."

He looked to see what effect his words had produced on Schweik, but all he could observe was unruffled composure.

"This chap doesn't move an eyelid," he reflected with a feeling of alarm. "That's his military training. If I was in his shoes and anyone was to say that to me, I'd feel pretty shaky about the knees."

"Tomorrow morning we're going to take you to Pisek," he announced with a casual air. "Have you ever been to Pisek?"

"Yes, in 1910, at the imperial maneuvers."

When he heard this answer the police sergeant's smile became still more winsome and triumphant. He was now thoroughly convinced that by this system of cross-examination he had surpassed himself.

"Did you go right through the maneuvers?"

"Not half I didn't, seeing that I was a footslogger."

And again, with the same tranquil air as before, Schweik gazed at the police sergeant, who wriggled with delight and could not refrain from rapidly entering this in his report. He called his right-hand man and told him to take Schweik away. Whereupon he completed his report thus:

His plan was as follows: Having wormed his way into the ranks of the 91st Infantry Regiment, he intended to volunteer for the front immediately and at the first opportunity he would then get into Russia, for he had observed that owing to the alertness of the authorities the return journey would otherwise be impossible. It can be readily understood that he would get on well in the 91st Regiment, for on his own admission, which was extracted from him after a lengthy cross-examination, he went right through the imperial maneuvers in the neighborhood of Pisek, as an infantryman, as far back as 1910. From that it is clear that he is extremely efficient in his own special branch. I may add that all the items of incriminating evidence were the result of my system of cross-examination.

The police sergeant then proceeded to the guardroom. He lit his pipe and gave Schweik tobacco to fill his with; the right-hand man put more coal on the fire, and amid the advancing winter twilight the police station was transformed into the coziest spot on the globe for a friendly chat.

But no one had anything to say. The police sergeant was following up a train of thought, and at last he turned to his right-hand man and said, "If you ask me, I don't think they ought to hang spies. A man who sacrifices his life for his duty, for his country, as you might say, is entitled to a more honorable end with powder and shot. What do you think?"

"Yes, that's the ticket. Shoot 'em, don't hang 'em," agreed the right-hand man. "Supposing we was told to go and find out how many machine guns the Russians have got in their machine-gun corps, we'd change our togs and go. And then if I got nabbed, would it be fair to hang me, as if I'd done someone in and robbed him?"

The right-hand man got so excited that he stood up and shouted, "I say he's got to be shot and buried with military honors."

"Yes, that's all right," Schweik chimed in. "The only trouble is that if a chap's smart enough, they can never prove anything against him."

"Oh, can't they!" declared the police sergeant with emphasis. "They can, if they're as smart as he is, and if they've got a method of their own. You'll have a chance of seeing that for yourself.

"Oh, yes, you'll see it for yourself," he repeated in a mild tone, and with an affable smile he added, "Nobody ever managed to bamboozle us, have they?" And he turned to his right-hand man.

The right-hand man nodded assent and remarked that people who did that sort of thing were playing a losing game and that it wasn't any use for a man to pretend he didn't care a damn, because the more he tried that dodge on, the more he gave himself away.

"Oh, you've got the hang of my method, that you have," declared the police sergeant proudly. "Yes, it's all very well to keep a cool head, but it's nothing more than a bubble, as you might say. And when it's only a bit of sham, it's a *corpus delicti*."

Whereupon, breaking off this disquisition on his theory, the police sergeant turned to his right-hand man and asked, "Well, what have we got for supper tonight?"

"Ain't you going out to The Tomcat for a meal, sir?"

This question confronted the police sergeant with another difficult problem which called for immediate settlement. Suppose this man were to take advantage of his temporary absence to escape? His right-hand man was reliable and cautious enough, although he had once let two tramps slip through his fingers.

"We'll send the old woman out to fetch our supper, and she can take a jug with her for the beer," was how the police sergeant handled the difficult problem. "It'll do the old girl good to stretch her legs a bit."

And the old girl who waited on them did, in fact, stretch her legs a bit. After supper there was a continual going and coming on the road between the police station and The Tomcat Inn. The extremely numerous traces of the old woman's very large boots on this line of communication bore witness to the fact that the police sergeant had consoled himself in full measure for his absence from The Tomcat. And when at last the old woman arrived at the taproom with the message that the police sergeant sent his best respects and would they please send him a bottle of brandy, the landlord's curiosity knew no bounds.

"Who've they got there?" replied the old woman. "Some suspicious man. Just before I left 'em, they was both holding their arms around his neck and the police sergeant, he was stroking his head and calling him his dear old pal and whatnot."

Later on, well after midnight, the police sergeant's right-hand man was reclining in full uniform on his truckle bed, sound asleep and snoring loudly. The police sergeant himself, on the other hand, with the remainder of the brandy at the bottom of the bottle, was holding his arms around Schweik's neck. Tears were flowing over his florid face, his beard was sticky with brandy, and he mumbled unsteadily, "You've got to admit the brandy in Russia ain't as good as this stuff. Then

228

I can toddle off to bed with an easy mind. You got to admit that like a man."

"No, that it ain't."

The police sergeant rolled on top of Schweik.

"It's a fair treat to hear you admit it. That's how a cross-examination ought to be. If I'm guilty, what's the good of denying it?"

He rose and staggered off with the empty bottle into his own room, muttering, "If I'd made only a sin-single sl-slip, it might have s-spoiled everything."

He then took his report out of his desk and endeavored to supplement it with the following material:

I must add that on the basis of paragraph 56 Russian brandy . . .

He made a blot, licked it up, and with a fatuous smile he flopped in full uniform onto his bed and slept like a log.

Toward morning the sergeant's right-hand man, who was lying on the bed by the opposite wall, started such a salvo of snoring, accompanied by a nasal buzzing, that it woke Schweik up. He left his bed, shook the right-hand man, and lay down again. The cocks then began to crow, and when the sun rose shortly afterward, the old woman, who had also overslept herself as a result of so much running to and fro on the previous night, arrived to light the fire. She found the door wide open and everyone plunged into profound slumber. The oil lamp in the guardroom was still smoking. The old woman raised an alarm, dragging Schweik and the right-hand man from their beds. To the latter she said, "You ought to be ashamed of yourself, that you did, going to sleep with all your clothes on as if you was so much cattle," and finally she ordered him in emphatic terms to go and wake up the sergeant, adding that they were a lot of lazy varmints to sleep the clock around like that.

"You're in nice company and no mistake," she muttered to Schweik, when the right-hand man had gone to wake the sergeant up. "A fine pair of boozers. They'd drink their shirts off their backs. They owes me my wages for the last three years, and if I says anything to 'em about it, the sergeant he answers me back. 'You'd better keep quiet,' he says, 'or I'll have you run in. We know your son's a poacher and sneaks wood from the private estates.' And for four blessed years they've been worrying the life out of me." The old woman heaved a sigh and went on grumbling. "You be careful with that there sergeant. He's an artful devil, he is, and a bigger rascal you never set eyes on. He bullies and locks up everybody he can."

It was a hard job to wake the police sergeant up. His right-hand man had all his work cut out to persuade him that it was morning. At last he stared about him, rubbed his eyes and began to remember what had happened the previous day. Suddenly a horrible idea struck him and with an unsteady glance at his right-hand man, he expressed it thus: "Has he slung his hook?"

"Not him. He's a regular sport."

The right-hand man began to walk to and fro. He looked out of the window, came back, tore a piece from a newspaper on the table and crumpled it into a pellet between his fingers. It was evident that he wanted to say something.

The police sergeant looked at him uneasily, and presently, anxious to make quite sure of what he could only guess at, he said, "Don't be afraid to get it off your chest. I suppose I must have carried on pretty badly again last night, eh?"

The right-hand man gazed reproachfully at his superior officer. "If you only knew, sir, the things you said to him yesterday. You did let yourself go and no mistake."

He bent down toward the police sergeant's ear and whispered, "You told him that the Czechs and the Russians was brothers, that the Grand Duke Nikolay Nikolayevitch would get to Bohemia by next week, that Austria wouldn't hold out, and that when he came up for trial he was to deny everything and just get them muddled up with some cock-and-bull story so as to keep things going until the Cossacks came and set him free. And then you said the Emperor was a knock-kneed old buffer who was going to peg out before very long and that the Kaiser was a skunk and that you'd send him some money so as he could have an easier time in prison, and a lot more things like that."

The right-hand man moved away from the police sergeant and continued, "I can remember all that because at first I wasn't very tight. Afterward I got a bit squiffy myself, so the Lord alone knows what you said then."

The police sergeant looked at his right-hand man. "And I can remember," he declared, "that you said we was no match for Russia, and then, right in front of the old woman, you yelled, 'Three cheers for Russia!'"

The right-hand man began to pace to and fro nervously.

"You yelled it at the top of your voice," said the police sergeant. "Then you just flopped across the bed and began to snore."

The right-hand man came to a standstill by the window, and drumming on the pane, he remarked, "You didn't mince your words either, in front of the old woman, and I remember you saying to her, 'Don't you forget that every emperor and king only thinks of their pockets and that's why they have wars.' And then you cleared off into the yard to spew."

"You do come out with some choice language, I must say," demurred the police sergeant. "And where did you get the fatheaded idea from that Nikolay Nikolayevitch was going to be King of the Czechs?"

"I don't remember that," murmured the right-hand man uneasily.

"I shouldn't think you would, considering you was blind to the wide, and when you wanted to go out, you crawled onto the stove instead of going through the door."

There was a lengthy silence. At last the police sergeant said, "I've always told you that booze is ruin. You can't stand it and yet you will drink it. Supposing that chap had done a bunk? A fine mess we'd have been in then. Holy Moses, my head don't half feel dizzy.

"I'll tell you what," continued the police sergeant. "If he hasn't done a bunk, that only shows how dangerous and artful he is. The thing's as plain as a pikestaff. Of course, when they come to cross-examine him, he'll swear blind that the place was open all night, that we was boozed, and that he could have cleared off if he'd been guilty. It's a good thing nobody'll believe a man with his record, and when we give our evidence under oath, we can say that it's a pack of lies from beginning to end, and that'll be another point against him. Not that one more or less makes any difference in his case. I only wish I hadn't got such a damned headache."

There was a pause. Then the police sergeant said, "Fetch the old woman here.

"Now just you listen to me," said the police sergeant to the old woman when she was brought in. He gave her a very stern look right between the eyes, and continued, "Go and get a crucifix that'll stand up, and bring it here."

From his desk he took two candles containing traces of the sealing wax with which he sealed up official documents, and when the old woman came scurrying in with the crucifix, he placed it between the two candles on the edge of the table, lit the candles, and said solemnly, "Sit down."

The terrified old woman sank down on a sofa and stared with frightened eyes at the police sergeant, the candles, and the crucifix. She was startled out of her wits, and beneath her apron her hands and knees could be seen trembling.

The police sergeant walked gravely twice around her, and then, coming to a standstill in front of her, he declared in a solemn voice, "Yesterday night you witnessed some very important things that happened here. I don't expect you've got enough intelligence to understand what it was all about. That soldier was a spy."

"My goodness gracious me!" exclaimed the old woman. "The Holy Virgin and—"

"Stop that row, will you? Now, we had to say all sorts of things to egg him on and get him to say something, too. Did you hear the funny things we said?"

"Yes, sir, if you please, sir, I did," said the old woman in a shaky voice.

"Now, the only reason we said all those funny things was to get him to own up. And we did, too. We made him tell us everything. We nabbed him fair and square."

The police sergeant interrupted his speech for a moment to adjust the wicks of the candles, and then he continued in solemn tones, and gazing sternly at the old woman. "You was there and so we let you into our secret. But it's an official secret. You mustn't breathe a word about it to a living soul. Not even on your deathbed, or there'll be no Christian burial for you."

"Holy Virgin!" moaned the old woman. "I wish I'd never set foot here. I'm that worried, I—"

"Hold your row, will you? Get up and stand in front of the crucifix. Now raise two fingers of your right hand. You're going to take an oath. Say it after me."

The old woman staggered to the table and kept on moaning, "Holy Virgin, I wish I'd never set foot here."

And from the cross the tortured countenance of Christ gazed down upon her, the candles became smoky, and everything seemed to her uncannily supernatural. She felt quite stunned, her knees quaked, her hands trembled. She raised her fingers and the police sergeant recited for her benefit in a solemn and emphatic voice, " 'I swear to God Almighty and

232

to you, Sergeant, that right up to the day of my death I will never breathe a word to anyone about what I have heard and seen here, even if anyone asks me. So help me God!'

"Now kiss the crucifix," ordered the police sergeant, when the old woman, amid immense sobs, had repeated the oath and crossed herself piously.

"That's right. Now take the crucifix back to where you borrowed it from and tell them I needed it for a cross-examination."

The old woman, now completely crushed, tiptoed out of the room with the crucifix, and through the window she could be seen continually looking back at the police station, as if she wanted to make sure that it was not a dream, but that she had really just been through a ghastly ordeal.

Meanwhile, the police sergeant was rewriting his report, which in the night he had supplemented with blots, and which, through having been licked, now looked as if it had been smeared with marmalade. He rearranged the whole thing and remembered there was one detail he hadn't asked about.

He therefore had Schweik sent for and inquired of him, "Can you take photographs?"

"Yes."

"Why haven't you got a camera with you?"

"Because I haven't got one," was Schweik's clear and straightforward answer.

"But if you had one, you'd take photographs, wouldn't you?" asked the police sergeant.

"Pigs might fly if they had wings," replied Schweik, and he blandly eyed the questioning expression on the face of the police sergeant, whose head was now aching so badly again that the only other question he could think of was:

"Is it hard to photograph a railway station?"

"That's easier than anything else," replied Schweik, "because it don't move and keeps in the same place, so you don't have to tell it to look pleasant."

The police sergeant could accordingly conclude his report thus:

With further reference to report Number 2172, I beg to add—

And this is what he begged to add:

—in the course of my cross-examination he stated that he could take photographs, and those of railway stations for

233

preference. Though no camera was found in his possession, it may be conjectured that he is hiding it somewhere and therefore does not carry it with him so as to avert attention from himself, which is borne out by his own admission that he would take photographs if he had a camera with him.

The police sergeant, whose head was heavy with the effects of the previous day's events, became more and more entangled in his report on photography, and continued:

There can be no doubt that, according to his own admission, only the fact he has no camera with him prevented him from photographing the premises of the railway station and, in fact, all places of strategic importance, and there can be no question that he would have done so if he had had with him the necessary photographic apparatus which he had hidden. It is due only to the circumstances that no photographic apparatus was available that no photographs were found in his possession.

"That'll be enough," said the police sergeant, and he signed his report. He was thoroughly pleased with his work and he read it with great pride to his right-hand man.

"That's a neat bit of work," he said. "That's the way to write reports. You've got to put everything in. A cross-examination isn't a simple job, let me tell you. No, sir. It's not much use unless you can shove the whole lot into your report, so that it makes the coves at the top sit up and take notice. Bring that chap in, and let's settle up with him.

"Now this gentleman's going to take you off to the superintendent at Pisek," he announced grandly to Schweik. "According to regulations, we ought to put handcuffs on you. But I think you're a decent sort of chap, so we won't put them on this time. I'm pretty certain you won't try to give us the slip on the way."

The police sergeant was evidently moved by the sight of Schweik's good-natured face, for he added, "And don't bear any grudge against me. Now take him along. Here's the report."

"Well, goodbye," said Schweik tenderly. "Thanks for all the trouble you've taken on my account. I'll write to you if I have the chance, and if I'm passing this way again at any time, I'll pay you a call."

Schweik accompanied the right-hand man on to the high-road, and all the people who saw them so deeply immersed in friendly conversation thought they must be very old acquaintances who happened to be going the same way to town.

"I'd never have thought," remarked Schweik, "that I was going to have so much trouble to get to Budejovice. It reminds me of a butcher I know who one night got as far as the Palacky monument and then kept walking around it till morning, because the wall didn't seem to have any end to it. It upset him so much that in the morning he came over quite faint and so he began to shout 'Police!' and when the police came running up, he asked them the way home to Kobylin, because he said he'd been walking for five hours alongside some wall or other, and there was no end to it. So they ran him in and he smashed the cell up for them."

They were just passing a pond and Schweik inquired with interest whether there were many fish poachers in the neighborhood.

"The place fairly swarms with 'em," replied the right-hand man. "They tried to chuck the other sergeant into the water. The pondkeeper up there on the dike peppers their backsides with buckshot, but it's no use. They shove a piece of sheet-iron inside their breeches."

The right-hand man went on to talk about progress and how there's nothing people don't think of, and how one gets the better of the other, and then he expounded a new theory to the effect that the war was a great stroke of luck, because in all those scrimmages not only the honest men would be knocked out but the rogues and vagabonds as well.

"As it is, there's too many people in the world," he declared. "They're squeezed together like a lot of blessed sardines, and the way they breed is something awful."

They were now approaching a wayside inn.

"It's damned windy today," said the right-hand man. "A little drop of something wouldn't do us any harm. You needn't tell anyone I'm taking you to Pisek. That's a state secret."

In his mind's eye the right-hand man saw the instructions of the central authorities concerning suspects and of the duty of every police officer "to isolate them from the local population and to take strict precautions, when conveying them to the higher authorities, to prevent any unnecessary verbal communications with the public."

"They mustn't be told who you are," the right-hand man

continued. "It's nobody's business what you've been up to. There mustn't be any panic.

"Panic's a bad thing in wartime," he went on. "Somebody passes a remark and before you know where you are, it's spread like wildfire all over the neighborhood. See what I mean?"

"That's all right," said Schweik. "I won't spread any panic."

And he kept his word, for when the landlord started talking to them, he went out of his way to remark, "My brother here says we shall be at Pisek in an hour's time."

"Is your brother on leave?" the busybody landlord asked the right-hand man, who, without moving an eyelid, answered as bold as brass:

"Today's his last day.

"We diddled him all right," he observed to Schweik with a smile, when the landlord was out of earshot. "No panic, if you please. There's a war on."

When the right-hand man before entering the inn had expressed his belief that a little drop of something wouldn't do them any harm, he had been optimistic, because he had overlooked the possibility of applying the principle on a larger scale. And when he had reached the twelfth drop, he declared in a very decided manner that up to three o'clock the superintendent would be at lunch, so it would be useless to get there earlier, apart from the fact that a snowstorm was just starting. If they got to Pisek by four in the afternoon, there'd be loads of time. Why, up to six o'clock there'd be time enough. They'd get there in the dark with weather like that. Not that it mattered whether they started then or later; Pisek wouldn't run away.

"We ought to think ourselves lucky we're in a nice warm spot," he declared. "In this sort of dirty weather the chaps in the trenches are worse off than we are by the fire."

It was quite dark by the time the right-hand man decided that they could start off for Pisek. In the snowstorm they could not see a yard ahead of them, and the right-hand man said, "Follow your nose till you get to Pisek."

He said this again and then again, but when he was saying it for the third time, his voice no longer sounded from the highroad, but from some lower place, where he had slipped along a snow-covered slope. With the aid of his rifle, he laboriously clambered onto the highroad again. Schweik heard him chuckling to himself in muffled tones: "A regular toboggan slide."

Five times the right-hand man repeated this performance. He was like an ant that, whenever it falls anywhere, stubbornly climbs to the top again. When he reached Schweik at last, he said in perplexed and despairing accents, "I might very easily lose you."

"Don't you worry about that," said Schweik. "The best thing we can do is to tie ourselves together. Then we can't lose each other. Have you got any handcuffs?"

"Every policeman always has to carry handcuffs with him," said the right-hand man earnestly, as he floundered in a circle around Schweik. "That's our daily bread, as you might say."

"Well, shove 'em on, then," urged Schweik. "Let's see how they work."

With a masterly movement the guardian of the law fastened one handcuff on Schweik and then attached the other end to his own right wrist. They were now linked together like Siamese twins. They floundered inseparably along the highroad, and whenever the right-hand man tumbled, he pulled Schweik with him. The result of this was that the handcuffs began to cut into their flesh, and at last the right-hand man announced that he couldn't stand it any longer and that he'd have to undo the handcuffs.

After long and vain attempts to separate himself from Schweik, he sighed, "We're fastened together forever and ever."

"Amen," added Schweik, and they continued their troublesome journey. The right-hand man became terribly depressed and when, after appalling torments, they reached the police headquarters at Pisek late in the evening, he was in a state of complete collapse.

On the staircase he said to Schweik, "Now there's going to be ructions. We can't get away from each other."

And ructions there were when the station sergeant sent for the superintendent, Captain König.

The captain's first words were, "Breathe on me.

"Aha, I've got you taped all right, my man," said the captain, whose keen and experienced sense of smell had unerringly fathomed the situation. "Rum, cognac, toddy, cherry brandy, grog, gin.

"Sergeant," he continued, turning to his subordinate, "here's an example of how not to do it. He's handcuffed himself to

237

the prisoner. He's arrived dead-drunk. There'll have to be an official inquiry into this. Take off their handcuffs.

"What's that?" he asked the right-hand man, who was saluting the wrong way around.

"I've brought a report, sir."

"A report, eh? There's going to be a report about you, my man," said the captain curtly. "Sergeant, lock them both up, and in the morning bring them up for cross-examination. Have a look through that report from Putim and then send it on to me in my quarters."

The captain studied the "report" which the police sergeant at Putim had drawn up on the subject of Schweik. Before him stood his own sergeant, who was privately cursing the captain and all his reports because his friends were waiting for him to make up a whist party.

"I told you not so long ago, Sergeant," said the captain, "that the police sergeant at Protivin is the biggest bloody fool I've ever known, but the sergeant at Putim with this report of his beats him hollow. The soldier who was brought along here by that boozy blackguard of a policeman isn't a spy. I expect he's just a common or garden deserter. This report is full of such awful twaddle that a child could see at a glance that the chap was as drunk as a lord when he wrote it."

He had another look at the report from Putim and ordered Schweik to be brought to him immediately. Also, a telegram was to be sent to Putim instructing the sergeant there to come to Pisek the next day.

"What regiment did you desert from?" was the greeting with which the captain received Schweik.

"I never deserted from any regiment."

The captain looked hard at Schweik and beheld such a lighthearted expression in his tranquil countenance that he asked, "How did you get hold of that uniform?"

"Every soldier gets a uniform when he joins up," replied Schweik with a bland smile. "I'm in the Ninety-first Regiment and I never ran away from it. It's all the other way around."

He accompanied the latter phrase with such emphasis that the captain's jaw dropped as he inquired, "What do you mean by all the other way around?"

"It's as simple as A B C," explained Schweik confidentially. "I'm on my way to my regiment. I'm looking for my regiment, not running away from it. All I want is to get to my regiment as soon as possible. Well, I suppose the thought of it made me so flurried that I keep moving away from Budejovice, although that's where they're all waiting for me. The sergeant at Putim, he showed me on the map that Budejovice is in the south, but then he goes and sends me to the north."

The captain made a gesture implying that the sergeant at Putim did worse things than send people to the north.

"So you can't find your regiment, eh?" he said. "And you went to look for it?"

Schweik explained the whole situation to him. He mentioned Tábor and all the places through which he had passed on his way to Budejovice: Milevsko, Kvetov, Vraz, Malcin, Cizová, Sedlec, Horaždovice, Radomyśl, Putim, Stekno, Strakonice, Volyne, Dub, Vodnany, Protivin, and then Putim again.

With tremendous gusto Schweik described his struggle with destiny and how, with might and main, regardless of obstacles, he had endeavored to reach his regiment, the 91st, at Budejovice, and how all his efforts had been in vain.

He spoke with fiery zeal and the captain mechanically sketched with a pencil a diagram of the vicious circle from which the good soldier Schweik had failed to extricate himself when trying to get to his regiment.

"Talk about Hercules," he said presently, when he had listened with relish to Schweik's account of how upset he had been at failing to reach his regiment. "Why, it must have been a marvelous sight to see you patrolling Putim."

"I might have managed it then," remarked Schweik, "if it hadn't been for the sergeant there. It's an unlucky sort of place, sir, if you ask me. You see, he never bothered to inquire what my name or my regiment was, but somehow or other he thought there was something very fishy about me. He ought to have had me taken to Budejovice and at the barracks there they'd have told him whether I'm Schweik who's looking for his regiment, or whether I'm a suspicious character. Why, I might have been with my regiment, doing my military duties, this very day."

"Why didn't you point out to the people at Putim that it was all a mistake?"

"Because I saw it wasn't any use talking to them. Old Rampa, who kept a pub down at Vinohrady, always used to say, when a customer wanted a drink on tick, that there's times when a man's as deaf as a post, no matter how you try to make him hear."

The captain made a rapid decision and, showing a due concern for all the beauties and niceties of official diction, he had the following letter typed in the office:

To the C. O.
Imperial Royal Infantry Regiment, No. 91.
Budejovice.
Herewith beg to transmit Josef Schweik, the same claiming to be a private in your regiment, and detained, according to his statement, at Putim, by the police, on suspicion of desertion. The aforesaid declares he is proceeding to his regiment, as above. The individual in question is short and thickset, symmetrical features and blue eyes, without any distinguishing marks. Please find herewith enclosure B.l., this being account for expenses incurred in rationing aforesaid individual, which kindly forward to War Office and acknowledge receipt of individual in question. Beg also to send enclosure C.l. for your acknowledgment, this being list of government property in possession of aforesaid individual at the time of his arrest.

Schweik accomplished the journey from Pisek to Budejovice by train, briskly and punctually. He was escorted by a young constable, who had recently joined the force and who kept his eyes glued on Schweik for fear he might run away.

In due course they reached the barracks.

At the time of their arrival Lieutenant Lukash had been on duty for two days. Suspecting nothing, he was seated at the table in the orderly room, when Schweik was brought to him with the appropriate documents.

"Beg to report, sir, I'm back again," said Schweik, saluting with a solemn demeanor.

The whole of the ensuing scene was witnessed by Ensign Kotatko, who, later on, used to describe how, after this announcement of Schweik's, Lieutenant Lukash jumped up, clutched his head in his hands, and fell back headlong on top of Kotatko, and how, when he had been brought to, Schweik, who had remained at the salute the whole time, repeated, "Beg to report, sir, I'm back again," whereupon Lieutenant Lukash, as white as a sheet, with trembling hands had taken the documents referring to Schweik, had signed them, and told everyone to go outside, after which he had locked himself with Schweik in the orderly room.

Thus concluded Schweik's Budejovice anabasis. . . .

Schweik and Lieutenant Lukash looked hard at each other.

In the lieutenant's eyes there was a sort of baleful and desperate glare, while Schweik gazed at the lieutenant tenderly and affectionately, as if he were a sweetheart who had been lost and then found again.

The orderly room was as quiet as a church. From the corridor could be heard the footsteps of a passer-by. Some conscientious volunteer officer who had stayed in barracks on account of a cold in the head, as was evident from his voice, was snuffling the military lore which he was learning by heart. The following filtered through plainly:

"What reception is to be accorded to members of the royal family when they visit fortresses?

"As soon as Their Majesties reach the vicinity of the fortress in question, the guns in all bastions and ramparts are to fire a salute. The commanding officer will receive Their Majesties, sword in hand, and mounted, and will then—"

"Oh, shut that row!" the lieutenant yelled into the corridor. "And for God's sake, go to hell. If you're seedy, why the devil don't you stay in bed?"

The conscientious volunteer officer could be heard departing, and like a quiet echo from the end of the corridor came a snuffling recitative:

"Simultaneously with the commandant's salute, the volley is to be repeated, and this must be carried out for the third time when Their Majesties leave their conveyances."

And again the lieutenant and Schweik looked at each other silently, till at last Lieutenant Lukash remarked with harsh irony, "Delighted to see you, Schweik. You've turned up again like a bad penny. It looks as if there's no getting rid of you. Well, they've already issued a warrant against you and you'll be up tomorrow in the regimental orderly room. I'm not going to waste any more breath swearing at you. I've had more than enough annoyance on your account, and my patience is exhausted. When I think that I managed to put up with an idiot like you for so long—"

He paced up and down the room.

"Really, it's appalling. The marvel to me is that I didn't shoot you. What would they have done to me? Nothing whatever. I should have been acquitted. Do you see what I'm driving at?"

"Beg to report, sir, yes, I do, sir."

"Now don't start again with any of your antics, Schweik,

241

or there'll be ructions. You carried your lunacy too far, and so there's been a regular bust-up."

Lieutenant Lukash rubbed his hands. "Yes, Schweik, you're for it now."

He went back to his table and wrote a few lines on a piece of paper, called the sentry who was on guard in front of the orderly room, and told him to see that Schweik was taken to the warder with the chit.

Schweik was led away across the barrack square and with undisguised joy the lieutenant saw how the warder unlocked the door bearing, on a black and yellow slab, the word *Regimentsarrest,* how Schweik vanished behind the door and how, after an interval, the warder emerged from the door by himself.

"Thank heaven for that," said the lieutenant aloud to himself. "Now he's safe under lock and key."

In the dark regimental dungeon Schweik was heartily welcomed by a portly volunteer officer who was lolling on a straw mattress. He was there all by himself, and after two days of this solitary confinement he was feeling thoroughly bored. Schweik asked him what he was there for and he said it was a mere trifle. By mistake he had punched the head of an artillery officer one night when he had drunk a drop too much. Or rather, he had not exactly punched his head, but only knocked his cap off.

"Of course," he admitted, "there was a bit of a scrimmage and I daresay there was a certain amount of punching as well. But I don't think that ought to count, because, as I explained at the time, it was all a mistake. I thought he was somebody else—a friend of mine. He looks just the same from behind. They're both a couple of undersized little blighters."

The volunteer officer now asked Schweik what he had been up to.

"Looking for your regiment, eh?" he said. "You had a regular Cook's tour. And you're for it tomorrow. Brother, we're in the same boat. We shall meet again in the shadow of the gallows. Colonel Schröder's going to have the time of his life. You wouldn't believe what a fuss he makes over any little shindy in the regiment. He rushes about the barrack square with his tongue hanging out like a rabid bulldog. And you ought to see him making speeches and chewing the rag generally. He dribbles at the mouth like a camel with an attack of the mumps. Once he gets started, there's no end to it, and you'd think the whole blessed barracks was going to fall to pieces."

The door opened and admitted the warder, who brought a quarter of a portion of army bread for the two of them, together with some fresh water. Without rising from the straw mattress, the volunteer officer addressed the warder as follows:

"Welcome, benevolent angel, whose heart is overflowing with pity. You are laden with baskets of food and beverages to alleviate our distress. Never shall we forget the kind services you have rendered us. You are a beam of radiance amid our gloomy captivity."

"They'll knock all that nonsense out of you in the orderly room," growled the warder.

"Now then, don't get shirty, you old stick-in-the-mud. By Jove, if I was Minister of War, you wouldn't half have a rough time of it."

The warder glared at him, shook with rage, and went out, slamming the door.

"This is a mutual aid society for the abolition of warders," said the volunteer officer, dividing the bread rations into two equal halves. "According to paragraph sixteen of the prison regulations, prisoners are supposed to get army rations until they're sentenced. But this is a place where only the law of the jungle holds good. First come, first served, where the prisoner's grub is concerned."

They sat down on the bench and gnawed at the bread.

"That warder," the volunteer officer continued his deliberations, "is a good example of how the army turns a man into a brute. I daresay that before he joined the army he was a young man with ideals, a fair-haired cherub, kind and gentle to everyone and always taking the part of the underdog. I wouldn't mind betting that everyone looked up to him. But now— By Jove, wouldn't I like to land him one in the jaw or shove him headfirst into the latrine. And there's another proof for you how absolutely brutal a man gets in a military atmosphere."

The key again grated in the lock and the warder lit the oil-lamp in the passage.

"Lighten our darkness, we beseech Thee, O Lord," exclaimed the volunteer officer. "Enlightenment is finding its way into the army. Good night, old boy; remember me to all the N.C.O.'s, and I hope you'll have pleasant dreams. Perhaps you'll dream about the five crowns that I gave you to buy cigarettes with and that you spent in drinking my health. Sleep well, you brute."

The warder could be heard growling something about the orderly room next day.

"Alone once more," said the volunteer officer. He yawned. "Well, we're for it tomorrow, so we'd better have a good night's rest. Three cheers for the army. Good night."

He lay down under the coverlet, but began to move about from side to side. Presently he asked. "Are you asleep?"

"No," replied Schweik, who was on the other mattress. "I'm thinking."

"What about?"

"About the large silver medal for bravery that was won by a cabinetmaker down our way, named Mlicko, because he was the first man in his regiment to have his leg blown off by a shell at the beginning of the war. They gave him an artificial leg, and then he began to swank about with his medal everywhere and make out he was the first cripple in the regiment since the war started. One day he went to the Apollo Café and had a row with some chaps from the meat market, and they pulled off his artificial leg and banged him on the head with it. The chap who pulled it off didn't know it was an artificial one, and he was scared out of his wits. Anyhow, they put the leg on again at the police station, but after that, Mlicko couldn't stand the sight of his big medal for bravery and took it to the pawnshop. Well, they took him in charge there, medal and all, and he got himself into a regular mess. The end of it was that they took the medal away from him and then condemned him to lose his leg in the bargain."

"What for?"

"Why, one day there was some committee came to tell him he didn't deserve to wear an artificial leg. So they unfastened it and took it away."

"From this it follows," said the volunteer officer, "that all glory is as the grass of the field. Also," he added after a short silence, "it strikes me that the military spirit is declining among us. I therefore suggest, my beloved comrade, that amid the darkness of night, in the stillness of our captivity, we should sing about Bombardier Jaburek. That'll help to foster the military spirit. But we'll have to yell, if we want to make ourselves heard all over the barracks. I therefore suggest that we should take up our position by the door."

And presently the windows in the passage rattled to the strains of:

> "And by his gun he stood
> And kept on loading, loading,
> And kept on keeping on.
> A bullet came up quickly
> And took his arms off slickly,
> He never turned a hair
> But kept on loading, loading,
> As he kept standing there,
> And kept on keeping on."

Steps and voices could be heard across the barrack square.

"That's the warder," said the volunteer officer, "and that's Lieutenant Pelikan with him. He's on duty today. He's a reserve officer, a pal of mine. Let's go on yelling."

And again they shouted:

> "And by his gun he stood—"

When the door opened, the warder, evidently agitated by the presence of the orderly officer, snorted, "This isn't a menagerie, let me tell you."

"Excuse me," replied the volunteer officer, "this is a charity concert for the benefit of incarcerated warriors. The first item on the program has just started: 'Martial Symphony.' "

"Stop all that," said Lieutenant Pelikan, with an appearance of severity. "I believe you know you've got to lie down at nine o'clock and not kick up a row. Your singsong can be heard right in the middle of the town."

"Beg to report, sir," said the volunteer officer, "we've spent a lot of time over rehearsals, and if we're not actually out of tune—"

"He carries on like this every evening, sir," said the warder, endeavoring to rouse feeling against his enemy. "In fact, his whole behavior's something shocking, sir."

"Beg to report, sir," said the volunteer officer, "I'd like to say something to you in private. The warder can wait outside."

When this was done, the volunteer officer said in a free-and-easy tone, "Out with those cigarettes, old chap. . . .

245

What, only gaspers! And you a lieutenant too. Well, they'll do to go on with. Thanks. And now some matches."

"Gaspers," said the volunteer officer contemptuously, after his departure. "A man ought to do things in style even when he's on his beam-ends. Well, have a smoke before you turn in for the night. Tomorrow's our day of judgment."

Before going to sleep, the volunteer officer warbled one more ditty, about mountains and valleys and the girls he left behind him.

Meanwhile Colonel Schröder was among his fellow officers in the hotel, listening to Lieutenant Kretschmann, who had returned from Serbia with a damaged leg (he had been butted by a cow) and who was describing an attack on the Serbian position, as seen from staff headquarters. Colonel Schröder listened with a benign smile.

Then a young officer sitting near him, anxious to impress upon the colonel what a ruthless warrior he was, said in loud tones to his neighbor, "Consumptives have got to be sent to the front. It does 'em good, and, besides, it's better for us to lose the crocks than the fit men."

The colonel smiled, but suddenly he frowned and, turning to Captain Wenzl, he said, "I'm surprised that Lieutenant Lukash gives us such a wide berth. He's not joined us once since the day of his arrival."

"He's writing poems," announced Captain Sagner scornfully. "He hadn't been here a couple of hours before he fell in love with a Mrs. Schreiter, the wife of an engineer, whom he met at the theater."

The colonel stared in front of him with a scowl. "I've heard he's good at singing comic songs."

"Yes, when he was at the cadet school he was quite a dab at comic songs. He used to make us roar with laughter. And he knows no end of funny yarns, too. It's a fair treat to listen to him. I can't make out why he isn't here."

The colonel shook his head sadly. "Nowadays there's no real comradeship among us. I can remember the time when every officer tried to do his bit toward amusing the company. There was one, I remember, a Lieutenant Dankl, he used to strip himself naked, lie on the floor, stick a herring tail to his backside, and pretend to be a mermaid. Then there was another chap, a Lieutenant Schleisner, who could waggle his ears and neigh like a stallion, besides imitating the meowing of a cat and the buzzing of a bluebottle. And then I remember Captain Skoday. He always used to bring some girls to the officers' club whenever we wanted him to. They were three sisters and he'd got 'em trained like dogs. He put 'em on a table and they used to undress in front of us, taking their time from him. He had a sort of little baton, and I must say he was a first-rate conductor."

At this reminiscence Colonel Schröder smiled blissfully.

"But nowadays? Do you call this amusement? Why, even the man who can sing comic songs hasn't turned up. And nowadays the young officers can't take their liquor like men. It isn't twelve o'clock yet, and there's five of 'em under the table, blind to the wide. Why, there were times when we kept it up for two days on end, and the more we drank, the soberer we were, though we kept on shifting beer, wine, and liqueurs. There's no such thing as a real military spirit. God alone knows why it is. You never hear anything witty now— always the same old endless rigmarole. Just listen to them at the other end of the table, talking about America."

A solemn voice could be heard saying, "America can't enter the war. The Americans and English are at loggerheads. America isn't prepared for war."

Colonel Schröder sighed. "That's the sort of balderdash the reserve officers talk. It's a damned unpleasant business. Yesterday, fellows of that type were adding up figures in a bank or selling nutmeg and blacking, or teaching kids a lot of tommyrot, and today they fancy they're on a level with pucka officers. They think there's nothing they can't do and they want to poke their noses into everything. And what can you expect, when we've got pucka officers like Lieutenant Lukash who never set foot among us?"

Colonel Schröder went home in a bad temper, and when he woke up in the morning he was in a worse temper, because the newspapers which he had been reading in bed contained several references to Austrian troops withdrawing to positions prepared beforehand.

And such was the frame of mind in which at ten o'clock in the morning Colonel Schröder went to preside over what the volunteer officer had, perhaps with some justification, styled the day of judgment.

Schweik and the volunteer officer were waiting for the colonel on the barrack square. With them were the N.C.O.'s,

247

the orderly officer, the adjutant, and the sergeant major from the orderly room with the documents concerning the culprits.

At last the colonel, looking very gloomy, came into view. He was accompanied by Captain Sagner and was nervously knocking his riding crop against the sides of his high boots.

Having received the report, he walked several times, amid a sepulchral silence, around Schweik and the volunteer officer, who faced eyes right or eyes left according to the flank which the colonel was reaching at that particular moment. They did this with extreme thoroughness, and as it went on for a considerable time, they nearly sprained their necks.

At last the colonel came to a standstill in front of the volunteer officer.

"What were you before you joined the army?" he asked curtly. "An undergraduate, eh? What were you studying? What's that? Ancient philosophy? Bah! A boozy student, eh?

"Captain Sagner," he then shouted, "bring all the volunteer officers along here, will you?

"Of course," he continued his conversation with the volunteer officer, "that's the kind of scum we have to soil our hands with. An undergraduate. Studying ancient philosophy, if you please. About turn. I thought so. Your tunic's all rumpled up. Anyone'd think you'd just been with a tart or sprawling about in a brothel. I'll make it hot for you, my fine fellow."

The volunteer officers had now entered the barrack square.

"Fall in, two deep, will you," commanded the colonel. And they did so.

"Just look at this man," bellowed the colonel, pointing with his hunting crop at the volunteer officer. "He's been bringing discredit on you with his drunken pranks. And has he got any excuse? None whatever. Just look at him. No excuse, and he was an undergraduate before he joined the army. Studying ancient philosophy. Ancient bunkum!"

The colonel spat with contempt.

"Studies ancient philosophy and then gets tight and then knocks off an officer's cap at night. Man alive, think yourself lucky it was only an artillery officer.

"Nevertheless," continued the colonel, "such conduct must receive exemplary punishment. Orderly room!"

The sergeant major from the orderly room came forward solemnly, with documents and a pencil.

The stillness was like that in a court of justice during a

murder trial, when the judge asks, "Gentlemen of the jury, have you agreed upon your verdict?"

And it was in precisely such a tone of voice that the colonel passed sentence: "Volunteer Officer Marek is condemned to twenty-one days in cells, and after serving his sentence will be transferred to the cookhouse to scrape potatoes there."

Then, turning to the volunteer officers, the colonel gave the order to re-form ranks. They rapidly formed fours and marched off, whereupon the colonel told Captain Sagner that it wouldn't do at all and that in the afternoon he was to give them another dose of quick marching on the barrack square.

"When they march, it's got to sound like claps of thunder. Oh, and there's something else I nearly forgot. Tell them that all volunteer officers are to have five days' c.b. so as they shan't forget their ex-comrade, that skunk Marek."

And that skunk Marek stood side by side with Schweik with an air of complete satisfaction. He had got just what he wanted. It was decidedly better to scrape potatoes, roll dumplings, and parcel out chops, than, with the wind properly up, in the middle of a withering enemy fire, to yell "Fix bayonets!"

Colonel Schröder then stationed himself in front of Schweik and looked at him attentively. At this moment Schweik's whole personality lay in his broad, smiling countenance, bounded by a large pair of ears which projected from underneath his cap, pressed down tightly upon his head. The general impression was that of a man who is altogether at peace with the world and blissfully unconscious of any transgression on his part. His eyes seemed to ask: "I haven't done anything wrong, have I?"

The colonel summed up the results of his observations in a brief question which he addressed to the sergeant major from the orderly room: "Daft?"

Whereupon the colonel saw the mouth belonging to the unruffled countenance open before him.

"Beg to report, sir, daft," replied Schweik, on behalf of the sergeant major.

Colonel Schröder beckoned to the adjutant and went on one side with him. Then they called the sergeant major and inspected the material relating to Schweik.

"Aha," said Colonel Schröder, "so that's Lieutenant Lukash's orderly, who, according to his report, got lost at Tábor. It seems to me that officers ought to attend to the

249

training of their own orderlies. If Lieutenant Lukash chose to have this chronic imbecile for his orderly, he must put up with the nuisance of looking after him. He's got plenty of spare time for that. He never goes anywhere. Have you ever seen him with us? Well, there you are, then. He's got enough spare time to lick his orderly into shape."

Colonel Schröder came up to Schweik and, looking at his good-humored countenance, said, "You blithering idiot, take three days in cells, and when it's over, report yourself to Lieutenant Lukash."

Thus it came about that Schweik met the volunteer officer again in the regimental guardroom, and Lieutenant Lukash enjoyed a special treat when Colonel Schröder sent for him and announced, "About a week ago, on joining the regiment, you made an application to me for an orderly, because your own orderly had got lost at the railway station in Tábor. However, as he has now come back—"

"But, sir—" began Lieutenant Lukash imploringly.

"—I have decided," continued the colonel meaningly, "to detain him for three days in cells and then send him back to you."

Lieutenant Lukash, utterly crushed, reeled out of the colonel's office.

During the three days which Schweik spent in the company of Volunteer Officer Marek, he enjoyed himself immensely. Every evening they arranged patriotic demonstrations on the benches in their cell.

Voices were then heard warbling "God Preserve Our Emperor for Us" and "Prince Eugene the Cavalier." They also went through a program of soldiers' ditties, and when the warder arrived, he was greeted with a special musical tribute:

> *"Our warder's a jolly good fellow,*
> *And he'll never, never die.*
> *But the devil himself will come from hell*
> *To fetch him by-and-by.*

> *"He'll come with a carriage to fetch him*
> *And he'll wallop him on the spot,*
> *And then the devils will shove him in the fire*
> *To keep hell nice and hot."*

And while they were thus annoying the warder, much as an Andalusian bull is annoyed at Seville by means of a red cloth, Lieutenant Lukash, with a sinking heart, was awaiting the moment when Schweik would make his appearance to report himself for service again.

3.

Schweik's Adventures at Kiraly-Hida

THE 91st Regiment was transferred to Bruck-on-the-Leitha,
and from there to Kiraly-Hida.

Just when, after three days' incarceration, Schweik was
within three hours of being released, he was conveyed with
the volunteer officer to the main guardroom and then led
under escort to the railway station.

"Well," said the volunteer officer on the way, "we knew
they'd send us to Hungary sooner or later. That's where the
drafts are going to be formed. And the troops'll be trained
in field musketry, they'll have some free fights with the Magyars, and then off we'll go to the Carpathians. And the Magyars'll take our place in this garrison and the breeds'll get
mixed. Some people think that the best way to improve the
stamina of one race is to violate the girls belonging to another
race. The Swedes and the Spaniards tried it in the Thirty
Years' War, and so did the French under Napoleon. And now

the Magyars'll do the same thing here. Not that there'll be anything violent about it. It'll simply be a sort of exchange. The Czech soldiers will go to bed with the Magyar girls and the Czech girls, poor wenches, will have to take the Magyar militiamen to their bosoms, and in a few hundred years the scientists will wonder why they find people with high cheekbones on the banks of the Malshe."

"It's a rum business with this here crossbreeding," remarked Schweik. "In Prague there's a black waiter named Christian. Well, his father was an African king, and he used to perform in a circus. There was a schoolmistress who wrote poems to the papers, all about shepherds and streamlets in the forest and things like that, and she fell in love with this nigger chap and went to a hotel with him and committed fornication, as they say in the Bible. And she had the surprise of her life when she had a white baby. Yes, it was absolutely white. But after a fortnight it began to turn brown. It got browner and browner, and a month after that it began to turn black. In six months it was as black as its grandfather, the African king. She took him to the skin hospital to see if they couldn't bleach him or something, but they told her that it was a genuine nigger skin and nothing could be done for it. It so upset her that they had to put her into an asylum and the little nigger chap was sent to an orphanage, and they had some fun with him there, too. After that he got a job as a waiter and went about dancing in night clubs. He's produced quite a lot of Czech mulattoes, only they ain't as dark as he is. There was a doctor chap who used to go to The Flagon, and he told us it's not as simple as it looks. A half-breed has more half-breeds, until you can't tell them from people like you and me. But all of a sudden a buck nigger pops up quite unexpected. That's rough luck and no mistake. You marry a girl, say. Well, she's quite white, and then one day the wench produces a nigger baby for you."

They were now approaching the railway station, where the people of Budejovice had assembled to take leave of their regiment. It was not an official ceremony, but the square in front of the railway station was crowded with people who were awaiting the arrival of the troops.

As usual, the dutiful soldiers marched behind and those under the escort of bayonets were in front. The dutiful soldiers would later be squeezed into cattle trucks, while Schweik and the volunteer officer were to be accommodated in a special prisoners' compartment which, in troop trains, was always attached immediately behind the staff carriages.

Schweik felt that he really must hurrah and wave his cap to the crowd. The effect was so stimulating that a surge of cheering spread across the square. The corporal of the escort was quite upset and shouted to Schweik to shut up. But the cheering gathered strength like an avalanche. There was a great brandishing of hats and caps. It developed into a regular demonstration. From the windows of the hotel opposite the railway station some ladies waved their handkerchiefs and shouted "Hurrah!" One enthusiast seized the opportunity to yell "Down with the Serbs!" but in the ensuing scrimmage he got somewhat trodden underfoot.

Schweik, amid his accompaniment of bayonets, waved affably to the crowd, while the volunteer officer saluted with grave dignity.

Thus they reached the railway station and were on their way to the train when the band of the fusiliers, the conductor of which was considerably bewildered by the unexpected demonstration, was just about to strike up the Austrian hymn. But just at this moment, Father Lacina, chaplain of the Seventh Cavalry Division, suddenly made his appearance in a billycock hat and proceeded to put things right.

His story was an exceedingly simple one. He had arrived at Budejovice on the previous day and had managed to attend a little party arranged by the officers of the departing regiment. He ate and drank for a dozen, and then in a more or less sober condition he had strolled into the officers' mess to wheedle a few leavings from the cooks. After consuming many dumplings and much gravy, he got into the kitchen and discovered rum there. He swilled rum till he began to hiccough, and then returned to the farewell party, where he distinguished himself by a new round of libations. In the morning it occurred to him that he really ought to go and make sure that the first battalion of the regiment got a proper send-off. He thus arrived in front of the station just in time to snatch the baton from the bandmaster of the fusiliers at the moment when he was about to conduct "God Preserve Our King and Emperor."

"Halt," he said. "Not yet. Wait till I give the sign. Now stand at ease, and I'll come back presently."

He entered the station and attached himself to the prisoners' escort, who stopped him with a shout of "Halt!"

"Where are you going to?" inquired the corporal severely.

Here Schweik intervened good-humoredly. "They're taking us to Bruck, your Reverence. If you like you can ride along with us."

"So I will, then," announced Father Lacina, and turning around to the escort, he added, "Who says I can't come? By the right, quick march!"

When the chaplain had got into the prisoners' carriage, he lay down on the seat, and the kindhearted Schweik took off his greatcoat and put it under Father Lacina's head. Thereupon, the chaplain, comfortably stretched out on the seat, began to expound thus:

"Mushroom stew, gentlemen, is improved by the addition of mushrooms. In fact, the more of them there are, the better it is. But the mushrooms must first be braised with onion and then you add a laurel leaf and onion—"

"You've put onions in once," demurred the volunteer officer, amid the horrified glances of the corporal, who saw that Father Lacina was drunk, but recognized him as his superior officer. The corporal was in a very tight fix.

"Yes," remarked Schweik. "His Reverence is quite right. The more onions, the better. I used to know a publican and he always put onions in his beer, because onions make you thirsty. Onions are good for you in every way. Fried onions are useful things if you've got carbuncles."

Meanwhile Father Lacina was murmuring half aloud, as if in a dream, "It all depends on the seasoning you put in and how much there is of it. There mustn't be too much pepper, or too much curry—"

His voice became slower and fainter.

"—or too much mushroom, too—much—lemon—too—much nutmeg—too—much—clove—"

His voice died away and he fell asleep, whistling through his nose when, from time to time, he stopped snoring. The corporal gazed at him fixedly, while the men of the escort sniggered.

"He won't wake up in a hurry," remarked Schweik presently. "He's as tight as can be.

"That's all right," continued Schweik, when the corporal nervously beckoned to him to keep quiet. "You can't do anything about it. He's tight as per regulations. He's got a captain's rank. All these army chaplains, whatever their rank,

255

have got a sort of special gift from heaven, and you'd be surprised at the amount they can shift. I used to be orderly to old Katz, and he could drink like a fish. Why, this chap's nothing to what he was. We once pawned the monstrance to pay for booze, and I expect we'd have pawned the Kingdom of Heaven if we could have found anybody to lend us money on it."

Schweik went up to Father Lacina, turned him to the wall, and said with the air of an expert, "He'll go on snoring all the way to Bruck."

He then returned to his seat.

The corporal, now in a desperate plight, remarked, "Perhaps I'd better go and report the matter."

"You'd better not," said the volunteer officer. "You're in charge of an escort and you're not allowed to leave us. And according to the regulations you're not allowed to send any part of the escort on an errand unless you've got someone to replace him. You see, you're in a bit of a fix. And you can't give a signal by firing your rifle because there's nothing wrong here. On the other hand, the regulations say that there mustn't be anybody in the prisoners' carriages except the prisoners and their escort. No intruders are allowed. And I don't quite see how you can cover up the traces of your slackness by throwing the chaplain out of the train when nobody's looking, because we've got witnesses here who saw you let him in where he has no business to be. I can see you losing your stripes, Corporal."

The corporal, in a terrible flurry, urged that he hadn't let the chaplain into the carriage, but that the chaplain had come in of his own accord and the chaplain was his superior officer.

"You're the only superior officer here," insisted the volunteer officer, and Schweik amplified this statement by declaring:

"Why, if the Emperor himself wanted to get in here, you couldn't allow him in. It's the same as when the orderly officer asks a recruit on sentry-go to run and fetch him some cigarettes and the recruit wants to know what sort he's to bring. Chaps who do that get shoved into a fortress."

The corporal falteringly objected that Schweik had been the first to tell the chaplain he could join them.

"I'm allowed to do that, Corporal," replied Schweik, "because I'm daft, but nobody'd think you could be such a fool."

"Have you been long in the army?" asked the volunteer officer in an offhand manner.

"This is my third year. I'm just going to be promoted to sergeant."

"You better get that idea out of your head," said the volunteer officer callously. "You take it from me, you're going to lose your stripes."

"It's all the same," observed Schweik, "whether you get done in as an N.C.O. or a private. Only you've got to remember that when a chap loses his stripes, they shove him into the front line."

The chaplain began to stir.

"He's snoring," announced Schweik. "I bet he's dreaming about a good old guzzle. Now, old Katz, who I was orderly to, he was a one, he was. I remember once . . ."

And Schweik began to give such a detailed and interesting account of his experiences with Otto Katz that nobody noticed the passage of time. But after a while the volunteer officer reverted to his former topic.

"It's a wonder to me," he said to the corporal, "that we haven't had any inspector yet. According to regulations, you ought to have made a report about us to the train commandant at the railway station and not waste your time fussing around with a boozy chaplain."

The unhappy corporal maintained a stubborn silence and stared at the telegraph poles which were whizzing past.

"Moreover," continued the volunteer officer, "according to the instructions issued on November twenty-first, 1879, military prisoners must be conveyed in a carriage provided with barred windows. We've got the barred windows all right. But the instructions go on to say that the carriage must also be provided with a receptacle containing drinking water. You've not carried out that part of the regulations. And, by the way, do you happen to know where the rations are going to be served out? You don't know? I thought as much. You simply aren't fit for your job."

"You see, Corporal," remarked Schweik, "it's no joke to escort prisoners like us. You've got to look after us properly. We ain't just ordinary soldiers who can shift for themselves. We have to have everything brought to us. That's what the regulations say, and they've got to be kept to, or else where's your law and order? And then there's another thing," continued Schweik, with a friendly glance at the corporal. "Perhaps you wouldn't mind letting me know when it's eleven o'clock."

The corporal gazed interrogatively at Schweik.

"I expect you wonder why you've got to tell me when it's eleven o'clock. You see, it's like this. After eleven o'clock, my place is in the cattle truck."

Schweik spoke with deliberate emphasis and continued in solemn tones, "They gave me three days in cells. Well, I started to work it off at eleven o'clock, and so I've got to be let out today at eleven o'clock. After eleven I've got no business here. Soldiers mustn't be kept locked up longer than what they've been sentenced to, because there's got to be order and discipline in the army."

The wretched corporal was quite overwhelmed by this blow and when he had somewhat recovered himself, he murmured something about not having received any documents.

"Documents, Corporal?" exclaimed the volunteer officer. "You don't expect documents to find their way to you by themselves. If the mountain won't come to Mohammed, the leader of the escort has to go and fetch the documents. This is a new phase of the matter and it complicates things for you. It's quite clear you can't detain a man who's entitled to his release. On the other hand, according to the regulation, nobody's allowed to leave the prisoners' carriage. Really, I don't quite see how you're going to get out of such an awkward fix. It's getting worse and worse. The time now is half past ten."

The volunteer officer put back his watch.

"Well, Corporal," he said, "I wonder what you're going to do in half an hour."

"In half an hour," insisted Schweik gently, "my place is in the cattle truck."

Whereupon the corporal, now quite dazed and bewildered, said to him, "Look here, if it's all the same to you, I reckon you're much more comfortable here than you'd be in the cattle truck. I reckon—"

He was interrupted by the chaplain, who from the midst of his slumbers exclaimed, "More sauce!"

"He's asleep," said Schweik indulgently, laying beneath his head the tip of the overcoat which was falling down from the seat. "Let him go on dreaming about grub, like he was before."

And the volunteer officer began to sing:

> "*Sleep, my child, sleep, and close your eyes.*
> *You shall be lulled by an angel from the skies.*"

The corporal, now reduced to the depths of despair, said no more. He stared out of the carriage window and let the disorganization of the prisoners' carriage take its course unhindered.

Suddenly the chaplain fell off the seat and continued his slumbers on the floor. The corporal gazed at him blankly and then, while all looked on with bated breath, he lifted him back to the seat without any assistance. It was clear that he had lost all authority, and when he mumbled feebly, "You might give me a hand with him," the men of the escort just stared at each other, without lifting a finger.

"You ought to have let him go on snoring where he was," remarked Schweik. "That's the way I always used to treat my chaplain. I just left him wherever he happened to be when he fell asleep. Once it was at home in a wardrobe, another time in somebody else's washtub. He used to snooze in all sorts of places."

The corporal suddenly became brisk and resolute. He wanted to show that he was the master and he therefore said in a bullying tone, "You shut your mouth and keep quiet, will you? All you batmen have got too much to say for yourselves. You're a bloody nuisance, that's what you are."

"Ah, you're right there, Corporal," replied Schweik, with the composure of a philosopher who desires peace on earth and good will unto men but who nevertheless embarks upon the most perilous controversies. "I am a bloody nuisance, and you're God Almighty."

"Almighty God," exclaimed the volunteer officer, clasping his hands together, "fill our hearts with love for all N.C.O.'s, that we may not behold them with repugnance. Bless our assembly in this den upon wheels."

The corporal flushed angrily and jumped up. "Here, you stop passing those remarks. I won't have it."

"Corporal," said the volunteer officer, "as you sit there watching the rustling hills and the fragrant forests, you remind me of Dante. The same noble and poetical countenance, a man of gentle heart and mind, susceptible to all magnanimous feelings. Remain seated in that attitude, I beg you.

It suits you so well. You gaze upon the landscape with such an expression of spirituality, devoid of all posing or posturing. I am sure you are thinking of how delightful it will be in the springtime, when these bare expanses will be covered with a many-hued carpet of field blossoms—"

At this moment the train steamed into the station where the inspection was to take place.

The military staff had appointed Dr. Mráz, a reserve officer, as train commandant. Reserve officers were always dropped upon for absurd jobs of that kind. Dr. Mráz had got everything muddled up. Although in civil life he was a teacher of mathematics at a secondary school, there was one carriage which, try as he would, he found it impossible to account for. Also, he could not make the nominal roll, which he had received at the last station, tally with the figures which were reported after the troops had entered the train at Budejovice. Also, when he examined his documents, it seemed to him that there were two field kitchens too many, though for the life of him he couldn't make out where they had come from. Also, it made his flesh creep to discover that the horses had increased by some mysterious process. Also, among the officers, two cadets were missing and he had failed to run them to earth. Also, in the regimental orderly room which was installed in the front carriage a typewriter had disappeared. Now, as a result of this wholesale muddle, Dr. Mráz had a splitting headache. He swallowed two aspirins, and was now carrying out the inspection of the train with a very wry face.

When he entered the prisoners' carriage with his orderly, he looked at the documents and after receiving the crestfallen corporal's report, he once more compared the figures. Then he looked around the carriage.

"Who's that you've got with you?" he asked sternly, pointing to the chaplain, who was sleeping flat on his stomach and whose posterior was challenging inspection.

"Beg to report, sir," stammered the corporal, "that we sort of—"

"Sort of what?" growled Dr. Mráz. "Why don't you express yourself plainly?"

"Beg to report, sir," interposed Schweik, "this chap who's asleep on his belly is a chaplain and he's a bit squiffy, like. He joined in with us and got into our carriage, and him being our superior officer, we couldn't very well chuck him out, or

260

it would have been an infringement of superordination, as they say. He must have mistook the prisoners' carriage for the staff carriage."

Dr. Mráz heaved a sigh and gazed into his documents. The nominal roll contained no reference to any chaplain who was to proceed with the train to Bruck. His eyes twitched nervously. At the last station there had been a sudden increase of horses and now a chaplain had turned up from nowhere in the prisoners' compartment.

All he could do was to tell the corporal to turn the sleeper over, as in his present posture it was impossible to ascertain his identity.

After a certain amount of effort, the corporal managed to turn the chaplain over on his back, the result being that the latter woke up and, perceiving Dr. Mráz, he said, "Hello, old boy, how are you? Supper ready yet?"

Whereupon he closed his eyes again and turned toward the wall.

Dr. Mráz, who saw that it was the same gluttonous fellow who had eaten himself sick in the officers' mess on the previous day, heaved a sigh.

"You'll report yourself to the orderly room for this," he said to the corporal. Just as he was on the point of departure, Schweik detained him.

"Beg to report, sir," said Schweik, "this ain't my place now. My time's up today at eleven o'clock. I got three days in cells and now I ought to be with the others in the cattle truck. It's past eleven now, sir, so perhaps you wouldn't mind seeing that they put me on the line or take me into the cattle truck or send me to Lieutenant Lukash. That's my proper place."

"What's your name?" asked Dr. Mráz, inspecting his papers again.

"Beg to report, sir, Schweik, Josef."

"H'm, then you must be *the* Schweik," said Dr. Mráz, "and in that case you most certainly ought to have been let out at eleven o'clock. But Lieutenant Lukash asked me not to let you out till we get to Bruck. He said that would be safer and would keep you out of mischief on the way."

When Dr. Mráz had gone, the corporal remarked gloatingly, "You see, Schweik, it didn't help you damn all to go blabbing to an officer. If I'd wanted, I could have made it hot for the pair of you."

At this moment the chaplain awoke in all his beauty and

261

dignity. He sat up and asked in astonishment, "Good gracious me, where on earth am I?"

The corporal, perceiving that the great man had waked up, replied cringingly, "Beg to report, sir, you're in the prisoners' carriage."

A flash of amazement darted across the chaplain's countenance. He sat speechless for a moment and pondered deeply. In vain. An ocean of obscurity lay between what had happened to him overnight and his awakening in the railway carriage with the barred windows. At last he asked the corporal, who was still cringing before him, "But at whose orders was I—"

"Beg to report, sir, at nobody's orders."

The chaplain stood up and began to walk to and fro, mumbling to himself that he couldn't make head or tail of it. He then sat down again, saying, "Where are we going to?"

"Beg to report, sir, to Bruck."

"And what are we going to Bruck for?"

"Beg to report, sir, all the Ninety-first Regiment, that's ours, sir, has been transferred there."

The chaplain again began to rack his brains as to what had happened to him, how he had got into the carriage and why he was on his way to Bruck of all places, with the 91st Regiment, accompanied by a kind of escort. He had now sufficiently recovered from his fuddled condition to perceive the presence of the volunteer officer, to whom he now addressed himself.

"You seem to be an intelligent fellow. Perhaps you can tell me, without any beating about the bush, how I got among you."

"By all means," assented the volunteer officer amicably. "You joined us at the station this morning simply because you had a bit of a head."

The corporal looked at him severely.

"You got into our carriage," continued the volunteer officer, "and there you were. You lay down on the seat, and Schweik here put his greatcoat under your head. When the train was inspected at the last station you were, if I may say so, officially discovered and our corporal is going to be had up in the orderly room on your account."

"I see, I see," sighed the chaplain. "At the next station I'd better make a move into the staff carriage. Do you happen to know whether lunch has been served yet?"

"Lunch won't be served till we get to Vienna," announced the corporal.

"So it was you who put the greatcoat under my head," said the chaplain to Schweik. "Thanks very much."

"Don't mention it," replied Schweik. "I only did what anyone'd do when he sees his superior officer with nothing under his head and a little bit tiddly, like. It's the duty of every soldier to respect his superior officer, even if he's not quite himself. I'm what you might call a dab at handling chaplains, because I was orderly to Otto Katz. They're all fond of a spree and they're good sports, too."

As the result of emerging from the effects of his yesterday's carouse, the chaplain felt in a hail-fellow-well-met mood, and producing a cigarette, he handed it to Schweik, saying, "Have a fag.

"I hear that you're going to be had up in the orderly room because of me," he then said to the corporal. "But don't you worry. I'll get you out of that scrape all right."

He turned to Schweik again. "You come along with me. You'll have the time of your life."

He became exceedingly magnanimous and promised he'd do them all a good turn. He'd buy chocolate for the volunteer officer, rum for the men of the escort; he'd have the corporal transferred to the photographic section attached to the staff of the Seventh Cavalry Division; in fact he'd see that they all had an easy time and he'd forget nobody.

"I don't want any of you to bear a grudge against me," he said. "I know lots of people and as long as I keep an eye on you, you won't come to any harm. If you've done anything wrong, why, you'll bear your punishment like men, and I can see you're cheerfully putting up with the burden that God has laid upon your shoulders.

"What was the reason for your punishment?" he asked, turning to Schweik.

"What God laid upon my shoulders," replied Schweik piously, "came from the orderly room, on account of me being late for my regiment through no fault of my own."

"God is merciful and just," said the chaplain solemnly. "He knows who should be punished, for it is thus that He reveals His omnipotence. And why are you here?" he asked the volunteer officer.

"Because of my overweening pride," answered the volunteer

263

officer. "After I have atoned for my guilt, I shall be sent to the cookhouse."

"Wonderful are the ways of God," declared the chaplain, whose heart expanded at the sound of the word "cookhouse." "Yes, there's plenty of scope in a cookhouse for a man to make his mark, if he's got anything in him. The cookhouse is the very place for people who've got their wits about them. It's not so much the cooking itself, but the proper way of mixing the various parts of a dish, the arrangement and so on. A man must have his heart in it to do that sort of thing properly. Take sauces, for example. Now an intelligent man, when he's making onion sauce, will take all kinds of vegetables and steam them in butter, then he'll add nutmeg, pepper, more nutmeg, a little clove, ginger, and so on. But a common or garden cook just takes some onions and boils them, and then pours some greasy gravy on top. I'd like to see you get a job in an officers' mess. Last night in the officers' club at Budejovice they gave us, among other things, kidneys *à la madeira*. May God forgive all the sins of the man who prepared that dish. He knew his job thoroughly. And I've eaten kidneys *à la madeira* in officers' mess of the 64th Militia Regiment, but there they put caraway seeds into it, just like in common eating houses when they do them with pepper. And what do you think the cook who prepared them like that was in civil life? He used to feed cattle on an estate."

After a brief silence the chaplain turned to the subject of culinary problems in the Old and New Testament. Those were the times, he said, when they attached much importance to the preparation of tasty dishes after prayers and other religious ceremonies. He then called upon them all to sing something, whereupon Schweik, with his usual propensity for doing the wrong thing, struck up:

> *"Oh, Mary, from Hodonin town she went,*
> *And the beery old parson was hot on the scent."*

But the chaplain did not mind in the least.

"It's a pity we haven't got a little rum here. There's no need to be beery, is there?" he said with the broadest of friendly smiles.

The corporal cautiously thrust his hand into his greatcoat pocket and produced a flat bottle of rum.

"Beg to report, sir," he said in a muffled voice which

showed what a great sacrifice he was making. "I hope there's no offense if I—"

"No offense at all, my boy," replied the chaplain with a chuckle in his voice. "Here's to our journey."

"Crikey!" exclaimed the corporal to himself when he saw that, after the chaplain had taken a good swig, half the contents of the bottle had disappeared.

The chaplain had another good swig at the bottle, and then handing it to Schweik, he said in a dictatorial manner, "Have a go at that."

"War is war," said Schweik indulgently to the corporal, as he returned the empty bottle to him.

"And now I'll just have a bit of a snooze till we get to Vienna," said the chaplain. "You might just wake me up when we get there."

"And you," he continued, turning to Schweik, "you go to our mess, get a knife and fork and the rest of it, and bring me some lunch. Tell them it's for Father Lacina and see that you get double helpings. After that, bring me a bottle of wine from the kitchen and take a mess tin with you and get them to pour some rum into it."

Father Lacina fumbled in his pockets.

"Look here," he said to the corporal, "I haven't any change. Lend me a gulden. That's it, there you are. What's your name?"

"Schweik."

"Very well, Schweik, there's a gulden for you to go on with. Corporal, lend me another gulden. Now then, Schweik, you'll get the other gulden when you've carried out all my instructions. Oh, yes, and afterward get some cigarettes and cigars for me. If there's any chocolate going, collar a double share, and if there's any tinned stuff, ask them to let you have some tongue or goose liver. And if they're handing out any Emmenthaler cheese, see they don't palm off on you a piece near the rind. And similarly, if there's any salami, no end pieces, if you please. Get it well from the middle where it's nice and meaty."

The chaplain stretched himself out on the seat and in a moment he was fast asleep.

"It strikes me," said the volunteer officer to the corporal, amid the snoring of the chaplain, "that you ought to be very pleased with our foundling. He seems to have found his feet all right."

"Yes, Corporal," remarked Schweik. "There's no flies on him. He's up to snuff, he is, and no mistake."

The corporal struggled with himself for an instant and then, throwing aside all his humility, he said sullenly, "He's a pretty cheap specimen."

"That wheeze of his with the change he hasn't got," interposed Schweik, "is like a chap named Mlicko, down at Deivice. He was a stonemason and he never had any change, till at last he got head over heels into debt and was had up for pinching money. He got through pots of money but he never had any small change."

"In the Seventy-first Regiment," remarked a man from the escort, "there was a captain who spent all the regimental funds in booze before the war, and he was cashiered. Now he's a captain again. Then there was a sergeant major who pinched the supplies of cloth for facings, more than twenty bales of them there was. He's a staff sergeant now. And not long ago a footslogger was shot in Serbia for eating up his rations of bully beef that was supposed to last him for three days."

"What do you want to drag that in for?" demanded the corporal. "All the same, he goes and cadges two gulden from a corporal who can't afford to pay his tips for him."

"Here's your gulden," said Schweik. "I don't want to make money at your expense. And if he gives me the other gulden as well, I'll let you have it back too. So you needn't start sniveling about it. You ought to be glad to have the chance of lending money to your superior officer. You're a close-fisted chap, you are. Here you are making all this fuss about a measly couple of gulden. I'd like to see what you'd do if you had to sacrifice your life for your superior officer, if he was lying wounded in no man's land and you had to try and save him and carry him away, with them firing shrapnel and shells and God knows what all at you."

They were now approaching Vienna. Those who were not asleep looked through the window at the barbed wire entanglements and fortifications around the city.

"That's the style," said Schweik, looking at the trenches; "that's just as it should be. The only thing is that the Viennese might tear their trousers when they go for an outing. They'll have to be careful."

The train passed through a station, where the strains of the Austrian hymn became audible behind them. Evidently the band had gone there by mistake, for some time elapsed before they reached the station where the train stopped, rations were distributed, and the troops received a ceremonious welcome.

But things had changed since the beginning of the war, when the troops on their way to the front overate themselves at every railway station and where they were welcomed by young ladies with absurd white dresses and even more idiotic faces and utterly stupid bouquets and an even more stupid speech by a lady whose husband is now an out-and-out republican.

On this occasion those present to welcome the troops comprised three ladies who were members of the Austrian Red Cross, two ladies who were members of some Viennese female war league, one official representative of the Viennese magistracy, and a military representative.

The faces of these people all showed signs of weariness. Troop trains were passing through day and night, ambulance trains with wounded were arriving every hour, every moment there were railway carriages full of prisoners being shunted from one line to another, and these members of all these various bodies and associations had to be present on all these occasions. It went on, day after day, and the people who had originally been enthusiastic now began to yawn.

The soldiers peeped out of the cattle trucks with the hopeless expression of those who are being led to the gallows. Ladies came up to them and distributed gingerbread decorated with inscriptions in sugar: *"Sieg und Rache," "Gott strafe England,"* [1] and so forth.

After that they received orders to go and fetch their rations by companies from the field kitchens, which were installed at the back of the railway station. There was also an officers' kitchen, to which Schweik proceeded in accordance with the chaplain's instructions, while the volunteer officer waited behind to be fed, two men from the escort having gone to fetch rations for the whole of the prisoners' carriage.

Schweik duly carried out his orders, and as he was crossing the railway track, he caught sight of Lieutenant Lukash, who was strolling along the track and waiting for whatever might be left over for him in the way of rations. He was very awkwardly situated, because at the moment he was sharing an orderly with Lieutenant Kirschner. The orderly attended solely

[1] "Victory and revenge," "God punish England."

to the wants of Lieutenant Kirschner, and exercised complete sabotage as far as Lieutenant Lukash was concerned.

"Where are you taking that to, Schweik?" asked the unfortunate lieutenant when Schweik had deposited on the ground a vast store of comestibles which he had managed to secure in the officers' mess and which he had wrapped up in a greatcoat.

"Beg to report, sir, that's for you. Only I don't know where your compartment is, and then I don't know whether the train commandant wouldn't cut up rough if I was to join you. He's a regular brute, he is."

Lieutenant Lukash gazed questioningly at Schweik, who, however, with complete good humor continued, "Oh, yes, he's a brute and no mistake. When he came around to inspect the train, I reported to him that it was past eleven o'clock and that I'd served my full three days and that I ought to be in the cattle truck or else with you. And he ticked me off properly and said I'd got to stop where I was so that I couldn't cause you any annoyance on the journey, sir." Schweik assumed the air of a martyr. "As if I'd ever caused you any annoyance, sir.

"No," continued Schweik, "you can take it from me, sir, I never caused you any annoyance. And if there's been any unpleasantness at any time, why, it was just a matter of chance, an act of God, as old Vanicek said when he'd finished his thirty-sixth spell in quod. No, I've never done anything wrong on purpose, sir. I've always wanted to do something good and smart and it ain't my fault if neither of us got any advantage from it, but only a lot of bother and worry."

"All right, Schweik, don't take it so much to heart," said Lieutenant Lukash gently, as they drew near to the staff carriage. "I'll see to it that you can be with me again."

"Beg to report, sir, I ain't taking it to heart. But I was sort of sorry that we're both having such a bad time of it in the war and it's not our fault. It's rough luck when you come to think of it. I've always tried to keep out of harm's way."

"Now then, Schweik, don't upset yourself."

"Beg to report, sir, that if it wasn't against subordination, I'd say I'm upset and always will be upset and there's an end of it. But as it is, I suppose I'll have to fall in with your orders and say I'm not a bit upset now."

"All right. Schweik. Now hop into this carriage."

"Beg to report, sir, I am hopping in."

The camp at Bruck was wrapped in the silence of night. In the huts for the rank and file the men were shivering with cold and the officers' huts were so overheated that the windows had to be opened.

Down in Bruck-on-the-Leitha lights were burning in the imperial royal tinned meat factory, where they were busy day and night modifying various forms of offal. As the wind was blowing from that direction toward the camp, the avenues around the huts were filled with the stench of putrefying sinews, hoofs, trotters, and bones which were being boiled as ingredients for tinned soup.

Bruck-on-the-Leitha was resplendent, and on the other side of the bridge Kiraly-Hida was equally radiant. Cisleithania and Transleithania. In both towns, the Austrian and the Hungarian gypsy orchestras were playing, the windows of cafés and restaurants shone brightly, there was singing and reveling. The local bigwigs and jacks-in-office had brought their ladies and their grown-up daughters to the cafés and restaurants, and Bruck-on-the-Leitha and Kiraly-Hida formed one vast Liberty Hall.

In one of the officers' hutments in the camp, Schweik was waiting that night for Lieutenant Lukash, who had gone to the theater and had not yet returned. Schweik was sitting on the lieutenant's bed, and opposite him, on the table, sat Major Wenzl's orderly.

The major had returned to the regiment when his complete incompetence had been demonstrated on the Drina. It was said that he had been responsible for the removal and destruction of a pontoon, while half his battalion were still on the other side of the river. Now he had been put in charge of the rifle range at Kiraly-Hida and he also had a finger or two in the camp commissariat. It was common talk among the officers that Major Wenzl was now setting himself up.

Mikulashek, who was Major Wenzl's orderly, an undersized, pock-marked fellow, sat there dangling his legs and grousing. "Why the deuce isn't that old blighter of mine back yet? I'd like to know where the old codger goes gadding about all night. If he'd only let me have the key of the room I could lie down and have a good binge. I've got plenty of booze in there."

"I've heard he pinches things," remarked Schweik, placidly puffing away at a cigarette belonging to the lieutenant, as the latter had forbidden him to smoke a pipe in the room. "You

269

must know something about it. Where does the booze come from?"

"I just go where he tells me to," said Mikulashek in a ready voice. "I get the chit from him and go to the hospital to fetch the doings and I bring them home."

"And if he ordered you to sneak the regimental funds, would you do it?" asked Schweik. "You call him names now, but when he's here you shiver in your shoes."

Mikulashek's little eyes twinkled. "I'd have to think it over a bit."

"It's no use thinking it over, you silly young chump," shouted Schweik, but then he stopped, because the door opened and Lieutenant Lukash entered. It was at once obvious that he was in a good temper, as his cap was on the wrong way around.

Mikulashek was so scared that he forgot to jump down from the table, but saluted in a sitting posture, quite overlooking the fact that he had no cap on his head.

"Beg to report, sir, everything's all right," announced Schweik, assuming a stern military demeanor according to regulations, but omitting to remove the cigarette from his mouth.

Lieutenant Lukash did not even notice this, and made straight for Mikulashek, who with startled eyes watched his every movement, continuing to salute and remaining seated on the table.

"I'm Lieutenant Lukash," said the lieutenant, approaching Mikulashek unsteadily, "and what's your name?"

Mikulashek said nothing. Lieutenant Lukash drew up a chair to the table, sat down, looked at Mikulashek, and said, "Schweik, fetch me my service revolver from my trunk."

While Schweik was searching in the trunk, Mikulashek stared in mute horror at the lieutenant.

"Man alive, what's your name? Are you deaf or what?" shouted the lieutenant.

Mikulashek still remained silent. As he explained later, the lieutenant's unexpected arrival produced a sort of numbness in him. He wanted to jump down from the table, but could not; he wanted to answer, but could not; he wanted to stop saluting, but failed.

"Beg to report, sir," announced Schweik, "the revolver isn't loaded."

"Then load it."

"Beg to report, sir, we haven't got any cartridges, and it'd be a hard job to shoot him off the table. I take the liberty of mentioning, sir, that it's Mikulashek, orderly to Major Wenzl. He always gets tongue-tied if he sees any of the officers. He's just too bashful to speak. He's a silly young chump, in fact, he's what you might call a whipper-snapper. It ain't as if there was any need for him to have the wind up, for he ain't done anything."

Schweik spat to show his complete contempt for Major Wenzl's orderly and his unmilitary behavior.

"Sling him out, Schweik."

Schweik dragged the trembling Mikulashek into the passage, shut the door behind him and said, "Well, I've saved your life, you young chump. When Major Wenzl comes back, you scrounge a bottle of wine for me and bring it here. And mind you do it, too. I've saved your life, remember. When my lieutenant's tight, he's a tough customer, I tell you. I'm the only one who can manage him when he's like that."

"I'm—"

"You're a little tick," said Schweik contemptuously. "Now sit down on the doorstep till your Major Wenzl comes back."

"You've kept me waiting long enough," said Lieutenant Lukash when Schweik had returned to him. "I want to talk to you. There's no need for you to stand at attention in that idiotic manner. Sit down, Schweik, and never mind about the regulations. Hold your tongue and listen to what I've got to say. Do you know where Sopronyi Street is? Now don't start any of your 'Beg to report, sir, I don't know.' If you don't know, say you don't know and have done with it. Now then, write down on a piece of paper: Sixteen Sopronyi Street. It's an ironmonger's shop. Do you know what an ironmonger's shop is? For God's sake, don't keep saying, 'Beg to report, sir.' Say 'Yes' or 'No.' All right, do you know what an ironmonger's shop is? You do? Very well, then. Now this shop belongs to a Magyar named Kákonyi. Do you know what a Magyar is? Holy Moses, do you or don't you? You do. Very well, then. He lives above the shop on the first floor. Do you know that? You don't know, but damn it all, I'm telling you, aren't I? Do you understand now? You do? All right. If you didn't, I'd have you shoved into clink. Have you made a note of this chap's name? Kákonyi, I said. Very good. Now then, tomorrow morning at about ten o'clock you'll go into town, you'll find this place, you'll go upstairs to the first floor, and you'll hand this note to Mrs. Kákonyi."

Lieutenant Lukash opened his pocketbook and with a yawn he gave Schweik a white envelope bearing no address.

"This is an extremely important matter, Schweik," he went on. "A man can't be too careful, and that's why I haven't put any address, as you see. I rely on you to hand the note to the proper person. Oh, and just bear in mind that the lady's name is Etelka—write it down: Mrs. Etelka Kákonyi. And let me also tell you that you're to hand the note over very discreetly, whatever you do, and wait for an answer. Is there anything else you want to know?"

"Supposing they don't give me an answer, sir, what am I to do then?"

"Tell them you've got to get an answer, whatever happens," replied the lieutenant, with another wide yawn. "But now I'm going to bed. I'm fagged out. By Jove, we did shift some liquor. I think anybody'd be fagged out after a night like that."

Originally Lieutenant Lukash had not intended to stop anywhere. He had gone into town that evening because he wanted to visit the Magyar theater in Kiraly-Hida, where a musical comedy was being played, the chief parts in which were taken by plump Jewesses, who distinguished themselves wonderfully by kicking their legs up in the air when they danced and not wearing any tights or drawers.

Lieutenant Lukash, however, was not enthralled by this interesting display, because the opera glasses which he had borrowed were not achromatic, and instead of thighs he could see only some violet surfaces moving to and fro.

In the interval after the first act his attention was attracted by a lady who was accompanied by a middle-aged gentleman. She was pulling him toward the cloakroom and saying that they were going home immediately and that she was not going to look at such a disgraceful performance. She was making these remarks very loudly in German, whereupon her companion replied in Magyar, "Yes, my angel, let us go. I quite agree. It's really most disgusting."

"*Es ist ekelhaft,*" [1] said the lady angrily, when the gentleman had helped her on with her opera cloak. And as she spoke her eyes flashed with indignation at such scandalous goings on, large, dark eyes which were quite in keeping with her

[1] "It's disgusting."

handsome presence. She also glanced at Lieutenant Lukash, as she insisted with great emphasis: *"Ekelhaft, wirklich ekelhaft."* [2]

That proved decisive. The romance had started.

Lieutenant Lukash learned from the person in charge of the cloakroom that this was Mr. and Mrs. Kákonyi, and that Mr. Kákonyi kept an ironmonger's shop at 16 Sopronyi Street.

"And he lives with Mrs. Etelka on the first floor," said the person in charge of the cloakroom with the precision of an ancient procuress. "She's a German lady from Sópron and he's a Magyar. In this town everything's mixed."

Lieutenant Lukash removed his greatcoat from the cloakroom and went into the town, where, in the Archduke Albrecht, a large wineshop and café, he met some officers of the 91st Regiment.

He did not talk much, but made up for it by the amount he drank, as he pondered over what he ought to write to this lady who was so severe, so moral, and so handsome, and who attracted him far more than did the whole pack of bitches on the stage, as the other officers styled them.

He was in a very good temper when he made his way to the St. Stephen's Cross, a small café, where he entered a private room and after chasing away a Rumanian girl there who offered to take off all her clothes and let him do whatever he liked with her, he ordered ink, pen, and writing paper, as well as a bottle of cognac, and after careful reflection, he wrote in his best German the following missive, which struck him as being the finest thing he had ever penned.

DEAR MADAM,

Yesterday evening I was present at the theater and saw the play which aroused your indignation. Throughout the first act I noticed you and your husband, and I could not help seeing that your husband—

"I may as well lay it on thick," reflected Lieutenant Lukash. "What business has a chap like that to have such a damn fine wife? Why, he looks like a baboon who's had a shave."

He continued his letter:

—evinced considerable appreciation of the disgusting antics which were being performed on the stage, and which met

[2] "Disgusting, really disgusting."

273

with your strong disapproval, because, far from being artistic, they pandered only to man's baser instinct.

"She's got a damn fine figure," thought Lieutenant Lukash. "Now I'd better come straight to the point."

I hope you will pardon me, a stranger, for addressing you in this direct manner. In the course of my life I have seen many women, but none of them made such an impression upon me as you did, because your views and your outlook on life are identical with my own. I feel sure that your husband is completely selfish and drags you with him—

"That won't do," said Lieutenant Lukash, and crossing out "drags you with him," he continued as follows:

—in his own interests takes you to theatrical performances which appeal only to his personal tastes. I like to be frank, and while not desiring to intrude upon your private life, I should very much like to speak to you privately on the subject of art in its purer aspects—

"I shan't be able to manage it in the hotels here. I suppose I shall have to trot her along to Vienna," meditated the lieutenant. "I'll wangle special leave."

For this reason I venture to ask you whether you would kindly make an appointment so that we could meet and become better acquainted on honorable terms, and I feel sure you will not withhold this favor from one who before very long will be facing the perils of warfare and who, should you give your consent, will preserve amid the terrors of the battlefield the most wonderful memory of a soul between whom and himself there was complete mutual understanding. Your decision will be my law. Your answer will constitute a decisive factor in my life.

He signed his name, drank what was left of the cognac, and ordered another bottle. As he drank glass after glass and re-read what he had written, he was moved to tears by almost every sentence.

It was nine o'clock in the morning when Schweik woke Lieutenant Lukash.

"Beg to report, sir, you're on duty and you've overslept yourself and I've got to go now to this here Kiraly-Hida. I woke you at seven o'clock and then at half past seven and then at eight, just when they was going past on their way to parade, but you just turned over onto the other side. Beg to report, sir—here, I say, sir—"

For Lieutenant Lukash, mumbling to himself, was about to turn over again on to the other side. But he did not succeed in doing so, because Schweik shook him mercilessly and bawled, "Beg to report, sir, I'm just going to take that letter to Kiraly-Hida."

The lieutenant yawned. "That letter? Oh, yes, that letter of mine. Mum's the word about that, you know. It's strictly between ourselves. Dismiss."

The lieutenant again wrapped himself up in the bedclothes, from which Schweik had dragged him, and continued his slumbers, while Schweik proceeded on his way to Kiraly-Hida.

It would not have been difficult for him to find 16 Sopronyi Street, if by chance he had not met Sapper Voditchka. Voditchka had lived years ago in Prague, and so the only thing they could do to celebrate their meeting was to go to The Red Lamb in Bruck, where there was a Czech barmaid.

"Where are you off to?" asked Voditchka.

"That's a secret," replied Schweik, "but as you're an old pal of mine, I'll tell you."

He explained everything to him in great detail, and Voditchka declared that he was an old sapper, that he wouldn't leave Schweik in the lurch, and that they would go and deliver the letter together.

They had a good long talk about old times, and when, shortly after twelve, they set out from The Red Lamb, everything seemed natural and easy to them. Moreover, they had a deep-rooted conviction that they were afraid of nobody. All the way to 16 Sopronyi Street, Voditchka was dwelling upon his vast hatred of the Magyars and kept telling Schweik how he was always coming to blows with them.

At last they found Mr. Kákonyi's ironmonger's shop at 16 Sopronyi Street.

"You'd better wait here," said Schweik to Voditchka in front of the doorway. "I'll just pop up to the first floor, leave the letter, and wait for an answer. I'll be back again in a jiffy."

"What, and me leave you in the lurch?" demurred Voditchka. "You don't know the Magyars. You got to keep a sharp eye on them. I'll give him such a biff in the eye."

"Stow it," said Schweik in a serious tone. "Magyar be blowed. It's his wife we're after. Didn't I tell you when we was in that pub where that Czech barmaid is that I'm taking a letter to her from my lieutenant, and that it's a dead secret? My lieutenant made me swear blind I wouldn't tell a living soul, and didn't the barmaid say he was quite right, because it's the sort of thing you got to keep to yourself? Didn't she say that it'd never do if anyone found out that the lieutenant had written to a married lady? And didn't you yourself nod your head and say it was quite right? I've told you all the ins and outs of it and how I'm carrying out my lieutenant's orders to a T, and now you've taken it into your head to come up with me."

"Ah, you don't know me, Schweik," replied Sapper Voditchka very solemnly. "Once I've said I'm coming with you, remember I mean what I say. It's always safer when there's two."

"Not always it isn't," said Schweik. "Don't you run away with that idea. I used to know a locksmith named Vobornik, and one day when he'd been on the spree, he came home, and brought another chap with him who'd been on the spree, too. Well, he stayed in bed for a long time, sleeping it off, and every day when his wife came to bandage the bruises on his head, she said to him, 'If there hadn't been two of you, there'd only have been one rumpus, and I shouldn't have chucked the weighing machine at your head.' And when he was able to talk, he said, 'That's right, old girl, and the next time I go out on the spree, I'll come home by myself.'"

"I don't advise any Magyar to chuck anything at our heads," demurred Voditchka. "I'd take him by the throat and sling him downstairs in double-quick time, too. When you come across these Magyar chaps, you got to treat 'em rough. It's no good shilly-shallying about."

"Here, steady on," objected Schweik. "Don't forget we've got to be careful not to go looking for trouble. If anything goes wrong, I shall cop out."

"You don't know the Magyars," repeated Voditchka. "Don't say you're going to cast me off, now that we've met again after all this time."

"All right, come along then," agreed Schweik, "but be careful what you do. We don't want to get ourselves into a mess."

"Don't you worry, chum," said Voditchka, as they went toward the staircase. "I'll biff him one—" And, in lower tones, he added, "You'll see, we'll have an easy job with this Magyar fellow."

Schweik and Voditchka stood at the door of Mr. Kákonyi's abode. Schweik rang the bell, whereupon a maid appeared and asked them in Magyar what they wanted.

"*Nem tudom,*" said Voditchka contemptuously. "Why don't you learn Czech, my girl?"

"*Verstehen Sie deutsch?*" [3] asked Schweik.

"*A Pisschen.*" [4]

"Then tell the lady I want to speak to her. Say that there's a letter from a gentleman, outside."

"I'm surprised at you," said Voditchka, as he followed Schweik into the passage, "talking to a baggage like that."

They stood in the passage and Schweik remarked, "It's nice and comfortable here, I must say. Why, they've got two umbrellas on the hatrack, and that picture of Jesus Christ ain't a bad bit of work, either."

The maid now returned from the room, where the rattling of spoons and the clattering of plates could be heard, and said to Schweik in broken German, "The lady says she's got no time. If there's anything for her, you're to give it to me with a message."

"All right," said Schweik solemnly. "Here's a letter for her, but keep quiet about it."

He produced Lieutenant Lukash's letter.

"I," he said, pointing to himself, "will wait for the answer here."

"Why don't you sit down?" asked Voditchka, who had taken a seat in a chair by the wall. "Here's a chair for you. You're standing there as if you was a beggar. Don't make yourself cheap in front of these Magyars. We're going to have a bit of a dust-up with him, but I'll biff him properly."

Presently he asked, "Where did you learn German?"

"All by myself," replied Schweik.

Again there was silence. Then a great uproar could be heard in the room into which the maid had taken the letter. Somebody was hitting the ground with a heavy object, then

[3] "Do you understand German?"
[4] "[*Ein Bisschen*] A bit."

the noise of glasses being thrown about and plates being broken could be distinctly recognized, and amid it all somebody was making angry noises in Magyar.

The door flew open and in dashed a gentleman with a serviette around his neck and brandishing the letter which had just been delivered.

Sapper Voditchka was nearest to the door, and it was to him that the excited gentleman first addressed himself.

"What's the meaning of this?" he demanded in German. "Where's the damned blackguard who brought this letter?"

"Here, steady on, governor," said Voditchka, standing up. "You're making a devil of a noise. Keep your hair on, and if you want to know who brought this letter, just ask my chum here. But keep a civil tongue in your head, or you'll get slung outside in double-quick time."

It was now Schweik's turn to sample the rich eloquence of the excited gentleman with the serviette around his neck. He was gabbling at random, and from the rigmarole of words emerged the statement that they were just having lunch.

"We heard you having lunch," agreed Schweik in broken German.

The excited gentleman, who as a result of his brisk gesticulations was now holding the serviette by only one tip, went on to say that at first he thought the letter was about billeting troops in the house which belonged to his wife.

"You could get plenty of troops in here," said Schweik, "but the letter ain't about that. I suppose you know what's in it?"

The gentleman clutched at his head and let loose a regular volley of curses, adding that he himself was a reserve officer, that he'd like to be in the army, only his kidneys were out of order. And as for the letter, he'd send it to the C.O., to the War Office, to the newspapers.

"Look here," said Schweik with dignity. "I wrote that letter. It wasn't the lieutenant who wrote it. The signature's a fake. I signed it. I've taken a fancy to your wife. I'm fairly mashed on her, as the poet Vrchlický used to say. A damn fine woman, that she is."

The excited gentleman was about to hurl himself at Schweik, who stood there in front of him as cool as a cucumber, but Sapper Voditchka, watching his every movement, tripped him up, snatched the letter out of his hand (he was still brandishing it), and put it in his pocket. And when Mr. Kákonyi recovered his balance, Voditchka caught hold of him, dragged him to the door, opened the door with one hand, and in a trice some heavy object could be heard rolling down the stairs.

The whole thing was done with as much dispatch as in the fairy tales, when the devil comes to fetch someone.

The only relic of the excited gentleman was the serviette. Schweik picked it up, knocked politely on the door of the room from which Mr. Kákonyi had emerged five minutes previously and where the sound of female weeping could now be heard.

"Here's your serviette," said Schweik courteously to the lady who was sobbing on the sofa. "It might get trodden on. Good day to you, ma'am."

He clicked his heels together, saluted, and went out into the passage. On the stairs there was not the slightest trace of any struggle; everything had gone off with the utmost ease, just as Voditchka had said it would. But at the outer doorway Schweik discovered a collar which showed signs of having been wrenched off. Evidently it was there that the final act of the tragedy had occurred, when Mr. Kákonyi had desperately clung to the doorway to save himself from being dragged into the street.

And in the street itself there was quite a rumpus. Mr. Kákonyi had been dragged into the doorway of the house opposite, where water was being poured upon him, while in the middle of the street Sapper Voditchka was fighting like a lion against some Magyar militiamen and hussars, who had espoused the cause of their fellow countryman. Sapper Voditchka was skillfully keeping his adversaries at bay by means of a bayonet strap which he was wielding like a flail. Nor was he alone. Side by side with him a number of Czech soldiers were engaged in the contest.

Schweik, as he afterward related, did not himself know how he got mixed up in the shindy. Nor could he tell how, having no bayonet, he obtained possession of a walking stick which had been the property of a scared spectator.

It lasted quite a long time, but all good things must come to an end. The patrol arrived and took them all into custody.

Schweik marched along by the side of Voditchka, holding the walking stick, which the commander of the patrol afterward fastened upon as a *corpus delicti*. He marched along complacently, with the walking stick at the slope, like a rifle.

Sapper Voditchka maintained a stubborn silence all the way. But when they were entering the guardroom he said to Schweik mournfully, "Didn't I tell you, you don't know the Magyars?"

4.

Fresh Tribulations

COLONEL SCHRÖDER was gloating over the pallid, hollow-eyed countenance of Lieutenant Lukash, who, in his embarrassment, was looking away from him, and stealthily peeped at the plan showing the disposition of the rank and file in the camp, which formed the sole decorative feature of the colonel's office.

On the table in front of Colonel Schröder there were a number of newspapers containing articles marked with blue pencil which the colonel scanned once again before turning to Lieutenant Lukash with the remark, "So you already know that Schweik, your orderly, is in custody and will probably be handed over to a divisional court-martial?"

"Yes, sir."

"That, of course," said the colonel meaningly, as he feasted his eyes on the lieutenant's pallor, "does not dispose of the matter. There can be no doubt that the whole of the business in which your orderly was mixed up has caused local feeling to run high, and your name is being mentioned in connection with it. The divisional command has already supplied us with certain material. Here are a number of papers which discuss this matter. Kindly read them aloud to me."

He handed Lieutenant Lukash the papers with the penciled articles, which the lieutenant began to read in a monotone, as if he were reading in a children's primer such a sentence as, "Honey is much more nutritious and more easily digestible than sugar":

"WHERE IS THE GUARANTEE FOR OUR FUTURE?"

"That's the *Pester Lloyd,* isn't it?" asked the colonel.
"Yes, sir," replied the lieutenant, and went on reading:

"The conduct of the war demands the cooperation of all classes in the Austro-Hungarian Monarchy. If we desire to attain the security of the state, all the nations must support each other and the guarantee for our future consists precisely in this mutual and spontaneous respect. The enormous sacrifices of our gallant troops at the front, where they are continually advancing, would not be possible, if the home front were not united, but harbored elements inimical to the harmonious structure of the state, undermining its authority by their malicious activities and thus threatening the joint interests of the nations in our Empire. At this historical juncture we cannot view in silence the handful of people who would like to impair the unified effort and struggle of all the nations in this Empire. We cannot silently overlook these odious signs of a diseased mentality which aims solely at destroying the unanimity in the hearts of the nations. Several times already we have had occasion to point out how the military authorities are compelled to adopt the severest measures against individuals in the Czech regiments who, heedless of glorious regimental traditions, by their disgraceful conduct in our Magyar towns have spread ill feeling against the Czech nation which, in its entirety, is not to blame and, indeed, has always been closely identified with the interests of this Empire, as is attested by the many distinguished Czech military leaders, such as the renowned Marshal Radetzky and other defenders of the Austro-Hungarian Monarchy. These noble figures are being besmirched by a few blackguards from the Czech rabble who are taking advantage of war conditions to enlist in the army and then imperil the united front among the nations in the monarchy, at the same time allowing their lowest instincts to run riot. We have already drawn attention to the disgraceful behavior of regiment No.— at Debreczin, whose outrageous conduct formed the subject of debate and condemnation in the Parliament at Budapest and whose regimental colors subsequently, at the front, were . . . (Deleted by censor). At whose door is this revolting offense to be laid . . . (Deleted by censor)? Who incited the Czech troops to . . . (Deleted by censor)? Some idea of the lengths to which the foreign elements in our midst will go, can be best inferred from the recent incidents at Kiraly-Hida. What is the nationality of those troops from the Bruck military camp close at hand who attacked and ill-treated Mr. Gyula Kákonyi, a tradesman in that town? It is obviously the bounden duty of the authorities to investigate this outrage and to ask the military command, which has doubtless already started making inquiries, what part in this unexampled bullying of Magyar citizens was played by Lieutenant Lukash, whose name is being mentioned in the town in connection with the recent disgraceful episode, as we are informed by a local correspondent who has already collected ample evidence on this matter which, at so grave an epoch as today, clamors for redress. We are sure that readers of the *Pester Lloyd* will follow with interest the further course of investigation and we shall certainly not fail to keep them acquainted with a matter of such eminent significance. At the same time, however, we await an official report on the outrage at Kiraly-Hida perpetrated against a Magyar citizen. It is obvious that the Parliament at Budapest will give the matter its closest attention, in order to make it plain that Czech troops, passing through the kingdom of Hungary on their way to the front, must not be allowed to treat the country of St. Stephen's crown as if it were their vassal. If any members of this nation which at Kiraly-Hida made such an exhibition of the unified spirit prevailing among all nations in this monarchy, still do not realize how things are, they had better keep very quiet about it, for in wartime it is the bullet, the rope, the jail, and the bayonet which will teach such persons to obey and to subordinate themselves to this highest interest of our joint country."

283

"Who's the article signed by?"

"Bela Barabas. He's a journalist and a Member of Parliament, sir,"

"Oh, yes, he's a well-known blackguard. But before the article got into the *Pester Lloyd* it had already appeared in the *Pesti Hirlap*. Now perhaps you wouldn't mind reading to me the official translation of an article in the *Sopronyi Napló*."

Lieutenant Lukash read aloud an article in which the writer had taken plenty of trouble to drag in as often as possible such phrases as: "an essential demand of political prudence," "law and order," "human depravity," "human dignity and honor trampled underfoot," "the feasting of cannibals," "the slaughter of mankind," "gang of ruffians," "behind the scenes," and so on, as if the Magyars were the persecuted element on their own soil. It read as if the Czech troops had intruded on the writer's privacy, had knocked him down, trampled on his abdomen with Wellington boots, whereupon he had howled with pain and somebody had taken it all down in shorthand.

"There are certain matters of prime importance [wailed the *Sopronyi Napló*] on which a significant silence is maintained and which nobody ventures to write about. We all know what the Czech soldier is like in Hungary and at the front. We all know what things the Czechs are doing and who is the cause of them. The watchfulness of the authorities, of course, is directed toward other important matters which, however, should be closely linked up with the general system of control, in order to prevent any recurrence of the scenes which recently took place at Kiraly-Hida. Fifteen passages in our yesterday's article were deleted by the censor. Accordingly, all we can do today is to announce that for technical reasons we feel no considerable urge to discuss in any detail the Kiraly-Hida affair. Our special report ascertained on the spot that the authorities are showing considerable zeal about the whole matter, which they are investigating with the utmost dispatch. Nevertheless, it seems to us rather curious that a number of persons who were present at the outrage are still at large. This applies particularly to the gentleman who, according to hearsay, is still enjoying complete freedom of movement in camp, and whose name was published the day before yesterday in the *Pester Lloyd* and *Pesti Napló*. We refer to the notorious Czech jingo, Lukash, concerning whose outrageous conduct a question will be asked in Parliament by Géza Savanyi, member for the Kiraly-Hida consitituency."

"There are equally pleasant references to you," said Colonel Schröder, "in the *Kiraly-Hida Weekly* and also in the Pressburg papers. But that won't interest you, because it's a rehash of the same old stuff. Still, you may care to see an article in the Komarno *Evening News* which says that you made an attempt to violate Mrs. Kákonyi at lunch in the dining room, in the presence of her husband, whom you threatened with your sword, forcing him to gag his wife with a napkin to stop her from screaming. That's the latest news about you."

The colonel smiled and continued, "The authorities are neglecting their duty. The censorship of all the papers here is in the hands of the Magyars, and they treat us exactly as they please. It was only after we had made urgent representations by a telegram from our divisional court-martial that the public prosecutor at Budapest took steps to arrest some of the editorial staff of all these papers. It's the editor of the Komarno *Evening News* who'll get it hottest. He'll have cause to remember that article till his dying day. The divisional court-martial have entrusted me with the task of cross-examining you and have sent me all the relevant documents. It'd be all right if it wasn't for that orderly of yours, that wretched fellow Schweik. With him there's a certain Sapper Voditchka, and after the rumpus, when they'd taken him to the guardroom, they found him in possession of the letter you sent to Mrs. Kákonyi. Your man Schweik declared, when cross-examined, that it wasn't your letter but that he'd written it himself, and when it was placed before him and he was asked to copy it so that the handwriting could be compared, he ate your letter up. Specimens of your reports were then produced to compare your writing with Schweik's, and here's the result."

The colonel turned over some documents and pointed out the following passage to Lieutenant Lukash: "The prisoner Schweik refused to write the dictated sentence, asserting that overnight he had forgotten how to write."

"Of course," went on the colonel, "I don't attach any importance to the evidence of Schweik or this Sapper Voditchka before the divisional court-martial. They both say that the whole thing was only a joke which was misunderstood, and that they themselves were attacked by civilians and that they defended themselves to vindicate their military honor. In the course of the proceedings it turned out that this Schweik of yours is a very queer fish indeed. Not all there, I should think, judging by his answers. I need hardly say that on behalf of the regimental command I've made arrangements for corrections of these disgraceful reports to be sent to all the papers concerned. They're being distributed today. I think I've worded it rather neatly. It runs like this:

"Divisional court-martial Number N. and the command of regiment Number N. hereby declares that the article published in your paper on the subject of alleged outrage committed by men of regiment Number N. is entirely without foundation and is a complete fabrication from beginning to end. Further, kindly note that the proceedings instituted against the offending papers will lead to the infliction of severe penalties upon the culprits.

"In its report to our regimental command," continued the colonel, "the divisional court-martial expresses the opinion that the whole business is nothing more or less than a systematic agitation against the military detachments proceeding from Cisleithania to Transleithania."

The colonel spat and added, "You can see for yourself what good use they've made of your adventure in Kiraly-Hida."

Lieutenant Lukash coughed with embarrassment.

"Now, tell me, as man to man," said the colonel in a confidential tone, "how many times did you sleep with Mrs. Kákonyi?"

Colonel Schröder was in a very good humor that day.

"And don't tell me you'd only just begun to correspond with her. When I was your age I spent three weeks at Erlau on a field-surveying course, and I give you my word I spent the whole of those three weeks doing nothing else but sleeping with Magyar women. A different one every day. Young ones, unmarried ones, elderly ones, married ones, whichever happened to turn up.

"Just begun to correspond . . ." The colonel tapped the lieutenant familiarly on the shoulder. "That won't go down with me. I know exactly how it all happened. You started playing about with her, then her husband got word of it, and that fellow Schweik, your blithering idiot of an orderly . . .

"But, all the same, you know, that chap Schweik is a regular card. That was really rich, the way he acted with your letter. I must say I'm sorry about him. He's a caution and no mistake. I think he showed a real sporting spirit. The court-martial proceedings have certainly got to be quashed. You got a dressing-down from the newspapers. They've made it too hot for you here. Within a week the draft will be on its way to the Russian front. You're the oldest lieutenant in the Eleventh Company and you'll be attached to it as company commander. That's all been settled with the brigade. Tell the sergeant major to find you another batman to replace this chap Schweik."

Lieutenant Lukash gazed gratefully at the colonel, who continued, "I'm attaching Schweik to you as company orderly."

The colonel rose, and shaking hands with the lieutenant, whose face had turned as white as a sheet, he said, "Well, that's all settled. I wish you all success and luck at the front. And if you should happen to come this way again, give us a look-up. Don't give us such a wide berth as you did at Bude-jovice."

All the way home Lieutenant Lukash kept repeating to himself, "Company commander, company orderly."

And before him arose the figure of Schweik.

When Lieutenant Lukash asked Sergeant Major Vanek to find him another batman instead of Schweik, the sergeant major said, "I thought you was entirely satisfied with Schweik, sir."

When he heard that the colonel had appointed Schweik company orderly of the Eleventh Company, he exclaimed, "Gawd help us!"

At the divisional court-martial headquarters, in a hut provided with gratings, they rose at seven in the morning, and in accordance with regulations, tidied up their paillasses, which were scattered about on the dusty floor. In a long compartment partitioned off by planks, they folded their bed-spreads on a straw mattress, and those who had finished this job sat on the benches by the walls and were either searching for lice or, if they had arrived from the front, were telling each other their experiences.

Schweik, with Sapper Voditchka, was sitting on a bench

near the door with a number of soldiers belonging to various regiments and units.

"Here, I say," remarked Voditchka, "look at that Magyar chap by the window. He's saying his prayers. A good biff on the jaw, that's what he wants."

"Oh, he's all right," said Schweik. "He's here because he wouldn't join up. He's against war, because he belongs to a sect or something, and he don't want to kill anyone. He wants to keep God's commandments, but he'll have a bellyful of God's commandments by the time they've finished with him. In Moravia there used to be a fellow named Nemrava, and he wouldn't even put a rifle on his shoulder when he was shoved into the army, because he said it was against his principles to carry a rifle. Well, they gave him a devil of a time in clink, and then they had another try to make him take the oath. But he wasn't having any. He wouldn't take any oath. He said it was against his principles. And he stuck to it, too."

"He was a damned fool," said Sapper Voditchka. "He might just as well have took the oath. What the hell's it matter? Oath be blowed!"

"I've taken the oath three times," announced an infantryman, "and this is the third time they've had me up for desertion. It it wasn't for the doctor's certificate that fifteen years ago I was off my chump and did my aunt in, this is the third time I'd have been shot at the front. But my dear old aunt, she's a friend in need, that she is, and I wouldn't mind betting that in the end she'll wangle me out of the army altogether."

"What did you do your aunt in for?" inquired Schweik.

"Why, the same as people always get done in for," replied this pleasant fellow, "for *oof*, of course. The old girl had five bankbooks and they'd just sent her the interest when I arrived on a visit, absolutely down and out. She was all I had in the whole wide world, as they say. So I asked her to do something for me, and the stingy old geezer said that a strong young chap like me ought to do some work. Well, one word led to another, and the end of it was that I started sloshing her across the head with a poker. And when I'd finished with her physiog, I'm blowed if I could tell whether it was my aunt or not. So I sat down near her on the ground and kept saying to myself, 'Is it auntie or ain't it auntie?' And that's how the neighbors found me the next day. After that I was in a lunatic asylum for a bit, till I went before a commission and they said I was all right again and I'd have to make up the time I'd still got to serve in the army."

"Oh, don't you worry," said Schweik. "You'll be all right in the end, just like Janetchek at Pilsen. He was a gypsy, and in 1879 they were going to hang him for robbery and murder. But he didn't worry and he kept saying that he'd be all right in the end. And so he was. Because at the last moment they couldn't hang him, because it was the Emperor's birthday. So they didn't hang him till the next day, when the Emperor's birthday was all over. But he was in luck's way again, because on the day after that he was reprieved and there was going to be another trial, on account of some new evidence that showed it was another fellow named Janetchek who'd done it. So they had to dig him up out of the prison cemetery and give him another, proper burial in the Catholic cemetery at Pilsen, and then it turned out that he wasn't a Catholic at all, but an evangelical, so they carted him off to the evangelical cemetery, and then—"

Footsteps could be heard in the corridor and the sentry shouted *"Zuwachs!"* [1]

"Let 'em all come," chuckled Schweik. "Perhaps they've brought some cigarette butts with them."

The door opened, and in trotted the volunteer officer who had been with Schweik in the guardroom at Budejovice.

"Praised be Jesus Christ!" he said as he entered.

Whereupon Schweik, on behalf of all present, replied, "For ever and ever, amen."

The volunteer officer eyed Schweik with satisfaction, put down the bedspread which he had brought with him, and joined the Czech settlement sitting on the bench. He unwound his puttees and having extracted the cigarettes which were artfully packed in their folds, he distributed them. Then, from his boots he took some matches, neatly cut in halves lengthwise, and a scrap of matchbox for striking them on. He struck a match, carefully lit a cigarette, gave everyone a light, and remarked in an offhand manner: "I've been sentenced for mutiny. I refused to clean the latrines."

"That's nothing," remarked Schweik indulgently. "It's a fair old lark, you take it from me. The best thing you can do is to pretend you're barmy. When I was in the detention barracks, there was a chap, a smart fellow he was, a schoolteacher, and he did a bunk from the front line, and there was going to be

[1] "Another!"

289

a devil of a big trial so as to get him hanged and scare the rest of us. Well, he got out of it as easy as winking. When the staff doctor examined him he said he'd never done a bunk but he'd always been fond of traveling, ever since he was a kid, and he always wanted to see far countries, as the saying is. Once he woke up and found he was in Hamburg, and another time in London, and he never knew how he got there. He said his father had always been on the booze and had done himself in before he was born—this chap I mean, of course—and his mother had been a tart and had died of the D.T.'s. He said his younger sister had drowned herself, and the elder one had chucked herself under a train, and his brother had jumped off a railway bridge, his grandfather had done his grandmother in, this chap's grandmother I mean, and had then soaked himself with paraffin oil and set himself alight, and his other grandmother had gone gallivanting about with the gypsies and had poisoned herself with matches in prison, and one cousin had been sentenced several times for arson, and had cut the veins in his neck open with a piece of glass, and a female cousin on his father's side had chucked herself from a sixth-story window, and he himself was very backward and couldn't speak till he was ten, because when he was six months old, when they had tied him in up on a table, and then gone away somewhere for a minute, a cat had pulled him off the table and he'd fallen down and bumped his head. He said he still had very bad headaches every now and then, and when they came on he didn't know what he was doing, and that was the state he was in when he'd left the front line, and he didn't properly come to, like, till the military police were running him in. Holy Moses, you ought to have seen how they fairly fell over each other to get him out of the army, and other blokes who was in the same cell with him made notes on a bit of paper like this, because they thought it'd come in handy:

" 'Father: boozer; Mother: tart.
" 'Sister no. 1: Drowned.
" 'Sister no. 2: Railway train.
" 'Brother: Jumped off bridge.
" 'Grandfather did grandmother in (paraffin oil, set himself alight.)
" 'Grandmother no. 2: Gypsies, matches.
" 'And all the rest of it.'

"And one of them started telling the tale to the staff doctor, but he didn't get any further than his cousin, when the staff doctor, who'd heard it all twice before, says to him, 'Oh, yes, I know all about you. You're the fellow whose female cousin on your father's side threw herself from a sixth-story window, and you've always been very backward, haven't you? Oh, yes, we'll put that right for you in the mental ward.' So they took him off to the mental ward and tied him up in a strait waistcoast. And it didn't take long before he got rid of his backwardness and his boozy father and his mother who was a tart, and he volunteered for the front mighty quick."

At this moment the key grated in the lock and the warder shuffled in.

"Private Schweik and Sapper Voditchka to go to the provost marshal."

They got up to go, and Voditchka said to Schweik, "See what rotters they are. Every day a cross-examination, and nothing ever comes of it. Why the hell can't they sentence us and have done with it, instead of messing us up like this? Here we are, just dawdling about every blessed day."

As they proceeded on their way to the cross-examination in the office, which was situated in another part of the building, Sapper Voditchka discussed with Schweik when they were likely to come up for a proper trial.

"Nothing but cross-examination," he grumbled, "and it wouldn't be so bad if it led to anything. They just use up piles and piles of paper and no signs of a trial at all. They just let you rot behind the bars. And the soup isn't fit to eat. And what about the cabbage with the frozen potatoes? Did you ever come across such awful grub? Blimey, talk about the Great War! That ain't my idea of a great war."

"Well, I must say I'm pretty satisfied so far," said Schweik. "When I was doing my regular service it used to be much worse than this. Our sergeant major, a chap named Solpera, he used to say that in the army every man's got to have his duties at his fingers' ends, as you might say, and then he'd give you such a biff in the jaw that you wouldn't forget in a hurry. Oh, I don't see much to grumble at now."

Sapper Voditchka mused for a while, and then remarked, "When you come up before this provost marshal bloke, Schweik, don't get flurried, but just pitch the same yarn as you did at the cross-examination, or else I'll be in a hell of a mess. The chief thing is that you saw those Magyar chaps go for me. Don't forget we share and share alike in this little rumpus."

"Don't you worry, Voditchka," said Schweik consolingly. "Just keep calm. It's no use getting excited. Why, there's nothing much in a divisional court-martial, is there? You ought to have seen the way a court-martial polished chaps off years and years ago. There was a schoolmaster serving with us, and he told me once, when we were in clink, that in the Prague Museum there's a book with records of a court-martial in Maria Theresa's time. Why, every regiment had its executioner, and he just chopped off heads at a dollar a time. According to this book, he sometimes earned as much as five dollars a day."

They were just entering the offices of the divisional court-martial, and a sentry at once took them to office Number 8, where, behind a long table containing stacks of papers, sat Provost Marshal Ruller. Before him lay a volume of the legal code, and on it stood a half-full cup of tea. On the right-hand side of the table stood an imitation ivory crucifix with a dusty Christ who was gazing in despair at the base of his cross, covered with ashes and cigarette ends. Provost Marshal Ruller was just causing the crucified deity fresh distress by knocking out a cigarette against the base of the crucifix, while with his other hand he was lifting the cup of tea, which had got stuck to the cover of the legal code. Having liberated the teacup from the cover of the legal code, he went on turning over the pages of the book which he had borrowed from the officers' casino. It was by F. S. Krauss and bore the promising title *Investigations into the Historical Development of Sexual Morality.*

He was contemplating the diagrams which so effectively supplemented the text, when he was interrupted by a cough. It was Sapper Voditchka.

"What's the matter?" he inquired, searching for more diagrams and sketches.

"Beg to report, sir," replied Schweik, "my chum Voditchka here has caught cold and now he's got a nasty cough."

Provost Marshal Ruller now looked at Schweik and Voditchka. He endeavored to impart a stern expression to his countenance.

"Oh, you've turned up at last, have you?" he said, burrowing among the papers on the table. "I sent for you at nine o'clock, and now it's nearly eleven. Is that the way to stand, you lazy lout?" The last question was addressed to Voditchka, who was casually standing at ease. "Until I tell you to stand at ease, you stand up properly to attention."

"Beg to report, sir," announced Schweik, "he's got rheumatism."

"You'd better keep your mouth shut," said Provost Marshal Ruller, "and don't answer back till I ask you something. Where the devil's that file got to? You two jailbirds are giving me a hell of a lot of work. But you'll find it won't pay you to cause all this unnecessary trouble."

From a stack of documents he now drew a bulky file labeled "Schweik & Voditchka" and said, "Just look at that, you mongrels. If you think you're going to fritter your time away at the divisional court-martial over a paltry rumpus, and dodge going to the front, you're damned well mistaken, let me tell you."

He sighed. "We're going to quash the proceedings against you," he continued. "Now you're going back to your units, where you'll be punished by the orderly room. Then off you'll go to the front. If you ever come my way again, you blackguards, I'll give you something you won't forget in a hurry. Take them away to Number Z."

"Beg to report, sir," said Schweik, "that we'll both take your words to heart, and we're much obliged to you for all your kindness. If we was civilians, I wouldn't mind calling you a jolly old sport. And we're both very sorry for all the trouble you've had because of us. We don't deserve it, and that's a fact."

"Oh, go to Hades!" the provost marshal yelled at Schweik. "If Colonel Schröder hadn't put in a good word for you, you'd have had a damned rough time of it."

As the military clerks in the office had gone to fetch rations, the soldier who was escorting them had to take them back to the cells, which he did to the accompaniment of much invective against the whole race of military clerks.

"They'll take all the fat from the soup again," he lamented, "and leave me nothing but gristle. Yesterday I had to escort a couple of fellows to camp, and somebody pinched half my bread rations."

"You chaps here think of nothing but your grub," said Voditchka, who was now his old self again.

When they told the volunteer officer how they had fared, he remarked, "On draft, eh? You've been invited to join the personally conducted trip to Galicia. Well, you can start on your journey without any misgivings whatever. And I hope you'll find yourselves attracted by the regions where you'll be introduced to the trenches. It's a fine country and extremely interesting. You'll feel quite at home there. The wide and valuable experiences of our glorious army while retreating from Galicia on its first trip will certainly prove useful when the program of the second trip is being arranged. Follow your noses straight into Russia, and fire all your cartridges into the air for sheer joy of living."

In the office they settled everything promptly. A sergeant major, his mouth still greasy from his recent meal, handed Schweik and Voditchka their papers with an exceedingly solemn expression. He also took advantage of the opportunity of delivering a speech, in which he made a special appeal to their soldierly spirit. His remarks were liberally embellished with elegant terms of abuse in his native Polish dialect.

The time now came for Schweik and Voditchka to take leave of each other.

Schweik said, "Well, when the war's over, come and give me a look-up. You'll find me in The Flagon every evening at six o'clock."

"You bet I will," replied Voditchka.

They parted, and when there was a distance of several yards between them, Schweik shouted, "Don't forget. I'll be looking out for you."

Whereupon Sapper Voditchka, who was now turning the corner by the second row of hutments, shouted, "Right you are. After the war, at six o'clock in the evening."

"Better make it half past, in case I'm a bit late," replied Schweik.

Then, at a great distance, Voditchka's voice could be heard: "Can't you make it six?"

And the last that Voditchka heard of his departing comrade was: "All right. I'll be there at six."

And that was how the good soldier Schweik parted from Sapper Voditchka.

5.

From Bruck-on-the-Leitha to Sokal

LIEUTENANT LUKASH, in a state of great agitation, was pacing up and down the office of Draft Number 11. It was a dark den in the company hutment, partitioned off from the passage by means of planks. A table, two chairs, a can of paraffin oil, and a mattress.

Facing Lieutenant Lukash stood Quartermaster Sergeant Vanek, who spent his time drawing up pay lists and keeping the accounts for the rations of the rank and file. He was, in fact, the finance minister of the whole company, and he spent the entire day in that dark little den, which was also where he slept at night.

By the door stood a fat infantryman with a long, thick beard. This was Baloun, the lieutenant's new orderly, who in civil life was a miller.

"Well, you've chosen a fine batman for me, I must say," said Lieutenant Lukash to the quartermaster sergeant. "Thanks very much for the pleasant surprise. The first day I sent him to the officers' mess for my lunch, and he ate half of it."

"Begging your pardon, sir, but I spilled it," said the bearded giant.

"All right, then you spilled it. You might have spilled some soup or some gravy, but you couldn't have spilled the roast meat. The piece you brought me was about big enough to cover my fingernail. And what did you do with the pudding?"

"I—"

"You ate it. It's no use saying you didn't. You ate it."

Lieutenant Lukash uttered the last three words with such solemnity and stern emphasis that Baloun involuntarily stepped two paces backward.

"I've made inquiries in the kitchen, and I've found out what we had for lunch today. First of all, there was soup with dumplings. What did you do with those dumplings? You took them out on the way, didn't you? Then there was beef with gherkins. What did you do with that? You ate that, too. Two slices of roast meat. And *you* only brought me half a slice, didn't you? Two pieces of pudding. Where's that gone to? You gobbled it up, you greedy hog, you. Come on, what did you do with that pudding? What's that? You dropped it in the mud? You damned liar! Can you show me the place where it's lying in the mud? What's that? A dog came up and ran away with it before you could stop him. For two pins I'd give you such a bloody good hiding that your own mother wouldn't know you. You'd try to make a fool of me in the bargain, eh, you low-down skunk, you! Do you know who saw you? Quartermaster Sergeant Vanek, here. He came to me and said, 'Beg to report, sir, Baloun's eating your lunch, the greedy hog. I was looking out of the window and saw him stuffing himself as if he hadn't eaten anything for a week.' Look here, Sergeant, really you might have found something better for me than this lousy fellow."

"Beg to report, sir, Baloun seemed to be the most satisfactory man on our draft. He's such a thickheaded idiot that he forgets all his drill as soon as he's taught it, and if we was to let him handle a rifle, he'd only do some more damage. The last time he was practicing musketry with blank cartridges, he nearly shot the next man's eye out. I thought he'd be all right as an orderly, at any rate."

"And eat up an officer's lunch," said Lieutenant Lukash,

"as if his own issue of rations wasn't enough for him. I suppose you'll tell me now that you're hungry, eh?"

"Beg to report, sir, I'm properly hungry. If anyone's got any bread left over from his rations, I buy it from him for cigarettes, and even then it don't seem enough, somehow. It's just the way I'm made. Just when I think I can't eat any more, I feel as if I'd got nothing inside me. If I see somebody eating, or just smell food, my inside comes over all empty, like. Why, when I feel like that, I could chew up nails. Beg to report, sir, I made one application to receive a double issue of rations, and I went before the M.O. at Budejovice, but he gave me medicine and duty and ordered them to give me nothing all day but a small bowl of plain soup. 'I'll teach you to be hungry, you impudent lout,' he says; 'just you come here again,' he says, 'and you'll be as thin as a rake before you get away again.' As soon as I see anything that's good to eat, it just makes my mouth water. I can't help it, sir. Beg to report, sir, I'd take it as a great favor if you'd let me have a double issue of rations. If it's not meat, something else'll do; some pudding, potatoes, dumplings, a little gravy—it all helps to keep you going."

"Well, of all the bloody impudence!" remarked Lieutenant Lukash. "Sergeant, have you ever come across a soldier with as much confounded cheek as this fellow? He eats my lunch, and then on top of that, wants me to let him get a double issue of rations! I'll see that you get a thundering big bellyache for this, my fine fellow.

"Now then, Sergeant," he continued, turning to Quartermaster Sergeant Vanek, "you take this man to Corporal Weidenhofer and tell him to tie him up for two hours near the cookhouse door, until the rations of stew are issued this evening. He's to tie him up properly, so that he can only just stand on tiptoe, and so that he can see the stew cooking in the saucepan. And tell him to keep the blighter tied up while the stew rations are being issued in the cookhouse, so that it'll make his mouth water like a hungry tyke sniffing outside a butcher's shop. And tell them to let someone else have his rations."

"Very good, sir. Come along, Baloun."

When they were on their way out, the lieutenant stopped them in the doorway, and looking at Baloun's horrified countenance, he remarked gloatingly, "You've done it this time, Baloun. Well, I hope you'll enjoy your feed. And if you try any more of those tricks on me, I'll have you court-martialed without any beating about the bush."

When Quartermaster Sergeant Vanek returned and announced that Baloun was already tied up, Lieutenant Lukash said, "You know me well enough, Vanek, to be quite sure I don't like doing that sort of thing. But I can't help myself. I can't have a low blighter like that around me. And it'll have a good moral effect on the rank and file when they see Baloun tied up. These fellows who're on draft and know they're going to the front in a day or two think they can do what they damn well please."

Lieutenant Lukash looked very upset.

"Don't you worry your head about that, sir," said Quartermaster Sergeant Vanek, trying to console him. "I've been on three different drafts and it was just six of one and half a dozen of the other, sir, not a scrap of difference between them. They all got cut to pieces with the whole battalion, and then what was left of us had to be reorganized. The worst of the lot was the ninth. Every man jack of them was taken prisoner, N.C.O.'s and company commander and all. And I'd have been taken as well, only I just happened to have gone to fetch the company's regular issue of rum, and that's what saved me."

"It strikes me," remarked Lieutenant Lukash, "that you're a bit of a boozer. But don't imagine that the next time we go into action you'll just happen to have gone to fetch an issue of rum. As soon as I spotted your red nose, I had you sized up all right."

"That's from the Carpathians, sir. When we got our rations up there, they were always cold. The trenches were in the snow; we wasn't allowed to make fires, and rum was the only thing we had to keep us going. And if it hadn't been for me, it would have been like in the other companies, where they hadn't got any rum and the men were frozen. The rum gave all of us red noses. The only drawback was that orders came from the battalion that only men with red noses were to be sent out on patrol duty."

"Well, the winter's practically over now," remarked the lieutenant meaningly.

"You can't do without rum, sir, in the field, whatever season it is. It keeps you in good spirits, as you might say. When a man's got a drop of rum inside him, he's ready to go for anyone. Hello, who's that knocking at the door? Silly ass, can't he read what it says on the door: 'Don't knock. Come in'?"

Lieutenant Lukash turned on his chair toward the door, and he saw the door open slowly and softly. And just as slowly and softly the good soldier Schweik entered the office of Draft Number 11.

Lieutenant Lukash closed his eyes at the sight of the good soldier Schweik, who gazed at him with much the same gratification as might have been displayed by the prodigal son when he saw his father killing the fatted calf.

"Beg to report, sir, I'm back again," announced Schweik from the doorway, with such frank informality that Lieutenant Lukash suddenly realized what had befallen him. Ever since Colonel Schröder had informed him that Schweik was being sent back to afflict him, Lieutenant Lukash had been hoping against hope that the evil hour might be indefinitely postponed. Every morning he said to himself, "He won't be here today. He may have got into trouble again, so perhaps they'll keep him there." But now Schweik had upset all these expectations by turning up in that bland and unassuming manner of his.

Schweik now gazed at Quartermaster Sergeant Vanek and turning to him, handed to him with a smile some papers which he took from the pocket of his greatcoat.

"Beg to report, Sergeant," he said, "I've got to hand you these papers that they signed in the regimental office. It's about my pay and rations allowance."

Schweik's demeanor in the office of Draft Number 11 was as free and easy as if he and Quartermaster Sergeant Vanek were old cronies.

The quartermaster sergeant, however, replied curtly, "Put 'em down on the table."

"I think, Sergeant," said Lieutenant Lukash, with a sigh, "that you'd better leave me alone with Schweik."

Vanek went out and stood listening at the door to hear what these two would say to each other. At first he heard nothing, for Schweik and Lieutenant Lukash held their peace. For a long time they looked at each other and watched each other closely.

Lieutenant Lukash broke this painful silence by a remark, to which he endeavored to impart a strong dose of irony. "Well, I'm glad to see you again, Schweik. It's very kind of you to look me up. Just fancy now, what a charming visitor!"

But his feelings got the better of him, and he gave vent to his bottled-up arrears of annoyance by banging his fist on the table, so that the inkpot gave a jerk and ink was spilled over the pay roll. He also jumped up, thrust his face close to Schweik, and yelled at him, "You bloody fool!"

Whereupon he began to stride up and down the narrow office, spitting whenever he came past Schweik.

"Beg to report, sir," said Schweik, while Lieutenant Lukash continued to pace up and down and kept furiously flinging into a corner crumpled scraps of paper which he snatched from the table each time he came near it, "I handed over that letter just as you told me. I found Mrs. Kákonyi all right, and I don't mind saying that she's a fine figure of a woman, although when I saw her she was crying—"

Lieutenant Lukash sat down on the quartermaster sergeant's mattress and exclaimed hoarsely, "When is this foolery going to stop, Schweik?"

Schweik continued, as if he had not heard the lieutenant's exclamation. "Well, then there was a little bit of unpleasantness, but I took all the blame for it. Of course, they wouldn't believe that I'd been writing letters to the lady, so I thought I'd better swallow the letter at the cross-examination, so as to put them off the scent, like. Then—how it happened I don't know, unless it was just a stroke of bad luck—I got mixed up in a little bit of a shindy, nothing worth talking about, really. Anyhow, I managed to get out of that, and they admitted I wasn't to blame, and sent me to the regimental orderly room and stopped all further inquiries into it. I waited in the regimental office for a few minutes, till the colonel arrived, and he gave me a bit of a wigging and said I was to report myself to you as company orderly, and told me I was to tell you to go to him at once about this here draft. That's more than half an hour ago, but the colonel didn't know they was going to take me into the regimental office again and that I'd have to hang about there for another quarter of an hour because I've got back pay coming to me for all this time, and I'd got to collect it from the regiment and not from the draft, because I was entered on the list as being under close arrest with the regiment. They've got everything here so muddled and mixed up that it's enough to give you the staggers."

When Lieutenant Lukash heard that he ought to have been with Colonel Schröder half an hour earlier, he hastily put on his tunic and said, "You've done me another good turn, Schweik."

He said it in such an utterly dejected and despairing tone

that Schweik endeavored to console him with a kindly word, which he addressed to Lieutenant Lukash as he was dashing out of the doorway. "The colonel don't mind waiting, sir; he ain't got anything to do, anyhow."

Shortly after the lieutenant had departed, Quartermaster Sergeant Vanek came in.

Schweik was sitting on a chair and throwing pieces of coal into the small iron stove, the flap of which was open. The stove smoked and stank, and Schweik continued his amusement without perceiving the quartermaster sergeant, who watched Schweik for a while, but then suddenly kicked the flap to, and told Schweik to clear out.

"Sorry, Sergeant," said Schweik with dignity, "but let me tell you that I can't obey your order, much as I'd like to, because I'm under higher authority.

"You see, Sergeant, it's like this," he added, with a touch of pride. "I'm company orderly. Colonel Schröder, he arranged for me to be attached to Draft Number Eleven with Lieutenant Lukash who I used to be batman to, but owing to my natural gumption, as you might say, I've been promoted to orderly. Me and the lieutenant are quite old pals. What was you in civil life, Sergeant?"

Quartermaster Sergeant Vanek was so taken by surprise when the good soldier Schweik addressed him in this free and easy, hail-fellow-well-met manner, that without standing on his dignity, as he so much liked to do when brought into contact with the rank and file, he replied as if he were Schweik's subordinate.

"I kept a druggist's shop at Kralup."

"I was apprenticed to a shopkeeper once," said Schweik. "I worked for a chap named Kokoshka, in Prague. He was a rum cove, he was. One day I put a match, by mistake, to a barrel of benzine in the cellar, and it all caught light, and he chucked me out, and the Shopkeepers' Association wouldn't get me another job, so just through a barrel of benzine I couldn't finish my apprenticeship. Do you make powders for cows?"

Quartermaster Sergeant Vanek shook his head.

"We used to make powders for cows and wrapped them up in pictures of saints. Our boss was as pious as they make 'em, and one day he read in a book that St. Peregrine was useful to cows when they've got spasms. So he had some pictures of St. Peregrine printed somewhere at Smichow and had them consecrated at the Emaus monastery for two hundred gulden. And then we wrapped them up in the packets of our powders for cows. You mixed the powder in warm water, and made the cow drink it out of a bucket, while you recited a little prayer to St. Peregrine that had been made up by Mr. Tauchen, our shopman. You see, when these pictures of St. Peregrine had been printed, there had to be a little prayer of some sort on the other side. So in the evening old Kokoshka sent for Mr. Tauchen and told him he'd got to make up a prayer to go on the picture for the cows' powders, and he'd got to have it ready when he came to the shop the next morning, so as it could be sent to the printers. It was wanted in a hurry because the cows was waiting for this little prayer. It was a case of take it or leave it, as you might say. If he made a good job of it, he'd have a gulden in hard cash, and if he didn't, he'd have a fortnight's notice. Well, Mr. Tauchen sat up all night in a regular sweat, and when he came to open the shop in the morning he looked absolutely washed out, and he hadn't written a line. In fact, he'd forgotten the name of the saint who made the powders do the cows good. And then our handy man Ferdinand helped him out of the fix. He was a smart chap, he was. He just said, 'Let's have a squint at it,' and then Mr. Tauchen sent for some beer. But before I was back again with the beer, Ferdinand had finished writing half of the prayer. It went like this:

> "Here I come from the skies so blue,
> And I bring good news to you.
> Whether you're a cow, a calf or a bull,
> You can't do without a packetful
> Of Kokoshka's powders if you're queer;
> They'll make your spasms disappear.

"Then when he'd had a drink and properly wetted his whistle, he finished it off in double-quick time, and very nice it was, too:

> "This was invented by St. Peregrine,
> And a packet costs you only one-and-nine.
> St. Peregrine, keep our cattle from harm;
> They like your powders because they act like a charm.
> The grateful farmers all sing your praises, oh,
> St. Peregrine, protect our cows from woe.

"Afterward, when Mr. Kokoshka arrived, Mr. Tauchen went with him into the countinghouse, and when he came out again, he showed us two gulden instead of the one that he'd been promised, and he wanted to go halves with Ferdinand. But when Ferdinand saw the two gulden, filthy lucre, as they call it, got the better of him. He said he wanted the lot or nothing at all. So Mr. Tauchen gave him nothing at all, and kept the two gulden for himself, and he took me into the stockroom and gave me a smack on the jaw and said I'd get a few dozen more like that if I ever told anyone it wasn't him who made up the prayer and wrote it down, and if Ferdinand was to go and complain to the boss about it, I was to say that Ferdinand was a liar. I had to swear I'd do what he said, in front of a keg of vinegar. But our handy man he got his own back over those cow powders. We used to mix them in large crates in the loft, and so he got together a lot of mouse droppings and mixed them into the powders. Then he went and collected horse dung in the streets, dried it at home, powdered it up in a mortar, and put that into the cow powders too, along with the picture of St. Peregrine. And that wasn't enough for him. He went up into the loft where those crates were and took down his trousers and—"

The telephone rang. The quartermaster sergeant clutched hastily at the receiver and then flung it down again, saying fretfully, "I've got to go to the regimental office. I don't like the look of that, at such short notice."

Schweik was alone again.

Presently the telephone rang again.

Schweik picked up the receiver. "Vanek? He's gone to the regimental office. Who's here? The orderly of draft Number Eleven. Who's that speaking? The orderly of Draft Number Twelve? Pleased to know you. What's my name? Schweik. And yours? Braun. You don't happen to have a relative named Braun at Karlin, a hatter? You haven't; you don't know him? I don't know him, either, but I once rode past his shop in a tram and the name just caught my eye."

"Any news?"

"Not as far as I know."

"When are we off?"

"I never heard we were going off anywhere. Where to?"

"To the front, of course, you chump."

"That's the first I've heard about it."

"You're a fine orderly. Don't you know that your lieutenant went to see the colonel?"

"Oh, yes, the colonel invited him."

"What difference does that make? Anyway, he went to see the colonel, and so did our lieutenant and the one from the Thirteenth Draft. I was just telephoning to his orderly. I don't like the look of all this running about. And don't you know whether the chaps in the band are packing up?"

"I don't know damn-all about anything."

"Oh, come off it! You ain't so soft as all that. Has your quartermaster sergeant been given his orders yet? How many chaps have you got in your company?"

"I don't know."

"You blithering idiot, do you think I'm going to bite your head off, or what?" (The man at the telephone could be heard saying to some third person: "Here, Franta, take the other receiver and you'll hear what a bloody fool of an orderly the Eleventh Draft has got.") "Hello, are you asleep, or what? Come along, answer up when a chap asks you a civil question, can't you? You don't know damn-all? Rats! that be blowed for a yarn. Didn't your quartermaster sergeant say anything about drawing the issue of tinned stuff? What, you never talked to him about things like that? You blithering ass. You don't care a damn one way or the other?" (There was a noise of laughter.) "You must have a tile loose somewhere. When you do get to know anything, telephone to the Twelfth Draft, you perishing imbecile. Where are you from?"

"Prague."

"You ought to be a bit quicker in the uptake, then. Oh, yes, there's something else. When did your quartermaster sergeant go to the office?"

"He was called away a little while ago."

"Well, why couldn't you have said so before? Ours went a little while ago, too. There's something in the wind. Have you had a word with the service corps?"

"No."

"Holy Moses, and you say you're from Prague? Why, you haven't got the foggiest idea about anything. Where the hell do you get to all day?"

"I only arrived from the divisional court-martial an hour ago."

"Oh, now you're talking. That accounts for it. I'll come and look you up today. Ring off twice."

Schweik was about to light his pipe, when the telephone rang again.

"Oh, to hell with the bloody telephone!" thought Schweik to himself. "I can't be bothered with it."

But the telephone went on ringing relentlessly, until at last Schweik lost patience. He took the receiver and bellowed into the mouthpiece, "Hello, who's speaking? This is Schweik, orderly of Draft Number Eleven."

Schweik then heard the voice of Lieutenant Lukash replying, "What are you all up to? Where's Vanek? Call Vanek to the telephone immediately."

"Beg to report, sir, the telephone rang not long ago—"

"Listen here, Schweik. I've got no time for gossip with you. In the army, messages by telephone have got to be brief and to the point. And when you're telephoning, drop all that beg-to-report stuff. Now I'm asking you whether you've got Vanek there. He's to come to the telephone immediately."

"Beg to report, sir, I haven't got him here. He was called away a little while ago to the regimental office, hardly a quarter of an hour ago."

"Look here, Schweik, I'll settle up with you when I come back. Can't you be brief? Now pay close attention to what I'm telling you. Do you understand clearly what I'm saying? Don't make the excuse afterward that there was a buzzing noise in the telephone. Now then, immediately, as soon as you hang up the receiver—"

There was a pause. Then the telephone rang again. Schweik picked up the receiver and was swamped by a flood of abuse. "You bloody, blithering, thickheaded, misbegotten booby, you infernal jackass, you lout, you skunk, you hooligan, what the hell are you up to? Why have you rung off?"

"Beg to report, sir, you said I was to hang up the receiver."

"I'll be back home in an hour's time, Schweik, and I'll make it hot for you. Now pull yourself together, and go and fetch a sergeant—Fuchs, if you can find him—and tell him he's to go at once with ten men to the regimental stores and fetch the issue of tinned rations. Now repeat what he's got to do."

"He's got to go with ten men to the regimental stores, and fetch the issue of tinned rations for the company."

"For once in a way you've stopped talking twaddle. Now I'm going to telephone to Vanek in the regimental office to go to the regimental stores and take charge there. If he comes

306

back in the meanwhile, he's to leave everything and go to the regimental stores at the double. Now hang up the receiver."

For some time Schweik searched in vain not only for Sergeant Fuchs, but for all the other N.C.O.'s. They were in the cookhouse, where they were gnawing scraps of meat from bones and gloating over Baloun, who had been duly tied up according to instructions. One of the cooks brought him a chop and thrust it between his teeth. The bearded giant, not being able to use his hands, cautiously took the bone in his mouth, balancing it by means of his teeth and gums, while he gnawed the meat with the expression of a wild man of the woods.

"Which of you chaps is Sergeant Fuchs?" asked Schweik, when he had at last succeeded in running the N.C.O.'s to earth.

Sergeant Fuchs did not even deign to announce himself when he saw that it was only an ordinary private who was asking for him.

"Look here," said Schweik, "how much longer am I to go on asking? Where's Sergeant Fuchs?"

Sergeant Fuchs came forward and, very much on his dignity, began to explain in the strongest of language how a sergeant ought to be addressed. Anyone in his squad who had the bloody cheek to talk to him as Schweik had done would get a biff in the jaw before he knew where—

"Here, steady on," said Schweik severely. "Just you pull yourself together without wasting any more time and take ten men at the double to the regimental stores. You're wanted there to fetch the tinned rations."

Sergeant Fuchs was so astounded that all he could do was to splutter, "What?"

"Now then, none of your back answers," replied Schweik. "I'm orderly of the Eleventh Draft, and I've just been talking over the telephone with Lieutenant Lukash. And he said 'with ten men at the double to the regimental stores.' If you won't go, Sergeant Fuchs, I'll report the matter immediately. Lieutenant Lukash particularly asked for you to go. There's nothing more to be said about it. Lieutenant Lukash said that messages by telephone have got to be brief and plain. 'When Sergeant Fuchs is told to go,' he said, 'why, he's got to go. In the army, especially when a war's on, all waste of time's a crime. If this chap Sergeant Fuchs won't go when you tell him, just you telephone to me at once, and I'll settle up with him. I'll make mincemeat of Sergeant Fuchs,' he said. My word, you don't know what a terror Lieutenant Lukash is."

Schweik gazed triumphantly at the N.C.O.'s, who were taken aback and also very much upset by his attitude. Sergeant Fuchs muttered something unintelligible and departed in a hurry, while Schweik called out to him, "Can I telephone to Lieutenant Lukash that it's all right?"

"I'll be with ten men at the regimental stores in a jiffy," came the voice of the departing sergeant, whereupon Schweik, without another word, left the N.C.O.'s, who were as astounded as Sergeant Fuchs had been.

"Things are getting lively," said Little Corporal Blazek. "We'll be getting a move on soon."

When Schweik got back to the office of the Eleventh Draft, he again had no time to light his pipe, for once more the telephone began to ring. It was Lieutenant Lukash who spoke to him once more.

"Where have you been, Schweik? I telephoned twice before and couldn't get any answer."

"I've done that little job, sir."

"Have those men gone yet?"

"Oh, yes, sir, they've gone all right, only I don't know whether they'll get there. Shall I go and have another look?"

"Did you find Sergeant Fuchs?"

"Yes, sir. First of all, he answered me back a bit offhand, like, but when I told him that telephone messages have got to be brief and—"

"Stop all that jabber, Schweik. Is Vanek back yet?"

"No, sir."

"Don't yell into the telephone. Have you got any idea where that confounded Vanek is likely to be?"

"I've no idea where that confounded Vanek is likely to be, sir."

"He's been in the regimental office, and then he went off somewhere. I shouldn't be surprised if he's in the canteen. Just go and look for him there, Schweik, and tell him to go to the regimental stores immediately. And then there's something else. Find Corporal Blazek immediately and tell him to untie that fellow Baloun at once. Then send Baloun to me. Hang up the receiver."

Schweik discovered Corporal Blazek, personally witnessed the untying of Baloun, and then accompanied Baloun on his way, as this led also to the canteen, where he was to search for Quartermaster Sergeant Vanek. Baloun regarded Schweik as his deliverer and promised that he would go halves with him in every parcel of food which he received from home.

"It's slaughtering time there now," said Baloun in tones of yearning. "Which do you like best, saveloys or liver sausage? Just you tell me, and I'll write home this very evening. I should reckon my pig weighs round about three hundred pounds. He's got a head like a bulldog, and that's the best kind. Pigs like that never let you down. That's a good breed, if you like. They can stand plenty of wear and tear. I bet the fat on that animal's a good eight inches thick. When I was at home I used to make the liver sausage myself and I always had such a rare old feed of it that I was fit to bust. The pig I had last year weighed over three hundred pounds.

"Ah, that was a pig for you," he continued rapidly gripping Schweik's hand as they reached the parting of the ways. "I brought him up on nothing but potatoes and I used to watch him growing visibly, as you might almost say. I put the ham into brine, and I tell you, a nice slice taken from the brine and fried with potato dumplings, soaked in pork dripping and some greens on top of it, that's a fair treat. And after a good blowout of that sort, you wash it down with a nice glass or two of beer. But the war's put a stop to all that."

The bearded Baloun sighed deeply and departed to the colonel's office, while Schweik made his way to the canteen through an old avenue of tall linden trees.

Quartermaster Sergeant Vanek was sitting at his ease in the canteen, and telling a staff sergeant major how much he was able to make before the war by selling enamel and varnish. But the staff sergeant major was no longer his usual self. That afternoon an estate owner from Pardubice, whose son was in camp, had been there and had tipped him handsomely, besides standing treat in the town the whole afternoon. He was now very listless and woebegone, because he had lost his appetite. He was not even aware what they were talking about and did not take the slightest notice of the quartermaster sergeant's remarks on the subject of enamel and varnish. He was engrossed in his own meditations and was mumbling something about a local train which went from Trebon to Pelhrimov and back.

When Schweik entered, Quartermaster Sergeant Vanek was making another attempt to explain to the staff sergeant major by means of statistics what profit could be made on one pound of varnish for building operations, whereupon the staff sergeant major, entirely bemused, replied, "He died on the way back, and all we found on him was some letters."

When he saw Schweik, he mixed him up with someone else, of whom he evidently did not approve, for he called him a bloody ventriloquist. Schweik, however, approached Quartermaster Sergeant Vanek, who was also somewhat fuddled, but very cheerful and friendly about it.

"You've got to go at once to the regimental stores, sir," announced Schweik. "Sergeant Fuchs is waiting there with ten men, and they're going to draw tinned rations. You've got to go at the double. The lieutenant's telephoned twice."

Quartermaster Sergeant Vanek burst out laughing. "Not if I know it, old chap. Do you think I'm barmy, or what? There's plenty of time, lad, plenty of time. The regimental stores won't run away. When Lieutenant Lukash has handled as many drafts as what I have, then he'll be able to talk, but he'll drop all that stuff about doing things at the double. A lot of useless worry, that's what it is. Why, many's the time I've received orders in the regimental office that we was off the next day and I was to go and draw rations there and then. And what I did was to come here and have a quiet drink and just take things easy. The tinned rations won't run away. I know more about regimental stores than what the lieutenant does, and when the officers have one of these here confabs with the colonel, I know the sort of stuff they talk. Why, for one thing, there ain't any tinned rations in our regimental stores, and there never was. All the tinned rations we've got is inside the colonel's noddle. Whenever we want tinned rations, we just get it in driblets from the brigade, or we borrow it from other regiments if we happen to be in touch with them. Why, there's one regiment alone we owe more than three hundred tins of rations to. Yes, sir! They can say what they like at their confab, but they're not going to bounce me. And the storekeeper himself'll tell 'em they're barmy when they go there for the doings. Why, there ain't a single draft yet as had any tinned rations issued to it when it left for the front."

"That's so, ain't it, you old pie-face?" he added, turning to the staff sergeant major, who, however, was either dropping off to sleep, or else was on the verge of a slight attack of delirium, for he replied:

"When she went for a walk, she always kept her umbrella open."

"The best thing you can do," continued Quartermaster Sergeant Vanek, "is not to worry about anything. Let 'em do what they damn well please. If they said in the regimental office that we're leaving tomorrow, they don't know what they're talking about. How can we leave, if there ain't any railway trucks? I was there when they was telephoning to the railway station. There ain't a single spare truck. It's just the same as it was with the last draft. We was hanging about in the railway station for two days, waiting for somebody to have pity on us and send us a train. And then we didn't know where we was going to. The colonel himself didn't know. After that, we had a ride all over Hungary and nobody ever knew whether we was going to Serbia or Russia. At every station they talked to the staff division direct. We was just a sort of flying squad, as you might say. No, take it easy, lad. Everything'll come right in time, but there's no need for any hurry. That's the ticket.

"They've got some first-rate drink here today," continued Quartermaster Sergeant Vanek, ignoring the staff sergeant major, who was stuttering to himself in German, "You take it from me, I've had a pretty thin time so far. I can't make it out."

"It ain't likely I'm going to worry my head about the draft leaving. Why, the first draft I was on got everything ready without a hitch, in a couple of hours. Then the other drafts after that started getting ready two whole days beforehand. But Lieutenant Prenosil, he was our company commander and a regular sport, he said, 'Don't you hurry yourselves, lads,' and we got everything done like clockwork. We didn't start packing till two hours before the train started. And if you take my advice you'll just sit down—"

"It can't be done," said the good soldier Schweik with a considerable effort. "I've got to get back to the office. Suppose someone was to telephone."

"All right, go if you want to, old chap, but it ain't sporting of you and that's a fact. A proper orderly has never got to be where he's wanted. You're too keen on rushing back to work.

311

There's nothing gets my goat more than an orderly with the wind up who wants to chuck his weight all over the bloody army."

But Schweik was already outside the door and was hurrying in the direction of his draft.

Quartermaster Sergeant Vanek was left by himself, for it could scarcely be said that the staff sergeant major was a sociable companion. He was now entirely isolated from the rest of mankind and toying with his glass, he was stammering a great jumble of incoherent remarks in Czech and German. "Many a time I have passed through that village and never even realized her existence. In six months my examinations will be over and I'll have my degree. I've become a thorough wreck, thanks to you, Lucy. They've been published in volume form, and very attractive the bindings are, too—some of you may remember what I mean."

Thoroughly bored, the quartermaster sergeant was drumming a tune with his fingers on the table, but his boredom did not last long, for the door opened and in came Jurajda, the cook from the officers' mess. He glued himself to a chair.

"We've had orders today," he babbled, "to draw our rations of brandy for traveling. All the bottles wrapped in wickerwork were filled with rum, so we had to empty one of them. That was a treat for us. The men in the cookhouse did themselves well, and the colonel turned up too late to get any. So now they've cooked him an omelette. I tell you, we're having a fine old time of it."

Jurajda lapsed into philosophic ponderings, as befitted his civilian occupation. Until the war broke out he was editing an occultist periodical and a series of books entitled *Secrets of Life and Death*. The colonel took a fancy to him as a kind of regimental freak, for there weren't many officers' messes that could boast of having as a cook a full-blown occultist, who, while scrutinizing the secrets of life and death, could dish up a first-rate roast sirloin or a tasty stew.

Jurajda, who could scarcely sit upright on the chair and reeked of a dozen or so tots of rum, now went on babbling at random.

"Yes," he said, "when there wasn't enough to go around and the colonel only saw some fried potatoes, he fell into what we call the gaki state. Do you know what that is? It means the state of hungry spirits. So I said to him, 'Well, sir, have you

312

got enough power to overcome the dispensation of fate that you didn't get any fried kidneys? It has been predestined by karma, sir, that you are to get a chopped calves' liver omelette for supper tonight.'

"My friend," he presently remarked to the quartermaster sergeant, with an inadvertent gesture of the hand which upset all the glasses within reach of him on the table, "all phenomena, all shapes, all objects possess disembodied qualities. Shape is disembodiment and disembodiment is shape. There is no distinction between disembodiment and shape; there is no distinction between shape and disembodiment. What is disembodiment, is shape, and what is shape, is disembodiment."

He then lapsed into silence, propping his head in his hand and contemplating the splashes and stains on the table.

The staff sergeant major went babbling on. Nobody could make head or tail of what he was saying. "The corn vanished from the fields. Vanished. Such was his mood when he received her invitation and went to call on her. The Whitsun holidays come in the spring."

Quartermaster Sergeant Vanek was still drumming on the table. From time to time he took a pull at his glass and remembered that ten men with a sergeant were waiting for him at the regimental stores. When he thought of this he smiled to himself and waved his hand airily.

When, at a late hour, he returned to the office of Draft Number 11, he found Schweik at the telephone.

"Shape is disembodiment, and disembodiment is shape," he murmured, and crawled, fully dressed, onto his mattress, where he immediately fell fast asleep.

But Schweik continued to sit by the telephone, because two hours previously Lieutenant Lukash had telephoned that he was still conferring with the colonel, but he had forgotten to tell him that he need not wait at the telephone any longer. Then Sergeant Fuchs telephoned to say that he had been waiting with ten men for hours and hours, but the quartermaster sergeant hadn't turned up. Not only that, but the regimental stores were locked. At last he'd given it up as a lost job and the ten men, one by one, had gone back to their huts.

From time to time Schweik amused himself by taking the receiver and listening in. The telephone was a new patent which had just been introduced into the army, and the advantage of it was that other people's conversations could be heard quite distinctly all along the line.

The army service corps was slanging the artillery, the engineers were breathing fire and slaughter upon the postal department, the school of musketry was snarling at the machine-gun section.

And Schweik still sat at the telephone.

The deliberations with the colonel were prolonged still further. Colonel Schröder was expounding the latest theories of field service, with special reference to trench mortars. He talked on and on, about how two months earlier the front had been lower down and more to the east, about the importance of precise communication between the various units, about poison gases, about antiaircraft, about the rationing of troops in the trenches; and then he went on to discuss the conditions inside the army. He let himself go on the subject of the relationship between officers and rank and file, between rank and file and N.C.O.'s, and desertion to the enemy at the front, which led him to point out that 50 per cent of the Czech troops were of doubtful loyalty. The majority of the officers were wondering when the silly old buffer was going to stop his chatter, but Colonel Schröder prated on and on and on about the new duties of the new drafts, about the regimental officers who had fallen, about zeppelins, about barbed wire entanglements, about the military oath.

While he was on the latter subject, Lieutenant Lukash remembered that the whole draft had taken the oath except Schweik, who had been absent from divisional headquarters. And suddenly he burst out laughing. It was a kind of hysterical laughter which had an infectious influence among several of the officers sitting near him, and as a result it attracted the attention of the colonel, who was just about to discuss the experience gained during the retreat of the German troops in the Ardennes. He got the whole subject mixed up and then remarked, "Gentlemen, this is no laughing matter."

They then all proceeded to the officers' club, because Colonel Schröder had rung up brigade headquarters on the telephone.

Schweik was dozing by the telephone when it started ringing and woke him up.

"Hello," he heard, "regimental office speaking."

"Hello," he answered, "this is Draft Number Eleven."

"Don't hang up," he heard a voice saying. "Take a pencil and take this message down."

314

"Draft Number Eleven."

This was followed by a number of sentences in a queer muddle, because Drafts Numbers 12 and 13 chimed in and the message got completely lost in the medley of sounds. Schweik could not understand a word of it. But at last there was a slight lull and Schweik heard, "Hello, hello! Now read it over and don't hang up."

"Read what over?"

"The message, of course, you jackass."

"What message?"

"Ye gods, are you deaf, or what? The message I just dictated to you, you bloody fool!"

"I couldn't hear it. Somebody kept interrupting."

"You blithering idiot, do you think I've got nothing else to do but to listen to your drivel? Are you going to take the message down or not? Have you got pencil and paper? What's that? You haven't, you thickheaded lout, you! I've got to wait till you find some? Christ, what an army! Now then, how much longer are you going to be? Oh, you've got everything ready, have you? So you've managed to pull yourself together at last. I suppose you had to change your uniform for this job. Now listen to me: Draft Number Eleven. Got that? Repeat it."

" 'Draft Number Eleven.' "

"Company commander. Got that? Repeat it."

"Zur Besprechung morgen.[1] Ready? Repeat it."

" *'Zur Besprechung morgen.'* "

"Um neun Uhr.[2] *Unterschrift.* Do you know what *Unterschrift* is, you chump? It means 'signature.' Repeat it!"

" *'Um neun Uhr. Unterschrift.* Do you know what *Unterschrift* is, you chump? It means "signature." ' "

"You blithering idiot! Signature: Colonel Schröder, fathead. Got that? Repeat it!"

" 'Colonel Schröder, fathead.' "

"All right, you swab. Who received the message?"

"Me."

"Good God, who's me?"

"Schweik. Anything else?"

"No, thank the Lord. Any news?"

"No. Still carrying on as before."

[1] "Conference tomorrow."
[2] "At nine o'clock."

315

"I bet you're glad, eh? I heard one of your chaps got tied up today."

"Only our lieutenant's batman, who ate his grub. Do you know when we're off?"

"The old man himself couldn't tell you that, chum. Good night. Have you got many fleas there?"

Schweik hung up the receiver and began to rouse Quartermaster Sergeant Vanek from his slumbers. The quartermaster sergeant offered a stout resistance and when Schweik began to shake him, he hit him in the nose. Nevertheless Schweik managed to make the quartermaster sergeant rub his eyes and inquire in alarm what had happened.

"Nothing so far," replied Schweik. "But I'd like to have a little confab with you. We've just got a telephone message to say that Lieutenant Lukash has got to go at nine o'clock tomorrow morning to the colonel for another *Besprechung.* I don't know what to do about it. Am I to go and tell him now, or wait till the morning? I couldn't make up my mind for a long time whether I ought to wake you up or not, when you was snoring so nicely, but at last I thought I'd better ask your advice and——"

"For God's sake let me go to sleep," moaned Quartermaster Sergeant Vanek, with a tremendous yawn. "Go there in the morning, and don't wake me up."

He turned over on the other side and fell fast asleep immediately.

Schweik went back to the telephone, sat down, and began to doze at the table. The telephone bell woke him up.

"Hello, is that Draft Number Eleven?"

"Yes, it is. Who's speaking?"

"Draft Number Thirteen. Hello! What do you make the time? I can't get onto the exchange. It seems to me I ought to have been relieved before this."

"Our clock's not going."

"Then you're in the same fix as we are. Do you know when we're starting? Haven't you been speaking to the regimental office?"

"They're like us. They don't know damn-all."

"Now then, none of that bad language. Have you drawn your tinned rations? Our chaps went to fetch them, but they didn't bring anything back. The regimental stores were closed."

"Our chaps never brought anything back, either."

"It's a false alarm, if you ask me. Where do you think we're going to?"

"Russia."

"I got an idea it's Serbia. Well, we shall know the worst when we get to Budapest. If they shunt us off to the right, that means Serbia, and if it's to the left, we're bound for Russia. I hear our pay's going to be raised. How many of you are there at the telephone? What, all by yourself? Give it a miss, then, and go to bed. Aha! they've just come to relieve me. Well, pleasant dreams."

And Schweik once more dropped quietly off to sleep, without hanging up the receiver, so that nobody could disturb his slumbers, and the telephonist in the regimental office used much strong language at not being able to get through to Draft Number Eleven with a new message that by twelve the next morning the regimental officer was to be informed how many men had not yet been inoculated against typhus.

Meanwhile Lieutenant Lukash was still in the officers' club with the M.O., one Schanzler, who, sitting astride a chair, kept hitting the floor with a billiard cue at regular intervals, and delivering himself of such remarks as these:

"The wounded, on whatever side they may be, must receive proper attention."

"The cost of the medicine and nursing which they receive must be defrayed by the other side."

"Wounded prisoners are to be sent back under protection and guarantee from the generals, or else exchanged. But they can then continue on active service."

While expounding these and similar principles relating to the treatment of the wounded in warfare, Dr. Schanzler had already smashed two billiard cues, and he was still in the thick of his recital.

Lieutenant Lukash drank the rest of his black coffee and went home, where he discovered Baloun busy frying some salami in a small pot over the lieutenant's spirit stove.

"Sorry, sir," stammered Baloun. "Beg to report, sir, that—"

Lieutenant Lukash looked at him. At that moment he was like a big baby, and Lieutenant Lukash suddenly regretted having had him tied up because of his huge appetite.

"Carry on, Baloun," he said, as he unstrapped his sword. "Tomorrow I'll get them to issue an extra bread ration to you."

He then sat down at the table, and under the influence of

his mood at the moment, began to write a pathetic letter to his aunt:

DEAR AUNT,
    I have just received orders to be ready with my draft to leave for the front. It may be that this is the last letter you will ever receive from me, for the fighting is very severe and our losses are great. It is therefore difficult to conclude this letter by saying "au revoir." I think I ought rather to send you a last farewell.

"I'll finish it off in the morning," decided Lieutenant Lukash, and went to bed.

When Baloun saw that the lieutenant was sound asleep, he again began to meddle and ferret about all over the place. He opened the officer's trunk and was nibbling at a stick of chocolate, when the lieutenant stirred in his sleep. He started up in alarm and hastily put the chocolate back. For a while he lay low and then he stealthily peeped at what the lieutenant had been writing. He read it through and was deeply touched, especially by the reference to a last farewell. He lay down on his straw mattress by the doorway; amid thoughts of home and the slaughter of pigs there he dropped off into an uneasy sleep. He dreamt that he was haled before a court-martial for taking a piece of meat from the cookhouse. And then he saw himself hanging on one of the lime trees in the avenue which led through the camp at Bruck-on-the-Leitha.

When Schweik woke up with the awakening morning which arrived with the smell of coffee essence boiling in all the company cookhouses, he mechanically hung up the receiver, as if he had just finished talking on the telephone, and started off on a short morning stroll through the office. He hummed a tune to himself with such gusto that Quartermaster Sergeant Vanek woke up and inquired what time it was.

"They sounded the reveille a little while ago."

"Then I won't get up till I've had some coffee," decided the quartermaster sergeant, who always had plenty of time for everything. "Besides, they're sure to chivvy us about again on some stunt or other, that'll only be a washout in the end, like they did yesterday with those tinned rations."

Quartermaster Sergeant Vanek yawned and asked whether he had been very talkative when he came home.

"Well, you was sort of flighty," said Schweik. "You kept on saying something about shapes, and that a shape ain't a shape, and what ain't a shape is a shape and this shape ain't a shape. But you soon got over that and began to snore so loud that it sounded as if somebody was sawing a plank."

The telephone rang. The quartermaster sergeant answered it and the voice of Lieutenant Lukash became audible. He was asking what had happened about the tinned rations. Then the sound of expostulation was heard.

"They're not, sir, I assure you," Quartermaster Sergeant Vanek shouted into the telephone. "How could they be? It's all a lot of eyewash, sir. The commissariat's responsible for it. There wouldn't be any point in sending the men there, sir. I was going to telephone to you about it. Have I been in the canteen? Well, yes, sir, as a matter of fact, I did drop in there for a bit. No, sir, I'm quite sober. What's Schweik doing? He's here, sir. Shall I call him?"

"Schweik, you're wanted on the telephone," said the quartermaster sergeant, and added in low tones, "If he asks you what I was like when I got home, tell him I was O.K."

Schweik at the telephone:

"Beg to report, sir, this is Schweik."

"Look here, Schweik, what's all this about those tinned rations? Is it all right?"

"No, sir, there ain't a trace of 'em."

"Now then, Schweik, I want you to report yourself to me every morning as long as we're in camp. And you'll keep near me until we start. What were you doing last night?"

"I was at the telephone all night, sir."

"Any news?"

"Yes, sir."

"Now, then, Schweik, don't start talking twaddle. Did anyone report anything of any importance?"

"Yes, sir, but not till nine o'clock. And I didn't want to disturb you, sir. Far from it."

"Well, for God's sake, tell me what it was."

"A message, sir."

"Eh, what's that?"

"I've got it written down, sir. 'Receive a message. Who's there? Got it? Read it.' Something like that, sir."

"Good God, Schweik, you're a devil of a nuisance. Tell me what the message was, or I'll give you a damned good hiding when I get at you. Now then, what is it?"

"Another *Besprechung* with the colonel, sir, this morning at nine o'clock. I was going to wake you up in the night, but then I changed my mind."

"I should think so, too. You'd better not have the cheek to drag me out of bed when the morning'll do. Another *Besprechung!* To hell with it! Call Vanek to the telephone."

Quartermaster Sergeant Vanek at the telephone:

"Quartermaster Sergeant Vanek, sir."

"Vanek, find me another batman at once. That hound Baloun has eaten up all my chocolate. Are you to tie him up? No; we'll send him to the medical corps. A hefty chap like that ought to be all right for carrying wounded out of the front-line trenches. I'll send him to you now. Get that settled in the regimental office and then go back to your company at once. Do you think we're starting soon?"

"There's no hurry, sir. When the Ninth Draft was supposed to start, they kept us messing about for four days. It was just the same with the Eighth. With the Tenth it was a bit better. In the morning we had our kit all ready, at twelve o'clock we got orders to start, and we were off in the evening. The only thing was that afterward they chased us all over Hungary and didn't know which hole on which front we were to be stuffed into."

Since Lieutenant Lukash had been commanding the Eleventh Draft, he had spent much time in endeavoring to reconcile conflicting opinions. He therefore said, "Yes, possibly, quite so, quite. So you don't think we're starting today? We've got a *Besprechung* with the colonel at nine o'clock. By the way, get me a list—Let's see, now, a list of what? Oh, yes, a list of the N.C.O.'s with their length of service. Then the company rations. A list of men according to nationality? Yes, that as well. But before you do anything else, send me a new batman. What's Ensign Pleschner doing today? Inspecting the men's kit? Accounts? I'll come and sign them after the rations have been served out. Don't let anybody go into the town. What about the camp canteen? For an hour after rations. Call Schweik.

"Schweik, you'll stay at the telephone until further notice."

"Beg to report, sir, I haven't drunk any coffee yet."

"Then go and fetch your coffee and stay there in the office till I call you. Do you know what an orderly is?"

"A chap who runs about, sir."

"Well, you've got to stop where you are till I call you. Tell Vanek he's got to find me another batman. Schweik—hello! where are you?"

"Here, sir. They've just brought my coffee."

"Schweik—hello!"

"I can hear, sir. My coffee's quite cold."

"You've got a good idea of what a batman is. Just you look him over and then let me know what sort of a chap he is. Hang up the receiver."

As Quartermaster Sergeant Vanek sat sipping his black coffee, into which he had poured rum from a bottle labeled "Ink" (for the sake of caution), he looked at Schweik and said, "This lieutenant of ours didn't half yell into the telephone. I understood every word. You must know him pretty well by now, I should think."

"You bet I do," replied Schweik. "Why, we're as thick as thieves. Oh, yes, we been through a lot together. They've tried over and over again to separate us, but we've always managed to get together again. He relies on me for every blessed thing. Sometimes I can't help wondering why. You heard him just now telling me to remind you again to find him a new batman, and I've got to look him over and make a report on him. Lieutenant Lukash is particular about what sort of batman he gets."

In summoning another conference of the officers, Colonel Schröder was prompted by his great desire to hear himself orate. Besides this, some decision had to be reached on the subject of Marek, the volunteer officer who had refused to clean the latrines and who had therefore been sent by Colonel Schröder to a divisional court-martial.

The previous night, Marek, who had returned from the divisional court-martial, had made his appearance in the guardroom, where he had been kept under close arrest. Together with him, an extremely muddled report from the divisional court-martial had reached the colonel's office. The report pointed out that this case could not be construed as mutiny, because the cleaning of latrines formed no part of a volunteer officer's duties, but that the accused had been guilty of "infringement of subordination," which offense could be made good by distinguished conduct in the field. For these reasons the accused was sent back to his regiment and the proceedings in respect of infringement of discipline were to be suspended until the end of the war, but should be renewed on the next occasion of any charge that might be brought against the accused.

Then there was another matter. Marek, on his arrival at the guardroom, was accompanied by a certain Teveles, a bogus sergeant. This gentleman had recently come under the notice of the regiment, to which he had been sent from the military hospital at Zagreb. He wore the large silver medal, the badges of a volunteer officer, and three stars. He told some stirring tales about the doughty deeds of the Sixth Draft in Serbia, of which he claimed to be the sole survivor. As the result of inquiries, it was discovered that at the beginning of the war there had been a Teveles in the Sixth Draft, but that he was not entitled to claim the rank of a volunteer officer. The brigade to which the Sixth Draft had been attached after retiring from Belgrade on December 2, 1914, reported that there was no Teveles on the list of names recommended for, or decorated with, silver medals. Whether Private Teveles, however, had been promoted to sergeant during the Belgrade campaign could not be ascertained at all, because the whole of the Sixth Draft, officers included, had got lost at St. Sava's Church in Belgrade. Before the court-martial Teveles had defended himself by the argument that he had been promised the large silver medal, and that he had therefore bought one from a Bosnian, while in the hospital. As regards the volunteer officer's badges, he had sewn them on while drunk, and he had continued to wear them because he was always drunk, owing to the weakening of his constitution by dysentery.

When the *Besprechung* started, before dealing with these two matters, Colonel Schröder emphasized the necessity for frequent deliberations before their impending departure. He had been informed by the brigade commander that they were awaiting divisional orders. The rank and file must be in fighting trim and company commanders must carefully see to it that nobody was missing. He once more repeated everything that he had uttered the previous day. He again gave a survey of recent military events and insisted that nothing must be allowed to impair the army's fighting spirit and eagerness for war.

On the table before him was fastened a map of the battle areas, with little flags on pins, but the little flags had been

322

disarranged and the battle fronts reshuffled. Pins with the little flags attached to them were lying about under the table.

The whole of the war areas had been scandalously disarranged in the night by a tomcat, the pet of the military clerks in the regimental office. This animal, after having relieved himself all over the Austro-Hungarian areas, had made attempts to bury the resulting mess and had dragged the little flags from their places and smeared the mess over the positions; whereupon he had wetted on the battle fronts and bridgeheads and soiled all the army corps.

Now Colonel Schröder was very shortsighted. With bated breath the officers of the draft watched Colonel Schröder's finger getting nearer and nearer to the small heaps.

"From here, gentlemen, to Sokol on the Bug—" began Colonel Schröder with a prophetic air, and thrust his forefinger by rote toward the Carpathians, the result being that he plunged it into one of the cat's attempts to impart a plastic character to the map of the war areas.

"It looks, sir, as if a cat's been—" remarked Captain Sagner, very courteously on behalf of all present.

Colonel Schröder rushed into the adjacent office, whence could thereupon be heard a terrible uproar and the grisly threats of the colonel that he'd have all their noses rubbed in it.

There was a brief cross-examination. It turned out that the cat had been brought into the office a fortnight previously by Zwiebelfisch, the youngest clerk. When this fact had been established, Zwiebelfisch gathered together all his goods and chattels and a senior clerk led him off to the guardroom, where he was to remain until further orders from the colonel.

This practically concluded the conference. When the colonel, very red in the face, returned to the assembled officers, he forgot that he still had to deliberate about the destiny of Volunteer Officer Marek and the bogus sergeant, Teveles.

He therefore said curtly, "I should be glad if you would kindly remain in readiness, gentlemen, and await my further orders and instructions."

And so the result was that the volunteer officer and Teveles remained in the guardroom, and when later they were joined by Zwiebelfisch they were able to play poker. After that they badgered the sentry in charge of them to catch the lice on their straw mattress. Later on, a Lance Corporal Peroutka of the Thirteenth Draft was added to their company. When on the previous day there had been a rumor in the camp that they were off to the front, he had got lost and was subsequently discovered by the patrol next morning at The White Rose in Bruck. His excuse was that before leaving he was anxious to visit the famous greenhouse of Count Harrach in Bruck, and on his return he had lost his way and, deadbeat, had only managed to discover The White Rose at the break of day. (Actually, he had spent the night with the barmaid of that hostelry.)

The situation became more and more perplexing. Were they leaving, or were they not? Schweik, sitting at the telephone in the office of the Eleventh Draft, overheard the most varied opinions, some pessimistic and some optimistic. The Twelfth Draft telephoned that somebody in their office had heard that they were going to wait till they had been trained in shooting at moving targets and that they would not leave until they had completed the usual course in musketry. This optimistic view was not shared by the Thirteenth Draft, which telephoned to say that Corporal Havlik had just come back from the town, where he had heard from a railwayman that the carriages were waiting in the station.

Quartermaster Sergeant Vanek snatched the receiver from Schweik's hand and shouted excitedly that the railway blokes knew damn-all, and that he'd just been in the regimental office.

Schweik sat on at the telephone with a genuine attachment to his job, and in reply to all questions his answer was that he knew nothing definite.

Then, when Lieutenant Lukash inquired, "Any news at your end?" Schweik replied in stereotyped terms, "Nothing definite come through yet, sir."

"You jackass, hang up the receiver."

Then came a series of telephonic messages which Schweik received after lengthy misunderstandings. In particular, there was one which could not be dictated to him during the night when he had failed to hang up the receiver and was asleep. This referred to those who had been, or who had not been, inoculated.

Then there was a belated message about tinned rations, companies, and regimental sections.

"Copy of brigade telephonic message number seven-five-six-nine-two. Brigade order number one twenty-two. When indenting for cookhouse stores the requisite commodities are to be enumerated in the following order: one, meat; two, tinned goods; three, fresh vegetables; four, preserved vegetables; five, rice; six, macaroni; seven, oatmeal and bran; eight, potatoes. In place of the foregoing: three, preserved vegetables: four, fresh vegetables."

When Schweik read this out to the quartermaster sergeant, the latter declared solemnly that he threw messages like that into the latrine. "It's only a stunt that some bloody fool on the staff has thought of, and then they send it out to every blessed division and brigade and regiment."

After that Schweik received another message which was dictated so rapidly that when he had taken it down it looked like something in cipher: "Subsequently closer permitted however has been nevertheless or thus has been notwithstanding the same to be reported."

"That's all a lot of useless bunk," said Quartermaster Sergeant Vanek, when Schweik, vastly astonished at what he had written, read it aloud three times in succession. "It's all damn nonsense. Christ knows what they think they're up to. Of course, it may be in cipher, but that's not our job. Chuck it away."

"You're about right, Sergeant," said Schweik. "If I was to report to the lieutenant that he's got to 'subsequently closer permitted however has been nevertheless or thus has been notwithstanding the same to be reported,' I don't mind betting he wouldn't like it.

"Some people are terribly touchy," continued Schweik, plunging into reminiscence again. "I remember once I was riding in a tram, and at one of the stopping places a chap named Novotny got in. As soon as I spotted him, I went over and joined him and started telling him we both came from the same town. But he started shouting he didn't know me and told me to go away and not to bother him. So then I started explaining to him how when I was a little boy I used to visit their house with my mother, whose name was Antonia, and my father's name was Prokop, and he was an overseer on a farm. But even then he still made out he didn't know me. So I started telling him some details, just to convince him, and told him how there were two chaps named Novotny in our town. Tonda and Josef. And Josef, so they told me, had shot his wife because she kept grumbling at him for going on the booze. And then he lifted his arm, and I dodged him, so that he smashed a large pane of glass in the tram, right close to the driver. So they ejected us from the tram and took us to the police station, and there it turned out that the reason he was so touchy was because his name wasn't Novotny at all, but Doubrava, and he'd come over from America to visit some relations."

The telephone interrupted his narrative and a hoarse voice from the machine-gun section again inquired whether they were leaving. The owner of the voice said that he'd heard there had been a *Besprechung* with the colonel that morning.

Then Cadet Biegler, the biggest jackass in the company, made his appearance in the doorway. He was extremely pale, and beckoned to Quartermaster Sergeant Vanek to follow him into the passage, where he had a long talk with him.

When Quartermaster Sergeant Vanek returned, he smiled contemptuously.

"He's a bloody fool, he is," he said to Schweik. "We haven't half got some rum specimens in this draft. He was at the *Besprechung* and at the end of it the lieutenant ordered all squad commanders to hold a rifle inspection and to make it a hot 'un. And now he comes and asks me if he ought to crime Zlabek for cleaning his rifle with paraffin."

Quartermaster Sergeant Vanek became quite heated about it. "He comes and asks me about that sort of flapdoodle, when he knows we're off to the front."

"Here," said Schweik suddenly, "what about that new batman you were told to get? Have you found one yet?"

"Talk sense," replied Quartermaster Sergeant Vanek. "All in good time. As a matter of fact I wouldn't mind betting that the lieutenant'll get used to Baloun. He'll sneak a bit of grub from him every now and then, but he'll drop all that when we get to the front. By that time neither of 'em'll have anything to eat. If I say that Baloun's got to stop, why, that's all there is to it. That's my job, and the lieutenant can't interfere. There's no hurry."

Quartermaster Sergeant Vanek lay down on his bed again.

At this juncture Lieutenant Lukash was in his den, studying a cipher message from the staff which had just been handed to him, together with instructions how to decode it and secret orders in cipher about the direction in which the draft was to proceed to the Galician frontier:

7217—1238—475—212135=Mazony.
8922—375—7282=Raab.
4432—1238—7217—35—8922—35=Komarom.
7282—9299—310—275—7881—298—475—7929=Buda-
pest.

As he decoded this rigmarole, Lieutenant Lukash sighed
and exclaimed, "To hell with it all!"

BOOK III

I

1.

Across Hungary

AT LAST the moment came for them all to be crammed into a railway truck in the proportion of forty-two men to eight horses. The horses, it must be said, traveled more comfortably than the men, because they could sleep in a standing posture. Not that it mattered. The important thing was that the military train was conveying to Galicia a fresh batch of mortals who had been hounded to the shambles.

On the whole, however, they felt rather relieved. Once the train had started, they knew a little more definitely how they stood. Hitherto they had been in a wretched state of uncertainty, racked with the strain of wondering whether they were starting that day or the next or the day after that. And now their minds were more at rest.

Quartermaster Sergeant Vanek had been quite right when he told Schweik that there was no hurry. Several days elapsed before they actually got into the railway trucks, and during

330

that time there was continual talk about tinned rations. The quartermaster sergeant, an experienced man, insisted that there was nothing in it. Tinned rations were a washout! A field Mass was a more likely stunt, because the previous draft had been treated to a field Mass. If they had tinned rations, there wouldn't be a field Mass. And, conversely, a field Mass was a substitute for tinned rations.

And surely enough, instead of tinned stew, Chaplain Ibl appeared on the scene, and killed three birds with one stone. He celebrated a field Mass for three drafts simultaneously, blessing two of them for service in Serbia and one for Russia.

On this occasion he delivered an impassioned address, containing material which he had obviously derived from military calendars.

It was such a stirring address that when they were on their way to Mozony, Schweik, who was with Quartermaster Sergeant Vanek in a truck arranged as an improvised office, remembered the chaplain's peroration and said to the quartermaster sergeant, "It'll be a fair treat, like the chaplain said, when the day is sinking toward evening and the sun with its golden rays sets behind the mountains and on the battlefield will be heard, like he said, the last breath of the dying and the groaning of wounded men and the wailing of the population, when their cottages are burning above their heads. There's nothing I enjoy more than to hear people talking good, thoroughgoing, out-and-out flapdoodle."

Quatermaster Sergeant Vanek nodded. "It was a damned nice heart-to-heart talk."

"It was a fine bit of speechifying," said Schweik, "and I shan't forget it in a hurry. After the war I'll tell all my pals at The Flagon about it. When the chaplain was well on the job, he'd got his legs so wide apart that I was afraid he'd slip and fall on top of the altar and bump his noodle against the monstrance. He was just telling us such a nice bit from the history of an army, about how the fire was mingled with the flush of eventide, and the barns were burning on the battlefield, just as if he'd seen it all."

And on the very same day Chaplain Ibl was already in Vienna and was narrating to another draft the edifying story to which Schweik referred and which had pleased him so much that he had described it as good, thoroughgoing, out-and-out flapdoodle.

Then Schweik began to discuss the famous army orders,

which had been read to them before they had entered the railway trucks. One was signed by Franz Josef and the other by the Archduke Josef Ferdinand, commander-in-chief of the eastern army. They both referred to the events at the Dukla Pass on April 3, 1915, when two battalions of the Twenty-eighth Regiment, officers and men, went over to the Russians amid the strains of the regimental band.

The two orders, which were read to them in a trembling voice, ran as follows:

Army Order of April 17, 1915

It is with profound distress that I order the Imperial Royal Infantry Regiment No. 28 to be effaced from my army for cowardice and treachery. The regimental colors will be removed from the dishonored regiment and placed in the military museum. From today onward, the regiment which was morally corrupted by its home surroundings when it marched to the field, ceases to exist.

Franz Josef I

Order of Archduke Josef Ferdinand

During this campaign the Czech troops have proved disappointing, especially in the recent hostilities. They have been particularly remiss in defending positions in which they had been entrenched for a considerable time, and the enemy has frequently taken advantage of this to establish contact and relations with worthless elements in the midst of these troops. Thousandfold shame, disgrace, and contempt upon those infamous scoundrels who have betrayed their Emperor and their country, and besmirched not only the honor of the renowned banners of our glorious and gallant army, but also the honor of the nation to which they belong.

Sooner or later they will be overtaken by the bullet or the rope of the executioner.

It is the duty of every single Czech soldier, who has any vestige of honor left in him, to denounce to his commander any such scoundrel, mischief-maker, and traitor. If he does not do so, he himself is a traitor and a scoundrel.

This order is to be read to all men belonging to the Czech regiments.

The Imperial Royal Regiment No. 28, by a decree of our emperor, has already been obliterated from our army and all deserters from the regiment who are taken prisoner will expiate with their blood the heinous crime they have committed.

"They read that to us a bit late," said Schweik to Quartermaster Sergeant Vanek. "I'm surprised they've only just read it to us, when the Emperor had it all ready on April seventeenth. It looks as if they'd got some reasons of their own for not reading it to us there and then. If I was the Emperor, I'd kick up a row at having my orders shoved on one side like that. If I was to make an order on April seventeenth, why, it'd have to be read to every blessed regiment on April seventeenth, even if hell was to freeze."

In the staff carriage, where the officers of the draft were assembled, there had been a curious hush from the very beginning of the journey. The majority of the officers were engrossed in a German book, bound in cloth and entitled *The Sins of the Fathers*, by Ludwig Ganghofer. They were all simultaneously absorbed in the perusal of page 161. Captain Sagner, the battalion commander, stood by the window, holding the same book, and his copy also was opened at page 161. He gazed at the landscape and wondered how he could best explain to them in the most intelligible manner what they were to do with the book. For it was a strictly confidential affair.

Meanwhile, the officers were wondering whether Colonel Schröder had now gone completely and irrevocably mad. Of course, they knew he had been a bit cracked for some time past, but they had not expected that the final seizure would be so sudden. Before the departure of the train he arranged a final *Besprechung* at which he informed them that they each were entitled to a copy of *The Sins of the Fathers*, by Ludwig Ganghofer, and that he had ordered the books to be taken to the battalion office.

"Gentlemen," he said with a terribly mysterious expression on his face, "whatever you do, don't forget page one sixty-one."

They had pored over page 161, but could make nothing of it except that a lady named Martha approached a desk, from which she extracted the acting version of a play and in a loud voice expressed the view that the public must sympathize with the hero of it. Then on the same page appeared a gentleman called Albert, who kept trying to crack jokes which, detached from the earlier part of the story, appeared to be such drivel that Lieutenant Lukash, in his annoyance, bit through his cigarette holder.

"The old boy's daft," was the general view. "It's all up with him. Now he'll be transferred to the War Office."

When Captain Sagner had arranged everything carefully in his mind, he left his place by the window. He was not excessively gifted as an instructor, and so it took him a long time before he had devised the scheme of a lecture on the significance of page 161. He began his lecture with the word "Gentlemen," just as the colonel did, although before they had entered the train he had addressed the other officers as "comrades."

"Gentlemen," he began, and went on to explain that on the previous evening he had received from the colonel certain instructions concerning page 161 of *The Sins of the Fathers* by Ludwig Ganghofer.

"This, gentlemen," he continued solemnly, "is entirely confidential information concerning a new system of telegrams in code for use on active service."

Cadet Biegler took out his notebook and pencil, and in an extremely zealous tone said, "Ready, sir."

Everybody stared at Cadet Biegler, whose zeal in the pursuit of knowledge bordered on idiocy.

"Look here," said Captain Sagner, "you keep quiet until I give you permission to speak. Nobody asked you to say anything. I suppose you think you're a damned smart soldier. Here am I, giving you absolutely confidential information and there are you, shoving it all down in your notebook. If you were to lose that notebook, you'd be liable for a court-martial."

Cadet Biegler, on top of all his other engaging qualities, was in the habit of always trying to persuade everyone by some plausible explanation that he, Biegler, was in the right.

"Beg to report, sir," he replied, "that even if my notebook were to get lost, nobody could make out what I've written. I take down everything in shorthand and nobody could read my abbreviations. I use an English system of shorthand."

Everybody gazed at him with contempt. Captain Sagner dismissed the matter with a wave of his hand, and continued his lecture:

"I have already referred to the new method of sending telegrams in code on active service. You may have found it difficult to understand why you were recommended to study page one sixty-one of *The Sins of the Fathers*, by Ludwig Ganghofer, but that, gentlemen, contains the key to the new code which has been introduced as the result of new instructions of the army corps to which we are attached. As you may be aware, there are many codes in use for sending important messages in the field. The latest which we have adopted is the method of supplemented numerals. Thus, you can now dispense with the codes which were served out to you last week by the regimental staff, and the instructions for deciphering them."

"Archduke Albrecht's system," murmured the assiduous Biegler to himself. "Eighty-nine twenty-two equals *R;* adopted from Greenfield's method."

"The new system is very simple," went on Captain Sagner. "Supposing, for example, we are to receive this order: 'On hill two twenty-eight direct machine-gun fire to the left'; we receive, gentlemen, the following telegram: 'Thing—with—us—that—we—look—in—the—promised— which—Martha—you — which—anxious—then— we—Martha— we—the—we—thanks— well—end—we—promised—really —think —idea—quite—prevails— voice—last.' As I say, it's extremely simple, no superfluous complications. From the staff by telephone to the battalion, from the battalion by telephone to the company. When the commander has received this code telegram, he deciphers it in the following way: He takes *The Sins of the Fathers,* opens it at page one sixty-one, and begins from the top to look for the word 'thing' on the opposite page one-sixty. Now then, gentlemen, the word 'thing' occurs first on page one-sixty and forms the fifty-second word, taking sentence by sentence. Very well. On the opposite page one sixty-one, he discovers the fifty-second letter from the top. Kindly notice that this letter is 'o.' The next word in the telegram is 'with.' That is the seventh word on page one-sixty, corresponding to the seventh letter on page one sixty-one, which is 'n.' That gives us 'on.' And so we continue, till we've deciphered the order: 'On hill two twenty-eight direct machine-gun fire to the left.' It's very ingenious, gentlemen, and very simple, and it absolutely can't be deciphered without the key which is *The Sins of the Fathers* by Ludwig Ganghofer, page one sixty-one."

They all gazed glumly at the fateful page and lapsed into anxious thought. For a while there was silence, till suddenly Cadet Biegler shouted in great alarm, "Beg to report, sir, God Almighty, there's something wrong."

And, indeed, it was extremely puzzling.

However much they tried, nobody except Captain Sagner discovered on page 160 the words corresponding to the letters on the opposite page 161 which supplied the key.

"Gentlemen," stammered Captain Sagner, when he had convinced himself that Cadet Biegler's desperate oratory was in accordance with the facts of the case. "What *can* have happened? In my copy of *The Sins of the Fathers* it's there all right, and in yours it isn't."

"I beg your pardon, sir." It was Cadet Biegler again. "I should like to point out," he continued, "that this novel by Ludwig Ganghofer is in two volumes. You will see for yourself, if you kindly turn to the title page. There you are: 'Novel in two volumes,' it says. We've got Volume One, and you've got Volume Two," explained the thoroughgoing Biegler. "It is therefore obvious that our pages one sixty and one sixty-one do not correspond to yours. We've got something quite different. In your case the first word of the decoded telegram should be 'on,' and we make ours 'bo.' "

It was now quite clear to everyone that Biegler was not such a fool as they thought.

"I received Volume Two from brigade headquarters," said Captain Sagner, "so there must be some mistake. It looks as if they got things mixed up at brigade headquarters."

Cadet Biegler gazed around triumphantly, while Captain Sagner continued, "It's a queer business, gentlemen. Some of the people in the brigade office are of very limited intelligence."

"I should like to point out"—it was again the unwearied Biegler who was anxious to display his wisdom—"that matters of a strictly confidential character ought not to pass from divisional headquarters through the brigade office. A message affecting the most secret affairs of an army corps should be notified by a strictly confidential circular only to commanders of parts of divisions and brigades, and of regiments. I know a coding system which was used during the Sardinian and Savoy hostilities, in the Anglo-French campaign at Sevastopol, during the Boxer Rebellion in China, and also during the last Russo-Japanese war. This system was based upon—"

"What the hell do we care about that?" said Captain Sagner, with an expression of contempt and repugnance. "There can be no doubt that the system which I have been explaining to you is not only one of the best, but also quite safe against discovery. It'll dish all the counterespionage departments of the enemy staff. They'll never be able to read our ciphers. Our system's quite unique. It's not based on any previous method."

The assiduous Biegler coughed meaningly.

"I should like to mention Kerickhoff's book on military ciphers," he began. "You can order it from the publishers of the *Military Encyclopedia*. It contains a detailed description of the system I mentioned to you just now. It was invented by Colonel Kircher, who served under Napoleon the First in the Saxon army. Kircher's code is based upon words and it was perfected by Lieutenant Fleissner in his *Handbook of Military Cryptography,* which can be obtained from the publishers to the Military Academy in Wiener-Neustadt. Just one moment, sir—" Cadet Biegler dived into his attaché case and produced the book he had been talking about.

He continued. "Fleissner quotes the same example as the one that's been given us. Here you are, you can see for yourselves:

" 'Telegram: On hill two twenty-eight direct machine-gun fire to the left. Key: *The Sins of the Fathers* by Ludwig Ganghofer, page one sixty-one, Volume Two.'

"And here you are again: 'Cipher: Thing—with—us—that—we—look—in—the—promised—which,' and so forth. Exactly as we were told just now."

There was no disputing this. The wretched Biegler was right. One of the generals on the staff had considerably lightened his labors. He had discovered Fleissner's book on military ciphers, and the thing was done.

While all this was being revealed, Lieutenant Lukash might have been observed grappling with a curious mental agitation. He was biting his lip, was about to say something, but in the end, when he did speak, he changed his mind and spoke about something else.

"There's no need to take it so seriously," he remarked in an oddly embarrassed tone. "While we were stationed at Bruck several changes were made in the system of coding telegrams. And before we leave for the front there'll be a fresh lot introduced, but personally I don't think we'll have much time at the front for solving conundrums. Why, before any of us could work out the meaning of a code message like that we, the company, the battalion, and the brigade would all be blown to smithereens. It's got no practical value."

Captain Sagner assented very reluctantly. "In actual practice," he admitted, "as far as my experience on the Serbian front goes, nobody had any time for solving ciphers. I don't say that codes had no value while we were in the trenches for any length of time. And, of course, they did change the systems."

Captain Sagner withdrew along the whole line of his argument. "One of the chief reasons why the staffs at the front are using codes less and less is because our field telephones don't work properly, and especially during artillery fire make it difficult to distinguish the various syllables of words. You can simply hear nothing, and that causes a hell of a muddle."

He paused.

"Muddle is the worst thing that can happen in the field, gentlemen," he added in oracular tones.

"Presently," he continued, after a fresh interval, "we shall be at Rabb, gentlemen. Each man will be served out with five ounces of Hungarian salami. Half an hour's rest."

He looked at the timetable.

"We leave at four-twelve. Everybody must be in the train by three fifty-eight. Alight by companies, beginning with Number Eleven. Rations to be issued one platoon at a time, from store Number Six. Officer in charge of issue: Cadet Biegler."

Everyone looked at Cadet Biegler, as much as to say, "Now you're for it, you young whippersnapper."

But the assiduous Cadet Biegler was already extracting from his attaché case a sheet of paper and a ruler; he drew lines on the paper to correspond with the number of squads, and asked the commander of each squad how many men there were in it, a detail which none of them knew with any exactitude. They could supply Biegler only with figures based upon vague jottings in their notebooks.

Meanwhile Captain Sagner began in sheer desperation to read the wretched *Sins of the Fathers*, and when the train stopped at Rabb, he closed the book with a jerk and remarked, "This chap Ganghofer doesn't write badly."

Lieutenant Lukash was the first to dash out of the staff carriage. He proceeded to the truck in which Schweik was installed.

"Schweik, come here," he said. "Stop all your idiotic jabber and come and explain something to me."

"Delighted, sir."

Lieutenant Lukash led Schweik away, and the glance which he bestowed upon him was highly suspicious.

In the course of Captain Sagner's lecture, which had ended in such a fiasco, Lieutenant Lukash had been developing a certain ability as a detective. This was not unduly difficult, for on the day before they started, Schweik had announced to Lieutenant Lukash, "There's some books for the officers, sir, up at battalion headquarters. I fetched them from the regimental office."

And so when they had crossed the second set of rails, Lieutenant Lukash said point-blank, "Schweik, I want to know some more about those books you mentioned to me yesterday."

"Beg to report, sir, that's a very long story, and it always seems to sort of upset you, sir, when I tell you all the ins and outs of anything. Like when you was going to give me such a smack in the eye that time when you tore up the circular about war loan, and I was telling you how I once read in a book that in olden times, when a war was on, people had to pay a tax on windows, so much for each window, and then so much on geese too—"

"We'll never get any further at this rate," said Lieutenant Lukash. He now proceeded with the cross-examination, after deciding that the strictly confidential part of the business would have to be kept entirely in the background, as otherwise that ruffian of a Schweik would only make further capital out of it. He therefore asked simply, "Do you know Ganghofer?"

"Who's he?" inquired Schweik with interest.

"A German author, you blithering booby," replied Lieutenant Lukash.

"Lord bless you, sir," said Schweik with the expression of a martyr, "I don't know no German author personally, as you might say. I once knew a Czech author personally, a chap named Ladislav Hajek. He used to write for a paper called *The Animal World* and once I palmed off a scraggy sort of tyke on him for a good-bred Pomeranian. He was a cheerful gentleman, he was, and a good sort, too. He once went to a pub and read a lot of his stories there. They were very sad stories and they made everybody laugh, and then he started crying and stood us drinks all around and—"

"Look here," interposed Lieutenant Lukash, "drop all that. That's not what I asked you about. All I wanted to know was whether you had noticed whether those books you mentioned to me were by Ganghofer."

"Those books I took from the regimental office to battalion headquarters?" asked Schweik. "Oh, yes, they were written by the fellow that you wanted to know whether I knew or not. I got a message by telephone direct from the regimental office.

You see, sir, it was like this: They wanted to send these here books to the battalion office, but everyone there was away, orderly officers and all, because they had to be in the canteen when they're off to the front and nobody knows whether they'll ever get another chance of going to the canteen. Well, sir, there they all were, drinking for all they was worth, and I couldn't get hold of any of them by telephone, and as you told me to stay at the telephone until Chodounsky was sent to relieve me, I stuck to my post and waited till it was my turn. The regimental office kept kicking up a row because they couldn't get any answer and so they couldn't pass on the message that the draft office was to fetch some books for the officers of the whole company. Well, sir, you told me that things have got to be done promptly in wartime, so I telephoned to the regimental office and said I'd fetch those books myself and take them to the battalion office. There was a regular sackful of 'em and I had quite a job to get them into the company office. Then I had a look at those books, and that gave me an idea. You see, the quartermaster sergeant in the regimental office told me that according to what the message said, the battalion office knew which volume of these books was wanted. Because, you see, sir, this book was in two volumes. One volume separate and another volume separate. Well, sir, talk about laugh! I never laughed so much in all my life. Reading ain't exactly in my line, as you might say, but I never heard of anyone starting to read the second volume of a book before the first. Anyway, the quartermaster sergeant says to me, 'There's the first volume and there's the second. The officers know which volume they've got to read.' So I thinks to myself, why, they must be all dotty, because if anyone's going to read a book like this *Sins of the Fathers*, or whatever it is, from the beginning, they got to start with the first volume, because we don't read books backward like what the Jews do. So then I telephoned to you, sir, when you got back from the club, and I reported about those books and asked you whether, being wartime, things was all topsy-turvy like, and books had got to be read backward, the second volume first and the first volume afterward. And you told me I was a silly chump if I didn't even know that the Lord's Prayer began with 'Our Father' and wound up with 'Amen.'

"Are you feeling queer, sir?" asked Schweik with concern, when Lieutenant Lukash turned pale and clutched at the step of a locomotive tender. His countenance, white as a sheet, showed no trace of wrath. But there was something of sheer despair in his expression.

"No, no, Schweik, that's all right. Get on with your story."

"Well, sir, as I was saying," continued Schweik in honeyed tones, "that's what I thought, too. Once I bought one of these thrillers all about the bloodthirsty bandit of the Bakony Forest and the first part was missing, so I had to guess how it started, so you see even in a tale like that, all about a bloodthirsty bandit, you can't do without the beginning. So it didn't take me long to see that there was no need for the officers to start reading Volume One afterward. What with one thing and another, it struck me that there was something very funny about those books. I knew that officers don't do much reading, anyway, and now with the war on and all that—"

"Oh, stop talking twaddle, Schweik," groaned Lieutenant Lukash.

"Well, sir, I at once telephoned to ask you whether you wanted the two volumes at one go, and you told me, the same as you did just now, to stop talking twaddle and did I think that they were going to lug a lot of extra books about with them. So I thought that if you felt that way about it, the other officers would, too. And then I asked our quartermaster sergeant, Vanek, because he's had some experience of the front. And he said that the officers seemed to think that the war was a sort of damned picnic, taking a regular library with them as if they was going away for their summer holidays. He said there was no time for reading, because they was always on the run. Well, after that, I thought I'd better get your opinion again, so I telephoned to ask you what I was to do about those books and you said that once I got something into my silly fat head, I never let go of it until I got a smack across the jaw. So then, sir, I only took the first volume of this tale to the battalion office and I left the rest in our company office. My idea was that when the officers have read the first volume, they could have the second volume served out to them, like in a lending library, but suddenly the order came that we was leaving, and a message was sent all over the battalion that the rest of the books was to go into the regimental stores."

Schweik paused, and then continued, "They've got all sorts of stuff in those stores, sir. Why, there's the top hat belonging to the choirmaster at Budejovice, the one he wore when he joined the regiment."

"Look here, Schweik," said Lieutenant Lukash, with a deep

sigh, "let me tell you that you can't realize the amount of harm you've done. I'm sick of calling you an idiot. In fact, what you are is beyond words. If I call you an idiot, it's downright flattery, that's what it is. What you've just done is so appalling that the worst offenses you've perpetrated since I've known you are angelic deeds in comparison. If you only knew, Schweik, what you've done! But you'll never realize it. And if at any time anything should be said about those books, don't you dare to breathe a word about what I said to you when I telephoned with regard to the second volume. If anything's ever said about the first and second volumes and how the mistake arose, you take no notice. You've heard nothing, you know nothing, you can remember nothing. And if you get me mixed up in it, why I'll—"

Lieutenant Lukash paused, as if shaken by throes of fever, and Schweik took advantage of this brief silence to ask innocently, "Beg to report, sir, but I don't see why I should never know what I've done wrong. I hope you don't mind me saying so, sir, but it's only because I could avoid doing it another time. They do say that we learn by our mistakes, just like a man I used to know, Adamec his name was, and he used to work in an iron foundry, and one day he drank some spirits of salt by mistake, and—"

He got no further with this modern instance, for Lieutenant Lukash interrupted him. "Oh, shut up, you ghastly jackass! I'm not going to waste time talking to you. Get back into your truck and tell Baloun that when we reach Budapest he's to bring me a roll and that liver paste that's at the bottom of my box, wrapped up in silver paper. Then tell Vanek that he's a thickheaded lout. Three times I've asked him to let me have the exact number of men. Today, when I needed the figures, I had to use the old list from last week."

"Right you are, sir," barked Schweik, and departed slowly to his truck.

Lieutenant Lukash walked to and fro on the tracks and thought to himself, "I ought to have given him a few smacks in the jaw, and instead of that I talked to him as if we were old friends."

Schweik entered the railway truck with great solemnity. He had quite a high opinion of himself. It was not an everyday occurrence for him to do something so appalling that he could never be allowed to discover what it was.

"Sergeant," said Schweik, when he was sitting in his place again. "It strikes me that Lieutenant Lukash is in a jolly good temper today. He told me to tell you that you're a thickheaded lout because he's asked you three times to let him know the number of men in the company."

"God Almighty," said Quartermaster Sergeant Vanek, flaring up. "I'll make it hot for those bloody sergeants. Is it my fault if they're too damned lazy to let me know the number of men in their squads? How the hell can I be expected to guess how many men there are? This draft's in a fine state, upon my word. But I knew it, I knew it! I guessed that everything'd be at sixes and sevens. One day there's four lots of rations missing from the cookhouse, and the next day there's three too many. They don't even let me know if anyone's in the hospital. Last month I had a chap named Nikodem on my list, and I didn't discover until payday that he'd died of galloping consumption in the hospital. And they kept drawing rations for him. A uniform was served out for him, too, but God knows where that went to. And then, on top of all that, the lieutenant calls me a thickheaded lout, just because he can't keep his company in order."

Quartermaster Sergeant Vanek strode up and down wrathfully.

"I ought to be company commander! I'd show 'em! I'd make 'em toe the line! I'd have my eye on every man jack of 'em. The N.C.O.'s'd have to report to me twice a day. But these N.C.O.'s are a washout. And the worst of the whole lot is Sergeant Zyka. He's all right at telling funny yarns, but when he's told that a man's been transferred from his squad to the A.S.C., he keeps on giving me the same figures, day after day. And then I'm told I'm a thickheaded lout. That's not the way for the lieutenant to get popular. A company quartermaster sergeant ain't a lance-jack that anyone can use to wipe his—"

Baloun, who had been listening with open mouth, now supplied the missing word before Quartermaster Sergeant Vanek had time to utter it.

"You shut your row," said the quartermaster sergeant testily.

"Here, Baloun," remarked Schweik, "I've got a message for you, too. The lieutenant says that when we get to Budapest you've got to take a roll to him and the liver paste that's wrapped up in silver paper at the bottom of the lieutenant's trunk."

Baloun's long arms, like those of a chimpanzee, suddenly

343

drooped, he bent his back, and he continued in this posture for quite a long while.

"I haven't got it," he then said in a low, despairing voice, with his eyes glued to the dirty floor of the railway truck.

"I haven't got it," he repeated brokenly. "I never thought . . . I unpacked it before we left. . . . I just sniffed at it. . . . To see if it hadn't gone bad. . . .

"I tasted it!" he exclaimed in accents of such genuine despair that it was clear to everyone what had happened.

"You ate it up, silver paper and all," said Quartermaster Sergeant Vanek, confronting Baloun. He was glad that a diversion had been created by the gluttonous Baloun and that the conversation now centered around a new set of tragic events. Quartermaster Sergeant Vanek felt a strong inclination to indulge in a little dour moralizing for Baloun's benefit, but in this he was anticipated by Schweik, who now intervened.

"Here, Baloun, you was telling me not so long ago that there was going to be slaughtering and curing done in your family and that as soon as we get to a place where letters can be sent, they'll let you have a parcel of ham. Now how would you like it if they was to send you this ham and then all the chaps in the company was to cut off a bit of it and have a taste, and then another bit, because we liked the taste of it, till that ham looked like a postman I used to know, a man named Kozel, whose bones started crumbling, and so first of all they cut off his leg below the ankle, and then below the knee, and then below the hip, and if he hadn't died in time they'd have gone on cutting bits off him till he looked like a stump of lead pencil. So just fancy what it'd have been like, Baloun, if we'd cut your ham up, like you gobbled up the lieutenant's liver paste."

Baloun gazed at them all very dejectedly.

"It's only because of me putting in a good word for you," said the quartermaster sergeant to Baloun, "that the lieutenant kept you as his batman. You was going to be transferred to the medical corps and carry wounded away from the front line. How'd you have liked that? Why, at the Dukla Pass there was three lots of stretcher-bearers sent out, one after another, to fetch back a wounded officer who'd been shot in the belly in front of the barbed wire, and the whole lot of 'em went west, shot right through the heart. The fourth lot managed to reach him, but before they got him to the dressing station it was all up with him."

344

Baloun could restrain himself no longer. He began to blubber.

"Why, you ought to be ashamed of yourself," said Schweik, contemptuously. "Call yourself a soldier?"

"I was never meant to be in the army," lamented Baloun. "I know I'm always thinking about food and I can never get enough of it, but that's because I've been dragged away from the life I'm used to. And it runs in our family, too. My father, he's dead now, but he once made a bet that he'd eat fifty sausages at a sitting and two loaves of bread, and he won his bet. I once made a bet I'd eat four geese and two plates of dumplings with cabbage."

"Well," said Schweik, "you've been tied up once, and now you deserve to be sent to the front line. When I was doing your job as orderly to the lieutenant, he could rely on me in everything, and I'd never have dreamed of eating anything that belonged to him. When something special was served out, he'd always say to me, 'Schweik,' he said, 'keep it for yourself,' or, 'Oh, I don't fancy that particularly; let me have just a scrap of it and do what you like with the rest.' And when we was in Prague and he used to send me sometimes to fetch his lunch from a restaurant, so as he shouldn't think he'd got a small helping because I'd eaten half of it on the way, when I thought the helping was too small, I bought an extra helping with my own money, so as he could have a proper feed and not think any harm of me. Till one day, he spotted what I'd been up to. It was like this: I always had to bring him the bill of fare from the restaurant and then he chose what he wanted. Well, that particular day he chose some stuffed pigeon. Now when I saw they gave me only half a bird, I thought he might think I'd eaten the other half on the way, so I bought an extra portion with my own money and brought him such a grand helping that Lieutenant Seba, who'd been nosing around after some lunch that day, and had just come to pay my lieutenant a call, was able to have a feed of it as well. But when he'd finished, he says, 'Don't tell me that's a single portion. Why, there isn't a restaurant on earth where you can get a whole stuffed pigeon on the bill of fare. If I can scrape together some money today, I'm going to send out to that restaurant of yours for some lunch. Now own up; that's a double portion, isn't it?' Well, the lieutenant asked me to bear him out that he'd only given me enough money for a single portion, because he didn't know that Lieutenant Seba was coming. So I said he'd only given me enough money for a single lunch. 'There you are,' says my lieutenant. 'And this ain't nothing,' he says. 'Why, the other day Schweik brought me two legs of goose for lunch. Just imagine Vermicelli soup, beef with horseradish sauce, two legs of goose, dumplings, and piles of cabbage and pancakes.' "

"Holy Moses!" exclaimed Baloun, and smacked his lips loudly.

Schweik continued. "Well, that was the cause of the trouble. Next day Lieutenant Seba sends his batman to fetch his lunch from our restaurant, and he brings him a tiny little dollop of chicken and rice, about as much as you could hold in the palm of your hand, just enough for two spoonfuls. So Lieutenant Seba went for him and said he'd eaten half of it. And he said he hadn't. So then Lieutenant Seba gave him a smack across the jaw and told him how much grub I was fetching for Lieutenant Lukash. Well, next day, when this chap who'd had a smack in the jaw for nothing went to the restaurant to fetch some lunch, he found out what I'd been doing, and told his boss and he told my lieutenant. So in the evening I was sitting having a read of the newspaper, all about the reports of the enemy staffs from the front, when my lieutenant comes in, as white as a sheet he was, and asks me point-blank how many of those double portions I'd paid for out of my own pocket, and he said he knew all about it and it wasn't any use for me to deny it and he'd always thought I was a jackass but he'd never supposed I was as dotty as all that. He said I'd disgraced him so much that he felt like first blowing my brains out and then his own. 'Well, sir,' I says to him, 'the first day I came to you, you said that every batman was a crook and a rotter. And they was giving such small portions in that restaurant, that you'd be bound to think that I was rotter enough to sneak your grub.' "

"Lord help us!" murmured Baloun, and bent down toward the lieutenant's box, which he took into the background.

"Then," continued Schweik, "Lieutenant Lukash began to search in all his pockets, but he couldn't find anything, so he fetches out his silver watch and gives it to me. He was quite overcome, as you might say. 'Look here, Schweik,' he said, 'when I draw my pay I want you to write down how much I owe you. You can keep this watch as an extra. And another time, don't be a bloody fool,' he says. But after that we was both of us so desperate hard up that I had to take that watch to the pawnshop."

"What are you up to, at the back there, Baloun?" inquired Quartermaster Sergeant Vanek.

Instead of giving any reply, the luckless Baloun hiccoughed. For he had opened Lieutenant Lukash's box and was gobbling up his last roll.

Shortly before this, a very tense conversation was taking place between Captain Sagner and Cadet Biegler.

"I'm surprised at you, Biegler," said Captain Sagner. "Why didn't you come and report to me immediately that those five ounces of Hungarian salami were not being issued? I had to go out personally and ascertain why the men were coming back from the store. And the officers, too, as if orders were so much empty talk. What I said was 'To the stores by companies, one platoon at a time.' That meant, that if no rations were served out, the men were to come back to the train one squad at a time as well. I told you to keep proper order, but you just let things slide. I suppose the fact is you were glad you didn't have to worry your head about counting out the rations of salami."

"Beg to report, sir, that instead of salami, the men received two picture postcards each."

And Cadet Biegler presented the battalion commander with two specimens of these postcards, which had been issued by the War Records Department in Vienna, at the head of which was General Wojnowich. On one side was a caricature of a Russian soldier, a Russian peasant with a shaggy beard who was being embraced by a skeleton. Underneath were the words:

The day upon which perfidious Russia is snuffed out will be a day of relief for our whole Monarchy.

The other postcard emanated from the German Empire. It was a gift from the Germans to the Austro-Hungarian warriors. On top was the motto *"Viribus unitis"* and underneath it a picture of Sir Edward Grey hanging on a gallows, with an Austrian and a German soldier blithely at the salute below. This was accompanied by a poem from Greinz's book *The Iron Fist*. The witticisms were described by the German papers as being so many strokes from a lash, full of rollicking humor and irrepressible wit. This particular stroke from a lash was as follows:

Grey

The gallows should on high display
Dangling now Sir Edward Grey.
It should have happened long ago;
Why did it not, then? You must know
That every single tree refused
As gallows for this Judas to be used.

Scarcely had Captain Sagner finished perusing this specimen of "rollicking humor and irrepressible wit" than Battalion Orderly Matushitch dashed into the staff carriage. He had been sent by Captain Sagner to the telegraph headquarters of the railway transport command to ask whether there had been any change of instructions, and had brought a telegram from the brigade. But there was no need to decode it. The telegram ran, *au clair:* "Quickly finish cooking then advance toward Sokal." Captain Sagner shook his head in perplexity.

"Beg to report, sir," said Matushitch, "the railway transport officer wants to see you. He's got another telegram there."

A conversation of a very confidential character then ensued between the railway transport officer and Captain Sagner.

The first telegram had to be delivered, in spite of the surprising message it contained. It was addressed *au clair* to the draft of the 91st Regiment, with a copy for the draft of the 75th Regiment, which was still further behind them. The signature was in order: Ritter von Herbert.

"This is a very confidential matter, sir," said the transport officer mysteriously. "A secret telegram from your division. Your brigade commander's gone mad. They took him off to Vienna after he'd been sending out dozens of telegrams like that from the brigade all over the place. You're pretty certain to find another telegram when you get to Budapest. Of course, all his telegrams'll have to be canceled, although we haven't received any instructions on that point yet."

Captain Sagner began to feel very uncomfortable.

"When does the train leave?" he asked.

The railway transport officer looked at his watch.

"In six minutes," he replied.

"Very well, then. I must be off," said Captain Sagner.

He returned to the staff carriage, where all the officers, except Cadet Biegler, were playing cards. Cadet Biegler was rummaging among a pile of manuscripts which he had started, all dealing with various aspects of the war. For he had ambitions to distinguish himself, not only on the battlefield, but also as a literary wizard. His literary efforts had promising titles, but he had got no further with them. They included the following:

Character of the Troops in the Great War; Who Began the War?; The Policy of Austria-Hungary and the Birth of the Great War; Observations on War; Popular Lecture on the Outbreak of the Great War; Reflections on Politics and War; Austria-Hungary's Day of Glory; Slavonic Imperialism and the Great War; War Documents; Documents Bearing on the History of the Great War; Diary of the Great War; Daily Survey of the Great War; Our Dynasty in the Great War; The Nations of the Austro-Hungarian Monarchy in Arms; My Experiences in the Great War; Chronicle of My War Campaign; How Austria-Hungary's Enemies Wage War; Whose Is the Victory?; Our Officers and Our Men; Noteworthy Deeds of My Soldiers; From the Epoch of the Great War; On the Battle Tumult; Book of Austro-Hungarian Heroes; The Iron Brigade; Collection of My Letters from the Front; Handbook for Troops in the Field; Days of Struggle and Days of Victory; What I Saw and Experienced in the Field; In the Trenches; The Officer Tells His Story; Enemy Airplanes and Our Infantry; After the Battle; Our Artillery, Faithful Sons of Our Country; And Even Though All Demons Ranged Themselves Against Us; War, Defensive and Offensive; Blood and Iron; Victory or Death; Our Heroes in Captivity.

Captain Sagner inspected all these things, and asked Cadet Biegler what he thought he was up to. Cadet Biegler replied with genuine gusto that each of these titles denoted a book which he was going to write. So many titles, so many books.

"If I should get killed at the front, sir," he said, "I should like to leave some sort of memorial behind me. In this I am inspired by the example of the German professor Urdo Kraft. He was born in 1870, but volunteered for the army and was killed on August twenty-second, 1914, at Anley. Before his death he published a book called *How to Die for the Kaiser! A Course of Self-training.*"

Captain Sagner led Cadet Biegler to the window.

"Let's see what else you've got. Your doings interest me enormously," he said with a touch of irony. "What's that notebook you're hiding under your tunic?"

"That's nothing," replied Cadet Biegler, blushing like a girl. "You can see for yourself, sir."

The notebook bore the following label:

CONSPECTUS OF GREAT AND FAMOUS BATTLES

Fought by the Austro-Hungarian Army.
Compiled from Historical Records by Adolf Biegler,
Officer in the Imperial Royal Army. With Notes and Comments.

By ADOLF BIEGLER, Officer in the Imperial
Royal Army

The conspectus was extremely simple.

From the Battle of Nördlingen on September 6, 1634, by way of the Battles of Zenta on September 11, 1697, Caldiera on October 31, 1805, Aspern on May 22, 1809, Leipzig in 1813, Santa Lucia in May, 1848, Trantenau on June 27, 1866, to the capture of Sarajevo on August 19, 1878. The diagrams of these battles were all alike. In each case Cadet Biegler had drawn plain rectangles on one side to represent Austro-Hungarian troops and dotted rectangles to represent the enemy. Both sides had a left wing, a center, and a right wing. Then at the back there were reserves, while arrows darted to and fro. The Battle of Nördlingen, just like the capture of Sarajevo, looked like the arrangement of the players at the start of a football match and the arrows showed which way each side was to kick the ball.

This idea immediately occurred to Captain Sagner, and he asked, "Do you play football?"

Cadet Biegler blushed still more and blinked nervously, so that it looked as if he were trying to keep back his tears.

Captain Sagner, with a smile, continued to peruse the notebook and paused at the comment on the diagram representing the Battle of Trantenau during the war between Prussia and Austria. Cadet Biegler had written:

The Battle of Trantenau ought not to have been fought, because the mountainous character of the terrain made it impossible for General Mazzucheli to extend the division menaced by the strong Prussian columns on the elevated areas surrounding the left wing of our division.

"According to you," said Captain Sagner, with a smile, re-

350

turning the notebook to Cadet Biegler, "the Battle of Trantenau could only have been fought if Trantenau were in a plain. It's very nice of you, Cadet Biegler, to try and get a grip of military strategy when you've been so short a time in the army. You remind me of a lot of kids playing at soldiers and calling each other General. Really, it's a real treat to see the way you've given yourself such rapid promotion. 'Adolf Biegler, Officer in the Imperial Royal Army'! Why, at that rate, you'll be a field marshal by the time we get to Budapest. The day before yesterday you were at home weighing cowhides in your father's shop. And now you're Adolf Biegler, Lieutenant in the Imperial Royal Army. Why, man alive, you're not an officer yet. You're a cadet. You're just floating in the air between the ranks of ensign and the N.C.O.'s. You're about as much entitled to call yourself an officer as a lance corporal sitting in a pub would be to let people call him a staff sergeant major."

Cadet Biegler, seeing that the conversation was at an end, saluted and, very red in the face, passed through the carriage to the corridor at the very end. He entered the lavatory, where he began to sob quietly. Later, he wiped his eyes and stalked out into the corridor, telling himself that he must be strong, damned strong. But he had a headache and he felt altogether out of sorts.

He passed through the last compartment when Matushitch, battalion orderly, was playing sixty-six with Batzer, orderly of the battalion commander.

He coughed as he went by. They turned around and went on playing.

"Don't you know what you ought to do?" asked Cadet Biegler sternly.

"Couldn't manage it," replied Batzer in the terrible dialect of German as spoken on the frontiers of Bavaria and Bohemia. "Hadn't got any trumps left.

"I ought to have played clubs," he continued, "high clubs, and then come out with the king of diamonds. That's what I ought to have done."

Cadet Biegler said no more, but lay down in his corner. When, later on, Ensign Pleschner came to give him a drink from a bottle of brandy, he was surprised to find Cadet Biegler engrossed in Professor Urdo Kraft's volume, *How to Die for the Kaiser! A Course of Self-training.*

Before they reached Budapest, Cadet Biegler was so tipsy that he leaned out of the carriage window and kept shouting to the deserted landscape, "Get a move on! For God's sake, get a move!"

Later, at Captain Sagner's orders, Matushitch and Batzer laid Cadet Biegler to rest on a seat, where he dreamed that he had the Iron Cross with bars, that he'd been mentioned in dispatches, and that he was a major who was proceeding to inspect a brigade. It puzzled him why it was that though he was in charge of a whole brigade, he was still major. He suspected that he ought to have been appointed major general, and that the "general" had somehow got lost in the post. Then he was in a motor car which, as the result of an explosion, reached the gates of heaven, for which the password was "God and Kaiser." He was admitted to the presence of God, who turned out to be none other than Captain Sagner, who was accusing him of masquerading as a major general. Then he floundered into a new dream. He was defending Linz during the War of the Austrian Succession. There were redoubts and palisades and Lieutenant Lukash dying at his feet. Lieutenant Lukash was saying something very pathetic and complimentary to him when he felt a bullet strike him so that he could no longer sit on his horse. He fell through space and landed on the floor of the railway carriage.

Batzer and Matushitch lifted him up and put him back on his seat. Then Matushitch went to Captain Sagner and reported that strange things had been happening to Cadet Biegler.

"I don't think it's the brandy that's upset him," he said. "It's more likely to be cholera. He's been drinking water at all the railway stations. I saw him at Mozony—"

"Cholera doesn't come on as quickly as all that. Go and ask the doctor to have a look at him."

The doctor who was attached to the battalion was a "war doctor" named Welfer. He had studied medicine at various universities of Austria-Hungary, and had walked all kinds of hospitals, but he had never taken his degree for the simple reason that there was a clause in his uncle's will by which a fixed annual amount was to be paid by the remaining heirs to Friedrich Welfer, medical student, until the said Friedrich Welfer received his doctor's diploma. As the fixed annual amount was about four times greater than the pay of a house physician, Friedrich Welfer, medical student, exerted himself honestly to stave off, to as remote a period as possible, the award of a medical diploma.

But when the war broke out, it dealt Friedrich Welfer a

treacherous blow from behind. He was taken by the scruff of his neck and shoved into the army, whereupon one of the heirs, who was in the War Office, arranged for the worthy Friedrich Welfer to be awarded a war-doctor's degree. This was done in writing. He received a number of questions to answer, and he answered them all with the stereotyped formula "rats." Three days later he was informed that he had been awarded a doctor's diploma. He was detailed to a military hospital, and with a bad grace he went. After a while it was discovered that he treated military patients with extreme indulgence, keeping them in the hospital as long as possible. His principle was: "What's it matter if they stay in the hospital or get killed in the trenches? May as well let 'em die in the hospital as in the fighting line."

It was then that Dr. Welfer was sent off with the Eleventh Draft to the front.

Captain Sagner, of course, felt vastly superior to this ex-medical student, and when Dr. Welfer came back from his examination of Cadet Biegler, he did not even condescend to notice him, but continued his conversation with Lieutenant Lukash on the subject of watermelons.

Dr. Welfer, however, came up and said with a smile, "There's nothing wrong with him. Young gentlemen who aspire in the course of time to become army officers and who brag of their expert knowledge of strategy really ought to be told that it's dangerous to eat up at a sitting a whole parcel of lollipops which their mama has sent them. Cadet Biegler, so he informed me, has managed to put away thirty cream puffs since we left Bruck. It reminds me of that verse in Schiller: 'Who saith that—' "

"Look here, Doctor," Captain Sagner interrupted him. "Schiller be blowed. What's up with Cadet Biegler?"

Dr. Welfer again smiled. "Cadet Biegler, your aspirant for military rank, has had a slight bodily mishap. It isn't cholera and it isn't dysentery. What with his thirty cream puffs and rather more brandy than he's used to—well, as I say, a slight bodily mishap."

"So it's nothing serious, then?" asked Captain Sagner. "All the same. If the news of it were to get about . . ."

Lieutenant Lukash stood up and said to Captain Sagner, "A damned fine platoon commander for you. I wouldn't take him as a gift."

"I pulled him around a bit," continued Dr. Welfer, with the

same irritating smile. "The battalion commander will do the rest. I'm going to have him sent to the hospital. I'll issue a certificate that he's got dysentery. A severe case of dysentery. Isolation. Cadet Biegler will be taken to the disinfection hut."

Captain Sagner turned to his friend Lieutenant Lukash and said in a strictly official voice, "Cadet Biegler of your company has been taken ill with dysentery and will remain at Budapest for treatment."

And thus it came about that the dauntless Cadet Biegler was conveyed to the military isolation hospital at Új Buda.

His trousers got lost amid the alarums and excursions of the World War.

354

2.

At Budapest

AT THE RAILWAY station in Budapest, Matushitch brought Captain Sagner a telegram from the command, sent by the wretched brigade commander who had been taken to a sanatorium. It was *au clair* and identical with the one delivered at the previous station: "Finish cooking promptly and advance on Sokol." To it was added: "Assign army service corps to eastern group. Reconnoitering work to be discontinued. Draft No. 13 to build bridge over River Bug. Further particulars in newspapers."

Captain Sagner at once proceeded to the railway transport headquarters. He was received by a fat little major with a friendly smile.

"This brigade general of yours has been up to fine old pranks," he said, chuckling with gusto. "I had to deliver the drivel to you because we haven't yet had any instructions from the division that his telegrams are to be kept back. Yesterday

355

the Fourteenth Draft of the Seventy-fifth Regiment passed through here and the battalion commander had a telegram to say he was to issue six crowns extra pay to each man as a bonus for Přzemysl, and also that of these six crowns two were to be deposited here in the office as subscription to war loan. From what I hear on good authority, your brigade general has got G.P.I."

"According to regimental orders, sir," said Captain Sagner to the railway transport officer, "we are to proceed to Gödölö. Each man is to be given five ounces of Emmenthaler cheese here. At the last stopping place they were to receive five ounces of Hungarian salami. But they got nothing."

"I expect that's what'll happen here, too," replied the major, still smiling affably. "I don't know anything about such orders, at least as far as the Czech regiments are concerned." He spoke the last words meaningly. "Anyway, that's not my business. You'd better apply to the commissariat."

"When are we leaving, sir?"

"In front of you there's a train with heavy artillery for Galicia. We're starting it off in an hour's time. On the third track there's a hospital train. That's leaving twenty-five minutes after the artillery. On track Number Twelve we've got a munition train. That leaves ten minutes after the hospital train and twenty minutes after that your train's leaving.

"That is, of course, if there are no changes," he added, still smiling in a manner which made Captain Sagner feel quite sick.

"Excuse me, sir," Captain Sagner then asked. "Can you explain to me why you know nothing about orders relating to the issue of five ounces of Emmenthaler cheese per man in the Czech regiments?"

"There's a special proviso about that," answered the railway transport officer at Budapest, still smiling.

"I suppose I was asking for it," thought Captain Sagner to himself, as he left the office. "Why the devil didn't I tell Lieutenant Lukash to call together all platoon commanders and go with them to the commissariat to fetch five ounces of Emmenthaler cheese per man?"

Before Lieutenant Lukash, commander of the Eleventh Company, could carry out the orders of Captain Sagner relating to the procedure to be followed in respect of the issue of five ounces of Emmenthaler cheese per man, Schweik made his appearance before him, accompanied by the wretched Baloun.

Baloun was trembling from head to foot.

"Beg to report, sir," said Schweik with his customary aplomb, "this is most important matter, sir. I'd take it as a favor, sir, if we could just step on one side to talk it over, like one of my friends who was best man at a wedding and while he was in church he suddenly wanted to—"

"Well, what is it, Schweik?" interrupted Lieutenant Lukash, who had already begun to pine for Schweik, as much as Schweik for Lieutenant Lukash. "We can just walk on a little."

Baloun followed behind them, still trembling all over. He had quite lost his composure and was dangling his arms in the last stages of despair.

"Well, what is it, Schweik?" repeated Lieutenant Lukash, when they had moved a little further on.

"Beg to report, sir," said Schweik, "that it is always better to own up to a thing before the row starts. You gave definite orders, sir, that when we got to Budapest Baloun was to bring you your liver paste and rolls.

"Did you get that order or not?" added Schweik, turning to Baloun.

Baloun began to dangle his arms still more, as if he were about to defend himself against the onset of an enemy.

"I'm sorry to say, sir," continued Schweik, "that your order couldn't be carried out. I ate your liver paste.

"I ate it," went on Schweik, nudging the horrified Baloun, "because I thought it might go bad. I've read over and over again in the papers that whole families have been poisoned with liver paste. There was one at Zderaz, another at Beroun, another at Tábor, another at Mladá Boleslav, another at Pribram. They was all finished off by the poison. Liver paste's shocking stuff."

Baloun, meanwhile, was standing on one side in a state of huge trepidation.

"What's the matter with you, Baloun?" asked Lieutenant Lukash.

"B-b-beg t-to re-re-port, s-s-sir," began the wretched Baloun, "I—I—I a-a-ate it."

"You see how it is, sir," said Schweik, as cool as a cucumber. "I was going to take the blame on myself, and then this silly ass blurts it all out and gives himself away. He's not a bad sort, you know, sir, but he eats up everything that's put in his

357

charge. I used to know another chap like that. He was a commissionaire in a bank. You could trust him with thousands. Why, one day he went to another bank to fetch some money and they gave him a thousand crowns too much and he took it back on the spot. But send him for a quarter of a pound of meat, and he'd eat half of it up before he got back. He was such a one for his grub that when the clerks used to send him to fetch liver sausage, he'd scoop lumps out with a pocketknife on the way and plug up the holes with court plaster that cost him more for five sausages than a whole sausage would have done."

Lieutenant Lukash sighed and walked away.

"Any more orders, sir?" Schweik shouted after him.

Lieutenant Lukash waved him aside and proceeded to the commissariat. The odd idea struck him that when the troops were eating liver paste belonging to officers, there wasn't much chance for Austria to win the war.

The signal was given for the train to start, and the men again returned without any rations. Instead of the five ounces of Emmenthaler cheese which was to have been served out, they each received a box of matches and a picture postcard issued by the Austrian War Graves Committee. Instead of five ounces of Emmenthaler cheese, they were provided with a picture of the Western Galician Military Cemetery, with a monument to some unfortunate militiamen which had been prepared by Scholz, a sculptor and a volunteer sergeant major, who had successfully managed to dodge the front.

There was quite a hum of excitement in the vicinity of the staff carriage. The officers of the draft had gathered around Captain Sagner, who was excitedly explaining something to them. He had just come back from the railway transport office, where he had received a very confidential (and genuine) telegram from brigade headquarters, a telegram containing news of far-reaching importance and accompanied by instructions as to how to act in the new situation which had arisen for Austria on May 22, 1915.

The telegram from the brigade stated that Italy had declared war on Austria-Hungary.

While they were still in Bruck, the officers during meals had frequently discussed, with their mouths full, the strange behavior of Italy, but on the whole nobody had expected that the prophetic words of that fool of a Cadet Biegler would be fulfilled. One night at supper he had thrust from him a plate of macaroni and declared, "I won't eat any of that stuff till I reach the gates of Verona."

Captain Sagner, having perused the instructions just received from the brigade, gave orders for the alarm to be sounded.

When the whole draft had assembled, the men were drawn up in a square, and Captain Sagner, in an unusually solemn voice, read them the telegraphic message which had reached him from the brigade.

"As the result of unparalleled treachery and greed, the King of Italy has forgotten the fraternal agreement by which he was bound as an ally of our monarchy. Since the outbreak of the war, the treacherous King of Italy has been playing a double game and carrying on secret negotiations with our enemies, and this treachery reached its climax on May twenty-second–twenty-third, by the declaration of war on our monarchy. Our supreme commander is convinced that our ever staunch and glorious troops will reply to this vile treachery on the part of a faithless ally with such a blow that the traitor will realize how, by having started war basely and treacherously, he was preparing his own destruction. We firmly trust that with God's help the day will soon dawn when the plains of Italy will again see the victor of Santa Lucia, Vicenza, Novara, Custozza. We desire to conquer, we must conquer, and assuredly we shall conquer!"

After that they gave the usual three cheers, and the troops got back into the train, feeling rather dazed. Instead of five ounces of Emmenthaler cheese, they had war with Italy foisted off upon them.

In the truck in which Schweik was sitting with Quartermaster Sergeant Vanek and Chodounsky the telephonist, Baloun, and Jurajda the cook, an interesting conversation had started on the subject of Italy's entry into the war.

"Well, now that we've got another war," remarked Schweik, "now that we've got one more enemy and a new front, we'll have to be more economical with the ammunition. 'The more kids there are in a family, the more canes are needed.' That's what old Chovanec used to say. He lived at Motol and he used to wallop all the kids in the neighborhood at a flat rate, as they say."

"All I'm afraid of is," said Baloun with great concern, "that this Italian business is going to mean smaller rations."

359

Quartermaster Sergeant Vanek reflected and then said gravely, "It's bound to, because now it'll take us a bit longer to win the war."

"What we want now," declared Schweik, "is another chap like Radetzky. He knew his way about in those parts and how to catch the Italians napping and what places to bombard and from what side to do it. It's an easy enough job to get into a place. Anybody can manage that. But getting out again, that's how a man shows if he's good at soldiering or not. When you find your way in, you've got to know everything that's going on all around you, or else all of a sudden you'll find your number's up and you're in what they call a catastrophe. But old Radetzky, he knew every inch of the ground, he did, and they could never get at him. Once I read in a book about him how he skedaddled from Santa Lucia and the Italians skedaddled too, and it wasn't until the next day that he discovered that it was really him who'd won, because he couldn't spot any Italians there, even though he had a squint through a telescope. So back he goes as large as life, and made himself at home in Santa Lucia. They made him a field marshal for doing that."

Quartermaster Sergeant Vanek had a sneaking regard for Italy. In his drugstore at home he did a side line in lemonade which he manufactured from decayed lemons, and he always obtained the cheapest and most decayed lemons from Italy. Now there wouldn't be any more lemons coming from Italy to Vanek's drugstore at Kralup. There could be no doubt that the war with Italy was going to produce many awkward surprises like that.

Baloun, meanwhile, had been laboriously pondering about something, until finally he asked Quartermaster Sergeant Vanek, in a scared voice, "Then you think, Sergeant, that all along of this war with Italy we're going to have smaller rations served out?"

"You bet we are," replied Quartermaster Sergeant Vanek.

"God Almighty!" exclaimed Baloun, sinking his head in his hands and squatting glumly in a corner.

This definitely concluded the debate on Italy.

In the staff carriage, the conversation on the latest turn of events, brought about by Italy's entry into the war, would certainly have been very dull, now that Cadet Biegler, that great expert on military strategy, was no longer there, if he had not been replaced, to a certain extent, by Lieutenant Dub of the Third Company.

In civil life Lieutenant Dub was a schoolmaster who taught Czech as a special subject, and even before the war he had displayed an extraordinary propensity for ramming his loyalty down people's throats on every possible occasion. The subjects for essays which he used to choose for his pupils were all taken from the history of the House of Hapsburg. He had once set the top class an essay on "Emperor Franz Josef I as a Patron of the Arts and Sciences," and the result of this had been that one pupil was disqualified from ever again entering a secondary school in the Austro-Hungarian Empire for having written that this ruler's finest achievement had been to establish the Franz Josef I Bridge in Prague.

He always made a point of seeing that on the Emperor's birthday and other imperial festivities all his pupils sang the Austrian anthem with due enthusiasm. He was disliked among his fellow townsmen because he was known to keep on the right side of the powers that be by telling tales about his colleagues. Among the local dignitaries he formed one of a trio composing the biggest imbeciles and bigots and consisting of himself, the district chief of police, and the headmaster of the local grammar school.

Lieutenant Dub now began to hold forth in the tones of a priggish schoolmaster. "On the whole I cannot say I am surprised at this action on the part of Italy. I expected this to happen three months ago. There can be no doubt that of recent years Italy has become extremely arrogant, in consequence of the successful war against Turkey. Moreover, she is placing too much reliance on her fleet and on the feeling among the population in our Adriatic areas and in south Tyrol. Before the war I used to tell our district chief of police that our government ought not to underestimate the Irredentist movement in the south. He quite agreed with me, because every farsighted man who is concerned about the preservation of this empire must long ago have realized what would happen to us if we were to show too much indulgence toward such elements. I well remember that about two years ago, in the course of a conversation with our district of police, I stated that Italy was only waiting for the next opportunity of making a treacherous attack on us.

"And now they've done it!" he bellowed, as if all the others were disputing his statements, although all the regular officers who were listening to his speech were wishing that the talkative temporary gentleman would go to blazes.

"It is true," he continued in quieter tones, "that in the vast majority of cases people were apt to forget our former relations with Italy, those great days when our armies were glorious and victorious, in 1848 and in 1866, which are mentioned in today's brigade orders. But I always did my duty, and just before the end of the school year, practically at the very beginning of the war, I set my pupils an essay on 'Our Heroes in Italy from Vicenza to Custozza, or—' "

And the driveling Lieutenant Dub solemnly added, " '— Blood and Life for Hapsburg, for an Austria Undivided and Uniquely Great.' "

He paused and waited for someone else in the staff carriage to express views on the new situation, so that he could show them that he had known five years previously how Italy would one day treat her ally. But he was grievously disappointed, for Captain Sagner, to whom Battalion Orderly Matushitch had brought the evening edition of the *Pester Lloyd* from the railway station, remarked from the depths of his newspaper, "Look here, that actress Weiner who was starring at Bruck when we were there, was playing last night at the Little Theater in Budapest."

And this concluded the debate on Italy in the staff carriage.

Battalion Orderly Matushitch and Batzer, Captain Sagner's orderly, viewed the war with Italy from a purely practical point of view, because, many years previously, when they were doing their regular military service, they had both taken part in maneuvers in south Tyrol.

"It won't half be a sweat for us, climbing about on those mountains," said Batzer. "Captain Sagner's got loads of boxes. There's mountains where I come from, but it's quite a different sort of stunt when you shove your gun under your coat and go to see if you can't bag a hare or two on his lordship's preserves."

"It's all according to whether they're going to send us off to Italy," said Matushitch gloomily. "I can't say as I'd be exactly keen on traipsing about on those mountains and glaciers and whatnot with messages. And then the grub down there, why, it's nothing but polenta and oil, oil and polenta."

"And I don't see why we should be the ones to do this mountain stuff," said Batzer, waxing indignant. "Our regiment's done its whack in Serbia and the Carpathians. I've done my share of carting the captain's box about in mountains. I lost 'em twice—once in Serbia and then in the Carpathians, when we were getting it fair in the neck. Maybe there's a third lot in store for me somewhere in Italy. And as for the grub—"

He spat with disgust.

Then he drew closer to Matushitch and said confidentially, "You know, in my part of the country we make small dumplings with raw potatoes, we boil 'em, soak 'em in egg yolk, stick plenty of bits of crust over 'em, and then fry 'em on bacon."

He pronounced the last word with mysterious solemnity.

"And they're just fine with sauerkraut," he added in melancholy tones. "I got no use for macaroni."

This completed their conversation about Italy.

As the train had now been standing in the station for more than two hours, the occupants of the other trucks believed to a man that the train was going to be turned around and sent to Italy. This was suggested by a number of queer things that had been happening to the echelon. All the men had again been chivvied out of the trucks, there had been a sanitary inspector with a disinfecting committee which had come and liberally sprinkled all the trucks with Lysol, a proceeding which met with great disapproval, especially in the trucks containing bread rations. But orders are orders. The sanitation committee had issued orders to disinfect all trucks of Echelon 728, and so they stolidly squirted Lysol over quantities of bread rations and bags of rice. This alone showed that something special was going to happen.

After that, everybody was chivvied back into the trucks because an aged general had come to inspect the echelon. Schweik, who was standing in the back ranks, remarked to Quartermaster Sergeant Vanek on the subject of this worthy, "There's an old perisher for you!"

And the old perisher trotted along the ranks, accompanied by Captain Sagner, and stopped in front of a young recruit. Apparently by way of encouraging the rank and file as a whole, he asked where the young recruit came from, how old he was, and whether he had a watch. The young recruit had a watch, but as he thought that he was going to get another one from the old gentleman, he said he hadn't got one, whereupon the aged general gave a fatuous smile, such as Franz Josef

363

used to put on whenever, on festive occasions, he addressed a few words to the mayors of towns, and said, "That's fine, that's fine," whereupon he honored a corporal, who was standing near, by asking him whether his wife was well.

"Beg to report, sir," bawled the corporal, "I'm not married."

Whereupon the general, with a patronizing smile, repeated, "That's fine, that's fine."

Then the general, lapsing still further into senile infantility, asked Captain Sagner to show him how the troops number off in twos from the right, and after a while, he heard them yelling, "One—two, one—two, one—two."

The aged general was very fond of this. At home he had two orderlies, and he used to line them up in front of him and make them number off: "One—two, one—two."

Austria had lots of generals like that.

When the inspection was safely over, and the general had lavishly expressed his approval to Captain Sagner, the men were given permission to move about within the precincts of the railway station, as a message had arrived that they were not leaving for another three hours. The men accordingly strolled about with an eye to the main chance, and as there were plenty of people in the station, here and there a soldier managed to scrounge a cigarette.

It was obvious, however, that the early enthusiasm which had evinced itself in the festive welcome extended to the troops in railway stations had sunk considerably and was being reduced to the point where cadging began.

Captain Sagner was met by a deputation from the League for Welcoming Heroes, consisting of two terribly jaded ladies who presented the gifts for the troops, to wit, twenty small boxes of throat pastilles (assorted flavors). These little boxes, which were distributed as an advertisement by a Budapest manufacturer of confectionery, were made of tin and on the lid was painted a Hungarian soldier shaking hands with an Austrian militiaman, with the crown of St. Stephen glittering above them. This was surrounded by an inscription in German and Magyar: "For Emperor, God, and Country." The manufacturer of confectionery was so loyal that he put the Emperor before God.

Each box contained eighty pastilles, which worked out, on an average, at five pastilles for three men. Besides the pastilles, the jaded and worried ladies had brought a bundle of leaflets containing two prayers written by Géza Szatmur Budafal,

Archbishop of Budapest. They were in German and Magyar, and contained the most dreadful imprecations against all enemies. According to the venerable archbishop, the Almighty ought to chop the Russians, English, Serbs, French, and Japanese into mincemeat. The Almighty ought to bathe in the blood of the enemy and slaughter them all as Herod did the babies. In his pious little prayers the worthy archbishop made use of such choice phrases as:

"May God bless your bayonets that they may penetrate deep into the entrails of your enemies. May the Almighty in His great righteousness direct your artillery fire upon the heads of the enemy staffs. Merciful God, grant that all our enemies may be stifled amid their own blood, from the wounds which we inflict upon them."

When the two ladies had handed over all these gifts, they expressed to Captain Sagner an urgent wish to be present at the distribution. In fact, one of them went so far as to say that on this occasion she would like to say a few words to the troops, whom she always referred to as "our brave boys."

They both looked terribly hurt when Captain Sagner refused them their wish. Meanwhile, the gifts were carted off to the truck which was being used as a store.

The worthy ladies passed through the ranks and one of them patted a bearded warrior on the cheek. Knowing nothing about the exalted mission of these ladies, the warrior remarked to his comrades after their departure, "There's a couple of brazen old tarts for you! Fancy those ugly, flat-footed old geezers having the sauce to try and get off with soldiers!"

The station was in a regular hubbub. The Italian complication had caused a certain amount of panic. Two echelons of artillery had been held up and sent to Styria. There was also an echelon of Bosnians who for some unknown reason had been left there for two days and completely overlooked. They had not drawn any rations for two days and were now going about the streets of Ujpest begging for bread.

At last the draft of the 91st Regiment was again got together and went back into the trucks. But after a while, Matushitch, the battalion orderly, came back from the railway transport office with the news that they were not starting for another three hours. Accordingly, the men who had just been collected were again let out of the trucks. Then, just before the train started, Lieutenant Dub entered the staff carriage in a very agitated state and asked Captain Sagner to have Schweik put under arrest immediately. Lieutenant Dub, who had been notorious as a talebearer among his fellow teachers, was fond of having conversations with soldiers, with the idea of getting at their opinions and also so that he could explain to them didactically why they were fighting and for what they were fighting.

While strolling around, he caught sight of Schweik standing near a lamppost behind the station buildings and examining with interest the poster of some charitable war lottery. This poster depicted an Austrian soldier impaling a scared and bearded Cossack against a wall.

Lieutenant Dub tapped Schweik on the shoulder and asked him how he liked it.

"Beg to report, sir," replied Schweik, "it's a lot of rot. I've seen plenty of footling placards in my time, but I've never seen any flapdoodle as bad as that before."

"What is it you don't like about it?" asked Lieutenant Dub.

"Well, sir, first of all I don't like the way the soldier is handling the bayonet that he's been trusted with and all. Why, he'll smash it against the wall like that. And, besides, there's no need for him to do it, anyhow, because the Russian's put his hands up. He's a prisoner and you got to treat prisoners properly. Fair's fair, when all's said and done. That chap'll cop out for what he's doing."

Lieutenant Dub continued his investigations into Schweik's views and asked him, "So you're sorry for that Russian, are you?"

"I'm sorry for both of 'em, sir. For the Russian because he's got a bayonet shoved through his inside, and for the soldier because he's going to cop out for it. What's the use of him smashing his bayonet like that, sir? Why, sir, when I was doing my regular service in the army, we used to have a lieutenant in our company and I bet the toughest sergeant major hadn't got the gift of the gab like that lieutenant. On the parade ground he'd say to us, 'When I say 'Shun, your eyes have got to start out of your head like a tomcat spewing into a saucer.' But apart from that he was quite a nice chap. Once at Christmas time he went dotty and bought a cartload of coconuts for the whole company, and ever since then I've known how easy it is to smash a bayonet. Half the company smashed their bayonets on those coconuts, and our colonel gave the whole company c.b. for three months, and the lieutenant was confined to his quarters."

Lieutenant Dub gazed cantankerously at the cheerful face of the good soldier Schweik and asked him in an angry tone, "Do you know me?"

"Yes, sir, I know you."

Lieutenant Dub rolled his eyes and stamped his foot. "Let me tell you that you don't know me yet."

Schweik again replied, with unruffled calm, "Beg to report, sir, I know you. You're on our draft."

"You don't know me yet!" yelled Lieutenant Dub. "You may know me from my good side, but wait till you know me from my bad side. If a man gets on the wrong side of me, I can make him wish he hadn't been born. Now, do you know me or don't you?"

"I do know you, sir."

"I'll tell you for the last time that you don't know me, you jackass. Have you got any brothers?"

"Beg to report, sir, I've got one."

Lieutenant Dub was infuriated by the sight of Schweik's calm, unruffled countenance and, unable to contain himself any longer, he bellowed, "Then your brother must be the same sort of damned fool as you are. What's he do for a living?"

"He's a schoolmaster, sir. And now he's got his commission."

Lieutenant Dub looked daggers at Schweik. Schweik bore Lieutenant Dub's savage glance with dignified composure and the interview between them concluded with the order "Dismiss!"

Each of them went his way thinking matters over from his own angle.

Lieutenant Dub, thinking of Schweik, decided that he would tell Captain Sagner to have him put under close arrest, while Schweik, for his part, reflected that he had come across some daft officers in his time, but Lieutenant Dub was the choicest specimen he had ever met.

Lieutenant Dub, who that day was particularly keen on training soldiers in the way they should go, found fresh victims behind the railway station. They were two soldiers from the 91st Regiment, but belonging to a different company, who under cover of darkness and in broken German were haggling with two of the streetwalkers who were swarming in the vicinity of the station.

As Schweik went his way he quite distinctly heard Lieutenant Dub's shrill voice:

"But I tell you, you don't know me.

367

"Do you know me?

"But when you do know me—

"I tell you, when you know me from the bad side.

"I'll make you wish you'd never been born, you jackasses.

"Have you got any brothers?

"Then they must be the same sort of damned fools as you are. What are they? In the army service corps? Very well, then. Just remember that you're soldiers. Are you Czechs? Do you know that Palacký said that if Austria did not exist, it would have to be created? Dismiss."

Lieutenant Dub's little stroll around, however, produced no positive results. He stopped three more groups of soldiers, but his educational endeavors "to make them wish they'd never been born" failed completely. His pride was hurt and that was why, before the train started, he asked Captain Sagner to have Schweik placed under arrest. He emphasized the necessity of isolating the good soldier Schweik by reason of Schweik's astoundingly impudent demeanor, and he described Schweik's frank replies to his last question as insulting remarks. If things were to go on like that, said he, the officers would be completely discredited in the eyes of the rank and file. Surely, he argued, none of the officers present could doubt that. He himself before the war had told the district chief of police that every person holding a superior position must aim at maintaining authority over his subordinates. The district chief of police had been of the same opinion. Especially now in the army during wartime, the nearer they got to the enemy, the more urgent it was to put the fear of God into the troops. For that reason he demanded that Schweik should be summarily punished.

Captain Sagner, who as a regular officer loathed all reserve officers, reminded Lieutenant Dub that proceedings of the kind which he was suggesting could be carried out only through the orderly room and not by any slapdash methods as if it were a case of haggling with a street hawker about the price of potatoes. As regards Schweik, the proper person to approach in the first instance was the person to whose jurisdiction Schweik was amenable, and that person was Lieutenant Lukash. Such things as these were done simply and solely through the orderly room. As perhaps Lieutenant Dub was aware, they passed from the company to the battalion. If Schweik had done anything he ought not to have done, he would be had up in the company orderly room and then, if he wished to appeal, the matter would be passed on to the battalion orderly room. If, however, Lieutenant Lukash was willing and if he regarded Lieutenant Dub's narrative as an official notification which should be followed by punitive measures, he had no objection to having Schweik brought up for cross-examination.

Lieutenant Lukash had no objection to this, but he pointed out that, as he was aware from what Schweik had told him on various occasions, Schweik's brother was actually a schoolmaster and he had a commission.

Lieutenant Dub wavered and said that he had asked for Schweik to be punished in the broader sense of the term and that perhaps Schweik was not capable of expressing himself properly and his answers only seemed to be impudent, insulting, and lacking in respect toward his superiors. Moreover, judging from the general appearance of the said Schweik, it was obvious that he was feeble-minded.

Thus, the thunderstorm passed over Schweik's head without touching him.

Before the train started, the echelon was overtaken by a military train containing specimens of various units. They comprised stragglers or soldiers discharged from the hospital and now sent to rejoin their regiments, and other suspicious characters returning from special stunts or spells in detention barracks.

Among the occupants of this train was Volunteer Officer Marek, who had been charged with mutiny for refusing to clean the latrines. The divisional court-martial, however, had discharged him and he now made his appearance in the staff carriage to report himself to the battalion commander.

Captain Sagner, on seeing the volunteer officer and receiving from him his documents which contained the confidential remark "A political suspect. Caution," was not altogether pleased.

"You're a regular slacker," he said to him. "You're a perfect pest. Instead of trying to distinguish yourself and attain the rank to which your education entitles you, you just loaf about from one detention barracks to another. You're a disgrace to the regiment. But there's a chance for you to make up for your past offenses. Show that you're devoted heart and soul to the battalion. Now look here. I'll tell you what I'll do. You're an intelligent young fellow, and I've no doubt you've got a ready pen. Every battalion in the field needs a man to keep a proper record of what it achieves at the front. What he has to do is to note down all the successful operations, all the cases of distinguished conduct in which the battalion is concerned, and in that way he gradually does his bit toward producing a history of the army. Do you follow me?"

"Beg to report, sir, yes, sir. It'll be a labor of love for me to place on record the gallant deeds of our battalion, especially now that the offensive is in full blast and the battalion is going into the thick of it."

"You will be attached to the battalion staff," continued Captain Sagner, "and you will keep an account of who is proposed for decorations, and then we will supply you with particulars which will enable you to record the marches testifying to the dauntless spirit and rigid discipline of the battalion. It's not an easy task, but I hope you've got enough powers of observation to give our battalion a better show than any other unit can put up, if I supply you with the proper hints. I'll send a telegram to regimental headquarters to say that I've appointed you keeper of the battalion records. Now report yourself to Quartermaster Sergeant Vanek of the Eleventh Company, so that he can make room for you in the carriage, and tell him to come to me."

Captain Sagner then had a brief talk with Quartermaster Sergeant Vanek. He merely reminded him that the keeper of the battalion records, Volunteer Officer Marek, would be in the same truck with Schweik.

"I may as well tell you that this fellow Marek is a political suspect. Of course, that doesn't mean much today. Lots of people are supposed to be that. But if he should start any talk of that kind, you know what I mean, just jump on him at once so that I shan't have the unpleasant job of inquiring into it. Just tell him to drop all that sort of talk and that'll be all right. But I don't want you to come running to me. Tell him off, but do it in a friendly way. A little coaxing like that is always better than a lot of idiotic speechifying. Anyhow, I don't want to hear anything about it, because— You see what I mean. That's the sort of thing that spreads all over a battalion."

When Quartermaster Sergeant Vanek got back, he took Marek on one side and said to him, "Look here, old chap, you're a suspicious character. Not that I care. But be careful what you say in front of Chodounsky, the chap at the telephone."

Scarcely had he said this than Chodounsky came staggering in and threw his arms around the quartermaster sergeant's neck. In a drunken voice he yelled, "We'll always stick together. Anything I hear in the telephone I'll come and tell you right away. A fat lot I care about their damned secrets."

Shortly afterward the order came that they were leaving in a quarter of an hour. As nobody would believe this, it came about that, in spite of all precautions, a certain number strayed away somewhere or other. When the train did start, eighteen men were missing, among them Sergeant Nasakl of the Twelfth Draft, who, long after the train had vanished beyond Isatarcsa, was squabbling in a small shrubbery behind the station with a streetwalker who was demanding five crowns for services rendered.

3.

From Hatvan to the Frontiers of Galicia

WHILE the battalion, which was to reap military glory, was being transported by railway as far as Laborc in Eastern Galicia, whence it was to proceed on foot to the front, the truck containing Schweik and the volunteer officer was again the scene of more or less treasonable conversations, and on a smaller scale the same sort of thing was happening in the other trucks. Indeed, even in the staff carriage there was a certain amount of discontent because at Füzes-Abony an army order had been received by which the wine rations served out to the officers were to be reduced by a quarter of a pint. Of course, the rank and file had not been forgotten and their sago rations had been reduced by one third of an ounce per man, which was all the more mysterious because nobody had ever seen any sago in the army.

At Füzes-Abony also, where it was intended to cook some stew, the discovery was made that one company had lost its field kitchen. Inquiries showed that the luckless field kitchen had never left Bruck and that it was still probably standing, chill and deserted, somewhere behind Hut Number 186. The fact was that the cookhouse staff belonging to this field kitchen had been locked up in the main guardroom for disorderly conduct in the town on the day before departure, and they had so arranged it that they were still under lock and key when their draft was traveling through Hungary.

The company minus its field kitchen was accordingly assigned to another field kitchen, and this caused a slight disagreement, because among the men from both companies who were put on to potato-scraping fatigue duties arose a controversy when one lot declared that they were not such damned fools as to work their guts out for the others. In the end, however, it turned out that the cooking of this stew was really only a sort of maneuver, so that by the time the troops were cooking stew in the field face to face with the enemy, they could get used to receiving the sudden order, "As you were," whereupon the stew would be thrown away and nobody would even get a taste of it.

So when the stew was about to be served out, the order came for the troops to return to their trucks, and off they went to Miskolcz. No stew was served out there, because a train with Russian trucks was standing in the station and the men were therefore not allowed out. Fantastic rumors now began to spread among the troops that the stew would not be served out until they left the train in Galicia once and for all, when it would be decided that the stew was rancid and unfit for consumption, whereupon it would be thrown away.

They then took the stew with them to Tisza-Lök and Zambov, and when nobody expected that the stew would be served out, the train stopped at Ujvaros near Satoral Újhely, where a fire was lit, the stew was warmed up and, at last, duly distributed.

The station was crammed with people. Two munition trains were to be sent off first, and after them two echelons of artillery, as well as a train with pontoon divisions.

Behind the station some Hungarian hussars were amusing themselves at the expense of two Polish Jews from whom they had filched a hamper of brandy, and now, instead of paying them, they were affably smacking their faces. This was evidently regarded as quite the thing to do, because their captain was standing close by and looking on with a broad smile, while behind the station depot a few other Hungarian hussars were putting their hands up the petticoats of the dark-eyed daughters of the Jews who were being castigated.

There was also a train with an aircraft division. On another set of rails could be seen trucks containing airplanes and guns, but in a very damaged state. These were the remains of aircraft which had been shot down and the shattered barrels of howitzers. While all the new material was being taken up to the front, these remnants of bygone glory were being conveyed inland for repairs and reconstruction.

Lieutenant Dub, however, was explaining to the troops who had assembled around the damaged guns and airplanes that this was war booty. He noticed, too, that a little further on Schweik was standing in another group and holding forth about something. He drew near and heard Schweik's hearty voice.

"You can take it how you like, it can't be anything but war booty. It may look a bit rum at first, when you read 'Imperial Royal Artillery Division' on a gun carriage. But I expect that the Russians collared that gun and we had to get hold of it again. Booty like that is a lot more valuable, because—

"Because," he solemnly continued, when he caught sight of Lieutenant Dub, "you must never leave anything in the enemy's hands. That's like the soldier who had his field bottle snatched away from him by the enemy while they were having a dust-up. That was during the wars with Napoleon, and in the night this soldier went off into the enemy's camp and brought his field bottle back, and he had the best of the bargain, because the enemy had drawn his brandy rations for the night."

All Lieutenant Dub said was, "Make yourself scarce and don't let me see you here again."

"Right you are, sir." And Schweik moved off toward another group of trucks.

Lieutenant Dub then continued to act the fool by pointing out to the soldiers an Austrian airplane which had been shot down and the struts of which distinctly bore the mark "Wiener Neustadt."

"We shot that down and captured it from the Russians at Lemberg," said Lieutenant Dub.

Lieutenant Lukash overheard this remark and coming nearer, he added, "Yes, and the two Russian airmen were burned to death." Then he went away again without saying another word, but thinking what a dreadful jackass Lieutenant Dub was.

Behind the second lot of trucks he encountered Schweik and endeavored to steer clear of him, because the face of Schweik, when he gazed upon Lieutenant Lukash, showed that there was much of which he desired to unbosom himself.

Schweik walked straight up to Lieutenant Lukash.

"Beg to report, sir, I've come to see if there are any more orders. Beg to report, sir, I've been looking for you in the staff carriage."

"Listen here, Schweik," replied Lieutenant Lukash, "the more I see of you the more convinced I am that you've got no respect for your superior officers."

"Beg to report, sir," said Schweik apologetically, "I used to serve under a Colonel Flieder von Boomerang, or something like that, and he was just about half your height. He had a long beard, and it made him look like a monkey, and when he got ratty he used to jump so high that we called him India-rubber Daddy. Well, one day——"

Lieutenant Lukash tapped Schweik amicably on the shoulder and said in a good-humored tone, "Now then, enough of that, you ruffian."

"Right you are, sir," replied Schweik, and returned to his truck.

After midnight the train jogged on toward Ladovec and Trebisov, where the Veterans' Association had turned out to welcome it, as they were under the mistaken impression that it was the Fourteenth Draft of the Hungarian militia, which had passed through the station in the night. The veterans had certainly drunk a drop too much, and when they yelled, *"Isten almeg a Király,"* [1] they woke up the whole echelon. Some of the more conscientious among them leaned out of the windows of the trucks and replied, "Go to blazes! *Eljen!*"

Whereupon, the veterans yelled till the windows rattled, *"Eljen! Eljen a tizennegyedik regimente!"* [2]

Five minutes later the train was approaching Humenné. Here could be seen plain traces of the fighting which had occurred when the Russians were marching into the valley of the Tisza. Primitive trenches flanked the hillsides, with here and there the remains of a burned farm, and where this was

[1] "God bless (the men of) Kiraly!"
[2] "Long live the Fourteenth Regiment!"

surrounded by a hastily constructed shanty, it showed that the inhabitants had returned.

Later, toward noon, when they reached Humenné, where the railway station also showed traces of fighting, preparations were made for lunch and the troops were able to have a glimpse into the public secrets of how the authorities treated the local population after the departure of the Russians, to whom they were akin by language and religion.

On the platform, surrounded by Magyar gendarmes, stood a group of Ruthenian prisoners. Among them were priests, teachers, and peasants from the length and breadth of the regions round about. They all had their hands tied behind their backs and they were fastened together in twos. Most of them had broken noses and bumps on their heads, as immediately after their arrest they had been thrashed by the gendarmes.

A little further on, a Magyar gendarme was having some fun with a priest. Around the priest's left foot he had tied a rope which he held in his hand, and with the butt end of his rifle he was making him dance a czardas, during which he pulled the rope so that the priest fell on his nose, and having his hands tied behind his back he could not get up, and made desperate attempts to turn over on his back, so that he might possibly stand up that way. The gendarme roared so heartily with laughter at this, that the tears came into his eyes and when the priest did at last manage to get on his feet, he pulled the rope again and once more the priest fell on his nose.

This amusement was stopped by a gendarme officer, who ordered the prisoners to be taken into an empty shed behind the station, so that they could be mauled and knocked about where nobody could see them.

These goings on were discussed in the staff carriage and on the whole they met with strong disapproval.

Ensign Kraus expressed the view that if the men were traitors they ought to be hanged on the spot, without any ill treatment beforehand, but Lieutenant Dub thoroughly approved of the whole business which he at once connected with the Sarajevo outrage. He talked as if the Magyar gendarmes at Humenné were avenging the death of Archduke Franz Ferdinand and his wife. In order to lend weight to his words, he said that he took in a monthly paper which even before the war, in the July number, had declared that the unexampled outrage of Sarajevo would leave a wound in human hearts which would not heal for many years to come. And so forth.

Lieutenant Lukash muttered something to the effect that probably the gendarmes at Humenné also took the paper which had published that touching article. He then left the carriage and went to look for Schweik. He had suddenly begun to feel disgusted with everything and all he wanted was to get drunk and forget his sorrows.

"Listen, Schweik," he said, "you don't happen to know where you could lay hands on a bottle of brandy? I'm feeling rather seedy."

"Beg to report, sir, that's the change of weather. I shouldn't be surprised that when we get to the front you'll feel worse. The further you get from your proper military base, the queerer you feel. But if you like, sir, I'll collar some brandy for you, only I'm afraid they'll leave here without me."

Lieutenant Lukash assured him that they wouldn't be leaving for another two hours and that brandy was being sold in bottles, on the Q.T., just behind the station. Captain Sagner had sent Matushitch there, and he'd brought back a bottle of quite respectable cognac for fifteen crowns. So there was fifteen crowns and Schweik was to go, and not to tell anyone that it was for Lieutenant Lukash, or that he had sent him, because, strictly speaking, it was not allowed.

"Don't you worry, sir," said Schweik. "That'll be all right, because I'm very fond of things that ain't allowed and I've been mixed up in lots of things like that without even knowing about it. Why, once when we were in barracks at Prague we was told not to—"

"About turn! Quick march!" Lieutenant Lukash interrupted him.

So Schweik went behind the station, repeating to himself all the main points of his expedition. The brandy must be good, so he would have to taste it first, and as it wasn't allowed, he would have to be cautious.

Just when he was turning aside from the platform, he again ran into Lieutenant Dub.

"What are you loafing about here for?" he asked Schweik. "Do you know me?"

"Beg to report, sir," replied Schweik, saluting, "I don't want to know you from your bad side."

Lieutenant Dub grew rigid with horror, but Schweik stood there as bold as brass, with his hand touching the peak of his cap, and continued, "Beg to report, sir, I only want to know you from the good side, so as you can't make me wish I'd never been born, like you was telling me a little while ago."

At this effrontery Lieutenant Dub shook his head and all he could do was to gasp forth in tones of fury, "Get out of my sight, you skunk. You'll hear more about this."

Schweik went beyond the platform and Lieutenant Dub, struck by an idea, set out after him. Past the station, just by the highroad, stood a row of baskets, placed topsy-turvy, and on top of them were some wicker trays containing various dainties which looked as innocent as though they were meant for school children on an outing. There were fragments of sugar sticks, rolled wafers, a large quantity of acid drops, with here and there some slices of black bread with a piece of salami, quite obviously of equine origin. But inside, the baskets contained various kinds of liquor, small bottles of brandy, rum, gin, and other alcoholic beverages.

Just beyond the ditch skirting the highroad was a shanty in which all the transactions in prohibited drinks were arranged.

The soldiers first struck a bargain in front of the wicker trays, and a Jew with side curls produced the brandy from beneath the tray which looked so innocent, and carried it under his caftan into the wooden shanty, where the soldier unobtrusively slipped it into his trousers or under his tunic.

This was the place to which Schweik directed his steps while Lieutenant Dub, with his talent for sleuthing, watched his movements.

Schweik tried his luck at the very first basket. First he selected some sweets, which he paid for and put in his pocket, while the gentleman with the side curls whispered to him in German, "I've got some schnapps, too, soldier."

A bargain was soon struck, Schweik went into the shanty, but handed over no money until the gentleman with the side curls had opened the bottle and Schweik had tasted the contents. However, he was satisfied with the brandy and having slipped the bottle under his tunic, he went back to the station.

"Where have you been, you skunk?" said Lieutenant Dub, standing in front of him as he was about to mount the platform.

"Beg to report, sir, I've been to fetch some sweets."

Schweik dived into his pocket and produced a handful of grimy, dusty sweets.

"I don't know whether you'd care to try them, sir. I've had a taste. They're not bad. They've got rather a nice, funny sort of flavor, something like raspberry jam, sir."

The curved outlines of a bottle stood out under Schweik's tunic.

Lieutenant Dub passed his hands over Schweik's tunic.

"What's that you've got there, you skunk? Take it out."

Schweik drew forth a bottle plainly and clearly labeled "Brandy" and containing a yellowish liquid.

"Beg to report, sir," replied Schweik, quite undaunted, "I pumped a little drinking water into this empty brandy bottle. I've still got a shocking thirst from that stew we had yesterday. But, you see, sir, the water from that pump is a bit yellow. I expect it's the sort of water that's got iron in it. That kind of water's very healthy and it does you good."

"If you're as thirsty as all that, Schweik," said Lieutenant Dub with a diabolical smile, "then have a drink, but take a good swig at it. Drink up the whole lot at one go."

Lieutenant Dub rather fancied that he was successfully piling up the agony. At last, he thought, he had driven Schweik into a corner. His forecast of events was that Schweik would drink a few gulps and would then give in, whereupon he, Lieutenant Dub, would triumph over him and say, "Give me that bottle and let me have a drink of it. I'm thirsty as well." And he pictured gleefully to himself how discomfited Schweik would be at that terrible moment, and then the various species of trouble into which he would be landed as a result.

Schweik uncorked the bottle, raised it to his lips, and gulp by gulp the contents vanished down his throat. Lieutenant Dub was dumbfounded. Before his very eyes Schweik drank up the whole bottle without turning a hair. He then threw the empty bottle across the road into a pond, spat, and said, as if he had just put away a bottle of lemonade, "Beg to report, sir, that water really does sort of taste of iron. I used to know a chap who kept a pub near Prague and he used to make a drink that tasted of iron for the summer trippers, by throwing old horseshoes into the well."

"I'll give you old horseshoes, you ruffian! You come and show me the well where you got that water from."

"It's just a few steps from here, sir, right behind that wooden hut."

"You go on in front, you skunk, so that I can see whether you can march properly in step."

"It's really most curious," thought Lieutenant Dub to himself, "but upon my word this wretched fellow seems quite all right."

Schweik went on in front, commending himself to the will of God. But he had a sort of inkling that there would be a well behind the hut, and so he was not surprised to find that there was one. In fact, there was a pump as well, and when they reached it, Schweik moved the pump handle up and down, whereupon out flowed some yellowish water, so that Schweik was able to announce with all due solemnity, "Here's the water that tastes of iron, sir."

At this juncture, the man with the side curls, now very much scared, came up, and Schweik told him in German to bring a glass, as the lieutenant wanted to have a drink.

Lieutenant Dub was so flabbergasted that he drank up the whole glass of water, which left in his mouth a flavor of horse urine and liquid manure, and, quite dazed by what had happened to him, he gave the Jew with the side curls a five-crown note and turning to Schweik, said, "What are you hanging about here for? Get back to your right place."

Five minutes later Schweik made his appearance in the staff carriage, and mysteriously beckoned to Lieutenant Lukash to come outside. He then said to him, "Beg to report, sir, that in five minutes, or ten at the most, I shall be as tight as a lord, but I'm going to lay down in my truck, so perhaps you wouldn't mind, sir, not calling me for another three hours and not giving me any orders until I've slept it off. There's nothing wrong with me, only I got nabbed by Lieutenant Dub, and I told him it was water, so I had to drink up the whole bottle of brandy right under his nose so as to prove to him that it was water. There's nothing wrong, sir; I never gave the game away, like you told me, and I was on my guard, but now I beg to report, sir, that I can feel my legs beginning to wobble. Of course, sir, I can stand liquor all right, because when I was with Mr. Katz—"

"Get out of it, you hog!" shouted Lieutenant Lukash, but he was not really angry with Schweik. On the other hand, his dislike of Lieutenant Dub was 100 per cent greater than before.

Schweik crept cautiously into his truck and as he lay down on his greatcoat and valise, he said to Quartermaster Sergeant Vanek and the rest, "Here's a chap who for once in a way has got tight and doesn't want to be woke up."

With these words he rolled over on his side and began to snore.

The vapors which he now began to exhale soon made their

380

presence felt, and Jurajda the cook, sniffing the atmosphere in the truck, remarked, "My God, what a stink of brandy!"

Marek, the volunteer officer, who at last, after all his tribulations, had managed to get a job as keeper of battalion records, was seated at the folding table. He was preparing an advance and reserve stock of heroic deeds for the battalion, and it was plain that this peep into the future was causing him much amusement.

Quartermaster Sergeant Vanek looked on with interest at the volunteer officer who, with a broad grin, was writing busily. Presently, he stood up and looked over the shoulder of the volunteer officer, who began to explain matters to him.

"This is no end of a lark, laying up stocks of history for the battalion. The chief thing is to go about the job in a systematic way. There's got to be system in the whole business."

"A systematic system," remarked Quartermaster Sergeant Vanek, with a more or less contemptuous smile.

"Yes," said the volunteer officer in an offhand tone, "a systematized, systematic system for writing the history of the battalion. It's no use coming out with great victories right at the very start. The whole thing's got to take its course gradually and according to a definite plan. One battalion can't win the war right off. The important thing for a painstaking historian like me to do is first of all to draw up a general scheme of the victories we're going to win. For example, this is where I describe how our battalion, about two months from now, nearly crosses the Russian frontier, which is strongly guarded, let us say, by some regiments of Don Cossacks, while a number of enemy divisions are about to surround us by a flanking movement. At first sight, it looks as if our battalion's done for and that they'll make mincemeat of us. But then Captain Sagner issues this order to the battalion: 'It is not God's will that we should perish here; let us retreat.' So our battalion takes to its heels, but the enemy division, which has now surrounded us, sees that we're really chasing after them, and so they begin to take fright and skedaddle, so that without firing a shot they get captured by our reserves. That's where the history of our battalion really begins. From quite a trifling event, if I may speak prophetically, Sergeant, matters of great moment develop. Our battalion passes from victory to victory. It'll be interesting to see how our battalion takes the enemy by surprise while they're asleep. Each man in the battalion will pick one of the enemy and with all his might will shove his bayonet through his chest. The bayonets, with their well-ground edges, will slide in as if they were cutting butter, and only here and there you'll hear a rib cracking. The bodies of the sleeping enemy will twitch, their eyes, horrified but already sightless, will bulge, they will make gurgling noises and then grow rigid. Blood and foam will appear on the lips of the sleeping enemy and that will end the whole business. Our battalion will score a victory. Or it'll be even better, say, in about three months' time, when our battalion captures the Czar. But we'll talk about that later on, Sergeant. In the meanwhile I must lay in a stock of little incidents giving proof of unexampled bravery. Thus, I'll write about the dogged self-sacrifice of our men when they are studded with bits of hand grenade. And then, through the explosion of an enemy mine, one of our sergeants, say, of the Twelfth or Thirteenth Company, will have his head blown off. And, by the way," continued Marek, with a gesture indicating sudden remembrance, "I nearly forgot to tell you, Sergeant, to get me a list of all the N.C.O.'s. Tell me the name of one of the sergeant majors in the Twelfth Company. Houska? Very well, then, Houska's going to have his head blown off by this mine. His head will fly off, but his body will go on walking for another few yards, he'll take aim and shoot down an enemy airplane. Of course, the royal family will have to arrange a special evening party in their own home to celebrate exploits of that kind. Quite a select affair, to be held in the apartment next to the Emperor's bedroom. The place will be lit up with candles only, because, as I expect you know, electric light is unpopular in court circles on account of our aged monarch's prejudice against short circuits. The festivities in honor of our battalion will begin at six P.M. At that hour the grandchildren of His Royal Highness will be in bed, and after the Emperor has proposed a toast to our draft, a few words will be said by the Archduchess Marie Valerie, who will refer to you, Sergeant, in terms of approval. I tell you, Austria's got lots and lots of battalions, but ours is the only one that'll distinguish itself to that extent. Of course, from the notes I have made, it is evident that our battalion will suffer severe and irretrievable losses, because a battalion without any dead can hardly be called a battalion. A fresh article will have to be written about our losses. Victories are all very well in their way, and I've got about forty-two of 'em on tap now. But the history of the battalion has got to be something more than a string of dry facts about victories. So, as I say, there's got to be plenty of losses as well. For instance, Sergeant, you're going west by the side of a brook, and Baloun here, who's squinting at us with such a queer look in his eyes, is not going to be done in by a bullet or by shrapnel or by a bomb. No, he's going to be strangled by a lasso chucked out of an enemy airplane just at the moment when he's guzzling Lieutenant Lukash's lunch. But don't get the wind up, Baloun. You'll be mentioned all right in the history of the battalion and there'll be an account of how you met death like a hero, grub in mouth, on the way from the officers' mess to the trenches. You'll be mentioned along with all the men of our battalion who fell for the glory of our empire, like Quartermaster Sergeant Vanek here."

"What sort of a death have you got me down for, Marek?"

"Wait a bit, Sergeant. Don't be in such a hurry. You've got to go slow with this sort of thing."

The volunteer officer lapsed into thought. Then he said, "You're from Kralupy, aren't you? Very well, then, you write home to Kralupy and tell them that you're going to vanish without a trace, but be careful how you put it. Or perhaps you'd rather be gravely wounded behind the barbed wire in no man's land. We can leave you lying there quite nicely with a broken leg all day long. In the night the enemy will get at our position with a searchlight and then they'll spot you. So they'll strafe you with plenty of bombs and shrapnel. You'll have rendered invaluable services to the army because the enemy will use up as much ammunition on you as on the whole battalion and your ingredient parts and accessories will sail about in the air and chant a great anthem of victory. And in the same way everyone in the battalion will have his turn at distinguishing himself, until, say somewhere in September, there'll be nothing left of us except these glorious pages of history which will thrill the hearts of all Austrians. And this is how I've wound up the whole thing, Sergeant: All honor to the memory of the fallen! Their love for our monarchy is the holiest love, for it culminates in death. Let their names, e.g., Vanek, be uttered with awe. And they who were most closely affected by the loss of their breadwinners—let them proudly dry their tears, for they who fell were the heroes of our battalion."

Chodounsky the telephonist and Jurajda the cook were listening with bated breath to the volunteer officer's account of the projected history of the battalion.

383

"Gather around, gentlemen," said the volunteer officer, turning over his collection of jottings. "I've got you all down. Here we are, page fifteen, Telephonist Chodounsky fell on September third, side by side with Jurajda the battalion cook. Just listen here to what I've written about you: 'Unexampled heroism. The former, at the risk of his life, protected the telephone wires in his bombproof shelter, remaining there at the telephone for three days without being relieved. The latter, seeing the menace from the enemy on the flank, hurled himself on the enemy with a cauldron of boiling soap, spreading terror and scalds among the enemy. Both died a glorious death. The former blown to pieces by a mine, the latter suffocated by poison gas. Both perished with the cry (in German): "Long live our battalion commander!" ' The supreme command can only show its gratitude by issuing orders acquainting the rest of the army with the gallantry of our battalion and urging them to take an example from us. Here's an extract from an army order which will be read to all detachments. I may say that it's very much like the order issued by Archduke Karl in 1805, on the day before he and his army got a devil of a walloping at Padua: 'I hope that the whole army will take the above-mentioned battalion as an example and in particular will gird itself with that spirit of self-reliance, self-confidence, and unwavering dauntlessness in the face of danger, that unexampled heroism, that attachment to and confidence in their superior officers, in short, with all those virtues by which this battalion distinguished itself and led it on to memorable exploits, to the welfare and victory of our Emperor.' "

From the spot where Schweik was reposing, he could be heard talking in his sleep. "You're quite right, Mrs. Müller. There's lots of people who looks like each other. At Kralupy there used to be a man named Jarosh who made water pumps and he was the very image of a watchmaker at Pardubice named Lejhanzl, and he again was as like another fellow named Piskor at Jicin, and the whole lot of 'em couldn't be told apart from the corpse of a stranger who was found in a pond, all rotting away, just near the railway line at Neuhaus." Snores were now heard, and then: "So they all had to pay a whopping big fine, and tomorrow, Mrs. Müller, I want you to cook me some noodles."

At this point Schweik rolled over onto the other side and went on snoring, while Jurajda and the volunteer officer started an argument on the future life.

While they were arguing about reincarnation and lizards and infusions, Lieutenant Dub popped his head in at the door, which was ajar.

"Is Schweik here?" he asked.

"Beg to report, sir, he's asleep," replied the volunteer officer.

"When I ask for him, it's your business to pull yourself together and fetch him."

"I can't do that, sir; he's asleep."

"Well, wake him up, then. I'm surprised that you didn't think of that at once. You ought to show more willingness to help your superior officers. You don't know me yet. But when you do get to know me——"

The volunteer officer began to wake Schweik up.

"Get up, Schweik. There's a fire."

"The time there was a fire at Odkolek's mills," mumbled Schweik, turning over onto the other side again, "the firemen came along from as far away as Vysocany."

"You see, sir," said the volunteer officer courteously to Lieutenant Dub, "that I'm waking him up, but it's no use."

Lieutenant Dub lost his temper.

"What's your name? Marek? Oh, yes; you're the volunteer officer who spends all his time under close arrest, aren't you?"

"Yes, sir. I've done all my training as a volunteer officer more or less in clink, but since being discharged by the divisional court-martial, where my innocence was established beyond the slightest doubt, I've reverted to my former rank and been appointed keeper of the battalion records."

"You won't be that long," yelled Lieutenant Dub, very red in the face. "I'll see to that!"

"I wish to be reported to the orderly room, sir," said the volunteer officer solemnly.

"Don't trifle with me," said Lieutenant Dub. "I'll give you orderly room. We'll meet again before long, and then you'll be damned sorry for yourself, because you don't know me yet; but you will."

Lieutenant Dub went out wrathfully, and in his annoyance he quite forgot that only a few moments previously he had fully intended to call Schweik to say to him, "Breathe on me," as a final method of establishing Schweik's unlawful alcoholism. He did not remember this until half an hour afterward, and it was then too late, because in the meanwhile the rank and file had been served out with an issue of black coffee with rum. When he got back to the truck, Schweik was already up and doing, and on being summoned by Lieutenant Dub, he skipped out of the truck like a lamb.

"Breathe on me!" Lieutenant Dub bawled at him.

Schweik breathed forth upon him the complete contents of his lungs, and it was like a hot wind sweeping the fragrance of a distillery into a field.

"What's this I smell, you brute?"

"Beg to report, sir, you can smell rum."

"Oh, I can, can I?" exclaimed Lieutenant Dub victoriously. "I've got you at last."

"Yes, sir," said Schweik without any sign of uneasiness. "We've just had an issue of rum for our coffee and I drank the rum first. But of course, sir, if there's some new regulation that we got to drink coffee first and rum afterward, I'm very sorry, and I'll see it don't happen again."

"And why were you snoring when I was here half an hour ago? They couldn't wake you up."

"Beg to report, sir, I couldn't sleep a wink all night for thinking of the times when I was in the maneuvers at Vesprem. That was when there was a first and second army corps crossing Styria and western Hungary and they surrounded our fourth army corps which was camping in Vienna and thereabouts where we'd got fortifications all around us, but they managed to outflank us and got to the bridge that the pioneers had built from the right bank of the Danube. We was supposed to start an offensive and be backed up by some troops from the north, and then, later on, by some more from the south, from Vosek. In the orders we read that a third army corps was coming to help us so as we shouldn't be cut to pieces between Lake Balaton and Pressburg when we started our big push against the second army corps. But it wasn't any use. Just when we was winning, they sounded the retreat, and it was the chaps with the white bands around their caps who won."

Lieutenant Dub, without saying another word, shook his head with perplexity and departed, but he immediately came back again and said to Schweik, "Just remember, all of you, that the time will come when I'll make you squeal for mercy." That was all he could manage, and he then returned to the staff carriage.

He felt the need to hear himself talk, and he therefore said to Captain Sagner in a confidential, free-and-easy tone, "I say, Captain, what's your opinion about—?"

"Excuse me a moment," said Captain Sagner, and got out of the carriage.

A quarter of an hour later they started off toward Nagy-Czaba, past the burnt-out villages of Brestov and Great-Radvány. They could now see that they were getting into the thick of it. The slopes of the Carpathians were scored with trenches, which stretched from valley to valley, and on both sides there were large shell holes. Across the streams flowing into the Labore, the upper course of which was skirted by the railway, they could see the new bridges which had been built and the charred beams of the old ones. The whole valley had been gouged and scooped out and the trampled state of the ground made it look as if hosts of gigantic moles had been toiling there. At the edges of the shell holes there were tattered shreds of Austrian uniforms which had been uncovered by downpours of rain. Behind Nagy-Czaba, on a charred old fir tree, in the tangle of the branches, hung the boot of an Austrian infantryman with a piece of shinbone left in it. The forests without foliage or pine needles, the trees without tops, and the isolated farms riddled with shot bore witness to the havoc which had been wrought by the artillery fire.

The train moved slowly forward along embankments which had been newly built, so that the whole battalion was able to feast its eyes on the joys of war, and by scanning the military cemeteries with their white crosses which formed gleaming patches on the devastated hillsides, they had an opportunity of preparing their minds gradually but surely for the field of glory which terminated with an Austrian military cap, caked with mire and dangling on a white cross.

Mezö-Laborcz was the stopping place behind a shattered, burnt-out railway station from the sooty walls of which twisted girders projected. A new long timber hut, which had been hastily constructed in place of the burnt station, was covered with placards bearing the inscription "Subscribe to the Austrian war loan" in various languages. Another long hut contained a Red Cross center from which emerged two nurses with a fat doctor, who, for their amusement, imitated various animal noises and made unsuccessful attempts to grunt.

At the bottom of the railway embankment lay a broken field kitchen. Schweik pointed it out to Baloun and said, "Look at that, Baloun, and see what's in store for us before very long. They were just going to issue the rations when a shell came across and upset the old apple cart."

387

"This is a shocking business," lamented Baloun. "I never thought anything of that sort was in store for me."

The men were informed that a meal would be served beyond Palota in the Lubka Pass, and the battalion quartermaster sergeant major, accompanied by the company cooks and Lieutenant Cajthaml, with four men as a patrol, proceeded into the parish of Meczi. They returned after less than half an hour with three pigs tied up by their hind legs, the squalling family of a Ruthenian peasant from whom the pigs had been requisitioned, and the fat military doctor from the Red Cross hut. He was vociferously explaining something to Lieutenant Cajthaml, who only shrugged his shoulders.

The controversy came to a head in front of the staff carriage when the military doctor began to tell Captain Sagner in downright terms that the pigs were reserved for the Red Cross hospital, while the peasant flatly contradicted this and demanded that the pigs should be restored to him, as they were his only property and he certainly could not let them go at the price which had been paid him. He thereupon thrust the money which he had received for the pigs into the hand of Captain Sagner, whom the peasant's wife was holding by the other hand; she was kissing it with the servility which has always been a prominent feature of that region.

Captain Sagner was quite startled, and it was a long time before he managed to shake off the old peasant woman. Not that it mattered, for she was replaced by her younger offspring, who again began to slobber over his hands.

Lieutenant Cajthaml, however, affirmed in very businesslike tones, "This fellow's got another twelve pigs, and he's been properly paid, according to the latest divisional instructions, Number one-two-four-two-zero, economic section. According to paragraph sixteen of the instructions, 'the price paid for pigs in localities unaffected by the war must not exceed one crown three hellers per pound of livestock, while in localities affected by the war fifteen hellers per pound of livestock may be added, making a total of one crown eighteen hellers per pound.' Note further the following: 'If it is ascertained in localities affected by the war that the supply of hogs which can be used as a source of food supply for the troops passing through the locality in question has remained intact, an extra payment of seven hellers per pound of livestock is to be made, as in the case of localities unaffected by the war. If the matter is not entirely clear, a commission is to be set up on the spot, comprising the owner of the livestock, the officer commanding the detachment concerned, and the officer or quartermaster sergeant in charge of the commissariat.' "

Lieutenant Cajthaml read all this from a copy of the divisional orders which he always carried about with him, and he practically knew by heart that in the zone of hostilities the regulation price per pound of carrots was increased to 15½ hellers and the price of one pound of cauliflowers for the officers' mess in the same zone was increased to 95 hellers. The gentlemen in Vienna who had drawn up these schedules seemed to imagine that the zone of hostilities was a land flowing with carrots and cauliflowers. But Lieutenant Cajthaml read his piece to the excited peasant in German and then asked him whether he understood it. When the peasant shook his head, he bellowed at him, "Do you want a commission, then?"

The peasant understood only the word "commission," wherefore he nodded, and while his hogs were dragged off to the field kitchen for execution, he was surrounded by soldiers with fixed bayonets, who had been detailed for the requisitioning, and the commission proceeded to his farm to ascertain whether he was to get one crown eighteen hellers per pound or only one crown three hellers. But scarcely had they set foot on the road leading to the village than the threefold mortal squealing of hogs could be heard from the field kitchen. The peasant realized that all was up, and shouted desperately in the Ruthenian dialect, "Give me two guldens for each of them."

Four soldiers edged close to him and the whole family dropped on their knees in the dust in front of Captain Sagner and Lieutenant Cajthaml. The mother and the two daughters clutched at their knees, calling them benefactors, until at last the peasant yelled at them to stand up. He added that the soldiers could eat the pigs if they wanted, and he hoped they'd die of it.

Accordingly, the idea of a commission was dropped, and as the peasant began to shake his fist angrily, each soldier hit him with the butt-end of his rifle, whereupon all the members of the family crossed themselves and took to their heels.

Twenty minutes later the battalion quartermaster sergeant major, assisted by Matushitch, the battalion orderly, was smacking his lips over a dish of pig's fry, and while he was gorging himself, he remarked gibingly to the military clerks, "I bet you wouldn't mind a feed like that. Oh, my lads, that's only for the N.C.O.'s. The livers and lights for the cooks, brains and breast for the quartermaster sergeant major, and double rations for the clerks from what the rank and file ought to get."

Captain Sagner had already issued instructions as regards the officers' mess.

"Roast pork with savory sauce. Pick out the best meat and see it isn't too fat."

And so it came about that when the rank and file received their rations in the Lubka Pass, each man discovered two tiny morsels of meat in his soup, and those who had been born under an unluckier star discovered only a piece of skin.

On the other hand, the clerks' mouths shone greasily and the stretcher-bearers puffed with fullness, while all around this divine plenty could be seen the unremoved traces of recent fighting. The whole place was littered with cartridge cases, empty tins, shreds of Russian, Austrian, and German uniforms, parts of broken vehicles, long, bloodstained strips of gauze and cotton wool which had been used for bandages.

A shell, which had not burst, had hit an old pine tree near the former railway station, of which only a heap of ruins remained. Fragments of shells were scattered everywhere, and it was evident that corpses of soldiers had been buried in the immediate vicinity, because there was a terrible stench of putrefaction. And on all sides lay lumps of human excrement emanating from all the nations of Austria, Germany, and Russia.

A half-smashed cistern, the wooden hut of a railway watchman, and, in fact, everything which had any walls, was riddled like a sieve with rifle bullets.

This spectacle of military delights was rendered even more complete by clouds of smoke which were rising from behind a hill nearby, as if a whole village were burning there. This was where they were burning the cholera and dysentery huts, to the great joy of those gentlemen who were concerned with the establishment of a hospital under the patronage of Archduchess Marie and who had filled their pockets by presenting accounts for nonexistent cholera and dysentery huts. Now one row of huts was being removed for all the rest, and amid the stench of burning paillasses the whole swindle of the archduchess's patronage was rising heavenward.

Behind the railway station on a rock the Germans had already hastened to set up a monument to the fallen Brandenburgers, with the inscription "To the heroes of Lubka Pass" and a huge German eagle, carved in bronze. The base of the monument bore an inscription to the effect that the eagle had been constructed from Russian guns captured during the liberation of the Carpathians by German regiments.

In these queer surroundings the battalion was resting after its meal, while Captain Sagner, with the battalion adjutant, was still unable to make head or tail of the cipher telegram from brigade headquarters on the subject of the further movements of the battalion. The messages were so muddled that it seemed as though they ought not to have entered the Lubka Pass, but should have proceeded in an entirely different direction from Neustadt, because the telegrams mentioned something about "Cap-Ungvar; Kis-Béreznaì Uzok."

Ten minutes later it turned out that the staff officer at brigade headquarters was a complete nincompoop, because a cipher telegram arrived inquiring whether the Eighth Draft of the 75th Regiment were speaking (military cipher G. 3). The nincompoop at brigade headquarters was astonished by the reply that it was the Seventh Draft of the 91st Regiment, and asked who had given orders to proceed toward Munkacevo, along the military railway line via Stryj, when the proper route was through the Lubka Pass via Sanok into Galicia. The nincompoop was staggered to learn that they were telegraphing from the Lubka Pass, and sent a cipher message: "Route unchanged, via Lubka Pass to Sanok, where further instructions."

When Captain Sagner returned to the staff carriage, a debate ensued on the muddle-headedness of the Austrian authorities, and hints were dropped that if it were not for the Germans, the eastern army group would be entirely at sixes and sevens. Lieutenant Dub thereupon proceeded to defend the Austrian muddle-headedness and came out with some twaddle to the effect that the region in which they had arrived was considerably devastated by the recent hostilities and it had therefore not yet been possible to restore the line to proper working order. All the officers looked at him pityingly, as much as to say, "It's not his fault that he's dotty." Finding that his views met with no contradiction, Lieutenant Dub went on jabbering about the magnificent impression which the battered landscape made upon him, for it bore testimony, he said, to the formidable character of our army's iron grip. Again nobody contradicted him, and he added, "Oh, yes, there can be no doubt that the Russians retreated here in a thorough panic."

Captain Sagner made up his mind that at the first opportunity, when they were having a hot time in the trenches, he would send Lieutenant Dub out on patrol duty into no man's land to reconnoiter the enemy positions.

It seemed as if Lieutenant Dub would never stop talking. He went on explaining to all the officers what he had read in the papers about these Carpathian battles and the struggle for the Carpathian passes during the Austro-German offensive on the San. He talked as if he had not only taken part in these operations, but had directed them himself.

At last, Lieutenant Lukash could stand it no longer, and remarked to Lieutenant Dub, "I suppose you discussed all this with your district chief of police before the war?"

Lieutenant Dub glared at Lieutenant Lukash and went out.

The train was standing on an embankment, and at the bottom of the slope various objects were scattered about, evidently thrown away by the Russian soldiers who had retreated through this cutting. There were rusty tea cans, cartridge pouches, coils of barbed wire, and more bloodstained strips of gauze and cotton wool. Above this cutting stood a group of soldiers, and Lieutenant Dub was not slow to perceive Schweik was among them, explaining something to the rest.

Accordingly he went there.

"What's the matter here?" inquired Lieutenant Dub sternly, coming to a standstill right in front of Schweik.

"Beg to report, sir," replied Schweik on behalf of all, "we're having a look."

"Having a look at what?" shouted Lieutenant Dub.

"Beg to report, sir, we're having a look down below into the cutting."

"And who gave you permission to do that?"

"Beg to report, sir, we're carrying out the orders of Colonel Schlager, who was our C.O. at Bruck. When he said goodbye to us, when we were leaving for the battlefield, as he said in his farewell speech, he said we was to have a good look at the places where there'd been any fighting so as we could see how the fighting was done and find out anything that might be useful for us to know. And now we can see in that ditch all the things a soldier has to chuck away when he's doing a bunk. Beg to report, sir, it shows us what a mug's game it is for a soldier to cart all sorts of useless junk about with him. It only loads him up without doing him any good. All it does is to make him tired, and when he's been dragging all that heavy stuff about with him, it stands to reason he can't fight properly."

A ray of hope darted through Lieutenant Dub's mind that at last he'd manage to get Schweik up before a court-martial for antimilitaristic and treasonable propaganda, and so he quickly asked, "So you think a soldier ought to throw away the cartridges that are lying about in this ditch, or the bayonets that we can see there?"

"Oh, no, sir, beg to report, sir, not at all," replied Schweik with a sweet smile. "But just have a look down there at that tin chamber pot."

And, right enough, at the bottom of the cutting lay defiantly a chamber pot with the enamel all chipped, eaten away with rust, among shards and other objects which, being no longer fit for domestic purposes, had been discarded by the station master as material for arguments in future centuries by archaeologists who, having unearthed this settlement, would go quite crazy about it, and school children would be taught about the age of enameled chamber pots.

Lieutenant Dub gazed at the object in question and he was unable to gainsay Schweik's designation of it. He therefore said nothing, and Schweik launched out into a long anecdote in which a similar object played a prominent part.

If Lieutenant Dub had followed his personal inclinations, he would have pushed Schweik over the edge, but he overcame this temptation, and interrupting Schweik's narrative, he shouted at the group of soldiers, "Don't stand there gaping at me like that. I tell you, you don't know me yet. But wait till you do get to know me!"

And when Schweik was moving away with the others, he bellowed, "You stay here, Schweik!"

So there they stood, looking at each other, and Lieutenant Dub tried to think of something really terrifying that he could say.

But before he had a chance to speak, Schweik remarked: "Beg to report, sir, I hope this weather'll last. It's not too hot in the daytime and the nights are quite pleasant. That's the best sort of weather for soldiering."

Lieutenant Dub took out his revolver and asked, "Do you know what that is?"

"Beg to report, sir, yes, sir. Lieutenant Lukash has got one just like that."

"Then just you remember, my fine fellow," said Lieutenant

Dub in solemn and dignified tones, "that something extremely unpleasant will happen to you if you keep carrying on this propaganda of yours."

And he departed, repeating to himself, "Yes, that's the best way to put it to him. Propaganda, that's the word I wanted; propaganda."

Before Schweik got back into his truck, he walked up and down a little longer, muttering to himself. "Well, I'm blessed if I know what sort of a label ought to be shoved on him."

But before he had finished his stroll, Schweik had devised a suitable designation for Lieutenant Dub. "Bloody old belly-acher."

After which discovery he returned to his truck.

Half an hour later they continued their journey toward Sanok. When they got beyond Szczawna, they again began to see small military cemeteries in the valleys. Below Szczawna there was a stone crucifix with a headless Christ, the head having been shot away during the bombardment of the railway line. The train now began to move at express speed as it pounded along down the valley toward Sanok. The horizon became wider and the number of shattered villages on both sides of the landscape increased accordingly. At Kulashna a Red Cross train, smashed to pieces, was lying in a stream at the bottom of the railway embankment from which it had tumbled. The funnel of the engine had got rammed into the embankment and peeped forth from it like the muzzle of a cannon. This sight attracted much attention in the truck where Schweik was. Jurajda the cook was particularly indignant.

"They're not supposed to shoot at Red Cross trains, are they?"

"They're not supposed to, but they can," said Schweik. "Whoever fired that shot scored a bull's-eye; and then they've always got the excuse that it was at night and they couldn't see the red cross. There's lots of things in the world that you're not supposed to do, but they can be managed all the same. When we were on maneuvers down at Pisek there came an order that soldiers wasn't to be trussed up while on the march. But our captain, he managed to get around it all right, because there's no sense in an order like that, and it stands to reason that if a soldier's trussed up, he can't march. Well, our captain, the way he managed it was, when a soldier was trussed up, he just had him shoved in an army service lorry, and there you are. So you see there's lots of things you're not supposed to do, but you can do them all the same, as long as you set about it with a will, so to speak."

"My friends," said the volunteer officer, who had been busily taking notes, "every cloud has a silver lining. This Red Cross train which has been blown up, half burned, and thrown over the embankment will enrich the glorious annals of our battalion by yet another heroic exploit of the future. I can imagine, say somewhere about September sixteenth, which is the date I've got noted down, that a few simple, untutored soldiers, under the leadership of a corporal, from each company of our battalion, will volunteer to put out of action an enemy armored train which is firing upon us and preventing us from crossing the river. These gallant fellows will fulfill their purpose disguised as peasants—

"What's this I see?" exclaimed the volunteer officer, suddenly breaking off his narrative and staring at his notes. "How on earth did our Quartermaster Sergeant Vanek manage to get into this little affair? Just listen, Sergeant," he continued, turning to Quartermaster Sergeant Vanek, "to the nice things I say about you in the history of the battalion. I rather fancy I mentioned you before, but this is altogether on a better and bigger scale."

And, raising his voice, the volunteer officer read:

"Heroic death of Quartermaster Sergeant Vanek. Among those who volunteered for the daring exploit of putting the enemy armored train out of action was Quartermaster Sergeant Vanek, who, like the rest, was disguised in peasant attire. He was stunned by the explosion which ensued, and when he came to, he saw himself surrounded by the enemy, who immediately conveyed him to their divisional headquarters where, with death staring him in the face, he refused to give any information about the strength of our army. As he was in disguise, he was condemned to death as a spy. It had been originally intended to hang him, but in view of his rank, this was commuted to execution by shooting. The sentence was at once carried out by the wall of a cemetery, and the gallant Quartermaster Sergeant Vanek insisted that he should not be blindfolded. When asked whether he had any special wish, he replied, 'Send my last greeting to my battalion and tell them that I die fully persuaded that they will pass on from victory to victory. Also let Captain Sagner know that according to the latest brigade orders the daily ration of tinned meat is increased to two and one-half pieces of meat per man.' Thus died Quartermaster Sergeant Vanek, who by the last words he uttered caused a panic among the enemy, who had supposed that, by preventing us from crossing the river, they would cut us off from our supply centers, reduce us rapidly to starvation, and thus cause demoralization in our ranks. The composure with which he looked death in the face is attested by the circumstance that before his execution he played nap with the enemy staff officers. 'Give my winnings to the Russian Red Cross,' he said, with the barrels of the rifles right in front of him. This nobility of character moved to tears the military representatives who witnessed his execution.

"I hope you don't mind, Sergeant," continued the volunteer officer, "the liberty I've taken with your winnings. I was wondering whether they oughtn't to be handed over to the Austrian Red Cross, but finally I decided that from a humanitarian point of view it didn't really matter, as long as they were given for a charitable purpose."

"Poor old Vanek," remarked Schweik, "he might have left his cash to the Prague municipal soup kitchen, but perhaps it's just as well he didn't, because the mayor might have spent it on liver sausage for himself."

"Yes, they all do their bit of scrounging," said Chodounsky, the telephone operator.

"And there's more of it goes on in the Red Cross than anywhere else," affirmed with bitter emphasis Jurajda the cook. "I knew a chap at Bruck who used to do the cooking for the messes there, and he said that the matron and the head nurses used to send home bags and bags of sherry and chocolate. That's the destiny of man. All of us pass through countless changes in the course of an endless life, and sooner or later, at definite periods of our activity, we all have to do our turn at scrounging. I've been through that particular period myself."

Jarajda, cook and occultist, took a bottle of brandy from his haversack.

"Here we have," he said, opening the bottle, "irrefutable proof of my assertion. I took it from the officers' mess before we left. It's one of the best makes of brandy and was supposed to be used for the icing on fancy cakes. But it was predestined to be scrounged by me, just as I was predestined to scrounge it."

"And it'd be a nobby sort of idea," observed Schweik, "if

we was predestined to join you in this particular bit of scrounging. Anyway, I sort of fancy that's how it'll turn out."

And it did indeed turn out that they were so predestined. The bottle was passed around, in spite of the protests of Quartermaster Sergeant Vanek, who declared that brandy should be drunk from a mess tin and properly shared out, because there was one bottle among five of them, and with an odd number like that it might easily happen that somebody would get a gulp more than the others.

Whereupon Schweik remarked, "That's quite right, and if the sergeant wants us to have an even number, perhaps he wouldn't mind falling out, and then we shan't have any rumpus about it."

Quartermaster Sergeant Vanek then withdrew his suggestion and made a new and generous proposal by which Jurajda, the donor, was to be allowed to have two swigs at the bottle, but this aroused a storm of opposition, because Vanek had already had one drink, having sampled the brandy when the bottle was first opened.

Finally they adopted the suggestion of the volunteer officer that they should drink in alphabetical order, after which they played cards, and when the game was over, Chodounsky had lost six months' pay in advance. He was very upset about it and the volunteer officer, to whom he owed the money, demanded a series of I.O.U.'s from him, so that he could receive Chodounsky's pay to square the debt.

"Don't you worry, Chodounsky," Schweik consoled him. "If you have any luck, you'll go west in the first dust-up we have, and then your I.O.U.'s will be worth damn-all to Marek. Sign for him and chance it."

The supposition that he might go west was extremely distasteful to Chodounsky, and he objected with emphasis.

"There's no likelihood of me going west, because I'm a telephone operator, and they're always in bombproof shelters."

The volunteer officer, however, expressed the view that telephone operators, on the contrary, are exposed to great danger and it was against them that the enemy artillery was chiefly directed. No telephone operator, he said, was safe in his bombproof shelter. Even if he was at a depth of thirty feet underground, the enemy artillery would spot him just the same. The telephone operators were being wiped out wholesale, and the best proof of it was that when they had left Bruck, the twenty-eighth course for telephone operators was just being started.

Chodounsky looked very down in the mouth, and seeing his woebegone expression, Schweik said to him affably, "You've been properly taken in."

And the volunteer officer said, "Let's see what I've got you down for in my notes on the history of the battalion. Ah, here we are: 'Chodounsky, telephone operator, buried by a mine, telephoned from his living tomb to the staff, "I die congratulating my battalion on its victory." ' "

"You ought to be satisfied with that," said Schweik. "What more do you want? Do you remember that telephone operator on the *Titanic* who kept telephoning into the kitchen while the boat was sinking and asking them when lunch would be ready?"

"Well, it's all the same to me," said the volunteer officer. "If you like, I'll make Chodounsky say, as he breathes his last, 'Give my best wishes to the Iron Brigade.' "

4.

Quick March

SANOK turned out to be the brigade headquarters of the "Iron Brigade," to which the battalion of the 91st Regiment belonged by virtue of its origins. Although the railway communication was unbroken from Sanok to Lemberg and northward as far as the frontier, it was a mystery why the staff of the eastern sector had arranged for the Iron Brigade with its staff to concentrate the draft battalions for a hundred miles behind the line, when at this particular period the front extended from Brody on the Bug and along the river northward toward Sokol.

This very interesting strategic problem was solved in a remarkably simple manner when Captain Sagner went to the brigade headquarters at Sanok to report the arrival of the draft there.

The orderly officer was the brigade adjutant, a Captain Tayerle.

"I can't make out," said Captain Tayerle, "why you haven't

been given definite instructions. It's all settled which way you've got to go, and, of course, you ought to have notified us beforehand about it. According to the arrangements made by the general staff, you've arrived two days too soon."

Captain Sagner's face flushed, but it never occurred to him to say anything about all the cipher telegrams which he had been receiving throughout the journey.

"I can't make it out," repeated Captain Tayerle, and mused somewhat. "By the way," he then continued, "are you a regular officer? You are? That's quite a different matter. A chap doesn't know where he is nowadays. We've had so many of these dud lieutenants passing through here. When we were withdrawing from Limanowa and Krasnik, all these temporary gentlemen got the wind up as soon as they set eyes on a Cossack patrol. We staff chaps can't stand all those hangers-on. They put on too much side just because they've passed some damn fool examination. They're a lot of bloody outsiders, that's what they are."

Captain Tayerle spat with contempt, and then confidentially patted Captain Sagner on the shoulder.

"You're staying here for about a couple of days. I'll show you around the town. We've got a few tasty bits of skirt here, I can tell you. There's a general's daughter, some hot baby she is. We all dress up in women's togs, and you ought to see the stunts she does then. She's a skinny piece, nothing much to look at, but, by Jove, she knows a thing or two. She's a saucy piece of goods. But you'll see for yourself.

"Excuse me," he broke off. "I must go out and spew. That's the third time today."

When he returned, he informed Captain Sagner, in order to show him what a jolly time they were having there, that it was the aftereffects of the previous evening's spree, at which the pioneer section had done their bit.

Captain Sagner soon became acquainted with the commander of this section. A lanky fellow in uniform with three gold stars dashed into the office, and without observing the presence of Captain Sagner, he addressed Captain Tayerle thus: "Hello, you dirty dog, what are you doing here? You made a fine old mess of the countess last night."

He sat down on a chair and, flicking his thin bamboo cane across his calves, he continued, with a broad grin, "The last thing I remember was you spewing into her lap."

"Yes," assented Captain Tayerle, "we had a jolly time last night."

He then introduced Captain Sagner to the officer with the bamboo cane, and they all three adjourned to the café. When they had installed themselves there, Captain Tayerle ordered a bottle of brandy and called for any of the girls who were disengaged to be sent in. It now turned out that the café was really a disorderly house, and as none of the girls were disengaged, Captain Tayerle flew into a temper and started bullying the manageress. He wanted to know who was with Miss Ella. When he was told that it was a lieutenant, he blustered more than ever.

The lieutenant who was with Miss Ella was none other than Lieutenant Dub, who, as soon as the draft had been billeted in the local grammar school, had called together his squad and made a long speech to them, particularly drawing attention to the fact that all along their line of retreat the Russians had left behind them brothels with diseased occupants, for the purpose of striking a treacherous blow at the well-being of the Austrian army. He therefore warned the troops against visiting such establishments. He added that he proposed to visit these places personally to see whether his orders were being carried out. They were now, he said, in the battle zone, and anyone caught infringing these regulations would be tried by court-martial.

So Lieutenant Dub had gone forth to see personally whether his orders were being obeyed, and as a starting point for his tour of inspection he had selected the sofa in Miss Ella's apartment, on the second floor of what was known as the "Municipal Café," and lolling in his pants upon this bug-infested sofa, he was having a thoroughly good time. While Miss Ella was telling him the tragic story of her life, the usual yarn about how her father had been a factory owner and her mother a teacher at a young ladies' college at Budapest, and how she had been driven to her present life by an unhappy love affair, Lieutenant Dub was helping himself freely to a bottle of gin which, together with two glasses, stood on a small table within reach.

By the time the bottle was half empty, Lieutenant Dub was quite fuddled, and thought that Miss Ella was Kunert, his orderly. He kept on addressing her in bullying tones: "Now then, Kunert, you brute, wait till you get to know me from the bad side—"

Meanwhile, Captain Sagner had returned to his battalion.

New divisional orders had been received, and it now became necessary to decide exactly where the 91st Regiment was to go because according to the new arrangements its original route was to be followed by the draft battalion of the 102nd Regiment. It was all very complicated. The Russians were retreating very rapidly in the northeastern corner of Galicia, so that a number of Austrian units were mingling there, and in places units of the German army were also being thrust in like wedges, while the resulting chaos was supplemented by the arrival of new draft battalions and other military formations at the front. The same thing was happening in sectors which were some distance behind the front, as here in Sanok, where a number of German troops, the reserves of the Hanoverian division, had suddenly arrived. Their commander was a colonel of such hideous aspect that the brigadier was quite upset by the sight of him. The colonel of the Hanoverian reserves produced the arrangements of his staff, by which his troops were to be billeted in the local grammar school, where the men of the 91st Regiment had already taken up their quarters. And for his staff he demanded the premises of the local branch of the Cracow Bank, which was occupied by the brigade headquarters staff.

The brigadier got into direct communication with divisional headquarters, to whom he gave an account of the situation. The cantankerous Hanoverian then had a talk with divisional headquarters, and the consequence was that the brigade received the following orders:

"The brigade will evacuate the town at 6 P.M. and will proceed in the direction Turowa Wolska-Liskowiec-Starasól-Sambor, where further orders will be received. The brigade will be accompanied by the draft battalion of the 91st Regiment, as escort, thus: The advance guard will leave at 5:30 P.M. in the direction of Turowa, with a distance of two miles between the southern and northern protecting flank. The rear guard will leave at 6:15 P.M."

So a great hubbub arose in the grammar school. An officers' conference was to be held, but was delayed by the absence of Lieutenant Dub. Schweik was detailed to go and look for him.

"I hope," said Lieutenant Lukash to Schweik, "that you won't have any trouble in finding him. You two don't seem to hit it off together, somehow."

"Beg to report, sir," said Schweik. "I'd like to have my

orders in writing. Then there won't be any mistake, and, as you say, sir, we don't seem to hit it off together."

While Lieutenant Lukash was jotting down on a leaf torn from his notebook a few words to the effect that Lieutenant Dub was to proceed immediately to the grammar school for the conference, Schweik continued, "Yes, sir, you can safely leave it to me, like you always can. I'll find him all right, because the troops have been told that brothels are out of bounds, and he's sure to be in one to make sure that none of the chaps in his company are anxious for a court-martial, which is what he generally threatens them with. He told his company himself that he was going to search every blessed brothel in the town, and if he copped anyone, they'd get to know him from his bad side and they'd be sorry for it. And, as a matter of fact, I know where he is. He's in that café, just opposite, because all his company watched him, to see where he'd go first."

The Municipal Café, the establishment to which Schweik referred, was divided into two parts. Visitors who did not wish to pass through the café itself could go around to the back of the premises, where an elderly lady who was basking in the sun would extend a polyglot invitation in German, Polish, and Magyar to inspect the female attractions of the establishment. When Schweik entered, he came into contact with this worthy person, who brazenly denied that they had any lieutenant among the visitors, whereupon Schweik thrust her aside and proceeded with dignified tread to mount the wooden staircase to the second floor. This caused the polyglot matron to set up a terrific hullabaloo, as a result of which, the proprietor of the establishment, an impoverished Polish aristocrat, appeared on the scene, rushed upstairs after Schweik, and tugged at his tunic, shouting to him in German that only officers were allowed on the second floor and that the place for private soldiers was down below. Schweik pointed out to him that he was paying a visit there in the interests of the whole army, and that he was looking for a lieutenant without whom the army could not proceed to the front. When the proprietor began to show signs of more obstreperous tactics, Schweik pushed him downstairs and went on his way to inspect the premises.

He discovered that all the rooms were empty, until he reached a door at the very end of the passage. In reply to his knock, he heard, first of all, Miss Ella's voice raised in squeaky protest, followed by the gruff voice of Lieutenant Dub, who, perhaps imagining that he was still in his quarters in camp, spluttered, "Come in!"

Schweik went in, went up to the sofa, and handing Lieutenant Dub the leaf torn from the notebook of Lieutenant Lukash, he said, with a sideway glance at the articles of clothing scattered about in a corner, "Beg to report, sir, you've got to get dressed and come at once along with me, like it says in these here orders I'm handing to you, back to the place where we're quartered, because there's going to be an important meeting there."

Lieutenant Dub goggled his eyes at Schweik, whom, through alcoholic mists, he just managed to recognize. He imagined that Schweik had been sent up before him in the orderly room and accordingly he said, "All right, Schweik, I'll settle—settle—settle—up—with—with—you—in a—jiff—jiff—jiffy. I'll sh-sh-show—you—what's—coming—to—you—"

And then, turning to Miss Ella, he shouted, "Kunert, another—little—drink—for—me."

He had his little drink and then, tearing up the paper containing the message, he laughed heartily.

"Is—that—a—note—of—excuse?" he babbled on merrily. "We—don't—accept—them—here. We're—in—the—army—now—and—not—at—school. Schweik—step—two—paces forward—in—what—year—did—Philip—of—Macedon—defeat—the—Romans? What's—that? You—don't—know—you—thickheaded dunce, you?"

"Beg to report, sir," continued Schweik relentlessly, "this is brigade orders, sir, and all the officers have got to get dressed and go to the battalion *Besprechung*. You see, sir, we're starting a big push, and they've just got to decide which company's going to be the advance guard and which the rear guard, and who's to be on the flank, and all that. That's what they've got to decide, sir, and it strikes me, sir, you ought to have something to say about it."

This diplomatic speech somewhat cleared Lieutenant Dub's mind, and he now began to perceive dimly that he was not in barracks. With some show of caution he asked, "Where am I?"

Schweik coughed. "Beg to report, sir, you're in a brothel. It takes all sorts to make a world, sir."

Lieutenant Dub sighed deeply, slipped down from the sofa, and began to hunt for his uniform. In this process he received assistance from Schweik, and when at last he was dressed, they went forth together. Before they emerged into the outer world again, however, Schweik returned, and ignoring Miss Ella, who quite misinterpreted the reason for his reappearance, rapidly finished what was left of the bottle of gin, and then joined Lieutenant Dub once more.

In the street the sultry state of the atmosphere caused Lieutenant Dub to lapse anew into befuddlement. He began to talk to Schweik completely at random, explaining to him that at home he had a pillar box from Heligoland, and that as soon as he had passed his matriculation he had gone to play billiards, and had not raised his cap to his form master. And after each remark he inquired, "See what I mean?"

"Of course I see what you mean, sir," replied Schweik. "The way you talk, sir, is just like a tinker I used to know, Pokorny his name was. If anyone asked him, 'Have you ate any mushrooms this year?' he'd say, 'No, but I hear the new Sultan of Morocco's a fine fellow.'"

Lieutenant Dub came to a standstill and blurted out, "Sultan of Morocco? He's a back number."

Whereupon he wiped the sweat from his forehead, and staring at Schweik with a glazed expression in his eyes, he muttered, "I've never sweated like this, even in winter. See what I mean?"

"Not half I don't, sir. There was an old gentleman who was a regular customer at The Flagon, he used to be on the county council, or something, but they'd pensioned him off, and he said exactly the same thing. He always said he was surprised how much warmer it was in summer than in winter, and he couldn't make out why nobody had looked into it."

At the entrance to the grammar school, Schweik left Lieutenant Dub, who reeled upstairs into the conference room, where he immediately reported to Captain Sagner that he was quite drunk. Throughout the proceedings he sat there with bowed head, but during the debate he stood up every now and then, and shouted, "Your opinions are quite correct, gentlemen, but I'm quite drunk."

When all the arrangements had been made for Lieutenant Lukash's company to form the advance guard, Lieutenant Dub gave a sudden jerk, stood up and said, "I wonder whether you gentlemen remember our old form master? Three cheers for our old form master! Hip, hip, hurray!"

It occurred to Lieutenant Lukash that the best thing to do would be to get Kunert, Lieutenant Dub's orderly, to put him into the physics laboratory, at the door of which a sentry was posted, probably to prevent anyone from stealing the rest of the collection of minerals which were in a glass case and half of which had already been pilfered. Brigade headquarters impressed the need for this upon all detachments which were quartered there. This precaution dated from the time when a battalion of Hungarian militiamen had begun to help themselves to the specimens in the glass case. They took a particular fancy to the collection of crystals and quartz which they slipped into their haversacks. And one of the white crosses in the military cemetery bore the inscription "Laszlo Gargany," this being the name of the Hungarian militiaman who was sleeping his eternal sleep there. During one of the inroads upon the collection of minerals he had drunk up all the methylated spirits from a receptacle containing a number of preserved reptiles.

When all the other officers had gone, Lieutenant Lukash sent for Kunert, who carried Lieutenant Dub out and deposited him on a sofa. Lieutenant Dub suddenly became quite boyish. He caught hold of Kunert's hand, began to examine the palm of it, saying that from the lines of the palm of Kunert's hand he could read the name of Kunert's future wife.

"What's your name? Take a notebook and a pencil out of the breastpocket of my tunic. So your name's Kunert? All right. Come back here in a quarter of an hour, and I'll give you a piece of paper with the name of your future wife on it."

Scarcely had he said this, than he began to snore, but he soon woke up again and started scrawling in his notebook. He tore out what he had written, threw it on the floor, and mysteriously putting his finger to his lips, he said in a fatuous voice, "Not yet, not for another quarter of an hour. You'd better look for the paper blindfold."

Kunert was such a good-natured fellow that he actually came back a quarter of an hour later, and when he undid the piece of paper, he read there, in Lieutenant Dub's scribble, "The name of your future wife will be Mrs. Kunert."

When, a little later, he showed this to Schweik, he told him to take great care of the piece of paper, because such keepsakes from big military men were very valuable. In the old days it wasn't like that. Officers never used to correspond with their orderlies and call them "sir."

When preparations had been completed for the advance to begin in accordance with the official plans, the brigade general, the same one who had been so neatly ousted from his quarters by the Hanoverian colonel, had the whole battalion drawn up in the customary square formation and delivered a speech to them. This man, who was very fond of orating, went on talking about anything that came into his head, and when his stock of ideas was exhausted, he suddenly remembered the field post.

"Soldiers," he thundered forth, "we are now approaching the enemy front, from which we are separated by only a few days' march. Hitherto, soldiers, being constantly on the move, you have had no opportunity of sending your addresses to those who are near and dear to you so that you could have the pleasure of receiving letters from those you left behind you."

He seemed unable to extricate himself from this train of thought, and he kept on repeating such phrases as, "those near and dear to you," "the ones you left behind you," "sweethearts and wives," etc. And anyone who heard his speech might have supposed that all these men in drab uniforms were to proceed with the utmost readiness to the slaughter simply and solely because a field post had been organized at the front, and that if a soldier had both his legs blown off by a shell, he was sure to die happy when he remembered that his field post was Number 72 and that perhaps a letter was awaiting him there from those he had left behind him, possibly together with a parcel containing a piece of salt beef, some bacon, and a few home-made cakes.

After the general's speech, the brigade band played the national anthem, there were three cheers for the Emperor, and then the various detachments of this herd of human cattle, destined for the shambles somewhere beyond the River Bug, set out successively on the march, in accordance with the instructions which had been received.

The Eleventh Company started at 5:30 in the direction of Turowa Wolska. Schweik toddled along right at the back with the ambulance section, while Lieutenant Lukash rode up and down the column, frequently inspecting the ambulance section at the rear in order to ascertain whether there was any improvement in the condition of Lieutenant Dub, who was being conveyed in a small cart, covered with tarpaulin, to fresh exploits in an unknown future. Lieutenant Lukash also relieved the monotony of the march every now and then by exchanging a few words with Schweik, who, stolidly shouldering his haversack and rifle, was telling Quartermaster Sergeant Vanek about how many years before he had been on a fine route march during the maneuvers at Velké Mezirici. After a while he began to trot sturdily along in step with Lieutenant Lukash's horse and started talking about the field post.

"That was a nice speech we heard and no mistake, and it must be a treat for everyone to get a nice letter from home when he's away at the front. When I was doing my service, years and years ago, I once got a letter sent to me in barracks, and I've still got it on me."

From a grimy pocketbook Schweik extracted a grease-stained letter, and still keeping in step with Lieutenant Lukash's horse, which had broken into a gentle trot, he read:

"You rotten blighter, you dirty, low-down crook. Corporal Kriz went to Prague on leave, and he told me you've been dancing with some boss-eyed little slut and that you've given me the push. All right then, we're through with each other. *Bozena*. And let me tell you that corporal is a regular sport, and he won't half lay you out. I asked him to. And let me tell you that when you come back on leave you won't find me in the land of the living.

"Of course," explained Schweik, keeping in step with the gentle trotting of the horse, "when I did come back on leave, I found her in the land of the living all right. Not half I didn't. There she was in a pub with a couple of soldiers, and one of 'em was so much in the land of the living that he was putting his hand under her bodice, as if he wanted, beg to report, sir, to pluck the bloom of her virginity, as they say."

"Well, Schweik, there's no getting away from it, you always manage to hit the nail on the head," said Lieutenant Lukash, and rode forward to the other end of the column. The men were now beginning to straggle, because after their long rest in the train the march in full equipment was making their limbs ache, and they eased themselves as best they could. They kept shifting their rifles from one side to the other and most of them went plodding along with bowed heads. They were all suffering from great thirst because, although the sun had already gone down, it was as sultry as in the middle of the day, and by now their water bottles were all quite empty. This discomfort, which, they realized, was a foretaste of the far greater hardships which were in store for them, made everyone become more and more slack and jaded. Earlier in the day they had been singing, but now this stopped entirely and

408

they began to ask each other how much further it was to Turowa Wolska, where they supposed that they were going to spend the night.

Meanwhile Lieutenant Dub, through being well shaken up in the two-wheeled cart, was slowly coming to. He could now raise himself into a sitting posture and more than five hundred yards ahead of him he saw clouds of dust, from which the shapes of soldiers dimly emerged. Lieutenant Dub, who now began to recover his martial enthusiasm, leaned his head over the side of the cart and yelled into the midst of the dust rising from the highroad.

"Soldiers, the lofty task before you is a difficult one; you are faced by all kinds of privations and hardships of every description. But I have the utmost faith in your endurance and your strong will. No obstacle, soldiers, is too great for you to overcome. Once more I will repeat that I am not leading you to any easy victory. It's going to be a hard job for you, but you'll manage it in the end, and your fame will endure through the ages."

And, at this point, Lieutenant Dub was very, very unwell indeed. He bowed his head over the dust of the highway, but after this interval of abasement, he exclaimed with new fervor, "Soldiers, keep up your spirits! Left, right, left, right, left, right."

After which he sank back onto the haversack of Chodounsky, the telephone operator, and slept soundly till they reached Turowa Wolska, where, at Lieutenant Lukash's orders, they helped him to his feet and lifted him down from the cart. He was still not quite his old self, because when he was moving off toward his squad, he said to Lieutenant Lukash, "You don't know me yet, but wait till you do, that's all!"

"You'd better go and ask Schweik about your queer behavior," replied Lieutenant Lukash.

So before rejoining his squad, Lieutenant Dub went to look for Schweik, whom he found in the company of Baloun and Quartermaster Sergeant Vanek. Being far from sure of himself, he asked them, "Well, are you having a good talk?"

"That we are, sir," replied Schweik. "We're just talking about lemon juice. There's nothing like a good talk for making a soldier forget his hardships."

Lieutenant Dub then asked Schweik to come along with him for a little way, because he wanted to ask him something. When they were out of earshot of the rest, he asked in an extremely faltering voice, "You weren't talking about me, were you?"

"Lord bless you, no, sir. We was just talking about lemon juice, like what I just said, sir."

"Lieutenant Lukash was just telling me that I've been behaving queerly and that you know all about it, Schweik."

Schweik replied in very solemn and emphatic tones, "You never behaved queerly, sir, not a bit of it. You was just paying a visit to a free-and-easy house. But I reckon there was some mistake about that. I expect, sir, you landed yourself in the wrong place because the weather was so hot, and if you ain't used to liquor, why, when it begins to get a bit warmer than usual, even ordinary rum'll get into your head, and you was drinking gin, sir. So I had orders to hand you a notice telling you to attend the officers' meeting that was going to be held before we started moving forward, and I found you upstairs with a young lady. And what with the gin and the hot weather and one thing and another, you didn't know who I was and you was lying undressed on a sofa. But you wasn't behaving queerly, sir, not by any manner of means. And as I was saying just now, sir, that's the sort of thing that might happen to anyone when the weather's hot. Some people can't stand it at all, and others take to it like a duck to water, as the saying is. If you'd have known old Vejvoda, a French-polisher he was, and he used to live down our way. Well, he made up his mind he'd never drink anything that'd make him tight. So off he goes one day to look for teetotal drinks. Just to give himself a proper send-off, like, he has a good glass of spirits before he starts. Well, at the first pub he comes to, he orders a vermouth, and in a cautious sort of way he begins to ask the landlord what it is the teetotalers drink. Because he thought, and he was quite right, too, that even teetotalers couldn't stand plain water. So the landlord explains to him that teetotalers drink soda water, lemonade, milk, cold skilly, teetotal wine, and other beverages without alcohol. Old Vejvoda rather takes a fancy to the teetotal wine and asks whether there was any teetotal brandy as well. Then he had some more vermouth and tells the landlord what a shame it is for a man to be always getting boozed, and the landlord says he can stand anything except a man who gets boozed in somebody else's pub and then comes to him for a bottle of soda water to clear his head, and then kicks up a row in the bargain. 'If you want to get tight,' says the landlord, 'get tight here in my pub, or you're no friend of mine.' So then, sir, old Vejvoda—"

"Look here," snappishly interrupted Lieutenant Dub, who as a result of Schweik's recital had become quite sober, "what are you telling me all this for?"

"Beg to report, sir, this ain't really got nothing to do with our official business, like, but I thought that as we was having a friendly little chat—"

At this moment it occurred to Lieutenant Dub that Schweik again insulted him, and he shouted at him, "One of these days you'll get to know what sort of man I am. What are you standing like that for?"

"Beg to report, sir, I ain't standing properly, and that's a fact. Beg to report, sir, I forgot to click my heels together, sir."

Schweik now remedied this omission in fine style.

Lieutenant Dub wondered what he was to say next, and finally he growled, "Just you pay attention to me once and for all and don't let me have to tell you about it."

And, as this seemed somehow inconclusive, he tacked onto it his ancient slogan: "You don't know me, but I know you."

He then sent for Kunert, his orderly, and instructed him to fetch a jug of water. To Kunert's credit be it said that he was a long time searching for a jug of water in Turowa Wolska. At last he succeeded in pilfering a jug from the parish priest and he filled this jug with water from a well which was almost completely boarded up, as the contents of it were suspected of containing typhus germs. Lieutenant Dub drank up the whole jugful without any untoward consequences, thus confirming the truth of the old proverb about ill weeds.

They were all very much mistaken in supposing that they were going to spend the night at Turowa Wolska.

Lieutenant Lukash called for Chodounsky, Quartermaster Sergeant Vanek, together with Schweik, the company runner, and Baloun. Their instructions were simple. They were to leave their equipment with the ambulance section, to make immediately for Maly Polanec across the fields, and then along the river, downward in a southeastern direction on the road to Liskowiec.

Schweik, Vanek, and Chodounsky were to act as billeting officers and to secure a night's quarters for the company, which would follow them an hour later, or an hour and a half at the outside. Meanwhile, on the spot where he, Lieutenant Lukash, was to spend the night, Baloun was to have a goose roasted and the other three were to keep a sharp eye on Baloun, to prevent him from gobbling up half of it. In addition to this, Vanek, in cooperation with Schweik, was to purchase a hog for the whole company, in proportion to the statutory allowance of meat. Stew was to be cooked that night. The billets must be clean. They were to avoid the vermin-infested huts so that the troops could get a proper rest, because the company had to leave Liskowiec at half past six in the morning for Kroscienko on the way to Starasól.

While the four of them were setting forth on their way, the parish priest turned up and began to distribute among the troops a leaflet containing a hymn in the various languages of the army. He had a parcel of these hymns which had been left with him by a high church dignitary who was making a motor trip through devastated Galicia, accompanied by a number of young ladies.

Now there were many latrines at Turowa Wolska, and before long all of them were clogged with these leaflets.

When it grew dark, the way became extremely unpleasant and the four of them who were to find quarters for the Eleventh Company got into a small wood above a stream which was supposed to lead to Liskowiec.

Baloun, who for the first time in his life found himself on an errand involving a journey into the unknown, and to whom everything—the darkness, and the fact that they were going on in advance to look for billets—began to appear uncanny, was suddenly gripped by a weird suspicion that all was not as it should be.

"Comrades," he murmured, as he stumbled along the road above the stream, "our lives have been sacrificed."

"What do you mean?" asked Schweik in quiet but gruff accents.

"Comrades, we mustn't make such a row," said Baloun imploringly. "I feel it in my bones they'll hear us and start shooting before we know where we are. I know what I'm talking about. They've sent us on in advance so as to find out whether the enemy are anywhere about, and when they hear the shooting, they'll know they can't go any further. We're what's called an advance patrol, comrades."

"Well, go on in advance, then," said Schweik. "We'll keep close behind you and when you're shot, just let us know, so as we can duck down in good time. You're a fine soldier, you

412

are, afraid of being shot at. Why, that's the very thing that ought to suit every soldier down to the ground. It stands to reason, the more the enemy fire at him, the quicker they'll use up their ammunition. Every time one of the enemy fires a shot at you, his chances of putting up a good fight get smaller. And at the same time he's glad he can fire at you, because he's got fewer cartridges to carry about, and it's easier for him to do a bunk."

Baloun sighed deeply. "What about my farm?"

"Farm be blowed!" said Schweik. "It's better for you to lay down your life for the Emperor. Haven't they taught you that?"

"They did say something about it," said the boobyish Baloun. "But I wish the Emperor'd fed us better."

"Well, you are a greedy hog and no mistake," objected Schweik. "Before going into action a soldier didn't ought to get anything to eat at all. Captain Untergriez used to tell us that, years and years ago. 'You damned gang of skunks,' he said, 'if ever there's a war, take good care not to overeat yourselves before you go into action. Anyone who overeats himself and then gets shot in the stomach is done for, because all the soup and army bread starts spurting out of his inside and the inflammation finishes him off on the spot. But if his stomach's empty, a wound like that is nothing at all, just a mere fleabite, only nicer."

Below, in the village where they were to find quarters for the company, it was pitch-dark, and all the dogs began to yelp, the result being that the expedition was brought to a standstill to discuss how these brutes could be dealt with.

"Suppose we went back?" whispered Baloun.

"If we did that," said Schweik, "you'd be shot for cowardice."

The yelping of the dogs became worse and worse, and Schweik yelled into the nocturnal gloom, "Lie down, you varmints, lie down, will you!" just as he used to yell at his own dogs when he was still a dog fancier.

This made them bark all the more, and so Quartermaster Sergeant Vanek said, "Don't yell at them, Schweik, or you'll set every blessed dog in Galicia barking at us."

As they descended toward the village, Schweik favored them with recollections of his experiences with dogs during the army maneuvers, and he also pointed out that dogs are afraid of lighted cigarettes at night. Unfortunately none of them had any cigarettes to smoke, so that Schweik's suggestion produced no positive results. It turned out, however, that the dogs were barking for joy, because they had pleasant memories of the troops who had previously passed that way and had always left them something to feed on. From afar they had scented the approach of people who would leave them bones and carcasses of horses. And so before Schweik knew where he was, four curs were fawning upon him, their tails wagging with delight.

Schweik stroked and patted them as he said in wheedling tones, "Well, here we are at last. We've come here to have a nice little snooze, a nice little feed. We'll give you some nice little bones and some nice little crusts, and tomorrow morning off we go again to fight the enemy."

Lights began to appear in the cottages and when they knocked at the door of the first cottage to find out where the mayor lived, a shrill and grating female voice was heard from within, announcing in a language which was neither Polish nor Ukrainian that her husband was fighting at the front, that her children had got smallpox, that the Russians had taken everything away with them, and that before her husband had gone to the front, he had told her never to open the door to anyone at night. It was only when they had emphasized their attack on the door by insisting that they had been sent to look for billets that an unknown hand let them in, and they then discovered that this was actually the residence of the mayor, who unsuccessfully tried to make Schweik believe that he had not imitated the shrill female voice. He explained that when his wife was suddenly waked up, she would start talking at random without knowing what she said. As regards quarters for the whole company, the village was so tiny, he said, that there wasn't room for a single soldier in it. There was no place at all for them to sleep. Nor was there anything on sale; the Russians had taken all there was. He suggested that if the gentlemen would kindly allow him, he would take them to Kroscienko, three-quarters of an hour further on. That was a place with large estates and they would find plenty of room there. Every soldier would be able to wrap himself up in a sheepskin, and there were so many cows that every soldier would be able to fill his mess tin with milk. There was good water, too, and the officers would be able to sleep in a mansion there. But here, in Liskowiec! A wretched, scabby, verminous place! He himself had once had five cows, but the Russians

414

had taken everything from him, so that when he wanted milk for his sick children, he had to go as far as Kroscienko.

In proof of this, the cows in the byre adjoining his cottage began to low and the shrill female voice could be heard abusing the unfortunate animals and expressing the hope that they might fall a prey to cholera.

But this did not nonplus the mayor, who said as he proceeded to put on his top boots, "The only cow we've got here belongs to my neighbor, and that's the one you've just heard. It's a sick cow, a wretched animal, worthy sirs. The Russians took her calf away from her. Ever since then she's stopped giving milk, but the owner feels sorry for her and he won't slaughter her because he hopes that the Blessed Virgin will put things right again."

During this speech he had been putting on his sheepskin coat.

"Now we'll go to Kroscienko, worthy sirs," he continued. "It's only three-quarters of an hour from here. No, what am I saying, wretched sinner that I am?—it's not as far as that; it won't take even half an hour. I know a short cut across the stream and then through a small birch wood around by an oak tree. It's a large village and they've got very strong vodka there. Let's go now, worthy sirs. You must not lose any time. The soldiers of your famous regiment must be given a proper and comfortable place to rest in. The soldiers of our King and Emperor who are fighting against the Russians need clean quarters to spend the night in. But here in our village there's nothing but vermin, smallpox, and cholera. Yesterday, in this cursed village of ours, three men turned black with the cholera. The most merciful God has cursed Liskowiec, worthy sirs."

At this point Schweik waved his hand majestically.

"Worthy sirs," he said, mimicking the mayor's voice, "I once read in a book that when the Swedish wars were on, and there was orders to billet the troops in such and such a village, and the mayor tried to get out of it and wouldn't oblige them, they hung him up on the nearest tree. And then a Polish corporal was telling me today at Sanok that when the billeting officers arrive the mayor has to call together all the chief men of the village and then he just goes around with them to the cottages and says, 'Three men here, four men there, officers in the parsonage, and everything's got to be ready in half an hour.'

"Worthy sir," continued Schweik, turning to the mayor, "whereabouts is the nearest tree?"

The mayor did not understand the meaning of the word "tree," and so Schweik explained to him that it was a birch or an oak, or something that plums or apples grew on, or, in fact, anything with strong branches. The mayor did not quite understand this either, but when he heard the names of fruit being mentioned, he became alarmed because the cherries were now ripe, and so he said that he knew nothing about that kind of thing, but that there was an oak tree in front of his cottage.

"All right, then," said Schweik, with an international gesture to denote hanging, "we'll hang you up in front of your cottage, because you've got to understand that there's a war on and we've got orders to sleep here and not in Kroscienko or wherever it is. You're not going to change our military plans, and if you try to, you'll swing for it, like in that book about the Swedish wars. I remember, gentlemen, there was a case like this during the maneuvers at—"

Quartermaster Sergeant Vanek interrupted.

"Tell us about that later," he said, and then, turning to the mayor, he added, "Now then, wake 'em all up and we'll find our billets."

The mayor began to tremble and stammered something about being anxious to do the best for the worthy sirs, but if it had to be, why, perhaps they could find room in the village after all, with everything to their satisfaction, and he'd bring a lantern at once.

When he had gone out of the room, which was very scantily illuminated by a small oil lamp underneath the image of some saint or other, Chodounsky suddenly exclaimed, "Where's Baloun got to?"

But before they could take proper stock of the place, the door behind the stove, which led to some outer place, quietly opened, and Baloun squeezed his way in.

He looked around cautiously to see if the mayor was still there, and then said snufflingly as if he had a terrible cold, "I've been in the larder and shoved my hand into something and took a mouthful of it, and now it all keeps sticking together. It ain't salty and it ain't sweet. It's dough for making bread with."

Quartermaster Sergeant Vanek flashed an electric torch on him, and they all agreed that never in their lives had they seen an Austrian soldier in such a ghastly mess. Then they had quite a scare, because they saw Baloun's tunic swelling up as if he were in the last stage of pregnancy.

"What have you been up to, Baloun?" inquired Schweik compassionately, as he prodded him in the bulging stomach.

"That's gherkins," wheezed Baloun, stifled by the dough, which wouldn't move up or down. "Be careful, that's salt gherkins. I ate three of 'em in a bit of a hurry, and brought the rest for you."

Baloun began to extract gherkin after gherkin from beneath his tunic and handed them around.

At this juncture the mayor appeared on the threshold with a light, and seeing what had happened, he crossed himself and lamented, "The Russians took everything, and now our soldiers are taking everything, too."

They then all proceeded into the village, escorted by a pack of dogs who clung most obstinately to Baloun and pranced at his trouser pockets, where he had a lump of bacon. This was another of his finds in the pantry, but for sheer gluttony he had basely kept it to himself.

As they went around in search of billets, they ascertained that Liskowiec was a large place but that it really had been reduced to dire straits by the turmoil of war. It had not actually incurred any damage by fire, as, miraculously enough, neither side had included it in the sphere of operations, but on the other hand the inhabitants of neighboring villages that had been destroyed were now crowded into it. In some huts there were as many as eight families living in the greatest misery, after all the losses they had suffered as a result of the pillage arising from the war, the first phase of which had swamped them like the turbulent waves of a flood.

The company had to be quartered partly in a small devastated distillery at the other end of the village, where half of them could be accommodated in the fermenting room. The rest, in batches of ten, were billeted on a number of farms, the wealthy owners of which had refused to admit any of the poverty-stricken rabble who had been reduced to beggary by being robbed of their goods and chattels.

The staff, with all the officers, Quartermaster Sergeant Vanek, orderlies, telephone operators, ambulance section cooks, and Schweik, quartered themselves in the parsonage, where there was plenty of room, because the incumbent had likewise refused to admit any of the families who had lost all their possessions.

He was a tall, gaunt old man in a faded and greasy cassock, who was so stingy that he would scarcely eat anything. His father had brought him up in great hatred of the Russians, but he suddenly got rid of his hatred when the Russians withdrew and the Austrian troops arrived, eating up all the geese and chickens which the Russians had not interfered with while a few shaggy Cossacks had been quartered on him. And his grudge against the Austrian troops had increased when the Magyars had come into the village and taken all the honey from his hives.

He now looked daggers at his nocturnal guests, and it did him good to be able to shrug his shoulders and declare, as he paced to and fro before them, "I've got nothing. I'm a complete pauper and you won't find so much as a slice of bread here."

Baloun looked particularly upset to hear of this distress, and it was a wonder he did not burst into tears. He found his way into the kitchen of the parsonage, upon which a sharp eye was being kept by a lanky youth acting as both handy man and cook to the incumbent, who had given him strict orders to see that nothing was stolen anywhere. And Baloun had found nothing in the kitchen except a little caraway seed wrapped up in paper inside a saltcellar. So he had made short work of that.

In the yard of the small distillery behind the parsonage the fires were alight under the field cookers and the water was already on the boil, but there was nothing in the water. The quartermaster sergeant and the cooks had searched the village from end to end for a pig, but no pig had they found. Everywhere they obtained the same answer: the Russians had taken and eaten everything.

Then they knocked up the Jew in the tavern. He tugged at his side curls and displayed enormous distress at not being able to oblige them. But in the end he induced them to buy from him an ancient cow, a relic of the previous century, a gaunt eyesore on its last legs, a sheer mass of skin and bone. He demanded an exorbitant sum for this appalling object, and tearing his side curls he swore that they would not find another cow like this in the whole of Galicia, in the whole of Austria and Germany, in the whole of Europe, in the whole world. He wailed, whined, and protested that this was the

418

fattest cow which had ever come into the world at Jehovah's behest. He vowed by all his forefathers that people came from far and wide to look at this cow, that the whole countryside talked about this cow as a legend, that, in fact, it was no cow at all, but the juiciest of oxen.

Finally, he kneeled down before them, and clutching at the knees of one after another, he exclaimed, "Kill a poor old Jew if you like, but don't go away without the cow."

He so bamboozled everybody with his howling that in the end the piece of carrion at which any knacker would have drawn the line was taken away to the field cooker. Then, long after he had the money safely in his pocket, he kept on wailing and lamenting that they had completely ruined him, destroyed him, that he had been reduced to beggary by having sold them so magnificent a cow at such an absurdly low price. He begged them to hang him up for having, in his old age, committed such a piece of folly which must make his fathers turn in their graves.

When, on top of this, he had wallowed in the dust before them, he suddenly shook all his grief aside and went home, where he said to his wife, "Elsa, my dear, the soldiers are fools, and your Nathan is a very shrewd man."

The cow gave them a lot of trouble. At times it seemed that they would never be able to skin the animal. When they tried to do so, they kept tearing the skin apart, and underneath they beheld sinews as twisted as a dried hawser.

Meanwhile, from somewhere or other, a sack of potatoes had been brought along, and hopelessly they began to cook the gristle and bones, while in the smaller field cooker a thoroughly desperate attempt was made to concoct from this piece of skeleton some kind of meal for the officers' mess.

This wretched cow, if such a freak can be called a cow, stuck in the memories of all who came into contact with it, and later on, if at the Battle of Sokol the commanders had reminded the troops of the cow from Liskowiec, it is fairly certain that the Eleventh Company, with terrible yells of wrath, would have flung themselves, bayonets in hand, upon the enemy. The scandal of the cow was such that it did not even produce any broth. The more the flesh was boiled, the tighter it stuck to the bones, forming with them a solid mass, as stodgy as a bureaucrat who has spent half his life feeding on official forms and devouring files and documents.

Schweik, who as a sort of courier kept up the lines of communication between staff and kitchen in order to make sure when the meal would be cooked, finally announced to Lieutenant Lukash, "It's no use, sir, the meat on that cow is so hard that you could cut glass with it. The cook tried to bite a piece of it, and he's broke a front tooth. And Baloun, he tried to bite a piece of it, too, and he's broke a double tooth."

And Baloun solemnly stepped forward in front of Lieutenant Lukash, and handing him the broken tooth wrapped up in a copy of the hymn which he had been given at Turowa Wolska, he stammered, "Beg to report, sir, I've done what I could. This tooth got broke in the officers' mess when we was trying to see if we could make some beefsteak out of that meat."

At these words, a woebegone form arose from the armchair by the window. It was Lieutenant Dub, who had been brought along in a two-wheeled cart by the ambulance section. He was a thorough wreck.

"Make less noise, please," he said brokenly. "I'm very unwell."

He sank back into the old armchair, every chink in which swarmed with bugs' eggs.

"I'm tired out," he said in tragic accents. "I am sick and ailing, so please don't speak about broken teeth in my presence. My address is Eighteen King Street, Smichov, and if I don't live until tomorrow, kindly see that the news is conveyed to my family in a considerate manner and that they don't forget to mention on my grave that before the war I taught in a school under His Majesty's Imperial Royal Government."

He then lapsed into a gentle snoring.

It was now decided that the troops had better have a nap before rations were issued, because in any case there would be no supper until morning.

In the kitchen, in front of a lighted stump of church candle, sat Chodounsky, the telephone operator, and wrote a stock of letters to his wife, to save himself the trouble later on. The first was as follows:

My DEER, DEER WIFE, MY BELOVED BOZENKA,

It is nite and I keep thinking of you my deer one and see you thinking of me as you look at the empty plaice in the bed beside you. Please dont be angry with me if the thort of this makes me think about Newmerus things. You no of corse I have bean at the frunt since the war started and I have herd Newmerus things from frends of mine who were wounded and went home on leeve and when they got home they wood rather have been under the Erth than find out that sum rotter had bean after their wives. It is Panefull for me deer Bozenka to rite to you like this I woodnt rite like this but you sed yourself I wasn't the ferst who was on close turms with you and before me there was Mr Kraus who lives down Nicholas Street well when I think of this in the nite that this Crock mite start making himself a Newsense to you I think deerest Bozenka I cood ring his neck on the spot. I kep this to myself a long time but when I think he mite start coming after you agane it makes my Hart ake and let me just tell you I wont stand any wife of mine running around like a Hoar with everybody and bringing Disgrace on my name. Forgive me deerest Bozenka for talking so plane but take care I dont here anything of that Sort about you. Or I shood have to do you both In because I am prepaired for anything even if it cost me my Life with lots and lots of Kisses best wishes to Dad and Ma Your own Tony.

P. S. Don't forget I gave you my name.

The next epistle which he added to his store ran:

MY DEEREST BOZENKA,

When you receeve these Lines you will no we have had a grate Battel in witch I am glad to say we came off Best. We shot down about 10 enemy airoplains and a general with a big Wort on his nose. In the Hite of the Battel when the shells were bersting above our Heds I thort of you deerest Bozenka and wondered what you were doing how you are and how everything is at Home. I allways remember how we were together at the beerhouse and you took me home and the next day you were Tired out. Now we are mooving on agane so their is no more Time for me to rite. I hope you have been Fathefull to me becos you no I wont stand any nonsense of that Sort. But now we are starting to March again with lots and lots of kisses deer hoping all will turn out Well your own Tony.

At this point Chodounsky began to nod and soon fell fast asleep on the table.

The incumbent, who was not asleep and who kept walking all over the parsonage, opened the kitchen door, and for the sake of economy blew out the stump of church candle which was burning at Chodounsky's elbow.

421

In the dining room nobody, except Lieutenant Dub, was asleep. Quartermaster Sergeant Vanek, who had received from the brigade headquarters at Sanok a new schedule relating to supplies, was studying it carefully, and he discovered that the nearer the troops got to the front, the less food they were given. He could not help laughing at one paragraph in the schedule which prohibited the use of saffron and ginger in the preparation of soup for the rank and file. The schedule also contained a remark to the effect that bones were to be collected and sent to the base for transfer to divisional stores. This was rather vague, as it did not specify whether it referred to human bones or those of other cattle which had been slaughtered.

When in the morning they left Liskowiec on the way to Starasol and Stambov, they carried the wretched cow with them in the field cooker. It had not yet been cooked, and they decided that this was to be done as they went along. Then, halfway between Liskowiec and Starasol, where they were to halt for a rest, they would eat the cow.

Black coffee was served out to the troops before they started.

Lieutenant Dub was again put into the two-wheeled cart of the ambulance section, because he had taken a turn for the worse. Lieutenant Lukash was on horseback, with Schweik as a close companion, marching forward so briskly that it looked as though he begrudged every moment's delay which kept him from coming into contact with the enemy.

As he stepped out thus, side by side with Lieutenant Lukash, he said, "I don't know if you've noticed it, sir, but some of these chaps here are a weak-kneed lot. What they got on their back don't weigh fifty pounds, and it's all they can do to stick it. Somebody ought to give 'em lectures about it like what Lieutenant Buchanek—he's dead now, poor blighter—did to us. He made us halt and gather around him like a lot of chickens around a hen, and then he begins to tell us what's what. 'You blackguards you,' he says, 'you don't seem to realize you're marching along the surface of the earth, you gang of boobies, it's enough to make anyone sick to look at you. Why,' he says, 'if you was marching along on the sun, where a man who weighs twelve stone on this planet would top the scale at more than two tons, that'd finish you off. That'd be something like marching,' he says, 'if you was carrying more than three hundredweight of stuff in your haversacks and your

422

rifle weighed close on two hundred pounds. That'd give you a grueling and make you hang your tongue out of your mouths like a lot of broken-winded dogs.' Well, there was a teacher chap on our squad and he ups and says, 'Begging your pardon, sir, but in the moon a man who weighs twelve stone here would only weigh about two stone. It'd be easier for us to march in the moon, because our haversacks would only weigh ten pounds there. In the moon we should just go floating along in the air, we shouldn't have to march at all.' 'Oh, you wouldn't, would you?" says poor old Lieutenant Buchanek. 'You wretched lout, you're asking for a smack in the eye. And think yourself lucky,' he says, 'that I'm only going to give you a common or garden smack in the eye, an earthly smack in the eye. If I was to give you one like you'd get on the moon,' he says, 'you'd be so light, you'd go sailing away to the Alps and you'd get smashed to smithereens against them. And if I gave you a heavy smack,' he says, 'like you'd get in the sun, it'd make mincemeat of your uniform and your head'd go flying away to Africa or somewhere.' So he gave him just a common or garden smack in the eye and then we marched on. And this teacher chap, he kicked up such a row about that smack in the eye, sir, that Lieutenant Buchanek had him up in the orderly room afterward and he got fourteen days and he had another six weeks to serve, but he didn't finish 'em off because he had a rupture and they made him do a circle on the horizontal bar and that settled his hash and he died as a malingerer in the hospital."

"It's a very funny thing, Schweik," said Lieutenant Lukash, "but, as I've told you several times before, you've got a strange way of poking fun at officers."

"Oh, no, sir," replied Schweik breezily. "I only wanted to show you, sir, how people get themselves into trouble in the army. That chap thought he was cleverer than Lieutenant Buchanek, and he wanted to score off him and take him down a peg or two in front of all the men, and so when he got that common or garden smack in the eye, we was all very much relieved. You take it from me, sir, we wasn't a bit sorry for him, in fact, we was all very pleased that the lieutenant answered him back and told him off properly and saved the situation, as you might say."

At this point Lieutenant Lukash seemed to be tired of the conversation, and he galloped his horse forward to overtake the vanguard.

Lieutenant Dub's condition had now so much improved that he was able to get out of the two-wheeled cart, and he began to address the company like a man in a dream. He delivered a long speech which made the troops feel wearier than did their packs and rifles. It abounded in such profundities as these:

"The attachment of the common soldier to the officer makes it possible for incredible sacrifices to be made. It does not matter, in fact, far from it, whether this attachment is something innate in the soldier, for if not, it must be enforced. This attachment is no ordinary attachment, it is a combination of respect, fear, and discipline."

All this time Schweik was marching along on the left, and while Lieutenant Dub was speechifying, he kept his head turned toward him, as if he had received the order "Eyes right!"

At first Lieutenant Dub did not notice this, and he continued, "This discipline, this compulsory obedience, this compulsory attachment of soldier to officer evinces itself very concisely, because the relation between soldier and officer is very simple: one obeys, the other orders. We have often read in books on military tactics that military brevity, military simplicity is the virtue at which every soldier must aim. Every soldier, whether he likes it or not, must be deeply attached to his superior officer, who in his eyes must be the ingrained paragon of an unswerving and infallible will."

At this point he perceived Schweik's fixed posture of "eyes right." It suddenly gave him an uneasy feeling that his speech was becoming very involved and that he could find no outlet from this blind alley of the attachment of the soldier to his superior officer. Accordingly, he bellowed at Schweik, "What are you staring at me like that for?"

"Beg to report, sir, I'm just carrying out orders, just like you yourself told me to. You said that when you was talking I was to keep my eyes fixed on your mouth. And because every soldier has got to be attached to his superior officer and carry out all his orders and always remember—"

"You look the other way!" shouted Lieutenant Dub. "And don't you let me catch you staring at me, you brainless booby."

Schweik changed over to "eyes left" and went on marching along by the side of Lieutenant Dub in such a rigid attitude, that at last Lieutenant Dub shouted out, "What are you looking that way for, while I'm talking to you?"

"Beg to report, sir, I'm carrying out your orders and facing eyes left."

"Good God!" sighed Lieutenant Dub, "what a devil of a nuisance you are! Hold your tongue and keep at the back, where I can't see you."

So Schweik stayed at the back with the ambulance section, and jogged comfortably along with the two-wheeled cart until they reached the place where they were to rest, and where, at last, they all had a taste of the soup and meat from the baleful cow.

"This cow," said Schweik, "ought to have been pickled in vinegar for a fortnight at least, and so ought the man who bought it."

A courier came galloping up from brigade headquarters with a new order for the Eleventh Company. Their line of route was changed so as to lead to Felstyn; Woralycz and Sambor were to be avoided because, owing to the presence of two Posen regiments, it would be impossible for them to find billets there.

Lieutenant Lukash immediately issued instructions. He told Quartermaster Sergeant Vanek, together with Schweik, to find a night's quarters for the company at Felstyn.

"And see you don't get into any mischief on the way, Schweik," said Lieutenant Lukash. "Above all, behave properly toward any of the people you come across."

"Beg to report, sir, I'll do my best. But I had a nasty dream when I dozed off early this morning. I dreamed about a wash-tub that kept slopping over all night in the passage of the house where I lived, till it had all dripped away and soaked the landlord's ceiling, and he gave me notice on the spot. The funny part of it is, sir, that something like that really happened. At Karlin, behind the viaduct—"

"Look here, Schweik, you'd better drop all that twaddle and have a look at this map and help Vanek to find out which way you're to go. From this village you bear to the right till you reach the river, and then you follow the river as far as the next village. From there, at the spot where the first stream, which you'll find on your right, flows into this one, you cut across the fields upward due north, and that'll bring you to Felstyn. You can't miss it. Can you remember all that?"

Schweik thought he could, and so he set out with Quartermaster Sergeant Vanek in accordance with these particulars.

It was the beginning of the afternoon. The landscape seemed

to be wilting in the swelter, and the stench of decay was wafted from the pits in which soldiers had been buried and not properly covered up. They now entered a region where fighting had taken place in the advance to Przemýsl and where whole battalions had been mown down by machine guns. In the small thickets by the river could be seen the havoc wrought by the artillery. There were large areas and slopes which had once been dotted with trees, but all that was left of them was jagged stumps jutting from the ground. And this wilderness was furrowed with trenches.

"This looks a bit different from Prague," said Schweik when the silence was becoming oppressive. And then, after a pause, he continued, "There'll be a fine harvest here after the war. They won't have to buy any bone meal. It's a good thing for farmers when they've got a whole regiment rotting away on their fields. There's no manure can beat it. That reminds me of Lieutenant Holub, who used to be in the barracks at Karlin. Everybody thought he was a bit dotty because he never called us names and always kept his hair on when he talked to us. One day we reported to him that our bread rations wasn't fit to eat. Any other officer would have made it hot for us, for having the cheek to grouse about our grub, but not he, oh dear no! He just stood there as cool as you please, he didn't call anyone a skunk or a swine or a bloody fool, and he didn't give anyone a smack in the eye. He just makes the men stand around him and says to them, as civil as could be, 'First of all,' he says, 'you must bear in mind that a barracks ain't a delicatessen store where you can get pickled eels and sardines in oil and assorted sandwiches. Every soldier ought to have enough sense,' he says, 'to eat his rations without any grousing, and he's got to show enough discipline not to make any fuss about the quality of the stuff that's given him to eat. Just suppose,' he says, 'there's a war. Well, the ground you get buried in after a battle don't care a damn what sort of bread you've been eating before you pegged out. Mother Earth,' he says, 'just takes you apart and eats you up, boots and all. Nothing gets lost, and from what's left of you there'll be a fresh crop of wheat to make bread rations for other soldiers, who'll perhaps start grousing like you except that they'll come up against someone who'll shove them into clink and keep them there till God knows when, because he's got a right to. So now,' he says, 'I've made it all clear to you, and I hope you'll bear it in mind and nobody will come here with any more

426

complaints.' Well, it got the men's back up, the way he kept a civil tongue in his head. 'Why don't he tell us off properly?' they says to each other, and so one day they picked me out to go and tell him that we all liked him but we didn't sort of feel we was in the army as long as he never told us off properly. Well, off I goes to call on him and I asks him not to be so smooth-spoken, because chaps expect to get it in the neck when they're in the army and they're used to being told every day that they're skunks and bloody fools, or else they don't have any respect for their superior officers. At first he wouldn't hear of it, and talked a lot of stuff about intelligence and how it ought to be a thing of the past for men to be ruled with a rod of iron, but in the end he saw my point and gave me a smack in the eye and kicked me downstairs, so as we should think all the more of him. When I told the other chaps what had happened, they was all very pleased, but then he went and spoiled everything the next day. He comes up to me in front of everyone and says, 'I acted a bit hasty yesterday, Schweik, so here's a gulden to drink my health with.' You can't get away from it, an officer ought to know better than that."

Schweik now inspected the landscape.

"It strikes me," he said, "that we've taken the wrong road. Lieutenant Lukash explained it to us all right. We've got to go up and down, then to the left and to the right, then to the right again, then to the left, and we're keeping straight on. I can see some crossroads in front of us, and if you ask me, I should say we ought to go to the left."

When they reached the crossroads, Quartermaster Sergeant Vanek affirmed that they ought to go to the right.

"Well, anyhow, this is the way I'm going," said Schweik. "It's a more comfortable road than yours. I'm going along by the stream where the forget-me-nots grow, and if you want to traipse along in the broiling heat, you can. I stick to what Lieutenant Lukash told us. He said we couldn't miss the way. So I'm going to take it easy across the fields and pick some flowers."

"Don't be a fool, Schweik," said Quartermaster Sergeant Vanek. "You can see from the map that we've got to go to the right, like I said."

"Maps are wrong sometimes," replied Schweik, as he strolled downhill toward the stream. "I know a pork butcher who tried to get home one night from Prague to Vinohrady and he followed a map, and the next morning he was found lying stiff and dead-beat in a cornfield near Kladno. If you won't take my word for it, Sergeant, and you're so cocksure you're right, why we'll just have to part, and we'll meet again when we get to Felstyn. Just look at your watch, and then we'll know who gets there first. And if you get into any danger, just fire into the air, so as I'll know where you are."

Later in the afternoon Schweik reached a small pond where he came upon an escaped Russian prisoner who was bathing there. When he saw Schweik he took to his heels, stark naked.

Schweik rather wondered how the Russian uniform, which was lying under the willow trees, would suit him. So he took off his own uniform and dressed himself in the clothes belonging to the unfortunate naked prisoner, who had escaped from the convoy that was quartered in the village on the other side of the forest. Schweik was anxious to have a good look at his reflection in the water, and so he lingered beside the brink of the pond for such a long time that he was discovered there by the field patrol who were looking for the Russian fugitive. They were Magyars, and in spite of Schweik's protests they took him off to the base at Chyruwa, where they put him

among a gang of Russian prisoners who were being sent to repair the railway line leading to Przemýsl.

The whole thing had happened so suddenly that Schweik did not realize until the next day what had happened to him, and on the white wall of the schoolroom where a part of the prisoners were quartered, he inscribed with a piece of charred wood:

Hear slept Josef Schweik of Prague, Company Orderly of the 11th Draft of the 91st Regiment who while looking for Billets was taken Prisoner near Felstyn by the Austrians by Misteak.

SIGNET CLASSICS by Russian Authors

Buy them at your local

bookstore or use coupon

on next page for ordering.

SIGNET CLASSICS by Russian Authors

(0451)

☐ **ANNA KARENINA by Leo Tolstoy.** New translation and Foreword by David Magarshack. (515404—$2.75)

☐ **THE DEATH OF IVAN ILYCH and Other Stories by Leo Tolstoy.** Translation by Aylmer Maude and J.D. Duff. Afterword by David Magarshack. Also includes *Family Happiness, The Kreatzer Sonata,* and *Master and Man.* (516761—$1.95)

☐ **WAR AND PEACE by Leo Tolstoy.** New translation by Ann Dun-nigan. Introduction by J.O. Bayley. Complete and Unabridged. (516613—$3.95)

☐ **FATHERS AND SONS by Ivan Turgenev.** Translation by poet George Reavey. Foreword by Alan Hodge. (515005—$1.95)

☐ **THE MASTER AND MARGARITA by Mikhail Bulgakov.** Trans-lated by Michael Glenny. (517016—$4.95)

☐ **ONE DAY IN THE LIFE OF IVAN DENISOVICH by Alexander Solzhenitsyn.** Translated by Ralph Parker. Introduction by Marvin L. Kalb and Foreword by Alexander Tvardovsky. (514564—$2.25)

Outstanding European Works in SIGNET and SIGNET CLASSICS

(0451)

- [ ] **CANDIDE, ZADIG, and Selected Stories by Voltaire.** Translated and with Introduction by Donald Frame. (516095—$2.25)
- [ ] **CHEKHOV: SELECTED STORIES.** Foreword by Ernest J. Simmons. (515277—$2.50)
- [ ] **BREAD AND WINE by Ignazio Silone.** Translated by Gwenda David and Eric Mosbacher. (517571—$2.95)
- [ ] **ANNA KARENINA by Leo Tolstoy.** Foreword by David Magarshack. (515404—$2.75)
- [ ] **WAR AND PEACE by Leo Tolstoy.** Translated by Ann Dunnigan. Edited and with an Introduction by J. O. Bayley. (516613—$4.95)
- [ ] **THE SORROWS OF YOUNG WERTHER and SELECTED WRITINGS by Johann Wolfgang von Goëthe.** Foreword by Hermann J. Weigand. Translated by Catherine Hutter. Glossary, Notes. (517369—$2.95)
- [ ] **CAT AND MOUSE by Günter Grass.** Translated by Ralph Manheim. (098552—$1.95)
- [ ] **THE GOOD SOLDIER SCHWEIK by Jaroslav Hasek.** Translated by Paul Selver. Foreword by Leslie Fielder. Illustrated. (516877—$3.95)
- [ ] **FONTAMARA by Ignazio Silone.** New translation by Eric Mosbacher. Introduction by Irving Howe. (515250—$2.95)
- [ ] **SILAS MARNER by George Eliot.** Afterword by Walter Allen. (516788—$1.75)
- [ ] **IVANHOE by Sir Walter Scott.** Afterword by Compton MacKenzie. Notes, Index and Glossary. (514963—$2.95)

Buy them at your local bookstore or use this convenient coupon for ordering.

NEW AMERICAN LIBRARY,
P.O. Box 999, Bergenfield, New Jersey 07621

Please send me the books I have checked above. I am enclosing $_____
(please add $1.00 to this order to cover postage and handling). Send check or money order—no cash or C.O.D.'s. Prices and numbers are subject to change without notice.

Name _____

Address_____

City_____ State_____ Zip Code_____
Allow 4-6 weeks for delivery.
This offer is subject to withdrawal without notice.